THE BEDLAM STACKS

NATASHA PULLEY

BLOOMSBURY PUBLISHING
LONDON • OXFORD • NEW YORK • NEW DELHI • SYDNEY

BLOOMSBURY PUBLISHING
Bloomsbury Publishing Plc
50 Bedford Square, London, WC1B 3DP, UK

BLOOMSBURY, BLOOMSBURY PUBLISHING and the Diana logo are trademarks of
Bloomsbury Publishing Plc

First published in Great Britain 2017
This edition published 2018

A catalogue record for this book is available from the British Library

ISBN: HB: 978-1-4088-7844-6; TPB: 978-1-4088-7845-3;
SPECIAL EDITION PB: 978-1-5266-0444-6; PB: 978-1-4088-7847-7; EBOOK: 978-1-4088-7846-0

2 4 6 8 10 9 7 5 3 1

Typeset by Integra Software Services Pvt. Ltd.
Printed and bound in Great Britain by CPI Group (UK) Ltd, Croydon CR0 4YY

PART ONE

ONE

Heligan estate, Cornwall
August 1859

ALTHOUGH I HADN'T BEEN shot at for years, it took me a long time to understand that the bang wasn't artillery. I sat up in bed to look out of the window, half-balanced on my elbows, but there was nothing except a spray of slate shards and moss on the little gravel path three floors below. There had been a storm in the night, huge, one of those that takes days and days to form and gives everyone a headache, and the rain must have finally worked loose some old roof tiles. In its bell jar, which kept damp from the mechanisms, the clock thunked around to twenty past seven. I sat still, listening, because I'd been sure the noise had been much louder than a few smashed tiles.

The bunches of plants drying in the rafters were pattering seeds into their paper bags. Somewhere above them, on the roof, the weathervane squeaked. Nothing else fell. Once my heart was convinced there was no gunfire, I tried to slide my cane out from under the dog.

'Gulliver.' I gave it a tug.

She rolled over and lay at an unnatural angle while I got dressed, paws crooked under their own weight. When I stroked her ears, she bumped her nose into my stomach, trying to herd me back into bed. Gigantic anyway and overfed, she was as heavy as me and almost managed it, but even with a cane I could still just about outmanoeuvre a sleepy St Bernard.

'No, sorry. Time for a walk,' I said. 'Let's see if the greenhouse is still in one piece.'

She snorted at me but padded through the door when I opened it for her, my head bowed because the rafters were low. Outside were six steep steps which she took at an old lady's pace, although in fact she was quite young. The way was so narrow that her sides touched the walls. There were polished parts on the wainscoting that represented a year of morning and evening passages, by far the most looked-after section of wall anywhere in the house. I eased down after her. My leg hurt but I got down four steps before I had to pause, which was a big improvement on six months ago.

Along the corridor were dislocated views over the gardens through windows whose panes had been made from patchworks of older stained glass, full of truncated bits of Latin and saints' robes, all of them rattly on the windward side. The cold and the damp seeped in round the edges. When I came home after a long time away it was always freshly horrible that there were happy slugs and moss in the inside grooves, but I'd been back for long enough now to have lapsed into a hopeless effort not to see it.

Down the dark stretch on the next stairs – ten steps, none quite the same height – I ran my hand along the wall to keep my balance. The door at the bottom stuck fast at less than halfway open. Gulliver had to squeeze through and I turned sideways. Though the landing looked just as poky as the last, it led out suddenly on to the main staircase, where all the portraits of previous Tremaynes and Lemons hung down the left-hand wall. Nearer the top were people in army uniforms and nicely rumpled silk whose names I didn't know, and down near the door of Charles's study were the few I would have recognised out of context: a couple of our mother's brothers, and the aunt who'd taught me to shoot. Last was our grandfather, who looked like me, blond and fast-ageing. A still-life of some fruit hung where our father should have been.

Now, there was a carpet of pine needles and broken bits of timber over the middle of the floor. I twisted round to see upward. Although there were, on my side, three floors to the house, on this side it was just galleries off the staircase. The ceiling was the roof. Being windowless, it was usually gloomy, with deep shadows between the vaults of the rafters, but now there was quite a big hole. Hanging down through it was a rotten branch still

Sketch Map of the

PROVINCE OF CARAVAYA

1859

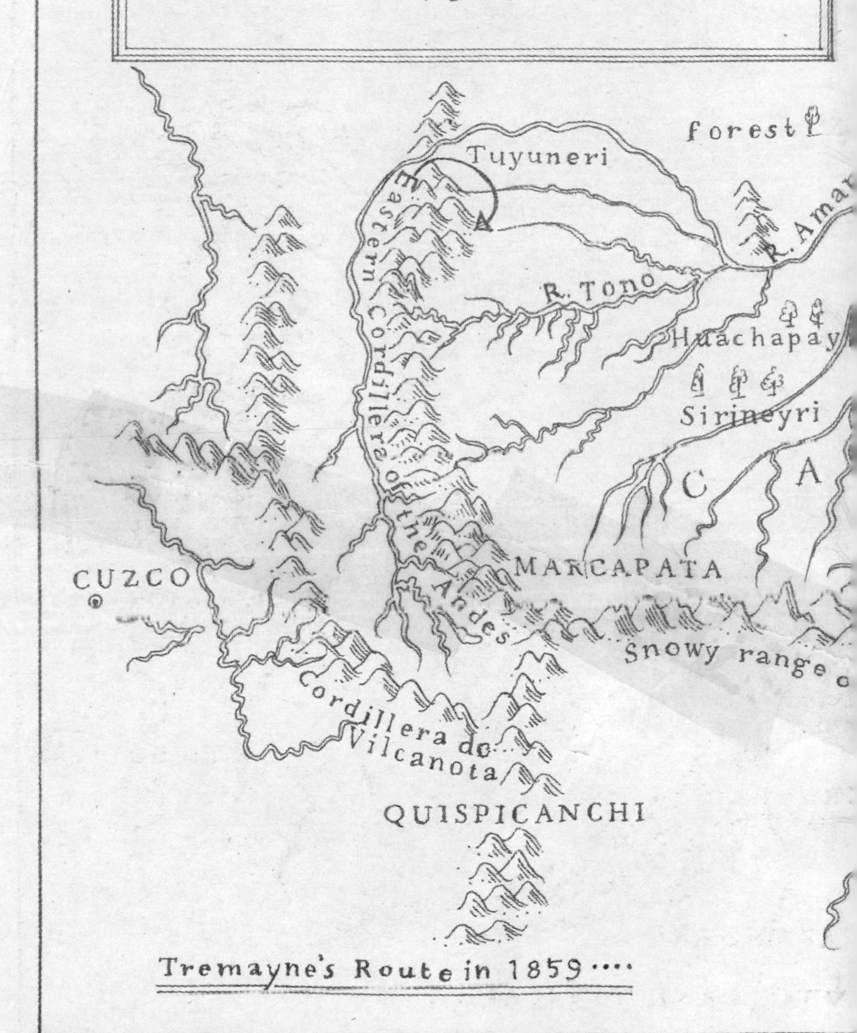

To Ruby

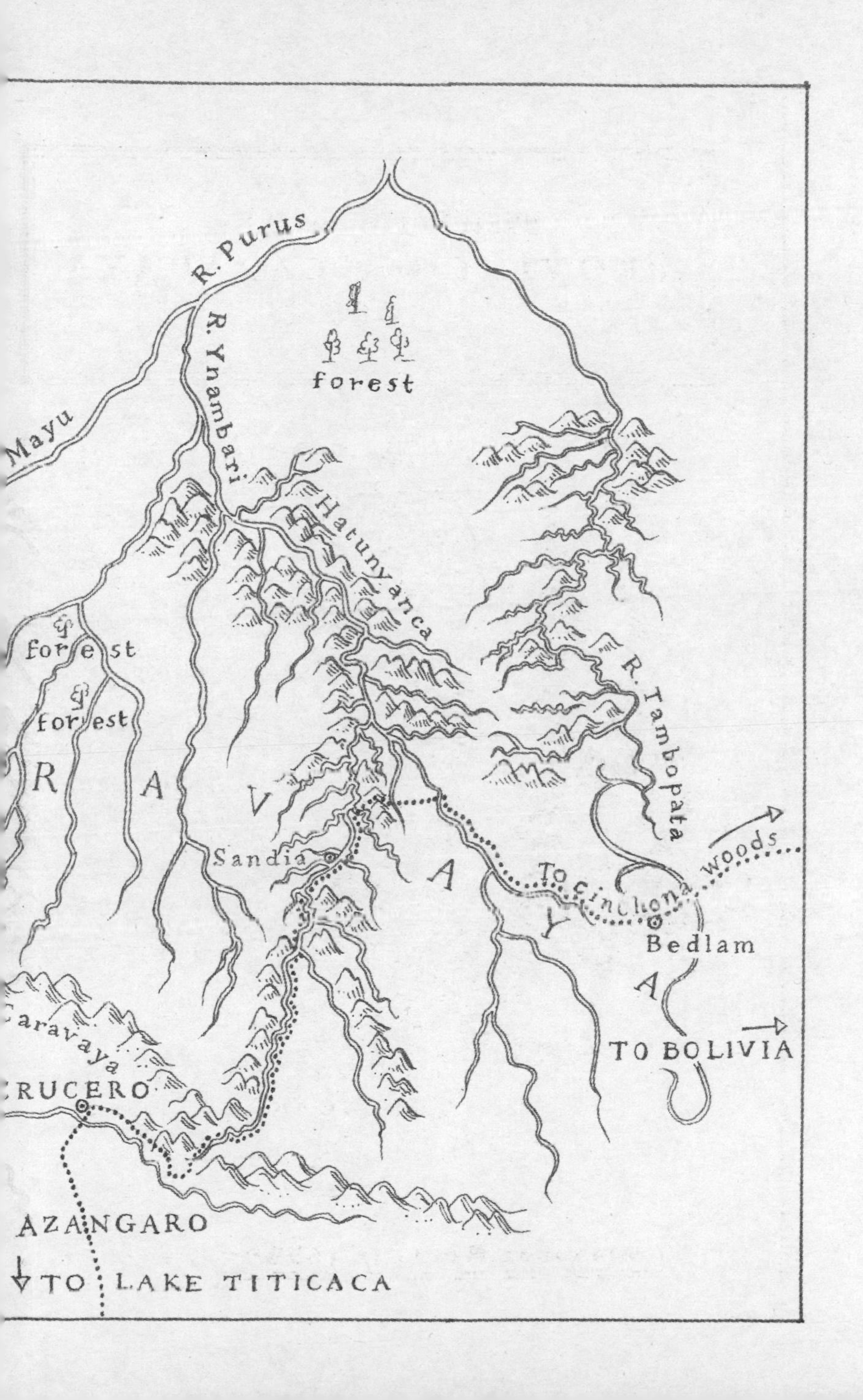

R. Purus
Mayu
R. Ynambari
forest
Hatunyanca
forest
forest
R. Tambopata
R
A
V
A
Y
A
Sandia
To cinchona woods
Bedlam
TO BOLIVIA
Caravaya
CRUCERO
AZANGARO
TO LAKE TITICACA

attached, just, to the old pine tree. It had been defying gravity for months.

I slid down the banister rather than bother with the stairs, and Gulliver lolloped down next to me. Through the hole in the ceiling, the old pine kept up its rain of needles. I watched it for a second before I went underneath, but nothing creaked.

Gulliver opened the front door by walking into it. She knew where she was going and trotted round to Charles's study window, where she swept her tail to and fro over the gravel and sprayed me with rainwater because the path was full of puddles. So was the lawn. They were reflecting the sky, lavender and grey. From outside, the tree seemed more or less all right, except for the rotten branch still suspended over the hole in the roof. I still had no idea what it was, the tree. Some kind of sequoia, but it was white, like a silver birch, and it had grown monstrous. Despite its size, it had a stunted list that suggested it ought to have been ten times bigger, the white bark full of awkward knots and abortive half-grown branches with no needles on them. Up in the canopy was a whole parliament of nests. Although it was noisy in the mornings usually, the crows must all have been out doing crow things for now.

I tapped on Charles's window. His shadow struggled up and swung across between his crutches. When he lined up with my reflection in the lilac morning light, we almost looked alike.

'I'll get some gardeners to go up and cut down that branch before it falls,' I said through the glass, then leaned back as he shoved it open. The frame stuck and it needed some force. 'What are we doing about the roof?'

'We're not doing anything about the roof,' he said, 'and I'd rather not have gardeners in the house.'

'I'd rather not have a tree in the house,' I said, 'so stay there and don't look.'

I heard a saw. There were gardeners by the tree, just beginning to cut the trunk. I hadn't seen from the front door, which stood at the wrong angle, but they had already tied ropes round the far side to guide the fall.

'What are they doing?' I said slowly.

'Cutting it down. You're right, it's not safe. And this way we can have some firewood we're not paying for.'

I didn't say that making firewood from that tree was like using pound notes for kindling, or worse, given the effort it had taken to bring it here. It was from Peru and our grandfather had built one of the greenhouses specially for it. But I knew what Charles would say. He would say it wasn't pound notes; it might have cost a lot to bring and to grow, but the tree wasn't worth anything now it was here. It would be like burning rupees if you never intended to go to India again and didn't know anyone else who would.

'Charles, you can't,' I tried, with no heart.

'We're past keeping things from sentiment.'

'As opposed to the ten generations' worth of rubbish taking up eighteen of twenty rooms inside—'

'Ridiculous thing to have planted by the house in any case. The roots are coming up through the kitchen floor, for God's sake.'

I let my breath out and tried not to feel angry. That I'd grown up among the roots of that tree, that Dad had climbed it with me and read me stories in the lowest branch; none of it meant a thing to him and there would be no making him understand. He had hated our father and that was that. He had hated him so much that if I said I hadn't, he couldn't conceive that it might be anything but a strange lie.

'They can save some of the timber to plank up the roof, then,' I said.

'Merrick, I told you, we can't afford to do anything about the roof; I can't have workmen in—'

'There's a hole in the bloody roof, Charles, and we've got timber. We've got eleven gardeners.'

'Don't swear at me. It should be done properly—'

'But we can't do it properly, you just said.'

'Just,' he said, 'leave it alone.'

I laughed. 'I'm not being rained on every time I come into the house because you're too proud to fix the roof. Talk about spiting your face.'

'I don't mind rain,' he said.

'Other people do.'

'Merrick. I said—'

'I heard what you said, but since what you said was stupid, we're not going to do that.'

He ignored me. 'There's a letter for you.'

I managed to hesitate only for a second when I saw the seal of the India Office before I folded it into my waistcoat. I liked fighting with Charles – if I was disagreeing with him it was proof I hadn't been beaten down altogether yet – but seeing the seal made the scar on my leg pang and I had to go more slowly.

TWO

GULLIVER LED THE WAY on the crooked path, which was sometimes gravel, sometimes cobbles, and sometimes only a flatter line of moss along the edge of the lawn. Once we were close to the big tree, the roots pushed up underfoot in bumps and contorted twists. There had used to be rainforest flora all around them: a great litter of orchids, plate-leaved lilies in the marshy patches, and clusters of carnivorous things with spines that closed fast if you poked one. Charles had had it all torn up when he moved the driveway to iron out the hairpin bend. It had made things difficult for the apple carts. I paused to tell the gardeners to save some timber for the roof. They snatched a glance between each other and said of course. They knew better than to ask why we couldn't bring in workmen from Truro for proper repairs.

Having found early on after coming home from China that I couldn't sit in the house all day, I'd gone exploring and rediscovered the old greenhouse. It was down in the valley, which hadn't seen any work since our grandfather had been alive. Because the wind funnelled right up from the sea sometimes, the trees there were blasted and strangely shaped. Some had leaves only on one side and one yew had bent right forward over the glass roof, old and dead and brittle. No matter how often I came in and out, the doors rained moss and spiders. When I'd found the place it had been overgrown. Nobody had asked for it back, so I stole it. I'd never be a gardener again, not like I had been, but although the loss of the profession had smashed over me like a tsunami, the interest behind it had turned out to be waterproof. I had forty-two types of fern and rescued tropical plants growing inside now, so densely that they pressed up against the walls.

The greenhouse stood on the edge of a tiny graveyard. The graves looked like somebody had dropped them there. They were a random, leaning clutter, some far spaced and some not, one half-hidden by the roots of a wind-warped tree that had spilled over the granite and tipped it sideways. There had once been a chapel, but all that was left of it were some stone steps and half a window frame. Dad's grave was the only one noticeable straightaway. There was a statue that looked down at the headstone, or it did usually. After the storm, one of the trees had fallen where the statue had been, but somebody prescient had moved it fifteen feet to one side.

When I got to the greenhouse, I saw that I'd left the door open, again. It worried me, because no matter how often I did it, I could never remember. I checked the inside lock without much hope. The key was gone, which wouldn't have mattered, but the same ring had my housekeys on it too. It was the third time I'd left it open since coming home, and the third time the crows had stolen the keys. It had taken me days to work out what had happened the first time and even then only when they brought the keys back to swap for a shilling I'd left on the bench.

I took down the jar of nails and coins on the shelf and sat for a while shining them up with turpentine. When they were gleaming I set them out on the step. I paused when I saw the floor was damp, dripped on, but there was nothing wrong with the roof. The little mechanisms that misted the air in the summer were bone dry. Not for the first time, I wondered if it hadn't been me who had left the door ajar at all, but someone else coming in to get out of the rain. But I'd asked before, and everyone had always said no.

In stealing the keys, the crows had knocked the map of Peru sideways. I straightened it up. I'd taken it from our grandfather's collection. It wasn't all of Peru, only the part he'd lived in. A district well into the interior, Caravaya. Half of it was beyond the Andes and after the line of the mountains there wasn't much, but he had sketched on a dragon with an amiable face and folded wings. At first glance it was a piece of whimsy but I knew why he had drawn it. There was a river there, in the shape of a dragon, but the territory was uncharted and he'd never taken the measure of the land. I only knew because whenever I saw the little picture, a nursery rhyme floated about at the back of my mind. It was about a dragon and a river and a mountain, but I couldn't fit the words into the tune any more.

Peru had been where I was meant to go, where I was meant to be now, if nothing had happened to my leg; I was supposed to be fetching cuttings from *calisaya* cinchona trees to begin a new plantation in India. The only cinchona forests in the world grew in Peru, and the only treatment in the world for malaria was quinine – derived from cinchona bark. Malaria was getting worse and worse in India, which was doing unpromising things to the trade revenue of the India Office. I'd put the map up when I'd thought I might recover enough to go. Still holding it between my fingertips I realised that all it was now was the fossil of a dead chance. I was never going to go. I propped it up on the floor instead, facing away.

Wanting to get it over with, I pulled open the letter and unfolded it against a tray of pansy seedlings. The paper was embossed and thick. Across it was my old manager's beautiful handwriting in dark black ink.

Tremayne,

Expedition to Peru going ahead. December start. Report to the India Office for November 15th at the latest.

Sing

I turned the paper over and cast around for the pencil I used for plant labels.

Dear Sing,

Cannot go to Peru. Cannot walk. Ask Charles Ledger, he's good.

Yours
Merrick

I stuffed it back into the envelope, readdressed it to India House, tied it up with string and dropped it in the spare plant pot to take out later.

A crow bumped into the glass in front of me. It fell on to the grass but hopped up again, ruffling its feathers. I tapped on the window to see if it was all right. It looked, bright-eyed and alert still. Another fluttered down next to it, and another shot overhead. There were dozens of them, everywhere, and most were fluttering in a great funnel above the graves. Some were far up in the sky, circling as though they were looking for something. I thought it was carrion at first. I went out.

'Anyone got my keys?' I called, then stopped walking, because I had almost come to what they were interested in. It was a broken amphora, the one that usually rested against the statue, but whoever had moved the statue had forgotten about it. It had spilled a spray of glass shells and tiny vials across the leafy moss. I frowned, because I hadn't known it had anything in it at all. The shells were bright and winking even in the drizzly sun. I went down on my good knee to pick one up. It came attached by a dead weed to three or four others, which plinked together and trickled old sand over my knuckles. Caught in the glass were burned imperfections and bursts of odd colour where scraps of iron or copper had been mixed up in it. There were dead sea things in two of them.

The vials were sealed shut. I broke the wax on one. Inside was something fine and white. I leaned down to it. Salt.

Not liking my being there, the crows wheeled away, towards the house and their nests in the big tree.

When I went back to the greenhouse, the crows had traded some glass shells for the pennies, but there was still no sign of my keys. Gulliver whined and nudged at me as I sat down. I stroked her ears. It made me jump when she barked. In the little space it was loud.

'Ow. What?'

She whined again and hid under the old couch. A couch is an odd thing to have in a greenhouse, but it had always been there. It was Regency, all twirling mahogany scrollwork and sun-faded upholstery. I couldn't tell what colour it had been, and some patches were so worn out that the calico lining showed through. I'd never sat on it – I couldn't lean back if I was sitting down now – but there was an impression of a person on the left side that must have been my father or his, which I liked.

I couldn't lean down from sitting either, so I had to take my feet off the ground and ease down on my hands to see underneath.

'Come on, girl.'

St Bernards have human mannerisms. They sigh a lot when they're fed up, and Gulliver, at least, always put her paw over her eyes when she was unhappy. I laughed, but then stopped when I saw what was by my hand. It was the watermark of a bootprint. The sole was a different pattern to mine, no pattern at all, and much bigger.

It shouldn't have worried me as much as it did, but I'd been skittish since I'd hurt my leg. I got up and took Gulliver twice round the greenhouse, then into the trees a little way in four directions, but we didn't find anyone or any sign of anyone. The only human shape was the statue, which kept catching my eye. In the end I gave up and tried to get on with things in the greenhouse, but the crawling feeling of being watched was heavy on the back of my neck and it wouldn't go away. I couldn't concentrate and when Gulliver nosed me, restless too, I took her out again and started back up the hill, thinking vaguely that we might both feel better for a cup of tea and a biscuit. Gulliver generally had the biscuit.

As we walked towards the house, I smelled something burning. It was so clear that I turned round twice, looking for smoke, but I couldn't trace where the smell was coming from and after a few seconds, in the way you lose sight of a star if you stare at it too long, I couldn't catch it at all any more.

It was only once we were on the driveway that it came back. Something bright half-blinded me and I looked up, worried there was a fire in the house, but the light wasn't coming from that way. It was in the tree. There were starry points all through the canopy. The glass shells were in the crows' nests, winking where the sun came down through the loose edges. Where one of them made a dot of brightness on the ground beside me, the pine needles were starting to smoke. They went up with an odd blue flame while I was watching. Gulliver squeaked and hid behind me. Points on the branches and the trunk were smoking too. Through the grey haze, more fires burned thin and chemical-looking. The gardeners weren't there; they were sitting on the kitchen steps with the tea that Sarah always provided at ten on the dot, unbeknownst to Charles.

'Tree's on fire,' I called.

The head gardener twisted back. I had a feeling his name was something brilliant, like Sisyphus, but although he had worked here since we were both children I wasn't confident enough to say it and we had never had a proper conversation. I'd been away too much. 'What?'

I pointed with my cane.

'Jesus!' There was a clatter as teacups clanked down on the steps. Men ran past me and I stood still so that I wouldn't get in anyone's way. 'How in God's name is it on fire?' Sisyphus demanded of the world more than of me. 'It pissed down in the night.' Then he flushed. 'Sorry, sir.'

I shook my head, although Charles had trained them too strictly not to swear for me to convince anyone I didn't mind. 'The crows have been collecting these, look.' I found the one I'd had in my pocket and showed him. The glass was thick enough that the spiral of the shell winked and lensed the light. The little spotlight it made on my palm felt warm. Sisyphus took it and moved it to and fro over a handful of pine needles, then gasped and dropped them when they caught alight with a hissing crackle. Gulliver nudged me further away from it.

Sisyphus was still embarrassed and when he spoke, the gorse and the ferns in his voice withered until there was almost no Cornwall left in it at all. It didn't matter that I wasn't well spoken. Charles was and, as far as the gardeners were concerned, I was only a taller, blonder extension of him. I'd never had the energy to sit them all down and explain I didn't go through their faults with him nightly over dinner. 'But that ought not be hot enough to – should it?'

'I don't know,' I said. 'The tree's from the Amazon. God knows what it should and shouldn't do.'

In the end there wasn't much they could do but put out what fell to the ground and hope nothing really got going. The fires only hissed damply, and after about ten minutes a misty rain started and we all stood just shy of the canopy, watching. Some of the smoking patches were on the rotten branch. Close to, the angle at which it hung above the house was mad. It was held on by nothing but one last string of wood and a pretty fungus.

'Better get it down sooner rather than later,' I said towards the cut the hawsers had made in the trunk. 'While it's raining.'

He nodded and called to some of the other gardeners. They were nervous, but they began to saw again anyway and I smiled, proud of them. Sisyphus watched too, his hands pressed over his kidneys.

'Sir – are you sure you should be living up near the attic?'

'I haven't got anywhere else to live.' I didn't want to explain Charles's refusal to clear out all the boxes of ancient gear and books on the first floor, or that it wouldn't change now just because there was a tree about to fall through my room; it hadn't when I'd nearly lost a leg, despite three sets of stairs. He was only asserting his ownership of the house, reminding me that living there didn't make anything mine, but it was so stupid that it didn't deserve any more oxygen.

'Honestly, I'd camp in the greenhouse if I were you. Even forgetting the tree, that roof could go at any minute. I mean, look at it.'

I inclined my head to say it was a fair point, then put two and two together and felt stupid. The gardeners must have been in the greenhouse because they'd moved the statue. 'By the way – can you tell whoever moved the statue, thanks?'

'What statue?'

'By Dad's grave.' Charles would have said old Sir John's grave. That sort of thing sounded right in his voice but not in mine. In mine it sounded like I had a rod down my spine.

He frowned. 'No one moved that. Christ – don't reckon you could move that thing with five men and a winch.'

'They must have. Someone moved it out of the way of the trees yesterday night before the storm. And someone was in the greenhouse.'

He gave me an odd look. 'Yesterday was Sunday. There was no one here but you and Sir Charles. No one came in till six this morning. The storm was all over by then.'

'Look, I don't mind if people use it – it's not mine, nothing here is mine, there's no need to cover for anyone. If they could just shut the door, though. Otherwise the crows steal my keys.'

'I'm not covering for anyone, I promise.'

'I'm sharing the greenhouse with a ghost, then. With boots bigger than mine. I found footprints.'

He was still frowning. 'There's . . . no one that tall here.'

'Well, there's someone out there,' I said. 'Has been for a while, I think.'

'We'll have a look through the valley. If we've got tramps drifting about the greenhouses, we need to know. There's valuable things lying about.'

I felt like a damselling idiot for not being able to help. 'Don't turf them out if there's no need. It isn't as though we're using that particular thousand acres.'

He looked like he might have argued with me, but he didn't have the chance.

It seemed to happen in slow stages, although it couldn't have. The gardeners were looping ropes around the trunk, ready for it to tip, but it leaned before they were ready, only a couple of inches, and the dead branch swayed. It fell, smouldering, straight down into the damaged section of the roof, which broke. Tiles slid down in a flint landslide and smashed on the drive. I was sure that I heard those sharp crashes well before the bigger, deeper bang of the branch smashing into the main stairway inside, for all that would have made Galileo wrong. There was a moment of quiet in which things seemed to settle and there was no sound but pine needles falling and the little hissing of the remaining fires in the rain. But then, inside the house, something exploded.

It blew out the windows nearest to us and dust and smoke plumed everywhere. We were just far away enough not to be hurt and for a second it was nothing but beautiful, because the peach-coloured sun was still filtering through the tree and now the light came down through the smoke like threads in a loom. The taste of burned paper and brick scratched the back of my throat. Men must have been shouting, but I couldn't hear anything except the crunch of the gravel where Gulliver had jerked in front of me. The first real thing I heard was when she barked.

She must have been able to see or smell something else through the smoke, because she ran around the house, towards the front door. I followed her as best I could and by the time I reached her, pacing up and down, the smoke was clearing; part of the wall had been blown clean through, and the one between the hallway and Charles's study.

'Come on, let's find him,' I said. I gave her a push inside.

She understood and hurried over the scattered bricks. Her normal pace was a sort of ooze, but she was quick now. I followed. There wasn't much to climb over and the doorways were more or less all right, but just inside the hallway now was what was left of the exploded branch. It had sprayed pieces of itself everywhere and each one burned like a phosphorous torch, smoke pouring from them. The hearts of the flames were bluish green. Gulliver barked again. She had found Charles; he was in the corner near the desk. She nudged him out towards me. He was all right, but he had banged his head and there was blood just under his hair. He was unsteady even with both crutches.

'Charles—'

'Of all the bloody juvenile things!' he shouted at me. 'What, you can't bear to see the wretched tree come down, so you douse the thing in turpentine?'

'I didn't do anything, don't be stupid.' I put my arm around him to help him over the rubble near the door.

'Get off me,' he snapped.

'Look, it takes something to go from sniping at each other to blowing someone up, doesn't it?'

'You'd do it in the right mood,' he said. 'And you know you would. Your idea of benign and acceptable violence is nearly crucifixion.'

'Look at this,' I said, gesturing to the brilliant fires.

He did look. Though he had shaken me off, he leaned on my arm while he stood still, the top of his dark head not quite to my shoulder. He was so frail it didn't feel like touching a human being. 'Why is it burning like that?'

'I don't know.'

Once we were safely out, I cast around for a decent-sized shard of wood. I found one just outside the door. It was warm when I picked it up. I held it to my nose, waiting to catch the smell of dynamite, but there was nothing until I tipped it to the light. It was honeycombed with tiny holes, minuscule. The combined surface area inside must have been vast.

'What is that, some sort of disease?' Charles murmured.

'I don't . . . God, feel that. It's light.'

I put it into his hand and his arm bobbed upward because it weighed so much less than it looked.

'There's nothing on it,' I said at last. I hooked my cane over my arm and found some matches in my pocket. He frowned but watched me hold a flame to the corner of the wood. Nothing ignited on the surface, but I threw it away from us, on to the grass, just in case. After a second it went off like a bomb and left a little crater in the lawn.

'It explodes,' he said slowly.

'Listen – you've got a concussion, your eyes aren't even. Sit down.'

He did as he was told. I perched on some of the ruined brick-work too. Gulliver put her nose on his knee. He didn't usually like her, but he stroked her ears. I rubbed some ash off his jacket. He smacked my hand.

'Don't,' he said. He sounded more tired of me than he ever had. 'How did this happen?'

'There was some glass on the ground. The crows took it, the sun was out . . .'

He seemed not to hear. 'What are we going to do about a hole in the wall?'

'Some of the bricks will be all right. We can board it up for now,' I said, knowing it wouldn't just be for now.

The rain turned harder and the fires in the main tree went out. The gardeners were in the hall with buckets. All that was left of the rotten branch were chunks of charcoal. I helped Charles around to the back of the house and the kitchen door, ashamed, because two years ago I could have carried him. I got him to sit down at the big table, where there was some abandoned dough because Sarah must have gone outside to see what was going on. I poured him some rum, some of the strong fantastic Jamaica kind. I bought it from smugglers in town. I could probably have bought it legally, but edging into the back of the Creely brothers' bakery was a tradition I was trying to keep alive from when Dad had taken me when I was tiny, and in any case, I liked the idea of bakers smuggling in rum from Calais.

He told me to stop fussing before long, but I left Gulliver with him. I went out into the rain to see if the gardeners were all right and rounded them up to count heads. They were all there, though some of the younger ones were shaken. Aware that Charles wouldn't like it but deciding that now was a nice moment not to care, I herded them all round to the kitchen to share the tea. In fact, Charles seemed relieved to see other people. The gardeners, big men for the most part, were just as relieved to have somebody fragile to be kind to and within a minute or so they were all talking as if they had always belonged together. Gulliver wagged her tail, pleased.

Sisyphus came to stand with me by the stove, where I had the small of my back propped against the hot part just above the oven. I didn't remember jolting anything, but something right under my spine hurt and the heat helped. He smelled of sweat and grass. I breathed in slowly, because I missed it, being fit enough and quick enough to sweat over real work.

'Where did you say that tree was from?' he said.

'Peru.'

'They must have problems out there.'

I smirked into my cup.

He was quiet for a while. Then, 'Right. I'll get them to have a look through the woods. Give them something to do, find your mystery man.'

I nodded and waited with Charles and Gulliver. It was nasty of me, but I liked Charles a lot better when he was upset than at equilibrium and we laughed together for the first time in years. But when the gardeners came back, they hadn't found anything. The greenhouse was empty and so were the woods, which were too overgrown to walk through without a struggle. Even the old charcoal pits were impenetrable. There was no one there and in the end I doubted what I'd seen. It must have been my own footprint in the greenhouse, but hazed and distorted as the water dried.

I felt uneasy when I went back out the next day, but the greenhouse was the only warm place I could go. By the time I came to open the glass door, I was convinced that I must have been telling myself stories. But someone had put the map of Peru back on its hook. I eased aside the ferns and looked under the couch. There was no one, but the statue had moved again. It was back by the grave, but not like it had been before the storm. It was facing me this time. No one would admit to having moved it.

THREE

When Charles tapped on the greenhouse door a few days later I got up too fast, worried, and swayed when my weight went too far on to my bad leg. I'd never known him venture so far from the house. Thinking that it must be an emergency, I pulled the door open for him and moved one of the wooden benches closer to the tiny ceramic stove I was burning twigs in. It gave off just enough heat to keep tropical things alive. He propped his canes against the pottery and sat down on the spare stool, then caught the edge of the workbench when it wobbled. He looked at his hand and brushed the earth off against his trouser leg.

'Good news,' he said, and it really must have been good, because he looked cheerful. 'I've a friend near Truro with a parsonage that's about to be empty. The parson is going to Bristol, apparently. He asked if you'd like to take it. The telegram just came.'

I didn't know what to say at first. I hadn't known he had been asking for me, or that he had wanted me out of the house so much. It was like being hit by a cricket ball, nowhere near a cricket pitch or players. I had to sit holding it before I could understand properly. Eventually I said, 'I can't be a parson. I thought Deuteronomy was the academic study of Germany till I was eighteen.'

'It's only Truro, we're not talking about Canterbury. There's a little cottage near the church. Own garden,' he added, nodding at the seed trays and the grafted saplings. He smiled, properly. He often smiled – he was a beautifully mannered man – but not in private and it made me feel like he hadn't quite recognised me. 'I said you'd be delighted, of course. Decent salary, and you can start next month.'

'I don't want to be a parson – where did this come from?'

His grey eyes turned hard. 'One of the gardeners has raised some concerns. I've told them all to keep an eye on you. He said that you thought the statue had moved.'

'It has. Someone moved it.'

'No one's moved it, Merrick. The thing must weigh a ton and a half at the inside.'

'I know that, but—'

'You're getting towards the age that Mama was,' he interrupted. 'And I'm sure she began by thinking her mind was hiccuping.'

'Well, if I'm going to go mad I'm sure I'll find something to fixate on, whether it's a statue or a tree near a parsonage or whatever. Why not sign me up to the asylum now?'

'I can't afford to. You know how much it costs to keep Mama at Brislington? They have silver pheasants wandering the courtyards, for Christ's sake.'

'I was joking,' I said flatly.

'I know you were. It was in such poor taste that I decided to ignore it,' he said. He looked out at the grave and the statue. 'It isn't good for you to be here, in any case. Perhaps you might fixate on something else, but that wretched thing means something to you and perhaps whatever that is will fade if you don't see it every morning. There is such a thing as out of sight, out of mind.'

'If you'd let me oversee the gardens it would bring in a lot more than a parsonage and I wouldn't be sitting here all day,' I said, though I knew it was dangerous.

'If I won't have you take after Mama, what in God's name makes you imagine I'd let you take after Jack?'

'I don't mean obsessive biannual trips to Peru, I mean keeping what we have. I mean *not* cutting down rare trees when there are people who would pay money to have cuttings, or even to come and see—'

'I'm not having anyone wandering through the grounds for no reason and I'm not having you up to your eyes in his memory, and if you ever mention it again, forget Brislington, I'll take you to the county asylum and let them try out all their interesting new electroshock therapies.'

'For God's sake.'

'I'm trying to keep you safe!' he snapped.

'Yes. The county asylum is very safe. I'll take the parsonage, thank you.'

'You wouldn't have to if you'd find yourself some proper work.'

'I couldn't stand up six months ago. I can barely get out here. Four hundred yards from the front door. I'm not going to get any better.'

'If you'd just pull yourself together—'

'I can't,' I said, gently, because he wasn't being vicious. Until two years ago, he had always been ill and I'd always been strong. That he had no one at all to lean on now had gone even harder with him than nearly losing the leg had with me. I was used to getting on with things by myself. He never had been. Somewhere deep and murky, I disliked him for having let himself get that way and for expecting help all the time when there was none, but I shouldn't have. Knowing that he had was what stopped me from making the same slide. 'If you run into a naval bombardment, that's the last running you're going to do. And you have to run, to do what I did. People don't always like East India Company expeditionaries stealing all the good tea and smuggling opium.'

'Parsonage or asylum, Merrick, choose, because I shan't have you here any longer,' he said, more angrily, because he knew he had been wrong.

'Can I not have a few weeks' grace in which not to go mad? You're going to need to hire someone or reshuffle Sarah's terms if I go, and you can't do that overnight.'

'What do you mean, hire someone? Who's Sarah?'

'The . . . kitchen girl,' I said. 'She leaves at five. Who do you think cooks dinner? It's only me here at that time.'

He looked honestly taken aback. 'Three weeks,' he said. 'And then I'm calling in a doctor.'

'I'm not mad now and I won't be mad then,' I said. 'Someone moved the statue.'

'Anyway, I'll be getting on,' he sighed. He didn't believe me.

I gave him his canes. 'I'm going to town later. Is there anything you want?' I said, to try and make peace before he went.

If he had been a hedgehog his spikes would have risen. 'You're doing much better if you can walk to Mevagissey.'

'No, I borrow one of the farm horses. Mr Tobin lets me take one when I need it as long as I saddle it myself.'

His focus passed straight through me. 'He's a tenant, Merrick. You can't borrow a horse from a sheep farmer, it—'

'Well, no dinner then,' I said, starting to laugh. 'You're a snob but there's no need to be a hungry snob.'

He stared at me and I stared back, and I think we both saw then what should have been obvious for years: that we belonged to different classes. He was a gentleman, and I never had been. His eyes filled with tears and then I looked away at the hopping crows so I could pretend not to have noticed.

'You've no pride, have you,' he said. 'There's nothing left for you to be proud of.'

'Well, hold on. We're neither of us down a tin mine. Own orchard. Large house. Or half of one. That's . . . pretty good.'

'I'm selling the orchard.'

Our grandfather had mortgaged a lot of the land for reasons we had never discovered. It hadn't been a catastrophic move in itself. It would have been nothing but a quirk in the family's financial history if our father had been canny with money, but he'd had no idea. He had come into the estate too young and made naive investments in the dying tin mines, and instead of paying off the original mortgage he'd had to increase it, to cover the house too. I hadn't known about any of the money problems for years – growing up, if a place is shabby it just is and I'd never thought twice – but after having left for a while and come back, it had been obvious and then I'd extracted it from Charles one Christmas. The only things we owned here were the plants. But I hadn't known he was struggling this much.

'This isn't really to do with me or the statue, is it? You have to sell the house.'

'Don't be ridiculous,' he snapped, but I didn't push. Although he was tempestuous it was only ever brief, and after his small storms he would freeze over; but the ice was never strong. I came away from the urge to break it and show him I could have and that I was usually quiet from tolerance, not meekness. His eyes were still glittering and he wouldn't talk to me again this year if he thought

I'd noticed. He pushed his hand over his mouth. 'Although – I am trying to find new positions for some of the gardeners. There's a new fellow at Trebah. Do you know anywhere else that . . .'

'There's another house next to that, big valley garden. Glendurgan.'

'They've a full staff. So does Trelissick.'

'I'll write to Kew, they know us. And some of the colleges at Oxford would take people, I imagine.'

He nodded and made an abrupt study of the floor, and I regretted having mentioned Oxford. He had gone to Christ Church College to read classics for three years in a beautiful set of rooms that overlooked the grounds and the almost-tame deer herds there. I'd gone to a naval academy in Bristol.

'This parsonage,' I said. 'Spare room?'

'I don't know, I hardly made specific enquiries.'

'Yours when you want if there is. No interior slugs, no sprouting doors, it'll be lovely. I might buy some chickens. Parsons do things like chicken competitions, don't they? You can't be a parson without prize bantams.'

'You sound like an Irishman,' he said, but he didn't say no. 'I'll see you at seven.' He hesitated in the doorway. 'No one's moved that statue, Merrick.'

I sat down, not wanting to loom, but I watched him go. He had an uneven walk because the polio had damaged his left leg more than his right, and there was something unsteady about it; there were always fractional moments where his weight swung just too far to the left and he looked like he should be falling.

After a while, I went out to the statue.

It had used to hold a candle when I was small and, having lit it, you had to make a wish. I took a candle from inside one of the greenhouse lamps and balanced it in the statue's open palm. I hoped more than wished not to go mad, and not to be seeing things, and that it had been the gardeners after all, or even Charles doing his best to convince me to get me out of the house and save his pride before he had to fold and say we couldn't afford to stay.

The statue closed its hand around the candle. It didn't otherwise move and I stood still for a long time, trying to tell if the motion was something I'd imagined after the fact, or if I had seen it. I shut my eyes and opened them again. But the statue was the same. I tried to move its fingers, but there was no give to them whatever and no sign that they had ever been intended to move. I leaned back in to take the India Office letter from its pot. I brought it with me when I went to town. The ride did me good. Being exhausted wasn't the same as being mad, and I was exhausted, had been for months. The loss of work, of the use of one leg, and the old independence from home and all its mouldering difficulties – none of that had done my mind any good. I was at two-thirds capacity, at best. It was amazing I hadn't started seeing things before.

I got a tight feeling in my chest whenever I went to the greenhouse after that, but the statue stayed where I'd left it.

FOUR

IT WAS A FEW weeks later that I found the door to the greenhouse already propped open one morning and the vapour from the sprinklers curling out into the cold. The lamps were on too, though hazy, because the glass walls had been made nearly opaque by condensation. The sun didn't reach over the trees until midday and it was still murky otherwise. I stopped shy of it.

Crockery chinked inside. Gulliver lifted her head and trotted through, nudging the door further open. It bumped into the frame again behind her. I heard a voice say something to her, a man's voice, but too quietly for me to make out the words or whether I knew the owner.

It was much warmer inside than out. The air was heavy with the smell of damp ferns. I'd put in a clockwork misting system last year, but I'd almost forgotten about it; it took time to set it going and at some point I'd given up. It kept a fine spray in the air near the door for about ten minutes every hour. Someone had turned it on. The stove, further inside, was lit and strong; the light was coming towards me, through the ferns, which cast piano-key shadows in the vapour as it spun.

'Come and sit down, the coffee's ready.'

I pushed aside one of the ferns with the knuckle of my middle finger. The smell of coffee met me over the woodsmoke. At the wobbly workbench, Clem grinned and burst to his feet to hug me. It was like being folded into a rainbow. He had bright red hair, so he had never suited dark colours, and instead all his waistcoats were purple or green, with peacock lining or tartan, and his ties were always done in fantastic paisley embroidery, and his handkerchief never matched. He smelled of smoke and green.

Where I'd lost it, he had put on weight; solid, broad, middle-aged weight. He was nearly twice my size. I had a sudden, weird realigning of perspective. Near Charles, who was so frail, I was big and clunky, but I felt fragile now, for all Clem was shorter. It must have shown too, because his gold eyebrows went right up. At any distance they were invisible and he always looked good-naturedly surprised.

'Merrick, old man, you look absolutely awful. Charles hasn't been withholding food, has he?'

'No – no,' I said, then laughed when I realised his wife was here too. She was almost his opposite and together they were like a pair of pheasants, the cock all bright and showy and the hen modest and brown. There were blonde streaks in her hair and she was tanned. 'Minna, it's lovely to . . . I'm sorry there aren't better chairs . . .'

'I'm happy to perch,' she said cheerfully. 'In fact I could sit on Gulliver, couldn't I? She's quite spacious.'

Gulliver snuffled at her, tail wagging interestedly. Her fur had puffed up almost at once in the humidity and she was nearly spherical now.

'What are you doing here?' I asked. I nearly said that I'd thought the statue had invited itself in and made some coffee.

'Fishing you out, old man. Consider yourself fished. And, er, playing with your clockwork. Sorry,' he added as a new puff of mist came from the nozzle next to me.

Clem and I had met in the Navy and bonded over a mutual interest in Peru, but we had lost touch after I went to the East India Company and he went off to be an expeditionary for the Royal Geographical Society. I hadn't thought of him or expected to see him again. He was Sir Clements Markham, in fact, and I had never been wholly convinced that we might really be friends. But when I came back from China in such a mess, he had arrived a few days later. I don't know how he heard I'd been injured, or how he even knew I was in England, but he'd burst into the house and announced he would be looking after me until I was upright again. And he had, cut short only when he was called off on an archeological expedition to some Incan ruins a month later.

He pulled the last stool out from under the bench, moved the old flowerpots, and put me on it. Sitting took me into the heat of the open stove. It was lovely. Minna smiled to say hello. Her eyes were dark and so she tended to sparkle even when she wasn't meaning to. Clem kissed the top of my head. 'You'll like this, it's proper coffee.'

'Do you take sugar, Em?' said Minna.

I tried to remember. I hadn't had coffee for years. It was expensive. 'No, I don't think so. When did you get in?'

'Oh, only about twenty minutes ago,' Clem said. 'Couldn't face going up to the house and talking to Charles, though. One of the gardeners said you'd be down here. Got lost twice,' he added. He was a geographer and losing his way was a novelty. 'And the house looked pretty chilly, what with the . . . enormous holes in the roof and the wall?'

'Yes. We had some accidents. The wood from the big tree near the house explodes.'

'Of course it does,' he laughed. He knew Heligan well enough to expect pointless bizarre things in the neglected corners.

Minna was arranging the coffee-making things across the bench, which she'd neatened up. I'd left a sprawl of seed trays and packets out and now they were all in a strict row along the side. A small hessian bag sat open, still mostly full of coffee beans that gleamed. A mortar and pestle I normally used for seeds still had some ground coffee in it – it looked much cleaner than it did usually – and by her elbow a percolator that wasn't mine stood fastened, steaming. It was bright bronze and it showed us all in colours warmer than we really were. They had brought their own cups too. She set one under the percolator and pushed a lever gently. The black coffee was silky and slow. She poured in the milk while she waited for it, so that it plumed brown, then gave the cup to me, still with rainbow coffee bubbles around the outside where the furling milk hadn't quite yet reached.

It was wonderful when I tried it. When I lifted my head, they were both watching me in the same concerned way.

'I don't look that bad,' I said, but not with much confidence. Next to the two of them, I could have been a tramp. My clothes were clean, more or less, but they had been washed in a sink, not boiled, and nothing had been ironed for a long time. Because I always had my sleeves rolled back, the cotton was a fresher, clearer white about halfway down my arms when they were rolled down.

'Well,' said Minna.

'Listen, we're not actually here for a jaunt,' Clem said. 'There's another wave of malaria in India. Price of quinine through the roof. The India Office are tired of buying it in from Peru and they want their own supply once and for all. They want us to try for the cinchona woods.'

'So you came via Cornwall?'

'When I say us I mean you too. They said you refused by letter a few weeks ago and I said they must have misunderstood.'

'No. I can't go on an expedition, Clem, I can't walk.'

'You'll be fine. Boat, horse, tent, easy. I'll show you the route.'

'I can barely make it down here from the house—'

'Of course you can't, you're living in the middle of nowhere with Vile Charles. Now do shut up and listen to me.'

I sat quietly. Minna kicked my ankle and nodded a little. I couldn't meet her eyes for long. I loved both of them, but they did tend towards over-optimism, having always had a lot of money and a lot of friends.

Clem lifted his bag into his lap to take out a folded map. When he unfolded it, it was a beautiful chart of southern Peru, covering much more territory than mine did. Lima was too far north for it, but near the coast was Arequipa, marked quite big, and then the great ragged shape of Lake Titicaca. He had already inked on the route around. It looped past the lake, north, to a pair of towns close together called Juliaca and Puno, then north again to Azangaro, where there was a drawing of what might have been a cathedral. After that, the Andes. Beyond them, there was nothing. None of the forest there was charted. The cartographer had put on intricate little etchings of tropical trees and the suggestion of mountains for the sake of not having white space, but that was all. Clem pinned the edges down with our cups when they tried to curl upward.

'Right. Now, I don't know what the situation was when you last looked into it, but according to the latest reports, the whole Sandia Valley – that's this bit here on the interior side of the Andes – and everything nearer the mountains has been completely stripped of cinchona. There's nothing left within easy reach, which sounds unpromising but in fact it's good. It means there's no quinine industry in the region. The supply regions are in the north, and the suppliers up there harvest lower-yield trees. But there are high-yield woods in the rainforest beyond Sandia, much harder to access. Technically, though, trying to get at them would be a violation of the monopoly, so we'll have to be—'

'Wait, wait,' I said. 'There's an official monopoly now?'

'Ooh, yes,' he said. 'The government run the supply as far as I can tell. Or rather, a group of violent criminals runs the supply, and the government enforces their monopoly for a cut of the very considerable profits. The point is to keep foreigners from taking anything.'

'What happens if they catch us?'

'Prison or shot.'

'Right. And – how do you know there are more trees further in?'

'Because the Dutch got out with a few. You remember, don't you?' he added, sounding a little shocked that I'd forgotten about it. 'The expedition who were killed by mad Indians last year. One of them survived, got out with some trees, remember?'

'But only a couple of the specimens survived the passage to the Java plantation,' I said slowly. The information came back as if I'd dreamed it rather than read it in the papers and argued to and fro by letter with India House about it. Finding the recollection again felt like having turned aside a stone to get at the thready roots of a few weeds only to find the ruins of a whole town. Something spidery walked down my back when I saw the extent of what I hadn't known I'd forgotten. I glanced around the greenhouse as if there might have been more crumbled half-memories clustered around it. 'And then the trees died once they were planted. The last British expedition were all killed too.'

'That's it. Are you all right?' Clem said.

'I'm . . . sorry. I do know. Too much time by myself not talking.'

'Happens to me whenever I visit my mother, I can quite imagine it's dreadful after months rather than days,' Minna said. She poured me some more coffee. 'I come back a veritable mute.'

I didn't say I thought it was something more serious than that. It was a miniature realisation, that I'd forgotten about the Dutch expedition, but it had lit a little miner's lamp somewhere in those lost places in the pit of my mind. The light echoed weirdly and I had a horrible feeling there were caverns there when I'd thought there were only a few caved-in corridors. Seams and forgotten seams.

Clem rubbed my shoulder. Some of it must have showed on my face.

'So – to be clear,' I said at last, because they had both been waiting for me to speak in a loaded silence that sounded a lot like they wanted to make sure I definitely could speak still. 'We are . . . being sent to steal a plant whose exact location nobody knows, in territory now defended by quinine barons under the protection of the government, and inhabited by tribal Indians who also hate foreigners and have killed everyone who's got close in the last ten years. Who was the British man?'

'Backhouse,' Minna said. 'Half a regiment of Peruvian soliders disappeared in the forest trying to help him.'

'Oh, did they, good,' I said. 'And you two think you'll get through it all if you go at the pace of someone with only one working leg?'

'Proper organisation, that's all that's required,' Clem said firmly. 'You don't mind a few mad Indians, do you?'

'It's more the two of you I'm worried about.'

'Kind but unnecessary,' he said, waving his hand. 'Anyway, you make it sound like we haven't the foggiest where to look. But we've got a pretty good idea of where the things are. It's round here.'

He was circling a point right on the edge of the map with his knuckle.

When I touched it too, my fingertip, rough from digging and seeds, scratched against the paper. I clenched my hand, then motioned between us. 'We would stand out, in the interior highlands of Peru. If the monopoly is what you say then they're watching for white men.'

'We say we're mapmakers. And we will be. The India Office has asked for an accurate map of the region as well as the plants. If we have to take any planty-type equipment, we're also collecting rare types of . . . something that grows in the same conditions at the same altitude?' he finished hopefully.

'Coffee,' I provided. 'But I doubt anyone would believe that.'

'Well, that brings me to what I wanted to ask you. Your father lived round there for a while, didn't he?'

'An Indian mission village called New Bethlehem. It's about here.' I touched the map just by the Bolivian border. 'My grandfather was collecting quinine for one of the early runs but he was caught and he had to hide for a while. They took him in. Dad went back for other things, orchids mostly. And some coffee, actually. Frost-resistant stuff up there. He used to live there four or five months of the year.' I hesitated. 'But we'd have to ask around for it, once we were over the Andes. Neither of them ever put it on a map. Dad said there are things that shouldn't go on maps. He got cross when I tried to make him tell me once. It's the only time he ever snapped at me that I remember.'

'Oh dear, how useful.'

'Oh, well.' I had to wave my hand to encompass all the things about Dad that hadn't been very useful. He had been made mostly of fly-fishing techniques and Peruvian stories, and since he wasn't a capacious person to begin with, there hadn't been much leftover room for cartography or finance. Getting annoyed about it was like blaming a butterfly for not being able to spin a web.

'Did he ever say why?'

'No.' I tried to think about it. At the time I'd taken it at face value. 'But he was born there. I think he was trying to protect the Indians. Or something.'

'Well, that's not an ignoble thing. We do have a habit of barging in and stealing all their cocoa. Do you suppose anyone there would still remember him?' Clem said. 'Anyone willing to help us?'

'Should do. But I wouldn't be confident of getting a letter out there,' I said, looking up.

'No need,' he said. 'We can sort out a guide and details when we arrive; in fact it's better that way. No paper trail, no letters, no evidence. We'll cross the Andes, find someone who can take us to the village, then we'll be roughly in the right place and if they recognise you they might just help. They don't know anyone else from Adam and we're going to need native help if we're going to find these wretched trees.'

'I'm not him. Even if the same people are there, I don't speak Quechua—'

'I do. Listen, I don't want you just for that. The idea is this. The guide and I will go up to the cinchona woods and bring back seeds or cuttings or whatever, and then you'll look after them from there on in. If the path is decent you could even come up to the woods with us.' He lifted his eyebrows at me, because I'd started to shake my head while he was still talking. 'I'd be a lot more confident about the specimens if I knew you'd chosen them. I suspect you know how to look after them?'

'I could make an educated guess,' I said, hedgingly.

'Good. So what do you think? Don't think about the leg. That isn't a reason not to do anything.'

'Well, it is.'

'I'm logistics. Let me worry about that,' he said over me. 'Merrick, the India Office put you at the top of the list. It isn't only me who wants you to do this. They haven't forgotten about you.'

'I'm sure they haven't. But I really can't walk. Perhaps it will be a bit better in good company doing something useful, but not much.'

'Can you ride?'

'Yes—'

'Good then. Em, I want your brain and your family connections. If you keep those in good order, I'll worry about getting the rest of you there. Don't think I imagine you'll spring up like a lamb, I know you won't, but the difficulty of getting you over there is paltry in comparison to the value of your presence – do you understand?'

'Do you mean it?'

'No, I'm lying, and so is the India Office, which of course is well known for its sentimental approach to all things.'

I looked between him and Minna and wanted to insist that it was a terrible idea. In the best of all possible worlds, Clem was going to realise it was a mistake and I'd have to stay like a fifth wheel in Arequipa or Azangaro to wait for him while he crossed the Andes, and in the worst, there was going to come a moment when we would have to run from someone with a gun and I wouldn't be able to.

'They're offering to pay a fortune if we get it right,' he added. He only flicked a look at the house, but it was clear enough.

'I imagine doing something like this has come to seem wholly impossible,' Minna said gently. 'But honestly, Em, we can get you there. Stop looking at it as an impossible thing and start looking at it as a thing that must be done.'

I was on the edge of saying no, but having almost decided on it made that future very clear. A parsonage in Truro while Charles amputated pieces of the grounds and the house until eventually there was nothing left and he was stuck with me in a spare room, surrounded by people he would never believe weren't beneath him. And me: I'd never see anything but Cornwall again, except maybe Clem's townhouse in London at Christmas. I'd be the quiet, tired person in the corner, and all those parts of myself I could feel crumbling now would be gone, and with any luck I'd never even remember that I'd been cleverer once and better, but I didn't generally have good luck. Minna frowned, worried. It tipped me over. It was better to get shot in the Andes than live for another forty years while they both looked at me that way.

'Christ, the two of you. All right. We can try,' I said. 'But I won't be magnanimous when it all goes wrong.'

Clem laughed. He had a huge, golden bubble of a laugh. It wasn't put on, just expansive. I'd never heard him sing, but I'd always had a feeling he could have easily filled a concert hall. 'Excellent. We're off in December; it'll be summer in Peru. Which we'll need, I tell you now. The highlands round Titicaca are bitter in winter. You wouldn't be able to get plants through it alive. What's it now, end of August – here, do you speak Spanish?'

I shook my head.

'Soon fix that. I've a fellow at the Spanish Embassy in London. Let's get you shacked up there until we go, he'll teach you. You'll learn in no time. It's as close to English as crumpets and cricket. God, it's lovely in here,' he exclaimed, surging to his feet again. He rubbed Gulliver's ears with both hands and she jumped up with a happy yip and walked round him twice, as pleased with him as I was. 'We've brought a picnic, shall we get cracking? You clearly haven't eaten properly in aeons. Honestly, Em, either look after yourself or marry someone who will.'

I laughed and didn't ask him if he had anyone in mind. Clem thought that marriage was something that happened naturally to a person, like starting to like olives; somebody would come along and that would be that, which was just how it had been for him. He had no notion that being a second son with nothing and no access to any particular society except a dog was any impediment and it seemed churlish to disagree. He laughed too and popped the cork on the wine. He snorted at himself when it foamed over his hand. He gave the bottle shamefacedly to Minna.

'There you are,' she said to me. She had had to hold the glass off to one side to keep the bubbles from dripping on a tray of pansies. 'Do wipe your hands on Markham.' She never called him Clem, though he insisted on it with everyone else. When she'd met him he had been Lieutenant Markham and she said she still couldn't altogether conceive of his having a first name.

I sank into a bright cushion of happiness. The wine was sweet and silvery, and the glass chimed when my fingernails touched it. Minna had brought everything in a hamper with leather straps. When she had finished pouring the wine, she took out a cake topped with icing flowers and a tumble of tropical marzipan fruit around a tiny iced signpost that said 'To Peru, 6,000 miles'. She turned it so that the sign pointed the right way. 'That's beautiful.'

'It was your birthday yesterday, wasn't it?' she said.

'Was it? What day is it?'

'It wouldn't be very good if I were to pat you on the head, would it.' Her deep laugh was thrumming up through her voice. 'Do you know how old you are? Oh, God, you're adding up in your head.'

'Thirty, I'm thirty, shut up.'

Minna blinked at me slowly. 'You know when a thing is so absurdly sweet it's hard not to—?' She smacked her hands together like she was killing a spider. 'Charm-rage.'

'Yes, perhaps don't sit next to her,' Clem stage-whispered.

'Oh, Christ. I need to talk to Charles,' I said suddenly.

Minna lifted her eyebrows at me. 'Why would you ever talk to Charles?'

'He arranged for me to be a parson in Truro. I need to ask him to delay the proceedings.'

'Try cancel,' Clem said. 'I'm not letting you come back here again, not on your life. Which is a shame, because it's gorgeous, but it would be a lot more gorgeous if you were to sling your brother off a cliff. You're not willing to have a go?'

'At homicide of the crippled and well meaning, no.'

'Fastidious liberalism.'

'Manners maketh man.'

Minna laughed and I smiled too.

'Well, never mind,' Clem said. 'Leave him to his farthing-harvests. He's a horrible little gnome. You need to get away from him. Tell you what, I'll take you to Peru.'

I rocked forward as I laughed, which brought into view a little clear patch of the glass wall unobscured by ferns. Outside, the statue had been moved again. It was right up close to the greenhouse now, looking in, as if it were hoping to catch what we were saying.

FIVE

ON THE SEVENTEENTH OF December, the *Hooper* waited on the Thames for the Greenwich time ball to drop, and the captain set both the ship's clocks to noon.

It was a little ship but modern, with a spacious hold and heating pipes that circulated through all the cabins. On the first morning we passed the Cornish coastline and home. I saw the little harbour at Mevagissey and, right up on the hills, a canopy of dark evergreens that I was nearly sure were our pines, at the top of the valley. It was a degree and a half of longitude away from Greenwich and so technically about twenty-five minutes behind, which I hadn't thought of before but Minna pointed out when we saw the first mate, who had nothing more pressing to do, resetting one of the clocks. It was too cold after that to linger outside and I retreated into the hold.

There, we had thirty Wardian cases, which were person-sized greenhouses shaped like Turkish lamps. Each one was big enough to hold a sapling tree, the glass thick enough to keep it sun-drenched and protected from the salt air. And in fact they did all have trees in them. I'd brought thirty apple trees for Clem and Minna to practise taking cuttings from.

'You're staring into space as though the ether is telling you things,' Minna said.

I'd been waiting for her and Clem with my back against three copper heating pipes, and a sapling apple tree in front of me. Because they had been force-grown, they were blossoming in the heat of the hold. When I opened the little door in the case, the blossom blew out in the warm draught and brought the smell of spring with it.

'Just vacancy – sorry. Have a pipe.'

She sat down next to me. 'Markham's on his way. How's your leg, is it painful?'

'The heating helps,' I said. I watched her for a second. 'You've gone green, are you seasick?'

'A bit. It's, um . . . it seems only to be in the mornings, though.' She didn't look pleased, only worried.

'Well, go gently, whatever happens,' I said, thinking of all the things it was possible to fall off or slip on: the ladders, the deck, which was slick with brine; the boxes stowed far short of Navy-fashion in the mess room.

'I'll lose it even if I sit perfectly still suspended in mid-air. I always lose them. Don't tell Markham. Horrible to get him excited and hopeful for nothing.'

'I won't.'

'Thank you. You don't – disapprove?'

'No. Christ, Minna, it's yours until it makes an appearance in the world. It's yours in the same way your liver is; you wouldn't catch me telling you what to do or not do about that. I'd suggest not drinking heavily or taking a lot of opium, but you know.'

She laughed. 'This is assuming I don't become hysterical soon and give the game away.'

'I can't imagine you hysterical.'

'Watch,' she said darkly.

'Morning all,' Clem said, sliding down the ladder with a happy spring that made both of us look at him a bit hard. He didn't notice. 'Right! Shall we get going with this cutting lark? Gosh, it's lovely down here,' he added. 'Hardly know it was a ship.'

I gave them both some barking knives. 'Right. The idea is, if you both learn to do this, there'll be three of us who can, whatever happens.'

I took them through how to take a scion cutting from one of the established branches, and then how to pack them properly. We used moss and one of Clem's map cases, because those were what we would have with us in Peru.

'God, it's fiddly,' Clem murmured. 'Can't we just take seeds?'

'No.' I paused while I checked his last cutting. It was jagged. '*Calisaya* cinchona seeds sport. Like apples and tulips. The daughter plant from a seed won't necessarily be the same type as the parent. It has to be cuttings.'

'Oh good. What a time to be a total arts and crafts duffer,' Clem said.

'You'll be all right. That's why I've got thirty apple trees. Plenty of practice – stop holding that knife like a hammer.'

'Right,' he said. 'Come on, let's try again. You were called to Leadenhall Street a few days ago, weren't you?' he said suddenly, which was his version of subtly.

My ribs caught, but I was too good at lying now to let it into my voice. After years with the East India Company I was an expert. 'I was. Just Mr Sing. He used to be my manager. It was a chat and a cup of tea, or he would have called you too. I think he just wanted to make sure I wasn't addicted to opium or anything.'

'Oh, of course,' he said, soothed. He hesitated. 'Only it – hasn't escaped me that it's odd for the India Office to have asked me.' Minna looked up too. 'I mean if the idea is to fetch out these trees, a geographer is a funny sort of choice.'

'A geographer who speaks Quechua and has lived in Peru on and off for years. There aren't many of those. You can't do this stuff without an interpreter.'

'I suppose,' he said.

'Let's try a new tree,' I said.

The telegram had arrived at the Spanish Embassy. I hadn't told anyone but Clem and Minna I was there and so I knew it was from Sing, though he didn't sign it.

The old East India Company had become the India Office, but really only in name. There were grand plans in Whitehall, said the papers, but for now it was even in the same building as it always had been. East India House was on Leadenhall Street, a vast place with a colonnaded front and a statue of a mounted Britannia on the roof. There was a confectionery shop next door and like always, the man at the main desk had a sugar mouse sitting in the middle of his ledger.

Nationalisation wasn't something any of us had thought would happen, but it had, last year. The East India Company, a private venture with the means and power of a country, a nation state of traders, had been taken almost overnight by the British Government and turned into a branch of the civil service. It had happened in the wake of the war in China; one war too many started by the Company and ended by the Navy. Parliament said they had made a de facto relationship law; Sing and the old traders called it the greatest robbery of the millennium. I kept quiet about it, because I was glad. It gave me a funny unfashionable confidence in Mr Palmerston and his government. Anyone clever enough to steal the EIC from a whole board and company of flick-razor bastards like Sing was certainly qualified to run an empire, just as much as anyone whose name had ended with Caesar.

I wasn't surprised to find Sing in exactly the same office I'd left him in, although if anyone was going to be shifted about in all the changes, it was him. He was a slight Oriental. In western clothes he should have looked like someone's butler, but he didn't have the eastern manner or its over-politeness. He sat like an Englishman, straight, with one forearm across the hem of his ribs and the other elbow resting against that wrist. If there was anything left of his own country, it was buried. He wouldn't say where he was from. His servant and his accent were Dutch and his first name was Iseul, but that only made me think of Cornish princesses.

'Tremayne, sit down,' he said, as if we hadn't been out of touch for nearly two years.

I sat, carefully, not wanting to look too exhausted from the tiny walk up through the building. But Clem was right; I had been getting better in London, much better. He kept the house warm and he had towed me out to buy new clothes because, he said, the Spanish Embassy didn't want me slouching about in a wax jacket that had probably seen action at Trafalgar, so now I was neat in black and grey, and a coat he had paid for with a blue cord collar. He had been buying gear for the expedition at the same time and it had been bizarre to see him order six shirts and four jackets all at once. I couldn't remember the last time I'd bought anything new and I'd forgotten how thick unworn cotton felt.

Sing studied me. Although he wasn't an expressive man I saw the dismay go through his eyes. I'd known I must have aged in the time we had been apart, but it was a shock to watch him notice it. He didn't mention it. 'So Markham seems like an idiot who signed up to all this in the interest of having a jolly good jaunt and discovering something irrelevant and Incan. Is that a fair summation?' he asked.

'He's a geographer-anthropologist, not an idiot. Of course he's interested in the Inca.'

'In the context of expeditions like these, anthropologist and idiot are wholly interchangeable terms.' His Dutch accent was gone now, except on perhaps one word in ten, where it could have been anything. He let his hands slip down to the file and rested his fingertips on the margins. 'So, I haven't invited him. I don't think I can stand to talk to someone like that at this time of the morning. I'd be in great danger of having him transported to Australia.' A ghost of a smile lined his eyes when I laughed. 'Anyway. Cinchona trees; tell me how you mean to do it.'

I sat forward so that I could talk with my hands and trace shapes along the edge of his desk. 'Seeds will sport, so we're going to take cuttings. Those cuttings will need to be about two feet long for trees like this. We'll pack them up in Clem's map cylinders. The difficulty is getting them back across Peru in time. They need to be planted within a month. We'll plant them in Wardian cases – those will be waiting for us at the port, in Islay; they're too delicate to transport inland on dust roads – and then ship them to India that way. Even in cases they won't survive very long at such low altitude, so the sea route is going to have to be direct.'

He frowned. 'You won't get many out in map cylinders.'

'The point is to bring out viable scion cuttings of high-yield plants. Quality over quantity. If those are successful, more cuttings can be taken from them once they're established in India. About Malabar? Clem said that's where we're going with them.'

'What about it?'

'Climate's wrong. Do we have land in Ceylon?'

'Yes.'

'There please. Sheltered ground, nothing rocky, rich soil, lots of ferns, between four and five thousand feet above sea level. They're very particular trees.'

'That's rather a—'

'I'm telling you the conditions required for their survival. I was at Kew yesterday, and they've only confirmed all this. Previous efforts at transplantation have failed because insufficient attention was paid to their natural environment. That's why the Dutch plantation in Java is such a catastrophe. It's on a rocky hillside, no shade, wrong elevation – of course they can't grow anything, even the hardy low-yield stuff. You'd do better trying to grow these things in a jar.'

He smiled a fraction and I realised he had wanted me to gardening-babble, to make sure I still could. 'So, Ceylon,' he said.

'Yes.'

'I'll arrange it, then.' Perhaps it was only that I was older now, but there was a fragility about him that seemed new; or perhaps it was new, and born of holding on to everything as the sand shifted under him. 'You don't look well,' he said.

'Well – I'm not fit enough to walk through the Amazon, no one's saying I am. Clem wanted me to supervise, that's all. But if you'd rather send someone else—'

'I don't care if you're preserved in a jar of turpentine if he can get you there,' Sing said. He paused. 'We're on the edge of quinine riots in India. The cost is madness now. We're having to sell it at a loss just to keep the tea plantations open. The monsoons last year – did you see in the papers?'

'No.'

'Vast. Malaria everywhere.' He shook his head once and then, in a way that sounded involuntary, 'I had it too. It's ridiculous. Half the plantation labourers have fled, the harvests are abysmal. Tea left on the plants because there's no one to bring it in. Do you know how much of the trade revenue of the British Empire comes from tea?'

'A lot.'

'A lot,' he said, tundra-arid and mostly to the file in front of him. He was quiet then and I saw him trying to decide whether or not to tell me anything else. Five years ago he wouldn't have, but he looked tired now. 'I think you'll do it. But nobody else involved has any such confidence. The new managers here have . . . no concept of the correlation of risk and gain. They're civil servants, not traders.' When he said trader, it had a weight; he meant it in the way other people would say statesman. 'What they know is what will fit into a morning briefing and that is as follows. The *calisaya* cinchona woods are remote in the extreme. The last expedition was Dutch; three men vanished in the rainforest and the survivor had to hide for so long that most of his trees died . . . only two made it to Java intact—'

'Two would have been enough if he had just taken care of the damn things properly.' Hasskarl was the worst gardener I'd met since one of my uncles had insisted ferns grew best in salt.

'Oh, you know that, I know that, but the new managers think we live in the pinnacle of human accomplishment and if it hasn't been done yet then it can't be. What they do know is that Charles Backhouse's whole expedition was lost before that, in 'fifty-one, along with fifty soldiers, to hostile Indians. Worse, they know we have no maps. Hasskarl didn't get any – he didn't go to the forest himself, and the men he sent in are dead. A guide brought him the trees. Said guide was then hunted by informers for the quinine suppliers and killed. Backhouse didn't send anything either. The Peruvians must have maps, of course, but they're hardly eager to provide us with nice charts to the only high-yield quinine forest in the world. So in their lofty and infinite W,' he finished, with the worrying fluency he sank into sometimes when he was talking to or about his colleagues, something he did to prove they weren't ever going to overshoot his understanding with slang or Latin, 'the India Office has written the idea off.'

I frowned. 'Then . . . how was this expedition ever approved?'

'Markham was chosen because he's a respected and capable member of the Royal Geographical Society, and he makes exceptionally good maps.' He watched me for a long moment. 'And you . . .'

He flicked his eyes to my cane. 'On paper you're going because your whole career with us has been difficult smuggling runs with difficult plants and because you have links to the area. But no one will be surprised if a crippled gardener can't get it done, and you've no proper family and no connections, so it doesn't cost us anything if you die out there. You're a way for this office to save face.'

I would have been quicker two years ago. I might even have seen it the moment Clem came to Heligan. 'This expedition isn't really about the trees at all, is it? It's about getting a decent map, for if – when – the army has to go.'

'Yes.' He wasn't the kind of man who would report his unsuccessful efforts, but hanging heavy in the air around him were meetings and meetings where he had argued against the appointment of an anthropologically inclined geographer. I knew the sort he would have wanted to lead the thing. It would have been one of the old expeditionaries from the Company, someone fast who could shoot well, ex-cavalry – a bodyguard for the gardeners. 'If you cannot reach the cinchona woods for whatever reason, then make a spark. There must be a political reason to send troops, however thin. You know how it is. Something small but inflammatory.'

'Get myself shot somewhere public?'

'No, get Markham shot somewhere public. A promising young knight of the realm with a pretty widow will make the front page. You wouldn't even be in the obituaries at the back.'

'He's my friend, you know. We were in the Navy together.'

'I know. I believe you met because he had you flogged.'

'You once had me kidnapped and traded for a racing camel, but I still wouldn't chuck you to a load of angry Indians.'

He sighed. I'd known him for years before he admitted that it hadn't been an accident and he did indeed have a policy about not promoting expeditionaries who couldn't get themselves back to Cairo from a Tuareg slave train in the desert. 'Just fetch the trees,' he said. 'That would be far simpler. On that note.' He opened the file he had in front of him. 'What do you know about New Bethlehem? Did your father and grandfather keep notes?'

'They didn't really. I know it's . . . a mission colony, or it was originally. It's high up, a good few thousand feet, and it's on the edge of an alpine section of the forest. There's a river, but I don't know the name of it. The cinchona trees nearer the Andes were killed off because traders barked them so badly, but if this place is as remote as I think, not many people will ever have reached it to look for more. It will be a decent starting place for an expedition further into the rainforest, anyway. And I know they'll know my name. My father was born there. But that's all.'

He had listened carefully. 'Did they ever have any problems with Indians? I mean forest tribes, not the villagers. Were they ever attacked?'

'Dad never mentioned anything like that. But I was eight when he died. I didn't get a very objective account. Honestly, though, if there are territorial tribes there, then tough,' I said. 'We'll have to cope. New Bethlehem is the only place we can ask for without being obviously there for quinine. It might just about fly that I want to find some coffee and visit people my father knew, but if we try to go anywhere else, no.'

He was quiet while he thought about it. 'Look, I know it sounds steep when we stack it up like this, but if you want to be paid, you need to bring back something. Whether it's the trees or the army's reason to go. I notice that Heligan is in danger of falling to ruin. Do this and I will see to it that you have work afterwards.'

'Sing,' I said, 'did you wait to do this so I'd be good and desperate when you asked me?'

'Yes,' he said.

I smiled. 'I missed you.'

'I'm glad you see it that way.' He settled forward on his forearms. 'Merrick. I would suggest that Backhouse's main problem was not Indians or quinine suppliers but that he was twenty-one and an idiot. You're old Company; you know how this sort of thing is done. If you can't go around, find someone to take you through those woods if you have to. Find some Indians, lie, cheat, bribe, use your father's name, sleep with the chief, I don't care. This is smuggling, like everything else we ever did. There's always a way.'

'I know.'

'Feeling all right about it?' he said, which he had never asked me before. 'Aside from having been chosen for exactly the wrong reason for what might be suicide.'

'I wish the papers weren't full of shipwrecks and frostbitten bits of the Franklin expedition, but you know.'

He smiled, but only enough to show his incisors. I realised suddenly that he must have had not just edges knocked off but whole walls blown through by the dissolution of the Company and its restructuring. It seemed ridiculous now that I hadn't written to him to ask how he was. 'You're not off to find the Northwest Passage on a thousand-mile plain of ice populated by six Esquimaux and an owl. It's only Peru.'

'No, I know.' The *Illustrated London News* had run an article a few days before, with pictures of things that were recovered. They had found a watch, some zigzag-pattern mittens, a pair of reading glasses, snow goggles, bone tools; ordinary things that people had had in their pockets, things made at home to help, things the natives had given them. Humanity on both sides of the Atlantic had tried to get the Franklin expedition to where it needed to go and the only real difficulty had been the weather. In the far north of Canada, there had been no one trying to shoot them, no animals that could hurt them, not around their guns, no diseases to slow them down. There would be no one trying to help us and the interior of Peru was even less charted than the Arctic. 'I'll try.'

He nodded. He would never tell me if someone in the upper management had threatened his job if this were to fail, but it was a pressure behind the quiet.

'The *Great Eastern* is launching today, did you see?' I said.

He tipped his eyes towards the window, more like his old self. 'Monstrous thing.'

'Have you been to look at it?'

'No,' he said, as if I'd asked him if he had been in a pornography shop.

'It's not monstrous. It's the biggest ship that's ever sailed, with the most powerful engine that's ever been on the sea. It could make the run to Australia without stopping to refuel, with four thousand passengers. Honestly, it's incredible. Come with me and see it off. It'll be good, there are people all up and down the river now.'

'I'll be impressed when the bloody thing sails to Mars. Send me a telegram the day before you go if all's running to time. I'll meet you in Ceylon in May.'

I frowned. 'You're coming?'

'This is the India Office. Its employees do occasionally make an appearance in India,' he said, annoyed to have been caught fretting. He sighed. 'Get it done, please. And stop waxing lyrical about maritime pedantry before the summer or I'll feed you to a tiger.'

So I took a cab up to Greenwich by myself, into the crowds there. The ship was impossible to miss. It was ten times bigger than anything else on the water, almost too big for the bends in the river. When the tugs guided it out, the cheer felt like it was coming up through the ground. There were four anchors chained to the prow, each one ten times the height of a person. Each link in each anchor chain was taller than me. Thousands of people stood on deck, waving and laughing. I had a horrible feeling that it was all too big and it would sink, but it didn't. It sailed gently out of sight, out towards Gravesend and looking wrong because it was so leviathan it didn't belong with anything else. I followed it in the papers because more and more it mattered that not every stupid endeavour ended frozen to a glacier with the *Illustrated London News* reporting what it had in its pockets. Off Dover there was a fire aboard, but the ship was so big that not even lightning would have bothered it and news came the following week that it had reached America seamlessly, ahead of schedule.

SIX

I MADE CLEM PRACTISE TAKING cuttings every day until we ran out of apple trees. He still couldn't do it very well, but he was seasick and I hoped it was the nausea making him unsteady, not his natural clumsiness. He kept to their cabin except at mealtimes and Minna moved into the mess room, where she took over the long table with charts and squashed the crew, who didn't know what to do with her, down one end.

'Evening,' she said when I stopped to sit down and have a rest between the hold and the kitchen on Christmas Eve. The crew had made an effort, which had surprised me, because left to myself I would have forgotten about it; but there were as many candles as the mate would allow, and wreaths on all the narrow doors, full of oranges pincushioned with cloves that made all the passageways smell of the holidays. The cook, who was German and had grown his moustache like Prince Albert's, had made nearly nothing but mince pies and mulled wine for three days and it was wonderful. I couldn't remember when I'd last eaten so badly or so happily. 'Eat my pie for me,' Minna added. 'I haven't wanted it. I'm off everything except tooth powder.'

'You'll have to call it Minty. What are you doing?' We had met some rough water, and above the table copper pots and pans swung on their hooks. Their shadows oscillated over the chart she had been looking at. A few of the candles tipped wax on it but we pretended not to notice. The mate was threatening to put them all out if they proved too hazardous. The pipes under the grille floor rattled as someone turned the heating up. Nearly at once, hot air drifted up round our ankles, pumped round from the engine furnace. Minna dropped her set of compasses when the table tipped and lifted her hands to surrender.

'I'm planning your route. I was trying to work out what would be quickest. And cheapest. The India Office accounting forms are formidable.'

I twisted my head so I could see it upside down. My spine twanged. I tried to ignore it. 'How long will it take, do you think? Cuttings are all right for a month but anything after . . .'

'All being well, from the coast to the Andes, it's about ten days. Through the Andes – it isn't too far as the crow flies but of course it will be longer. I can't find any record of how high the pass through the mountains is, so I don't know the real distance. But I'd say give that a few days as well. Then there's a river called the Tambopata – you're close when all the place names go into Quechua – and after that . . . no one knows. New Bethlehem isn't on any maps. It's too far into the interior. That's when you'll need a guide. So say three weeks there, three weeks back? But that's an absolute guess.'

'You keep saying *you*.'

'I can't come like this,' she said quietly. Her eyes went briefly past me to be sure Clem wasn't here yet. 'I don't think I'll be able to carry it to term anyway but . . . I don't want to take the chance of falling off a mule or drinking something horrible. I don't even know what the altitude does. Do you?'

'Do you think I've got a clutch of other female acquaintances in a cupboard somewhere? I haven't. I don't know anything about it.'

'Really? Handsome bachelors tend to know . . . sometimes . . .'

'No bastard children kicking round China, sorry. I'm not that exciting. What will you tell Clem?'

She looked pained. 'I'll make noises about there being no plumbing in Amazonian mission colonies, I suppose.'

'Say he shouldn't be worrying about both of us. Worrying about me is enough and I have to be there.'

'Are you sure?'

'You haven't an extensive history of minding about plumbing.'

'He's coming,' she murmured.

Clem dropped down on the bench next to me. 'This is not all right. I was never seasick in the Navy, was I?'

'No,' I said. 'But those were bigger ships and you were always outside.'

'Been outside,' he said. 'Got wet. Not worth it.'

Minna shifted with a tiny creak of the whalebone in her corset. It was almost exactly like the creak that rigging makes in a breeze and, although it actually represented something wholly unfamiliar, it was homely. 'Um . . . I've worked out your route, more or less.'

He noticed at once. '*Our* route? You're coming with us.'

'I'm not. I'd be a distraction if push came to shove.'

'Oh, what on earth do you mean?'

'I mean,' she said, 'that if you're arrested, you could fight your way out and take the cuttings. If I'm held hostage, you'll give up the cuttings in a heartbeat. Honestly, why do you think the East India Company loved unmarried childless men so much?' She inclined her head at me. 'What I will do is stay at Arequipa and arrange as fast a passage to Ceylon as our money can buy. I think we might need it.'

'I swore I'd never leave you behind just because it wasn't safe. We'd never have done anything together otherwise. You always said—'

'It's not about safety, it's about the integrity of the expedition. If I go, you're more likely to fail. You're hostage to the first person who works out that you'll drop it all if he grabs me, and I'm not big enough to reliably fight anyone off. If I don't go, you might just bluff it out with your cuttings intact.' She paused. 'And if it does all go wrong, you're going to need someone to come and fetch you out of prison.'

'Bugger prison. We've been everywhere, and you've never been kidnapped or thrown off a building or trampled by a llama, or anything—'

'Markham,' she laughed. 'You can't worry about Merrick and about me at the same time. While you ought not to be worrying about either of us, I know that you will, and this expedition hangs on *your* mind being on the job, and on someone knowing what it is you need to bring back.' She tipped her eyelashes at me. 'The expendable element in this equation is me.'

'I don't worry about Merrick! He's – perfectly capable.'

Although we had agreed for her to say it, it still stung to see what Clem thought. There was only a tiny pause before he rallied properly, but it was still a pause.

'Honestly, I don't worry about him. Minna, of course you must come.'

'I'm frightened,' she said. 'I don't think it's . . . people have died there, often, and I don't think it's any place for a woman.'

'Nonsense—'

'No, I mean any human who's five foot one and doesn't know how to shoot. I will slow you down, one way or the other. Listen, I did a bit of laundry earlier and I want to get it dried on the pipes while the wretched heating is still on, so I'd better . . . get to it,' she said, having to hop gently to get out from the bench, which was bolted into place. 'Can you bring the charts along with you, Markham?'

'Yes, of course,' Clem said. He stared after her. I could see the pressure fractures forming in his gold bubble. From the next room, the cook began to sing '*Stille Nacht*' in an unexpectedly fine tenor. Some of the other men at the far end of the table hummed along.

The ship swayed again and the copper pans pendulumed above us. I leaned into it. Clem looked queasy. I got on with finishing off a drawing I'd started at Kew. Tucked in the back of my journal, the letter my mother had given me tipped a little. I pushed it back in with the end of my pencil.

I'd gone up to Brislington before leaving for London. It was a picturesque place near Bristol, more hotel than asylum. Nobody there was gibbering. It was for subtle shades of madness: ladies who insisted they could control the weather or told marvellous lies for no reason. I'd never been to the men's side, but there was only a hedge between the two sections and when I arrived that morning, a badminton match was going on over the top of it, so it seemed unlikely that the policy was radically different there. Our mother was always in the same place, with a stack of books and some feed for the pheasants, which barely shuffled out of the way when I went over to her.

'I hear your brother's having to sell up,' she said. I shouldn't have been surprised that he had confessed to her and kept it from me. They were close. She didn't like me any more than he did. I couldn't remember having done anything particular, but having never known her especially it had never mattered much. Dad had died and she had been sent here within the same six months. I'd gone to school in Bristol after that, where the housemasters, ex-quartermasters all, were solid and kind. I called her Caroline.

'He's being cagey about it but I think so.'

'He writes that you're going to Caravaya.'

'If there's anyone you want me to look up, write a letter and I'll deliver it.'

She looked at me oddly. 'You can't afford to go to Peru. What on earth are you doing?'

'It's for the India Office. Quinine.' One of the pheasants pecked hopefully at my shoelaces.

'Is that really why, or is it some rubbish your father told you?'

'It – no. I don't remember anything he told me. I was eight.'

'Well, that's wholly for the best. No, I don't want anything to do with the wretched place.'

'All right.' I sprinkled some grain down for the pheasants, who cooed. She had the grain in a wine glass between us.

'Merrick,' she said.

I looked across.

'You don't mean to go . . . *looking* for anyone, do you?'

'What? Looking for someone, no.'

'Not out in the forest?' she said, unconvinced. She was watching me carefully.

'What are you talking about?'

'Nothing, I'm sure I'm only raving,' she said.

'Being mad isn't an excuse for being vague. Can we at least have specific madness?'

She ignored me. If you didn't catch it and understand it first time, she wouldn't go back. I knew why. Nobody had listened to her when she was sent here and so she tended now to wave something interesting under her interlocutor's nose, then snatch it away since they weren't listening anyway. Then, like she didn't want to but found she couldn't countenance not doing, she said, 'Your grandfather wrote a letter for the priest, so I suppose you had better take that. Your father never delivered it.'

Some gears in my mind clunked and made a grinding noise. 'But Harry was there eighty years ago,' I said, trying not to sound too gentle. There's something horrible about the way visitors speak to mad relatives. Madness of the Brislington kind was not a loss of reason but reason disorientated and funnelled in the wrong direction. 'It won't be the same priest.'

'Take it anyway. It will be in the top drawer of your father's desk, if Charles hasn't chopped it up for firewood.'

'He hasn't. And I will take it, but—'

'Well, you never know, it might help.'

'How?'

'Feed the pheasants, Merrick.'

I hadn't opened the old study door for years. Nobody had. It stuck at first. When it juddered open I expected the air to be stale, but it was fresh and cold because there was a hole in the ceiling and a spear of sunlight where some more roof tiles had fallen through. The desk wasn't locked. It had three top drawers along its width and the first I opened was full of farthing coins and odds and ends Dad must have turned out of his pocket: bits of interestingly knotted string, a few white pebbles. The next was empty except for the letter. Caroline had told me exactly what to look for, although it wasn't addressed. The envelope was old and much folded, the edges worn. One had torn a little and the creamy paper inside showed through. The only thing to say whose it had been was the seal on the back, from our grandfather's signet ring. When I picked it up, it exposed the corner of a little book that had been tucked underneath. I lifted the book out slowly. I'd seen it before.

It was a storybook my father had made for me when I was four or five years old. There was no writing inside – he'd told me the story, not read it – only ink pictures, dotted with gold. He drew beautifully and he had used to read it by candlelight, which had brought out all the gold flecks in among the black ink drawings, made when he'd still more or less had the money for gold ink. He had bound it and covered it too, in velvet rather than leather, to make it soft to hold. I opened it, carefully, afraid it would crack.

The story was about a woodcutter who lived on the edge of a great forest, the sort that we didn't have in England any more. The trees were drawn bleak and Schwarzwald-ish, in grey light. The woodcutter worked on the border and never strayed in, because it was dangerous, but one morning an elf came out and decided he quite liked the woodcutter's company and stayed for a while. But eventually he heard bells ringing for him inside the forest, and went back. He didn't forget about the woodcutter, but time being different for elves, he lost track, and when he came back, it was the woodcutter's grandsons he found working on the edge of the forest, the woodcutter having died years ago.

I could remember Dad turning pages for me. He'd always worn the same coat, which was too big for him because he had inherited it from his father, so he had rolled the sleeves back. The lining was an elderly but beautiful Indian chintz, brilliant complicated birds on a blue background that had faded from wear and sun to nearly white. I could remember those cuffs but not his face.

As I let the book fall closed, a page slipped forward, not attached to the others. It was another panel in the story. I didn't remember it. I couldn't make it out at first and I had to raise it towards the light.

It showed a man trapped in a growing tree. The bark and the roots had twisted around him, holding him upright, though he was asleep or dead. They had angled him upward a little, as if they were offering him to the sky. There were vines around the roots and they were flowering. Haloes of uninked spaces around them made them look like they were glowing. The petals were moulting, and in the air where they fell, they had left tiny wakes of light like firework embers, done in hairlines of white ink. There was no sun. The man was facing mostly away, his head resting against a loop of the vine that twined around his arm. It had pulled the collar of his shirt down over his shoulder. Along his collarbone were freckles, marked on in the very faintest sepia, like someone had flicked ink at him and he had scrubbed it off days ago but not all its ghosts.

I couldn't remember anything about a scene like that. In the story the elf had gone off to be with his friends and the woodcutter had, I supposed, lived happily ever after, since he'd had children and grandchildren. The way it was drawn was different from the other pictures in the storybook; more detailed, less like make-believe. I touched the ink, suddenly sure he had drawn it – or the man at least – from life. It was too good to be imaginary. Where he had pressed hard the thick paper was still furrowed. I turned it over but there was no note to say when or where he had done it.

I slid the extra drawing back into the book, then put the book into his desk again and closed the drawer. Not sure how else to keep it flat and from any more damage, I tucked the letter into the paper pocket inside the cover of my sketchbook. Easing over the crooked floor and out to Gulliver, who was sprawled at the top of the stairs, I wondered if there was a grimmer version of the story he hadn't told me: a dead man trapped in a tree somewhere and cradled in those glowing vines, somewhere so cold he was frozen perfect. The portrait had seemed like a memorial.

PART TWO

SEVEN

Peru
January 1860

We crossed Panama on a cart, very slowly to keep from damaging the Wardian cases, then set off on a Pacific and Orient ship which Minna had arranged for along the west coast. When we passed Lima, only its church spires showed above the cliffs, which formed in furrows like kapok roots. That wasn't even halfway down Peru; we were going much further south. It took three days in the little ship, and at night, incredibly, the aurora australis sang out above the wispy clouds. Clem and I had stared at it for a long time before Minna came out with a compass to show us how it was spinning. Solar storm; we had better not get lost.

There wasn't much of a port where we landed, just a little fishing town called Islay where the only food you could easily come by was guinea pig on a stick or some variation of ceviche, which was a kind of horrible fish thing marinated in something citrus until it tasted less like fish. Though they said at the inn that I'd be robbed if I wandered about by myself at the market, I risked it for pineapples and proper coffee, which they sold in abundance even though nowhere seemed to serve it as a drink. It was good to sit still in the baking courtyard with the innkeeper's incurious llama and a mortar and pestle to crush up the beans.

The first bigger place was Arequipa, miles inland. It was high up – the road had climbed all the way – and the sky was a blue I'd never seen in England. Minna found us a pair of Indian boys to help with the mules, then booked herself into an old inn where the foundations were made of the irregular polygonal stones the

Incas had built with. Although Clem tried to make her change her mind about not coming with us, she didn't. She went up on the roof terrace to see us off but, because the houses were dense and the tiny streets so steep, we soon lost sight of her in the jumble of bright shutters and the hanging tapestrywork in the roadside markets.

Clem watched me bleakly sometimes after that. Although he soon got his brightness back, it was thin enough to see through. I would have paid it more attention, but the boys seemed impressed and worried by the idea of going all the way to Caravaya, and it was hard to stop them telling it to complete strangers, as if Caravaya were on Jupiter. They were only twelve and fourteen and I'd promised their mother I'd look after them, and I couldn't think the chances of that would be better if the whole of Peru knew where we were going. A vicuña hunter rode with us for a while and the boys told him half-earnest and half-worried about how mad we were.

'I wouldn't,' he said to me. Ahead of us, Clem was already flagging from the altitude and in no fit state to talk to anyone. 'The forest there is haunted.'

'Is it. Brilliant.'

The journey was easy enough at first. It was all long, straight, beautiful Incan roads. They were dotted with post houses and inns where you could change horses and mules or stay the night for not very much money at all, which was just as well because high summer in the highlands was still hovering around freezing after dark. The boys said it was far colder in winter. It was a bizarre climate. The days were hot and we were all always halfway into or out of jackets, but we soon learned to keep them on, because the sun was ferocious and after fifteen minutes unshaded, even my hands were sunburned. Being so pale, Clem suffered much more. The grass plains were dead, and for a reason I couldn't understand, the local farmers had burned great tracts of it, so that the hills around us were a strange striped mix of yellow and soot black. But as soon as we came into any shade, at an inn or one of the bare twisted trees, it was hard to imagine being warm again and, being the least fit of everyone, I was shivering in a few minutes. It was fun though, until we reached Lake Titicaca.

By then, twelve thousand feet above the sea, I could feel the altitude too, a nasty pressure inside my ears as if someone were trying to crush the membrane inward. The towns became sorrier and fewer. Stopping was nearly always as miserable as pressing on. Scattered about were the ruins of much better-built places – drystone archways and tumbled pillars that led nowhere now except the water, where people bundled up in furs poled to and fro in boats and rafts made of reeds. Whatever the Incas had done to hurry along the economy was long gone now.

People in Arequipa had been burnished, but nobody looked healthy at the lake. They were all small but the poorest, the people who swept the courtyards of the run-down little inns, were tiny; some of the women barely reached my ribs and even Clem was a relative giant. We shared food at the inns, spread our money around, but I don't think we helped much. It made me nearly angry with them, because it would have been less effort to get everything together and just walk to somewhere gentler. There must have been something keeping them there, laws or relatives, but the waste of it and the inefficiency were hard to watch. There must have been minds there just like Sing's, people who could have been flint-hearted trader millionaires, but would never make a difference to anything because they were too occupied weaving the idiotic reed boats. Reeds, when the Amazon rainforest was just over the mountains. But there was no logging trade, or not a visible one. Three decent engineers and a proper businessman could have sorted it all out in a month, but something about the place made me think that they never would.

It took me a while to realise that we were irritable partly because of the altitude. It dragged at everything in a thick, chemical headache, but I could have lived happily enough with that if walking even for a few yards hadn't felt like sprinting a hundred. I woke up in the nights with my heart pounding like I'd run for my life and Clem was even worse. It meant we were both exhausted always, even before setting off in the mornings, and nothing drags at a journey like being too tired to look at anything. We tried not to push ourselves or the mules. They were industrious and enterprising in pursuit of the main scheme of their lives, which was escaping. It was difficult for Clem and the boys, but since there was about as much chance of my running after mules as skipping back to England, for me it was mostly a matter of finding a comfortable rock and something to read while I watched them rush about. We only managed a few miles each day and I started to worry about getting cuttings back. We'd only have a month on the return journey before they all died.

Although everyone else we saw was Indian, white men must have been common enough because there was no particular curiosity about us. People just smiled and kept on herding their llamas or their geese along the broad road. Before long I had the impression it was unobjectionable but still funny for us to be there, like camels in London.

On the far side of the lake was Azangaro, the last proper town before the Andes. What had been a pretty good dirt road became muddy in the light and frozen in the shade. A lot of people had passed through recently; it was to do with the war in Bolivia, though the boys were too young to know much about it. When the storm arrived, the sleet was cutting. It got down collars and into lamps where it made the flames flicker and hiss. By the time the town came into view, with its cobbled-together church spire that tipped at an angle, Clem had real altitude sickness and rode with his handkerchief clamped over his nose, blooming red every hour or so.

The town was a big cluster of doorless houses and straw roofs. Raggy curtains writhed over the thresholds, sometimes enough to see people inside, wrapped up and hunched round braziers on dirt floors. I sent the boys on ahead to find a post house. I hoped we hadn't gone too far east for them now. The idea of stopping in a mud hut instead of somewhere with a proper roof was terrible. The wind howled and I had to keep my head turned to one side.

Clem groaned and half-collapsed. I caught up with him just in time to get my arm under his shoulder and keep him more or less upright. We rode like that, awkwardly, until the boys came back with a man. He was Spanish, with a good coat and two Indians. It was just then, just before he met us, that we turned the corner into what must have been the main square. The houses had doors and windows and there was firelight inside most of them. It wasn't anywhere near dark yet, but the storm had folded everything into a twilight gloom.

'We've been expecting you!' the man called, and I was too cold and tired to ask who he thought we were. When he was close enough, he lifted Clem down. While they headed away, I started the painful business of getting down from the saddle too. I could do it, but the horse had to be understanding, because I had to dismount at a difficult angle and hold the reins to keep the weight off my bad leg. It hurt more each time.

'You'd better come in,' the man shouted back. 'It's not much but at least you won't freeze. It's just here.'

His was one of the houses opposite the crumbling church. In Lima or Cuzco it would probably have seemed poky, but here it was palatial. There were shutters on the windows and, when we went inside, deep rugs over a tiled floor. I leaned gratefully on my cane and held the door open for the boys and the two Indian men who had rescued our bags without being asked. They put the bags down in the hallway and went straight back out to see to the mules and the horses, nodding for me to go in alone. I pulled the door shut behind them. It fitted well and didn't let in a draught.

When I turned back, the hallway led out into a broad room with bearskin rugs everywhere and a fire tall enough to fill the big hearth, and candles all over the place, because the shutters were closed against the storm. In front of the fire was a table. They were halfway through a meal. Or, someone had been halfway through. It was only laid for one.

'Sorry to have disturbed you,' I said. I frowned into the effort that Spanish had become. I hadn't noticed before, but parts of my mind were shut off in the anorexic air.

'Don't be silly,' the Spanish man laughed. He was lifting Clem onto the couch near the fire. His face was broad, harsh strokes that would have been ugly if he hadn't had huge eyes and a sweep of well-cut hair. His clothes were meticulous too, his coat richly cut with a green velvet collar that would have been dandy on me but suited him. Everything about him was expansive and I had a feeling he might be the Spanish version of Clem.

'Thank you,' I said, feeling shabby and English in the falling-apart, ill-looking way English people always seem whenever you stand them next to someone from a healthier latitude. I moved to the side as the Indians came back in with the smell of damp leather from their coats. One of them had such long hair that the tip of his plait flicked my elbow as he passed.

'My name is Martel, I'm a trader here,' said our unexpected host, and something about the way he inclined his head said he could see that I felt shabby and wanted me not to. 'Will you give your coat to Hernandez there?' He nodded to the younger of the Indians. 'I know it seems cold now but you'll warm up in no time.'

I did as I was told and Hernandez took my coat. 'We can pay you for the night, if we can have some blankets and some floor.'

'My God, don't worry about money. There's a spare room, you can have a whole bed.' He was looking down at Clem. 'Well – he's fainted clean away, but he'll come round soon. It's just the altitude. Has someone got some coca?' For a second I misheard and thought he meant chocolate, which seemed inexplicable and benign, until the other Indian handed over a little canvas bag that rustled with dry leaves.

'You give it to him, I think, Hernandez, I don't know how much is right. Quispe – go upstairs and fetch Raphael out. Make sure he's fit for human company. Mr . . .?' he added to me.

'Tremayne. That's . . . Mr Markham. He's normally the one who makes the good conversation.'

'Oh, never mind, you and I shall manage. Come and sit down, there's plenty to go round.'

Almost as soon as I'd sat down, new crockery appeared in front of me, and a girl with more food. I gave the first serving to the boys and she looked perturbed, but fetched down two more bowls. I handed along the next one too and nearly fainted into the third. Martel motioned for the boys to sit by the fire. They knelt down with Hernandez to use the hearth as a table. If they were offended not to be invited to sit at the real table, they didn't show it.

'Actually, why don't you all go into the kitchen?' Martel said to them.

'I promised their mother not to let them out of my sight, if you don't mind,' I said quickly, in case the kitchen fire was less grand.

'They're grown men, I'm sure they don't need watching,' he laughed.

'I did promise.'

'I suppose the world would come to nothing whatever if we broke promises to people's mothers. Is she Spanish?' he said curiously. 'Are you mestizos, boys?'

'What does mestizo mean?' I asked before they could say anything.

'It means half-white and half-Indian.'

'Is that different to mulatto? My Spanish isn't very good, sorry. Especially . . . not up here,' I said.

'God, don't worry about that, of course it's hard. Arriving here for the first time is like breathing with one lung. Mulatto is half-black. Mestizo is half-Indian. And if one parent is mestizo and the other is Indian, that's something else again.' Martel smiled. 'We're so short of real white men out here that mestizos tend to be counted as white these days, I'm afraid. It's shocking, but . . . well, we're all Peruvian now, of course. No more Spain.'

I watched him while he was talking. I couldn't tell if he was the kind of person he would have been if he had said it in English in London, the kind who wanted to round up all the Jews and sink them in the Thames again. He was cheerfuller and gentler than that type at home. Although we had crossed Peru widthwise by then, we had never stopped anywhere for long enough to have a proper conversation with anybody, and I had only a hazy idea of where the walls built by the good men were, and what they walled in or out. The only thing I was sure of was that the boundaries would be different to the English kind. Not as different as China, I hoped, because that had been exhausting – to be friends with people who were kind and amiable to me but kept their wives like crippled prisoners in a back room somewhere – but it would be different.

'You look very thoughtful,' he laughed.

'No, I'm just slow.' I pushed my hand across my forehead. The altitude headache had become familiar and comfortable, but I could nearly see the fog. I would have been able to decide what sort of person he was at sea level, easily. I looked up when Hernandez set some coca leaves down by me too. Martel smiled a little as he leaned across and dropped them in a cup, which he filled with water from the kettle between us. A deep grassy smell steamed up from it.

'The Indians say it's a crime to have it as tea, but I think sometimes half the problem is the cold,' he explained. 'Just give it until it goes green.'

'Thank you,' I said again. I faded back in my chair, listening to my heart thump loud around the bones inside my ears, which hurt.

'Pardon me, but did you say your name was Tremayne?' Martel said. He had taken his coat off too and underneath he had a beautiful brocade waistcoat, the same red as the wine. 'I feel sure that sounds familiar?'

'My family have been here before. My grandfather came in . . .' The unexpected numbers pulled me up short. They never had in London. Like a fever echo, I heard how slowly I was talking. It wasn't unnatural, not like being drunk, but it was noticeable. I prodded the coca leaves with a spoon to hurry them along and tried a sip while I hauled together the names of the years. It tasted like any other herbal tea. 'Seventeen . . . eighty?'

Martel nodded encouragingly.

'He was stealing quinine bark. He got caught and he had to hide in an Indian village for a while, then got interested in Quechua and kept coming back for twenty years or so. My father was born there. He came for a few months every year.'

When he had mentioned Raphael, I'd thought Martel was talking about a dog, but Quispe came back with a man. Martel pushed out the chair opposite mine with his ankle but didn't introduce him and left a vague impression in the air of some kind of clerk or bodyguard, someone whose name wouldn't matter. The man didn't seem like either. He held himself very straight, not like a servant, in good but old clothes that must just have been ironed, because I caught the smell of hot cotton when he came in past me. He was Indian, but from a different nation to Quispe and Hernandez and the boys. He didn't have the Incan nose and his hair was cut short, and he was far taller. He moved so slowly it was ostentatious, the way very strong men do, and I wrote him off after about half a second as probably an arrogant bastard, although after meeting so many beaten-down people on the road, it was a relief to see someone who looked like he might punch anybody trying to make him sweep a yard.

He stopped when he saw me, just before reaching his chair. His expression opened as if he knew me, but then he saw he was wrong and sat down. Martel thumped him to say hello. It didn't sway him in the least and Martel looked as if he might have hurt his hand. Raphael was still watching me hard, taking measurements. Whoever he had mistaken me for, I must have been a good lookalike.

'Merrick Tremayne,' I said, when nobody introduced us properly.

They still didn't, and nor did he, but he shook my hand. He felt like he was made of hydraulics. He only glanced at me before his eyes skipped past my shoulder. Our boys were staring at him. Quispe was trying to give them some bread. The younger one shrank close to the older one, who finally noticed the bread and took it quickly. Hernandez rubbed the little one's hair and said something in Quechua to distract him. Raphael looked away from them and down at the edge of the table. That he knew he had frightened them was written across his face, but he seemed resigned too and I wondered if there was caste trouble I didn't know about, something that couldn't be made better by smiling.

'What was all that?' I asked him, but it was Martel who answered.

He was pouring me some wine. 'The Indian nations beyond the mountains are known for their savagery, you see. It's often hard to make any Indians from *this* side work with them. They call them all Chuncho. They say it means barbarian, but I think barbarian sounds rather more genteel than what it really is. Heard the term?'

'Viking,' I said, feeling odd, because I knew them from stories, but since Dad had put them in with elves and dragons I hadn't thought they were real. They were the men who came from the deep woods in winter and burned everything they didn't take, from Indians or from white men. They weren't either one, and nobody – not the Inca nor the Spanish kings – had ever made much of a dent in their lands beyond the mountains; if anyone tried, all that was left in the end was charcoal and salted ground. 'I mean . . . raiders.'

Martel laughed. 'No, that's good. Vikings. I'll steal that from you, if you don't mind. It's rather difficult to explain to foreigners what they are.'

Raphael looked away from us in a way that made it clear he thought it was all hyperbole. It was hard not to agree with him. If he was from one of the tribes in the rainforest, he was thoroughly hispanicised. His clothes were all Spanish and he had a rosary around his wrist; no tattoos, no native jewellery, not even an earring.

'But . . . you two are colleagues?' I said, not sure why Martel had called him down.

'Raphael works for me. He'll take you over the mountains.'

'Mr Martel,' I said in the pause that followed, struggling, 'you said before that you were expecting us. I'm . . . worried that you might have mistaken us for someone else.'

'No, no. Someone came up early last week from Lake Titicaca to tell me to expect a pair of Englishmen. I have a sort of . . . alert out,' he said ruefully. 'Anyone planning to go over the mountains comes this way; it's the only decent pass for miles. It can be dangerous for foreigners. This used to be quinine country and there are still men working for the northern suppliers who would shoot anyone who might threaten the monopoly, you see?'

'Sorry – what? Quinine monopoly?' I said. I only just had the thinking capacity to lie, and felt pleased to have managed it. The coca tea was clearing the haze, just. There were still some dry leaves left, so I made myself another cup. 'I didn't know any quinine came out of Caravaya now.'

'Well, it doesn't any more. It used to. It's mostly been harvested out – certainly there's nothing like enough trees to be of any commercial use – but the northern suppliers pay a great deal to make sure no one takes anything. Every so often we have expeditionaries coming through here trying for cuttings, and you only need the one tree for that. The Dutch are trying to raise a plantation in Java, apparently. There are rumours that the India Office are too.'

He and Raphael were both watching me hard. In spite of the altitude, gears I hadn't used for a long time clicked into place and my thinking sped up. It shouldn't have been remarkable, but I'd been worried that they were all rusted and I had a surge of happiness at hearing them whirr like new again.

'Oh. That sounds . . . complicated,' I said.

'Does it?' said Martel. 'God, I suppose I'm too used to the whole headache of it. Essentially . . . there are cinchona woods up and down Peru, as I'm sure you know.'

I nodded.

'But we're a poor country. In order to drive up the price, there is a monopoly. We make sure that no one but local suppliers take quinine or cinchona trees from Peru. If they did, our economy would be crippled overnight; it's quite as simple as that. Do you know what our largest export is? The one we'd rely on entirely without quinine.'

'No.'

'Guano. Oh, you laugh, but it is. Anyway, there are a few cinchona woods in Bolivia but it would be hard work to get through. Too much rainforest, not enough road. Peru is the only country in the world with a meaningful supply of cinchona trees. You follow so far?'

'I think so.'

'Now, it would be stupid to have everyone growing the stuff and selling it. There would be a huge supply and the price would go down. Not good. So it's run like the diamond trade. You let only a few diamonds out of the country at a time. There are cinchona forests elsewhere, but they're kept untouched now, except for one cluster in the north. If someone is caught trying to set up a cinchona farm or a quinine supply unauthorised . . .' He made a gun of his first two fingers and touched his own temple. 'So, members of the northern monopoly pay to keep people out of the southern regions. If someone catches you and convinces the right person that you're here for quinine, he would be paid a lot of money and you would be shot. It's an unfortunate place to be white at the moment, the Andes.'

'Oh. I didn't . . . how dangerous? Should – we not be here?'

'Well, may I ask why you are here?' he said gently.

'We – coffee.' I was good at being nervous. I'd always had the right face for it, and with my leg now, it suited even better. I pushed my hand through my hair. 'We're hoping to get into the Sandia Valley – towards a town called New Bethlehem. Something above five thousand feet anyway. We're hoping to find plants more resistant to colder weather.'

He swept his eyes down at the wine and then back up at me. 'That is exactly where the last of the cinchona woods are.'

'Yes, I . . . know that. I'm a gardener. God, I know what this must sound like. I knew they were an indigenous plant, I just – I didn't know about the politics around them.'

Hernandez and Quispe were listening too now. Over by the fire, the boys looked up, worried. Clem was still unconscious. I'd missed it often, but it came back with a nasty sharpness then, that I'd used to be as strong and slow as Raphael. I lifted my hands up from the cutlery and let them shake a little. It was easy; ever since China, they had had a tiny natural tremor when I was anxious, although usually I could stop it if I concentrated. It was much worse here than at home.

'I'm not who they'd send if it was something as dangerous as all that.'

Martel nodded. 'No, quite. But listen; I would hate for you to be offended, but have you any way of proving it's coffee you want, and not cinchona?'

'I can't prove a negative, all I – I can tell you how I know about the coffee, is all.'

'Go on.'

'I told you about my grandfather. He stayed at New Bethlehem and he brought back all kinds of things – orchids, white pines – and among them was a kind of coffee that showed some resistance to frost. The samples were lost, and there's been interest now from Kew and the India Office, so we were hoping for new ones. I've never heard of it anywhere else, so we came . . .'

Martel swivelled in his chair to Raphael, a theatric precise ninety degrees. 'Well? How are you for frosty coffee?'

'Well off,' he said.

'It exists?'

'I've got a garden full of it. You've had some. It tastes like chocolate.' The other Indians we had met, including the boys, spoke Spanish mixed with Quechua, but his was glassy. He was quiet too. It was elegant.

'Oh, that. God, I didn't realise it was coffee; I thought you just didn't know the Spanish for whatever it was.'

Raphael gave his wine glass a blank look and didn't say anything.

'Don't look like that. You didn't know the Spanish word for the cathedral, remember, the other day?'

'No,' he said, without looking up from the glass, '*you* didn't know. It's the Qorikancha in Spanish too.'

'It's Cuzco Cathedral.'

'And what do you call the much older place it's built over?' Over anything more than a sentence, he had a strange voice. It sounded like he was dragging it up through a shale quarry.

'The foundations,' Martel said firmly.

'For God's sake.'

I looked between them, prickling and sure that Martel had run on with that to keep me waiting for his verdict about my coffee story. Raphael lifted his eyes just enough to catch mine while Martel was still laughing. There was something bleak in them. He hadn't smiled once. My heart was going fast again. I couldn't tell if he didn't believe me or if he only would have preferred to be elsewhere.

Martel smiled at me. 'I frightened you, I'm sorry.' He put his glass down and leaned forward against the table, his forearms flat to the cloth. When they closed over mine, his hands were warm. I made an effort not to shy. 'I believe you, but I have to be careful, you understand? If you were here for quinine I'd have to turn you back or risk your life. And – as you can imagine, there would be trouble for me too, if the northern suppliers found out I'd let you through.'

'Yes, I'm . . . starting to see that.'

'Good.' He must have felt how cold I was, because he chafed my knuckles. I wanted to take my hands back, but I'd already offended people by not letting them kiss me. 'So, you see you must travel safely, with a proper guide. That's why Raphael is here now. I brought him so that he could take you over the mountains. He's from New Bethlehem, in fact.'

'Really?'

'There are only a few towns up that way,' Martel said. 'New Bethlehem is by far the biggest. I'm sorry to spring it on you, but it would be dangerous for you to ask around cold.'

I shook my head. 'Pardon my asking, but why are you helping us? If you'll be in trouble if I'm lying, you should be turning us away whether you believe me or not.'

He lifted his eyebrows. 'I don't think you realise how often this happens. It's at least once a year. I am very tired of sitting down to dinner one evening with a man, then hearing of his death a week later, whether he was here for quinine or pepper. Very tired. I'm damned if I'll live in fear of them over nothing but coffee.'

Raphael sat forward. It made the bones and muscles in his shoulders show. I leaned back without meaning to. It was like sitting across from a big animal. There was a right-angled nick in his eyebrow, not old. Someone had smacked him over the head with the butt of a gun. It was a scar I recognised, common in the Navy, common in all the expeditionary arms of the East India Company. I realised he had moved to get a little further away from Martel. He didn't want to be sent out with us.

'Would I be right in thinking Raphael is also there to keep an eye on us and make sure we don't try and dive off into any cinchona woods?' I said.

'You would,' Martel admitted. 'But – you do understand? Unless you go with him, I can't let you go at all. It wouldn't be safe. For any of us.'

'Of course I do. It's kind of you to have thought of it all. I'm afraid we must look very haphazard to you.'

He smiled, not all the way. 'You can't be expected to know what's going on here if all you were given is vague orders about coffee. Brave of you to come at all, in your condition.'

I touched my cane without meaning to. The fact was, and chivalrously he hadn't pointed it out, that he would have no trouble stopping a cripple and a man crippled by altitude sickness if we tried to make a run for it alone. We were stuck with Raphael now. Even if we did run off successfully, he lived in the place we were going to. How to get round him would have to be a problem we saved for New Bethlehem. I didn't mind. I was too tired to have all our problems stacked up here and now, and hopefully, New Bethlehem was a bit lower down and I might be able to think more like a human being there than a clever sheep.

'And you're happy to take us?' I said.

Raphael was staring into his wine, but his eyes came up when he realised I was talking to him. They were black, real black like I hadn't seen even in Asia. He set his glass down softly. The cross on the rosary around his wrist chimed against the crystal. 'Yes.'

'R . . . ight,' I said, not full of confidence. 'You don't sound very happy.'

He glanced at Martel. 'He'll burn my village down if I don't keep you safe.'

'Only way,' Martel said cheerfully. 'Firm hand. Negotiation not a Chuncho strong point.'

Raphael gave him a look full of threadbare hate. Resignation showed through the worn-out places. Martel saw it too and clapped the back of his neck, only gently. Raphael turned his head away but not fast. It looked like token resistance to me. Nearly like a joke between them.

'Are you allowed to do that?' I said to Martel.

'It's my land. It's all my land, out that way. The villagers all work for me. It's their only livelihood. I wouldn't like to burn it down, it's a charming place. Unless Raphael does something especially Indian to change my mind.'

'I'll show you especially Indian one day,' Raphael murmured, with no force.

Martel snorted. 'You get used to him.' He watched Raphael for a second or two, looking quietly pleased. Then he leaned across to share the last of the wine out between us all. 'Cheers. To coffee.'

I lifted my glass but didn't drink. Sitting down with nothing urgent happening, I was feeling the pressure inside my skull more and the wine looked like nothing but a thumping headache in a glass.

'Listen, what would be appropriate to pay you, for being our guide?' I said to Raphael.

'I don't need paying,' he said, as if the idea were halfway to alarming. 'Mr Martel looks after me.'

'There must be something,' I pressed. However glad I was to be able to do it, it felt grimy to lie to them, and the urge to be fair in my dealing, at least, was strong. 'Not money if that isn't right, but . . .?'

He waited for something from Martel, who nodded.

'A clock,' Raphael said. 'There's an antiques shop round the corner. Doesn't matter if it's working or not. Whichever one doesn't seem like robbery to you.'

I frowned. 'Is that all?'

'Two clocks if you feel generous.'

Martel had been holding Raphael's shoulder, which I'd seen men in charge doing to men not in charge all the way across Peru, and now he leaned on it more. 'Are you making bombs, my dear?'

Raphael inclined his head away. 'Leaving them in your wardrobe.'

'Clocks then,' I said.

'Thank you,' he said. He was losing his voice, even though he had hardly spoken. It must have happened often, because he didn't seem surprised. I wasn't either. Even at the start of the conversation it had sounded maltreated.

'Didn't you go to the antiques shop on Monday?' Martel asked, shooting me a little sideways look to say, watch this. I shifted, not wanting to see it, whatever it was.

'No, I said I'd go next Monday on the way home,' Raphael said. He moved his hand back, towards his shoulder, like he was pointing at something behind him. He hadn't spoken with his hands much before, but with his voice fading it must have felt the natural thing to do. 'And I *asked* you last Monday. You said no.' This time he brought his hand down in front of him, not too close. I was confused until Martel slapped his hand. Forward was the past, behind was the future.

'Don't talk about time in Spanish and think in Quechua, dear. It doesn't match and it gives me a headache.'

Raphael turned his head slowly to look at him properly. 'Can your superior Spanish brain not recognise ordinary things when they're backwards? You must be a menace around reversing horses.'

Martel laughed. 'Interesting, isn't it?' he said to me.

'Y . . . es,' I said, wishing I could think of an inoffensive way to say that as a rule Englishmen found bull-fighting awkward more than interesting.

'Anyway, I'm sure Quispe can go for the clock. You can't be expected to brave it across in sleet and ice.'

'I don't mind,' I said. There wasn't much I wanted to do less, but I needed a few minutes not speaking Spanish, and not trying to understand the strange way they were with each other. 'Is there a particular make? Of clock, I mean.'

'No – but decent mainsprings,' Raphael said. 'Do you know what a mainspring is?'

I nodded once. I knew them quite well, after a year with a clockwork-making interpreter in China. I tried not to think about Keita too much. 'Steel or gold mainsprings. Back in a minute.'

The shop was diagonally opposite and it didn't stock antiques, exactly, but viceroyalty tat that must have been increasing in value now that there was no supply of new things coming from Spain. There were cases and cases of Spanish books with gilt spines, and lots of dark furniture with lions' feet – the pointless sort, tiny tables that would only hold a wine glass or footstools so miniature that a decent heel would take your feet just as far off the floor. But next to the dust and the doorless shacks, it was good to see the bronze studs in the upholstery and the scrollworked mahogany. I paused at a table hung with well-made leather bags and a stack of books in Dutch, novels and monographs all jumbled. There was a beautiful microscope too, and a whole roll of archaeological excavation tools with a trademark that said Amsterdam on it. They were much newer than everything else, brightly out of place.

'You're not from here,' an old lady's voice said from the back of the shop.

'No. I'm looking for a clock.' I was breathless even from having crossed the street. 'It doesn't matter if it's working.'

'Lots of clocks,' she said. She passed me a couple over the counter.

'Mind if I see inside?'

'Why?'

'Springs. Is that a screwdriver – thank you.' I opened up the casing, pleased to have remembered the word for screwdriver. 'All right, good. Is there another?'

'That's five reales, just for that,' she said doubtfully.

'It's fine,' I said, though I hadn't been handling Peruvian money long enough to know if it was fine or ridiculous.

'Unless you're trading anything? Probably work out cheaper if you do.'

'No, just the money – do people normally trade?'

She nodded to the table of Dutch things. 'Last man to buy clocks brought all that.'

Something walked over the back of my neck. I had been admiring it all brainlessly without understanding that it was everything the missing Dutch expeditionaries had left behind last time. Raphael had been with them too.

'Just the money,' I said again. We found another clock, smaller. When she gave them to me wrapped in old newspaper, the clocks were heavy.

'Careful in the snow,' she said as I eased the door open with my elbow, my cane in one hand and the clocks under my other arm. Outside, little flurries spun thinly, just enough to sting. Quispe must have been watching for me, because he opened Martel's front door before I was even close to it. Martel and Raphael were where I'd left them at the table. I handed over the clocks.

'These are nice,' Martel murmured as they unwrapped them. Raphael lifted the second one away from him and put it out of his reach at the far end of the table. He had taken a small screwdriver from somewhere and now he was opening up the first one. His eyes flicked up when he found the steel mainspring.

'The other one's gold-plated,' I said. 'I hope it's not too soft, but everything else was rusty even on the outside.'

He looked sceptically pleased. I was on the verge of pointing out that the service he was about to do us was worth a hundred thousand steel mainsprings, but Clem stirred on the couch then and swore as he tried to sit up. I got up to go round to him, holding the edge of the table to keep myself steady, and Hernandez hurried away to the kitchen. When he came back, it was with a small cup of powerful black coffee, burned-smelling.

'Yes, off you go,' Martel murmured to Raphael, who ghosted away back up the stairs, chaperoned by Quispe again. There was only one tiny lamp at the top. Raphael faded into the gloom at first and then sharpened again as he climbed up into the shallow light. There was one silver bead in his rosary and it gleamed.

'I thought you'd died,' I said to Clem. I helped him prop himself up. 'Are you all right?'

'Apart from having the constitution of an invalid lady. Where are we?'

'Azangaro. This is Mr Martel, it's his house.'

Martel waved from the table. 'Coca's working. You might feel zingy for a while.'

Clem bumped back on to the cushions. 'Don't suppose I could have a bit more?'

At the top of the stairs, Quispe opened a door just off the landing, put Raphael inside, and locked it. He came down still fastening the keys back on to his belt.

The room upstairs had its own stove, which had no flue and which Quispe warned us to keep completely closed until the embers were dead, not just glowing. I promised I knew how not to poison myself. I meant it as a joke, but he seemed worried and backed out. Clem had dropped sideways across the bed.

'He's set us up with a guide,' I said. 'I think we're going out with him tomorrow morning, if you're all right.'

'A guide? You didn't tell him about—'

'No. I said coffee. The man's from New Bethlehem.' I paused. 'At some point we'll have to tell him what we want. There won't be cinchona trees just lying around up there.'

'You utter pigeon, Em,' he said sleepily. 'Of course we won't. We'll just go for a walk one morning. You do like to fuss.'

I tucked a blanket round him and then inched down on the foot of the bed, in the waving heat from the stove. The hook of my cane fitted nicely over the handle of one of the closed window shutters. Curious, I opened it a little way. There was glass in the frame. It was old and it rattled, and the cold seeped through its seals. We must have been at the side of the house, because the front faced the church and the back the way we had come over the plain. Outside now was the little tumble of the town and then, about thirty miles away, beyond more hills, the mountains. They were jagged and white, stretching in both directions until they were lost in the haze of bad weather. There was nothing inviting about them and no clear way through, although there must have been, if we were crossing them tomorrow. I pushed the shutter closed again and the glass stopped juddering now it was braced, but the wind hummed and howled in the roof. Something in the rafters made a kind of clucking rattle, and then there was a scuffle and a squeak.

'What is that?'

Clem was asleep, or not worried enough by it to open his eyes.

'Guinea pigs,' said a voice, in English. It came from beyond the wall against which the headboard of the bed rested, from the next room, and it was so to the left of anything I'd expected that almost as soon as I'd heard it, I convinced myself I couldn't have and there was a long silence while I tried to chase down the memory of the sound. If it had been real, it was so close to me that the man must have had his forehead against the wall.

I cracked. 'Did you say guinea pigs?'

'Listen. You need to go home. Or to another part of the country.'

I went to the wall. The house twisted and turned and I couldn't put together a map of it well enough to know whose room it might be, even if I'd known who was where. 'Why?'

'It's a waste of time,' he said softly. 'There is no way you'll ever get out of the cinchona woods alive and with live specimens.'

'We're here for coffee.'

'I just heard you talking, don't be stupid. You need to leave.'

I laughed, my temple against the plasterwork. It was new and white. My shadow put its fingertips up to meet mine. 'If I go home without having done this, I'll never work again. I'd rather be shot by a quinine supplier, if it's all the same to you.' I hesitated. 'Are you going to tell Mr Martel?'

'No.'

'Why?'

He didn't answer.

'Who is this? How come you speak English?'

There was silence after that. I waited, then jumped when there was a sharp thump that I recognised, right at a level with my head. It was the sound of someone throwing a cricket ball against the wall. I didn't hold many intermural conversations, but I thought that it probably meant go away.

Clem tugged the back of my shirt. 'Move, you're blocking the heat,' he mumbled.

I shifted to one side. 'Sorry. All right now?'

He pulled the blanket over his head. 'Sorry doesn't make you any less of a pain, you know. If all this fails and we get shot because you gave us away, you can explain it to the India Office. Were you talking to me just now?'

'No, there's a man in the next room,' I said. Clem was at an awkward angle, so I folded his pillow double and eased the new half under his head. The room was warming up, but slowly.

He was asleep. Wanting to let him spread out if he liked, I took the other pillow and the spare blanket and set up on the floor next to the stove.

It took me a long time to go to sleep. Somewhere in the ceiling, the guinea pigs scuffled. I still felt like I was having to push through mist to think. I wanted to believe that we had just stumbled over someone who hated the quinine suppliers enough to help strangers, and perhaps we had. But Martel had said the land at New Bethlehem was his, and he was rich, and Raphael had been with the Dutch, who had died in the forest. Those things spun and spun in my head but I couldn't make them link up, and it kept me awake because it was maddening. All the doors in my brain had come down and locked. In the end I slept badly, sourcelessly afraid, my heart drumming.

EIGHT

THE INDIAN BOYS RAN away in the night. There was no note and no message to say why. They had taken the mules and the horses too. I strayed out into the frosty street to see if they were still in view, because it was early when I noticed they were missing, but they must have gone hours ago. There weren't even tracks in the road; it had all been covered over by a new dusting of snow, disturbed only in one line of small footprints where a tiny girl wrapped up in a thick poncho and what must have been her father's leather hat was going into the church.

'It doesn't matter about the mules,' Raphael said when I told them over breakfast. Quispe looked disapproving that Martel had let him sit at the table with us. 'You'd never get them over the mountain passes and you don't want them on a boat.' He spoke more slowly than Martel did, and far more clearly. I'd been tired even at the idea of sitting at a table with people who only spoke Spanish so early in the morning – except for one mystery English-speaker, though I was starting to think I must have dreamed that – but Raphael was so easy to understand that his Spanish was only a bit more work than Edinburgh English. It was a tiny thing, but it went a small way to soothing the loss of the boys and the animals, and I felt less unsettled. I'd forgotten what a knife-edge my mood sat on in the first few weeks in a new country.

'I know, but I can't walk,' I said. I was opposite him again. They had set another place next to me for Clem, who was awake but hadn't come down yet. 'You might have to leave me here until I can find a horse.'

'There are horses here.' He glanced at Martel. 'Quispe can come with us and bring them back.'

Quispe stared at the floor.

'Fair enough,' said Martel, who was making something at a side table where there were steaming kettles and cups. 'But if any of them come back with a broken ankle, my dear, I'll break yours.'

'Yes,' said Raphael.

Martel stopped by me and gave me a cup of chocolate. I looked down at it and then up at him, surprised.

'It's good for you,' he said gently. He gave a second to Clem, who had just eased in, holding himself tentatively. 'You need to keep having something sweet at this altitude. Keeps your blood going.'

'Oh, lovely,' Clem murmured. I moved my cane, which I'd propped against his chair, over the back of mine instead, and put my hand out to give him something to lean on. He did and smiled, but it was watery.

'It's local,' Martel said. 'From my cocoa farm, actually.' He nodded towards Raphael to say he meant the one at New Bethlehem. 'Marvellous stuff. Grows back very fast if somebody sets it on fire too,' he said cheerfully. 'Doesn't it?'

He was talking to Raphael, who almost smiled. 'I don't know. I've never set your cocoa on fire.'

'Look, take care,' Martel said to him, more seriously. 'The weather's mad. It's going to be madder up on the passes.'

'I'll be careful with the horses.'

'I did mean with yourself too. Here you are. Sugar cake for the way. Make sure you don't give it all to other people.'

Raphael lost some of his usual stiffness and took it. Martel rubbed his shoulder. In his fine velvet waistcoat, he looked like the most accomplished sort of ringmaster, with a lion that was just getting used to him.

The way after Azangaro was frozen. That night we stayed at a horrible place called Crucero, huddled at the foot of the jagged mountains. When I boiled a cup of water and dunked a thermometer in it, the reading in Clem's logbook said we were at almost fifteen thousand feet. It had laid him out flat, although it was a variation, at least, on his nosebleeds. I was queasy too, and slow and tired. I couldn't think properly to read and even working out that I could put a shirtful of snow on my leg to keep it from hurting so much was a long, creaking exercise. I went through my bag to find an old shirt but then gave up when it occurred to me I'd have to go back outside again for snow.

When we arrived, Raphael had lifted me down from the saddle as if that were as ordinary and certain as taking down the bags. He must have been used to doing it for someone else, because he knew not to let it become nothing but a controlled fall. He took my whole weight until I was almost on the ground and then still kept it slightly more on the right while I found my uneven balance again. Usually I was too tall for anyone to help reliably but he didn't struggle. He seemed like he could have managed someone twice as heavy before it gave him any trouble, though he was a good few inches smaller than me.

'Thanks,' I said, surprised. I'd been about to ask Quispe to give me a hand.

He looked just as surprised to be thanked, and disapproving, but he didn't say anything and only dropped my bag into my arms by way of telling me not to get too used to it.

Inside the inn, I wedged myself into a corner with a blanket, near Clem, so that I'd notice if he stopped breathing. It was a bizarre feeling, having half my brain taken away, but it meant that to sit and do nothing was much less boring than it would have been usually. We were sharing the place with other people, Indians crossing back over the mountains after trading, so I watched them for a while. Closer to me, Raphael drove an old tent peg into the dirt floor and looped a piece of string around it. He had a book open in his lap in Spanish, and while he read, he tied knots into the string. After a while, I noticed that all the other Indians had crowded over the far side of the room, although there was plenty of space to sleep nearer to him if they had wanted to stretch out. Eventually, one of them came up to him and crouched down to give him a vial full of something white, and spoke in earnest Quechua. He nodded and put it into his bag. He saw me watching, but he didn't explain.

Beside me, Clem was almost translucent, his lips colourless. He was breathing hard.

'We need to get him down from here,' I said to Raphael, barely able to bring out Spanish at all now.

Raphael glanced across, too quickly to have taken in much but that Clem was lying down. 'He's fine.'

'No, look at him. I know you were born up here but he could die of this, for Christ's sake, people die—'

'No.' He left the knots and knelt down in front of me, and caught my shoulders. I shied, certain he meant to bang my head back against the wall to make me shut up.

'Don't—'

'Listen. I've seen men die of it. It doesn't look like that.' He nodded at Clem. 'This panic you're feeling is part of mountain sickness. It's nothing to do with him. Feel how fast your heart's going.' It was thundering when he put my hand against my chest.

'What?' I said weakly. That he hadn't hit me was confusing more than it was any relief.

'You can't get enough air,' he said, quiet and slow. 'That's all. You panic when you drown, you panic up here. It's the same but stranger, because you're still breathing. But neither of you is anything like close to dying. If you were, I wouldn't be sitting reading. Do you believe me?'

I nodded, shocked to find I was starting to cry. 'God, it's strong, isn't it.'

He dipped his head once and didn't seem surprised or annoyed that I was so upset. 'Very. You're right, it can kill you. But it's not going to kill you this minute.' He gave me some coca leaves. Like everyone he seemed to carry them around always. 'Take those.'

'How do you . . .?'

'Just chew. Keep them behind your back teeth.'

I took them from him like a little boy and concentrated while I tried them. It was a bitter grassy taste, much worse than the tea. He tucked the bag of it next to me under the hem of the blanket.

'Thank you,' I said, too grateful.

He studied me for a long objective moment. 'You're all right,' he concluded. 'And stop bloody lisping. I know it's a Madrid accent but someone's going to rob you. You sound queer.'

I laughed. As if I'd only needed to be told firmly enough, I calmed down and realised that Clem didn't look so bad after all. When I turned again to tell Raphael he was right, he had gone back to the nail in the floor and the knotted string.

The weather fined up the next morning just as we reached the top of the pass through the Andes. The way behind us stretched back for miles, bleak and snowy, the road a purer white line because it was flat. The cold was cutting. Up ahead, the pass plunged us down through ravines. Halfway down, a chunk of snow sloughed away from the surface under Raphael, who was leading his horse, but he didn't fall and only let himself glide for twenty yards or so.

'Well,' said Clem. He had stopped to wait for me. He hadn't talked yesterday, too ill, but he was better today. I was too, but shaky. I could remember having been frightened in the night and that Raphael had said something, but I couldn't think what. It was like a fever dream. The more I chased it, the less real it felt. 'Do you suppose he's a wronged but admirable man, or just a grumpy bastard?'

I laughed. 'Not sure.'

'Did you talk to him much at Martel's?'

'No. Martel locked him in his room straight after dinner.'

'Locked?'

'They seemed to think he might attack someone otherwise.'

'Or maybe he'd fuck off home before you idiots could remember what he looked like,' Raphael called back, and we both stopped, because he had said it in English. He had no accent, or rather, he had our kind of accent, with what might have been a foreign edge. 'Get down here. It's a way even to the river and we'll have ten miles on the boat after that.'

'Interesting English you've got there,' Clem said after a lag. 'Where did you learn?'

'Hurry up,' was all he said.

Clem lifted his eyebrows at me. 'Told us. Off we hop.'

I couldn't let the horse go any faster than I already was without the jolt hurting too badly to sit through, so I fell behind. Through a fog of altitude stupidity, I tried to think why Raphael had said one thing at Martel's table and then told us to turn back when he had spoken to me through the wall. It felt ominous, but in the end I couldn't decide why. Ahead of me down the slope, Clem's nose started to bleed again and he slung a handful of blood sideways to sprinkle vivid and steaming against the snow.

It was soon obvious why Raphael wanted us to go quickly. There was nowhere to stop. Even up to Crucero there had been inns, but there was nothing now. On one side of the road the cliffs rose up black, straight into clouds. They were a thousand feet at least, sheer and snowy. On the other side was a kingfisher-blue lake, and beyond that, the white mass of a glacier, which mumbled somewhere inside the ice. It must have been moving fast, because every half-hour or so another chunk fell from it and smashed over the rocks. It was all too huge to seem real. Before long I started to feel edgy. It didn't seem like the sort of place humans were meant to be. But only a couple of miles after the glacier, we found the farming terraces: gigantic steps eight feet broad built into the mountainside so that crops could be grown on the flat surfaces. They were Incan, abandoned, but the shapes of them were still clear. There were a hundred and five on one side, stretching up and up the cliff. It was bigger than anything I'd seen in China, any tea plantation or temple. Perched in impossible places were the ruins of houses. Clem knocked my arm. If he had still been annoyed with me for agreeing to a guide, it was all gone now and he had turned glowing and joyous.

'How about that? Eat your heart out, Emperor Hadrian.'

'I didn't know it was like this.' The terraces covered such a great swathe of land that although the grass and overgrown trees were nodding in the wind, the only things that really seemed to move across them were the shadows of the clouds. It was grand, but there was something horrible about it too.

'Like what?'

'I don't know. Just . . .'

'Actually brilliant, rather than comparatively brilliant?' He was grinning. 'I know. One's so used to saying, yes, your stick-man painting is marvellous, considering you're a pygmy in a mud hut.

They weren't pygmies in huts, though. They were as good and as strong as Rome. Historical fluke the Spanish ever managed to get the better of them.'

'How did they?' I said, wanting suddenly and badly to know.

'Smallpox,' he said. 'It wasn't strategy or anything like that. The Spanish brought smallpox with them when they landed in Mexico. It arrived in Peru before they did. And the Inca had built a wonderful, efficient road system for it to travel on. The royal family was obliterated in five years, the administration of the empire collapsed, and Pizarro took the whole thing with five thousand men. One of the most ridiculous confluences of bad luck in history.'

I'd never been interested before, not even a bit. Whenever Clem talked about South American history, it sounded as though there were a hundred uninteresting abortive empires kicking around and the Inca had blurred into it all, but they were almost still here. Someone must have been proud to live in those mad houses. There weren't ghosts – I don't believe in ghosts – but standing there I wished I did, because ghosts would have meant they were less lost.

'Do you know who built this?' Clem called to Raphael. 'Which king?'

'Won't have been a king. The royal estates are much bigger.'

'Bigger,' I echoed. I was lagging again.

'How's the leg?' Clem said.

'Fine,' I said, having decided we'd stop when I fainted and not before.

Raphael had decided something else. 'We're stopping, I'm starving. We're out of the wind here at least.'

'I thought you said we should hurry along?' Clem said.

'Not when there are grapes up here.' He climbed straight from his saddle up one of the terrace walls to sit on the edge of the second lowest level, where he snapped a handful of dusky grapes off a vine and hummed at me to catch my attention before he dropped them and a piece of Martel's sugar cake into my lap. 'Eat something sweet. We're still high up, you'll get tired fast.'

Clem looked up. 'Where are we now?'

'This valley is Sandia.'

He was right – the grapes were sweet and I did feel better for them. They were perfectly ripe, taut in their skins.

'Right, I see. Not much after this is charted,' Clem said to me. He was unfolding a piece of paper from his pocket, already sketched with the tentative shapes of the mountains and the rivers. Before Crucero he had wanted to work out latitudes with the sextant he'd brought, but the sky had been clouded over all night and there hadn't been even a glimmer of the pole star. It must have been getting towards noon now, but the sun was lost in haze. 'We'll have to start being more systematic soon.'

I eased down from my saddle onto the first step of the terrace, which was exactly at ankle height. The horse, an expensive mare, stayed more or less where she was to nose at some of the plants nearby. She ate them delicately. I rubbed her neck, missing Gulliver, who had good table manners too. Along from us, about twenty feet away, Quispe dropped down nearly as stiffly as I had.

Clem was hovering a pencil just above his sketch map. 'There's a river, isn't there, soon. What's it called?' he aimed at Raphael.

'Depends which village you're from.'

'Aren't you a fountain of information.'

Raphael only looked tired and swung his legs up onto the terrace. Because he was almost directly above us, he disappeared then. If he wanted to he could walk off and leave us. He could have been doing it then and we wouldn't see until he was a hundred yards away. Hoping Quispe knew the way too, I gave Clem some of the grapes. He sat down beside me and looked me over.

'Well, you're shiny and healthy at this generally atrocious altitude. Obnoxious, really. You couldn't develop some sort of awful complication with the leg so my fragile constitution looks less ladylike, could you?'

I wished he wouldn't lie. He wasn't very good at it. All he did was say the opposite of what he thought and hope for the best. I was sure I'd never looked worse. 'If Raphael will leave me a map, I can come after you at my own pace.'

'Does it hurt that much?'

'As long as I can take the weight off it sometimes it's all right,' I said, quietly because the old Navy feeling was coming from him that if I were to just buck up a bit, I'd forget about it.

'Yes, no, obviously,' he said. He looked away, embarrassed because, however much he didn't want to be, he was getting impatient. I looked down at my knees. We were both at half-capacity, but I was starting to think that only meant neither of us had the brain power for good lies. Even Quispe had folded up in an exhausted heap. His horse nudged at him to see if he was all right.

'Raphael, are you still there?' I said.

He dropped some more grapes at me to show that he was. When I looked up, the terraces above us were strung about with mist. It was forming in threads all along the valley. There was a sound like soft rain, but it was only the moisture dripping from the leaves of the overhanging plants.

It was uncomfortable that I was having to call him by his first name. 'And do you have a last name?'

'Not really.'

'Are you sure?' I said. It was hard to tell whether he was only being polite or if he was holding it back so that he didn't have to give us everything.

'What do you want?'

'Can you leave me a map and take Mr Markham on?' I said. 'I'm not going to be able to go quickly, I'm sorry.'

Clem didn't argue and glanced up with hope in his eyes.

'No,' Raphael said. 'Eat your grapes.'

'To be fair, a lazy Indian probably goes fifteen times slower than you ever would,' Clem said, resigned to it now.

I concentrated on the grapes. The sugar was chipping away at the tiredness. The wheedling bluebottley unease that had been whining close to me since the glacier faded. We were safe. It was almost warm. For the first time in days it felt nearly like the land had noticed it was supposed to be summer. I hoped the snow at Azangaro was just a quirk of local weather, not a wider thing to do with the solar storm. I was so tired of being cold already.

I was turning a grape over between my fingertips when I saw a man coming towards us from the direction we were heading in. Clem, who was sorting through his pack, didn't notice him. He was Spanish, wearing an old colonel's jacket over his ordinary clothes and a rifle slung over his shoulder. It was Dutch. He leaned down close to me. He stank of old brandy.

'I'll cut your feet off if you so much as touch a quinine tree.'

I pushed the handle of my cane up hard into his jaw. He reeled backwards.

'Jesus,' said Clem. 'Where did he pop up from?'

The man shoved me against the wall by the front of my shirt.

'*One* seed. Don't worry, everyone will be watching.'

From the edge of my eye I saw Raphael drop down beside us, his rifle against his shoulder.

'Manuel,' he said in his quiet way. 'Get your hands off him.'

'Oh, it's you,' said Manuel. He laughed. 'Don't trust him, boys, he's only in it to sell your guns to me. Hey?' He slapped me, not hard enough to spin my head but enough to make my teeth ache. I slapped him back, much harder. He looked indignant and pulled out a knife, and Raphael shot him in the head. Clem yelled, which made me jump where the gunshot hadn't. I held the back of my head where it had banged against the terrace behind me, waiting for it to stop pulsing.

'Did you have to do that?' Clem demanded.

'Since you didn't. Look at me,' Raphael said, much more gently than I would have thought he could speak. He tipped my head to either side to be sure my pupils were even. Close to, he was younger than I'd thought; some of the lines around his eyes weren't lines at all but the subsurface scars that boxers have.

It was shamefully nice to be paid the attention, though it had nothing to do with real concern. Seeing him close brought back a clearer memory of the night before and a bolt of shame went right through me for having let myself go so badly in front of him then. I put my fingertips on his chest and pushed. 'All right, no one's burning down your village. Who was he?' I said towards the body.

'He used to be a quinine farmer before all the trees were cut back round here. He just helps maintain the monopoly now. Makes threats to any white men who come through.' He put his rifle back over his shoulder and I caught the chemical tang of gunpowder. It was a good smell, one I'd forgotten I liked.

'Thank you,' I said, wishing I hadn't been churlish. 'I'll try and be less useless.'

That made him laugh for some reason, or almost. 'Get on your horse. Before his son comes. And you, Markham. Quispe, we're going,' he added in Spanish.

'And we're leaving the body here, are we?' Clem said.

'Feel free not to, but I am.' He rode away before Clem could argue.

Quispe was looking at the body with a quiet satisfaction that made me think the man must have had a history of worse things than threats. I sat looking at the Dutch rifle, holding the back of my head where it hurt.

'What if Raphael hadn't had a gun, hey?' Clem said once Raphael was out of earshot. 'Don't pick fights you can't finish, Em. We both could have been killed.'

I knew he was only annoyed with himself for having been slower than Raphael, but it stung anyway and before long I was lagging further behind them than ever. It was Clem who went ahead; Raphael waited to make sure I was still there and twice he turned down unexpected paths and left Clem to work out that we weren't following. Quispe must have known the way, because he dawdled well behind, walking rather than riding. When we turned down one steep valley, Raphael pretended not to notice how much I was struggling for a while, then touched my arm to stop me and pointed to a spray of great boulders across the mountainside. They looked like the petrified vertebrae of a huge spine.

'That's unusual,' he said. 'Lucky to see one these days.'

'What is it?' I asked, leaning forward in the saddle and suspecting he had invented it as a reason to stop.

'They're called chakrayuq.'

It sounded like a real word. He was watching the stones, not me, passing his rosary beads through and through his hands, the reins pinned under his knee.

'What does that mean?'

'It means owner-of-the-field,' Clem called. He must have just found the turning. He sounded annoyed. 'They're a kind of shrine. Very old. People used to think they were alive.'

'No,' Raphael said, too quietly for Clem to hear. 'That's etymology. It means . . .' His eyes went into the middle distance while he thought about it. I saw the moment he came up with what it should be, because he looked sad, like he hadn't thought of it that way before, the Quechua word being just a word. 'Giant,' he said. 'It's a dead giant.'

NINE

WHEN WE FOUND THE river, it was unexpected. There were no reeds or marshy patches to announce it; only the water, suddenly. It stretched off in either direction, already broad and slow. Clem looked up and down, disorientated. He asked Raphael where it came out at either end, but although they might have been talking about the same places, they were using different names and never overlapped, except at countries.

'Does it ever run into Bolivia?'

'Bolivia?' Raphael looked almost interested, but only as though Bolivia were a philosophical notion he had learned at school and hadn't come across very often since, rather than what it was, which was the Peruvian version of Wales. 'Where's the border?'

Clem was plainly having to do his best not to explode. 'You *live* on the Bolivian border and you don't know?'

'No. Bloody great forest in the way.'

I inclined my head at that, because he really was fluent. Unless he'd learned English as a child it would have been nearly impossible and even then, to have retained it after years of no use, or sporadic use at best, meant a spectacular memory. I'd lost all my Chinese already. He caught me looking and flared his eyes at me to ask why. I opened my hand gently away from myself like an orator, to say he spoke well. He frowned, but his shoulders tacked shyly.

'Can I borrow that scarf?' Clem said to me, then screamed into it when I gave it to him. When he handed it back, he kept his face straight. 'If I haven't strangled him by next Tuesday, I'm to be beatified. Write to the Pope.'

If Raphael noticed, he pretended not to. He had gone ahead of us, to a single stone pier. There was nobody there, no houses, no boats. At the end of it was a statue: seven feet tall, facing out towards the water like a person.

'What happens now?' Clem asked when we caught up.

'We wait for a fisherman.'

'Is there no ferry?'

He didn't snort, but he did show his teeth in something too humourless to be a real smile. There was a cruel curve to it, the kind of smile women call rakish before the owner abandons them pregnant in an asylum. 'No.' He dropped his bag on the ground and crouched down to take out a jar of wax and a brush with a bluish glass handle. With his wrists hanging over his knees, he looked up at the statue, then stood to scrub off the watermarks left by old rain and the splashes that reached it from the river. I'd thought the statue's clothes were stone like the rest of it, but they shifted when he ran the brush over them; real leather, all of them, bleached as pale as the marble by the weather. I watched him for a while and wondered why they bothered dressing statues. But then, most of the statues of Mary in churches on the way had been wrapped up in blue silk. I caught the smell of the wax on the breeze. Burned honey.

Quispe gathered together the horses and turned straight around again without saying goodbye.

When I sat down, a swarm of fish came to inspect the soles of my boots. Clem paced for a while but then gave up and we played skimming games with the flat pebbles that covered the shoreline. Along from us, Raphael was still waxing the statue's clothes. It seemed like a lot of work after riding as far as we had, but he was doing it carefully and something about the way he moved his arm made it look like a ritual with a specific set of motions. Clem had noticed too.

'St Somebody, is that?' he said.

'No.'

I've never seen anyone go from wary to delighted as fast as Clem did then. He nearly bounced onto his feet. 'You're joking! It's a markayuq?'

Raphael nodded ruefully. I had a feeling he had avoided saying the Quechua by way of discouraging Clem from it too.

'I've never seen an anthropoid version before, I thought they were always just outcrops of the bedrock—'

Raphael looked at him past the statue's shoulder. 'Quiet down.'

'You believe it's real?' Clem beamed. 'That it can hear us? Sorry, he?'

'Stop. Calm down.'

'But you're Catholic,' Clem said joyfully, impervious now. I smiled, glad he was happy again. 'But you still believe in the local . . .?'

Raphael let the silence go on for a second. 'Speak quietly,' he said, quietly himself.

'Sorry! May I look at him?'

'Look. Don't touch. But there are six in Bedlam. You'll have more time then.'

'Bedlam?' I said.

'New Bethlehem. Joke.' He didn't sound as though he found it especially funny. 'You'll see.'

'Six markayuq in one place?' Clem said over us. 'I thought it was one per village.'

'This village is special.'

'How?'

'Like Canterbury. He's here because he marks the pilgrimage route.' He pointed along the river, left to right. There was another jetty a good way off, almost out of sight, and on it the motionless figure of a man in heavy robes. Like the one on the pier it was fantastically real-looking and nothing like the blocky things I associated with South America. They were just like the statue at home. I didn't say anything. I would later, because I wanted to know why Dad had stolen a Peruvian shrine, but the sense of things I'd thought were unconnected connecting was too strange then.

'In that case,' Clem said, 'I shall leave him be. But they're all like this one, are they? Proper statues? They look like real people?'

'Yes.'

Clem grinned and sat down with me again. 'This is going to be much better than I thought.'

'What does markayuq mean?' I asked.

'Marka means village and yuq implies ownership, or being a vessel, something like that. It's the same yuq as in chakrayuq, but chakra means field. So owner-of-the-village, or similar. It's another kind of shrine, just a littler one for a littler place. Not that there's a village round this one, but there would be usually.'

'It means warden,' Raphael said. He didn't sound optimistic that he was going to be able to change Clem's translating habits.

'This is handy, a bilingual native speaker,' Clem said happily. He wrote 'markayuq' down on the corner of his map and marked the position of the shrine too.

Raphael finished his work on the statue and sat down next to his bag again to exchange the brush and the wax for his Spanish book. He fitted them neatly in, and when he lifted the book out, he was careful of the corners.

I scooped up another pebble. It glittered oddly and I paused, because it wasn't stone at all but bluish glass. I showed Clem, who frowned and shrugged, but when we leaned down to look along the shore, there were dozens of them, and perfect glass shells, occupied by river things whose inner workings the glass exposed. The sun came out and sparkled along them all.

'I found some of these at home,' I said to Clem. 'Dad must have brought them back.'

'We're going the right way, then. I wonder what the hell they are. How could anything form a shell from glass?'

I shook my head. We both looked along at Raphael, weighing up mystery versus asking him.

'Raphael,' Clem ventured at last.

He ignored us. He was holding the book open but his focus missed it. There were leather gaiters over his boots, black once and unevenly grey now, and he was just touching the water's surface with the buckle of one, holding it perfectly still while the fish came close to the shiny bar. The long stillness was unsettling, because it's usually something humans only do when they mean to kill something. He didn't. He only sat. Clem said his name again to exactly the same effect. Long after we had lost interest, I heard the scratch of paper as he turned a page.

We didn't quite wait an hour before a boat came, a little balsawood skiff with sails made of woven grass, carrying a cargo of sheepskin and one cheerful trader bundled up against the cold under a Russian-looking hat. I didn't think we would all fit on, but the trader sat on the sheepskin bale to make room for us. There wouldn't have been a spare inch for the mules. Thinking of the mules made me wonder again about the boys. Clem thought they had just decided against the unwelcoming weather, but they hadn't seemed unhappy to me before. It was Raphael they hadn't liked. As the boat drifted by cliffs that grew taller and taller, cut with fine waterfalls that fell from so high the sources were lost in the clouds, I tried to think of someone who might have made me run away as soon as I saw him – and not just run, but turn back from a good fire on a sleeting night. All I could think of was Irishmen talking quietly over dynamite boxes.

The stack of sheepskins was easily high enough to lean back against if you sat on the deck which, though balsawood splinters the second you introduce it to an overweight mouse, was properly layered and bolted together, and dry. There was a quiet conversation in Quechua going on somewhere over my head. Whatever the boys' anxieties about Raphael, the trader didn't share them and he was chatting, or I thought so at first. It was an elegant language. Every so often it hung mid-word like a ballet dancer where English would have rattled along on its tracks. It took me a good while, half-asleep, to realise that it wasn't Raphael on the other side of the conversation but Clem. I could hear his English accent next to the trader's dancing one. Now that I was paying attention, other things sounded wrong too. He was talking in an English word order. When I caught myself thinking that, I frowned, because I would have sworn to a jury I'd never learned any Quechua.

Something cold touched the back of my neck, then my hands. When I looked up, the air was grainy with snow, though the valley had narrowed so much that we were protected on either side for hundreds of feet. It was coming down heavily enough to have dusted the rocks along the banks already. I brushed the new flakes off my sleeves and got up unevenly, already stiff from the cold. Some of the rocks were the same almost-clear glass we had found on the shore by the pier, huge boulders of it smoothed into watery curves by the river. They were covered in white crystals – salt, though we must have been a thousand miles or more from the nearest sea. Raphael was sitting at the prow, half-hidden by the sail.

'Is that salt marsh?' I said, without much hope of getting any more of an answer out of him than we had before.

He did turn back this time. 'Mm. There's salt under the ground here. Used to be mines.' He was looking up at the snow, not quite frowning, but grim, though I couldn't see any particular reason to worry about it. In the grey light, there were red strands in his hair. It was long enough to tie back but short enough to be always falling down. I couldn't imagine him neat.

The white motes pottered about on their way down to the water, not driven by any wind. The thin sunbeams swam with them. I'd crossed my scarf over my chest and buttoned my coat on top of it, the collar turned up, but the cold was starting to bite through everything. The only bright thing nearby was a flock of parrots perched on the bank, all red and blue and tropical in the deepening cold. Whenever we turned a bend of the river, I caught a snatch of mountains up ahead, as jagged and vast as the range we had just crossed. The peaks were already white.

Clem had taken out his map and now he was sketching the shape of the river in pencil, to the interest of the boatman, who made him mark on a little town called Phara and looked disproportionately pleased when he did.

'This fellow's telling me he's originally from somewhere called Vangavilga – do you know where that is?' asked Clem. 'Is it round here? I think he wants me to put it on my map.'

Raphael looked across. 'Huancavelica. No. It's about four hundred miles away.'

'No, he said V—'

'Vangavilga is Huancavelica,' he said with unexpected patience. 'Huancavelica is how you spell it and how you'd say it in Spanish but we have a different accent round here. It's the start of the pilgrimage route. He means his family escaped here from the old labour draft. The mines killed so many people the young men used to run before the draft captains came round. Or after, to recover from the mercury poisoning.'

'I know where Huancavelica is,' Clem said, shocked. 'But that . . . the variation. It's not in the least reflected in the Spanish spelling. You can't read *vanga* for *huanca* in Spanish. That's ridiculous. Is it widespread? Are there other interchangeable consonants?'

'Plenty.'

'That's linguistic vandalism.'

'They say Wank'avilka in Cuzco. Huancavelica. What's the matter with it?'

'What does it mean?' I asked, to break their flow.

'Stone idol,' said Clem. 'There's a chakrayuq there, a huge one.'

Raphael looked like he might have laughed if he'd been younger and more cheerful. 'Why are you using the Jesuit dictionary?'

'How do you know what I'm using? And it's the only Quechua dictionary.'

'It's probably shrine,' I said, and then when Clem frowned, not understanding, 'not idol.'

Raphael nodded to me and I smiled, because he was taking it so gently. I would have burst out laughing if someone had translated Christchurch as Heathen God Temple in front of me.

Clem sighed and I wished I hadn't said anything. I'd always thought he was a languages genius – he was perfect in Spanish, at least. But Spanish and English aren't different languages, only extreme dialects of Latin. It's almost possible to translate word for word. Translation from a language unrelated to English is nothing to do with equivalent words. Whenever I'd tried to do that in Chinese I'd come out with unbroken nonsense. I had to forget the English, hang the meaning up in a well-lit gallery, stare at it hard, then describe it afresh. I was starting to think Clem was looking at Quechua like he would have looked at Spanish. He was trying to link, not translate. I couldn't think of a way to say so without sounding like a patronising twerp, so I stayed quiet.

'And to answer your previous question,' Clem said to Raphael, 'the *matter* with it is this. Spelling it Huancavelica, from the Cuzco dialect, crystallises *one* pronunciation and makes the others irretrievable unless you meet a native speaker, of which there will be none in two hundred years' time at this rate. Come on, you know very well what I mean.'

Raphael was unmoved. 'Spend a lot of time weeping over the lost phonemes of Pictish, do you?'

'Phonemes.' I murmured to no one, or to the river. I had no idea how in God's name he could have learned a word like that. I barely knew what it meant. Neither of them noticed.

'What's Quechua for "philistine"?' Clem said waspishly.

He thought about it. 'Philistine.'

'Oh, God, it just goes on, doesn't it.' Clem sighed and tapped his pencil against the map, still unhappy. 'And this river doesn't seem to have a name except "the river". Or something about glass, which I guarantee also isn't written anything like it's pronounced.'

'What's written Quechua like? Can't you write it that way?' I said. 'You know, in brackets.'

'There isn't any,' Clem said bleakly. 'There is no record whatsoever of an Incan writing system. The closest they had was a kind of knotting, for counting and so forth. Looks like very clumsy tapestrywork.'

'How can you have a whole empire without legal textbooks and public records?'

'Oral traditions, one supposes. Wiped out when the Spanish arrived.' Clem shook his head. 'It makes a horrible sort of sense. Writing evolves not when you want to wax lyrical about the daffodils but for tax purposes. Numbers. Nouns. Five sheep. No need for adjectives or adverbs or grammar, not at first.'

Raphael had covered his nearer eye with the heel of his hand so that he wouldn't have to look at us.

Clem finished putting down guessed names and tipped the map towards me. 'You're part homing pigeon – how does that look to you? More or less?'

He had sketched a long, rounded right-angle as the river veered south towards Bolivia. His compass was still balanced on his knee, but the solar storm must still have been churning around us, because the needle was skittering in no steady direction. I steepened the curve with my fingertip. The river was starting to meander, just little swerves at the moment, but because of that it was difficult to feel that it was tilting more broadly as well.

'Are you sure?' Clem asked, frowning.

'No,' I said, not wanting to start another fight. 'I just feel like we've strayed a bit further to the right.'

'Right isn't a cartographical term, darling,' he laughed.

'It looks like a dragon if you've got it right,' Raphael said. His eyes caught on Clem for too long. 'Darling' was the sort of thing Martel would have said.

'Nor are dragons,' Clem said, but he tipped the map to see if he could find one. I traced out the hump of a wing, one that would be there if it leaned more to the right. The meanders made paws. 'Oh, yes. Well, that's neat, isn't it? Have you got a map, then, Raphael, if you know what it all looks like?'

'At home I have.'

'Why didn't you bring it?'

'It's carved on the wall.'

'How useful,' Clem said. 'Just like the rest of you, hey?'

Raphael watched him with the same distance as when he shot Manuel. I vacillated for a long few seconds, but there were a hundred things out here he could claim to have no control over if Martel asked and, in the interest of his not ensuring that some of them happened to us, I shut my eyes and shoved Clem over the side. He landed with a splash and an explosion of swearing. I had to pretend I'd slipped, but Raphael smiled and looked more ordinary as he helped Clem back onto the boat, which only got him a round of his own accusations, although he hadn't been in arm's reach.

We all stopped talking when we saw the body on the cliff. It was hanging by its hair from a sturdy vine, not much but bones now. I couldn't see how anyone might have got it up there, much less how to take it down. There was a Spanish sign around its neck: *I stole quinine trees.*

'That's Edgar,' said Raphael. 'He used to live opposite. Took cinchona trees to a Dutchman.' He was watching me with the smallest cinder of a spark, as though he were quite looking forward to hearing how I meant to talk my way around that.

TEN

THE CLIFFS LEANED TOWARDS each other until the river was more of a creek. Even so, I didn't expect to see what we did when it tipped us round the last, sharp bend, past the deep caves with their salt stalactites and scatterings of glass boulders.

Where there used to be a bridge of land, the river had worn through and made three towering stacks. Clem worked out later that they were six hundred and twelve feet high. I couldn't see the tops of them properly, but around the bases were wharves, arranged like spokes, and then stairs and stairs and stairs, up to a tangle of wooden scaffolding that supported the corners of houses and spiralling gantries. As we came closer, I could see people moving; there was a man with a wheelbarrow full of pineapples.

The sun came out suddenly. Greenish blue shadows fell across the boat and turned the riverwater turquoise. The light was shining down through translucent parts in the stacks, which weren't rock but glass. It had been worn shiny and clear by the weather and the river. When I put my hand out to the coloured shadow beside me, the light was hot. The boatman steered us away from it but he didn't quite move quickly enough. Where the tip of the boom swung into the light, the grass sail caught fire. The boatman squeaked. Raphael, who had been drinking something from the cup of a flask, lobbed the contents at the little fire and put it out before it could spread. He didn't seem worried by it, but the boatman looked shaken and steered us square down a line of unlensed sunlight.

'My God,' Clem said. 'That's obsidian. Blue obsidian. It's formed in a strata over the – that isn't possible.' He said it in a nearly accusatory way towards Raphael, who was either too tired or too graceful to take him up on it.

'Black swans,' I said, fighting to stay mild. Raphael knew why we were really here. That he hadn't told anyone so far didn't mean he might not lose patience if we blamed him personally for one too many geological unlikelihoods or linguistic abnormalities. I would have told Clem to shut up if he had been Charles, but I wasn't afraid of Charles's temper. I'd forgotten I was afraid of Clem's. 'You know. More in heaven and earth. You don't know it's there until it pecks you.'

Clem snorted, still too annoyed with me to laugh. Raphael looked back slowly as if someone had walked over his grave. I frowned, but he shook his head to say it was nothing to do with me.

Where the light made the water clear, there were ruins on the riverbed, chunks of old masonry. I looked up again. The two bridges that connected the first and third stacks to the land were stone, but the middle ones, between the stacks, were wooden. They were recent. The whole great structure must have been eroding always.

I stood up by the prow as we reached the wharves. The river had carved out combes and caves that sang with drips as we passed. It smelled cleanly of hot salt. Rather than flowing straight between the stacks, it had cut deep gullies in the weak places and made a glass beach, almost the same as the rocky ones at home. But here the glass had been smoothed and worn into twisting shapes and dips that whirled the light and played perspective tricks. Nothing was sharp.

The trader steered us to a flat outcrop. Raphael stepped across easily. Clem struggled with it more, still pale from altitude sickness and wet from the river. The boatman held my elbow to help me down. I thought he would get out too to unload, but he only gave the beach an uneasy look and started back straightaway.

'He wasn't coming here, then?' I asked, confused.

'No, there's a warehouse back that way. Keep out of the sun,' Raphael added. He didn't sound like he thought we would listen.

We followed him in the cooler, safer, unlensed path of sunlight between the left-hand and middle stacks. On the far side, the river was much stronger and foamed over rocks and little crevasses, and from further away was a quiet roar that sounded like waterfalls. The cliffs stayed close after the stacks; a kayak would have made it through, but nothing substantial. Though I could just make out the green of trees at the top, it was impossible to see what sort they were or how dense.

I tripped into a well in the glass beach and thought for a long suspended instant that I was going to fall, but it was an illusion. The dip itself was only a few inches deep, but the glass was clear for about twenty feet. The bottom was a frozen riverbed. There were fish caught mid-turn around weed caught mid-furl. None of it was burned. I leaned down, but the surface was warped into wave-shapes, and everything blurred and distorted. It sharpened again when I straightened.

Nearer the wharves, the smooth glass turned pebbly and green-blue shells lay heaped everywhere. Most of them were stuck to rocks just like ordinary shells would have been. The rocks themselves were all either obsidian entirely or half-vitrified, great chunks of glass and stone all twisted together. The granite made shapes like ink unwinding in water. The boat had been cold, but the beach was so warm now that I had to take off my coat. When I strayed into a stronger patch of sunlight, having drifted sideways trying to get out of one sleeve, I had to jerk away. The heat was fierce there. The glass stratum was about two hundred feet high in the stacks and up to that point the cliffs were pockmarked with black spots and burns, like another waterline where the light was magnified. Birds, little black coot things, had all made their nests well above it. Except for the places exactly beside the stacks, where they were glass, the cliffs were ordinary rock. The obsidian had poured down in its own narrow stream when it was first formed and drawn a great glass stripe across the land. One of the mountains must have been a volcano.

Once we were well out of the hot shadows and in ordinary sun, Raphael stopped and waited.

'Right. Don't come down here around midday if it's sunny, you'll catch fire. In the forest there is a border marked with salt and animal bones; don't cross it. There are Indians in the woods and they do not like wandering foreigners. You'll never see them but they're there. Just stay away from them and they'll stay away from you.' He waited for us to nod. 'This place is a hospital colony. Most people up there are sick or deformed, so don't expect help carrying and lifting. You see to yourself, as much as you can. There are no servants.'

'We didn't expect to be waited on,' Clem said.

Raphael made an unconvinced sound and turned away towards the last stack and the wharves there.

'How quickly can we start out?' Clem said. 'For the coffee, I mean.'

'I'm interested to know when you're going to admit you're lying about the coffee and ask me where the cinchona woods are,' Raphael said over his shoulder. Like it often did, his voice came quiet at first and then strengthened. 'You're going to need to. This place is full of coffee but it isn't full of cinchona. Look around.'

'Now,' I said. 'Where are they?'

'Merrick,' Clem snapped.

Raphael looked back. 'This was shut down as a supply region years ago. Everything that could be harvested has been. Anything left is in Chuncho territory. I can take you round on the road they used to use, but it's old now and you might not find much even if it is passable. Why did you come here?'

'We have reports from a few years ago that imply there's something here worth going for,' I said.

He frowned. 'You're talking about the Dutch. And Backhouse's expedition. He brought an army battalion, and half those men were killed. You could have gone north. There's boatloads of the stuff up there.'

I shook my head. 'Those varieties have a two per cent quinine yield. What you have here is nine per cent at least. Look, we can pay. It will be worth your while, even if it is a trek.'

'As I say, I'll show you the path. But I don't think you'll find anything.'

'And if we do?'

'If you do – then there's going to need to be some negotiation.'

'Well, let's have that out now,' Clem said. 'How much do you—'

'We're not talking about it now.'

'Come on, man, a rough figure would be—'

'I said,' he interrupted, not loudly. He had never been loud. 'Not today. It would be a long talk. I'm tired enough already.'

'All right, all right,' Clem said. His crossness had taken on an edge of alarm. I felt it too. I had to step back. Raphael was too sharp and too strong, and he was standing side on to us as if he meant to punch one of us in the face. It might only have been how he happened to stop, but I was nearly sure he knew exactly what it looked like, and whether or not he was really thinking of hitting someone, standing close to him had made my spine fuse up. The need to back off was there in the air, like negative magnetism.

'Mr Martel will burn this place down if anything happens to you, and it's not safe for you to go off by yourselves,' he said quietly, more to me than to Clem, like I was an almost acceptable halfway mark. 'Do you understand? You don't go anywhere alone. I will take you round on the supply road in the morning. And you can see for yourselves that there's nothing left, and then you can get out of here before anyone guesses why you came.'

'Yes,' I said.

He didn't look as if he believed me, but he started towards the wharves again. We had to rush through the blue shadows of the stacks in the shade of boulders. The smell of steam hung in those places. The air writhed and the water boiled as it came in over the glass beach.

Chiselled on all the wharves were notices to keep out of the sun in Spanish and that odd, Spanish-phonetic Quechua. There was a barnacle-rough ladder and a set of steps. When we reached the top, there were more steps, far more, spiralling up the stack. They were stone for only a few yards, then the stone crumbled and was replaced by weatherbeaten wood. I thought Raphael would start up them, but he stopped instead by what I thought at first was a cargo winch whose pulley was a dot hundreds of feet above us. There was a loop at the end, the knot cemented into place by age and run through a straight metal bar to make a flat step, broad enough for two or three people to stand on or one to sit down on it like a swing. He nodded us across.

'On there and don't fall off.'

'Really?'

'It's higher than St Peter's. Walk if you like.'

I stepped on and wrapped my arm around the rope. Clem followed me, more unsteadily. He had never been a rigging sort of sailor. Raphael kicked a lever. As we started to rise, he stepped up with us. His weight made almost no difference to the speed. His clothes smelled of burned honey now, from the wax he had used on the statue.

After a few seconds we were well above the docks and passing the great twists in the glass. The winch had been built just where the strongest sun never reached, but there were still intensely hot patches, as hot as open ovens, while snow still feathered only forty feet away downriver. When we rose up beside the falling counterweight, it was an old Spanish cannon stamped with a pomegranate sigil.

'How big is the obsidian flow?' Clem said. He was still shivering from the river. 'If you ever stirred yourself to find out.'

'It comes from up there. Those mountains are all volcanoes. There are streams of it all around these hills, if you dig.'

By the time we were near the top, the view back down the river must have been fifty miles long. Further up, where it disappeared into steep turns and spars in the cliffs, the water churned white and was soon lost. Away in that direction, the mountains were flinty. Waterfalls made fine white lines down their faces, so far off that I couldn't see them moving.

The gantry was built just in front of a rock that had been carved into the shape of the nearest mountain, a sawtooth monster capped with what must have been permanent snow.

'Don't snigger too much,' Raphael said, 'but people are going to ask if I introduced you to the mountain and they'll think it's strange if I haven't.'

'Introduce us to the . . .?' Clem said.

Raphael motioned over his shoulder at the replica. 'Consider it an introduction to the local lord. If I have, everyone will know you're all right. Leave him an offering.'

'Like what?' I said. 'What do mountains like?'

'Silver. Shells. Salt. Nothing stupid; people will look to see what you left.'

I put down some of the glass shells I'd found and Clem turned out his pockets for his shinier coins.

'People believe the mountain is alive?'

'Mm.' He watched us. 'Stand straight, look polite. Cultural experience,' he added when we exchanged an uncertain look. 'This is the Inca tour.' He glanced towards the mountain and said something quiet in Quechua, which made Clem squeak.

'Did you call it Father?'

'Yes,' he said, drawing out the sibilant in a way that didn't in the least encourage any more questions. 'Shall we go? Before you freeze.'

As soon as Raphael had turned away, Clem beamed at me and made a hallelujah gesture at the sky, and then a little apologetic bow at the mountain. I laughed. Raphael was waiting at the corner where the path turned, not for us but for a pair of men and a wooden cart with one front wheel coming the other way. The cart was the one I'd seen from the boat, full of pineapples trussed down with a lattice of rope. One of the men had a withered arm and without being asked, Raphael pulled down the hook of the winch to loop it under some of the rope straps.

'Thanks very much, Father,' the carter said in what I only just recognised as Spanish, but he was speaking carefully, and he had only started after a glance towards us. 'Who are these gentlemen, then?'

'They're just visiting,' Raphael said. He was so much clearer than the carter that he might as well have been speaking English. 'Exploring. We were just introducing them to the mountain.'

'Oh, lovely,' the man said happily. He and his friend both glanced up at the mountain and then away again, just shy of an obeisance. He smiled at me. 'He's a good still mountain,' he explained. 'Not feisty at all. People here are very kind and steady.'

'Oh, right,' I said, feeling like an idiot. I'd understood all of the words and none of the sense. 'Thank you. It was . . . good to meet you.'

'Yes, yes,' he beamed.

Raphael helped them both on to the lift platform beside the hanging pineapples. They sank gently out of sight and lapsed into Quechua once they were away.

'Padre?' Clem echoed. 'Are you something to do with the mountain?'

Raphael held up his wrist to show him the rosary. 'I'm the priest.'

'You're a priest. Right. Good. These poor people.'

The path was a white line, the only flat place the snow had been able to settle properly. We passed houses set on broad steps hacked into the rock, and tiny gardens where goats watched us go and fishermen sat mending nets, and then there was a bridge to the next stack, which was a jumble of gantries and crooked buildings with red windmills spinning on the roofs. The bridge was so high that we were well above even the birds playing on the wind. The river was hardly anything but a shiny ribbon, curving steep off to the south and our right. A young condor was sitting on the banister of the bridge and hooted interestedly when we came by. It shuffled along with us and I went closer to see how tame it was. Very tame; it let me touch its feathers, then did a little happy dance. I laughed. It must have been someone's pet.

Clem thumped my arm and pointed up ahead of us. The condor flew away.

'What?' I said, disappointed.

'Look at that.'

On the opposite bank, beyond the stacks and the crooked spire of a small church on the mainland, was the forest. We were too high for tropical things; the trees were immense pines. They were almost like sequoia, but the trunks were, even in the gathering twilight, not red, but white as silver birches. They stood in a rank perhaps forty feet away from the edge of the cliff. There was no scrub or tangle of smaller plants – only the pines, hundreds of feet tall and with trunks as broad as the church. They were so different that it took me a long time to understand they were the same as the one we had at home. This was what they were supposed to be, at their natural altitude instead of stunted at the Cornish sea level. I'd never imagined they would be so vast, or so many. They sheared away down towards the next valley and then on and on into a thready mist which seemed not to care that it was sharing space with the snow. It looked like the sort of place where you should have heard wolves, but it was monkeys that were howling.

I had never really wanted to come to Peru, never been excited about it. There had been too much to worry about: walking, the journey, Clem, the altitude, and all the hundreds of stupid things that could have killed us before we even began. I'd thought that something was gone in me and I would never be uncircumspectly pleased with anything again. But all at once it came back. The place where my father had stood and my grandfather, a place that was in my bones and stories and home but had been as lost to me as Byzantium for years – here it was. I felt like I'd drawn a door on the wall at home in chalk and gone through into an imaginary place where the river was a dragon and somewhere in the forest was something stranger than elves.

'Come on, it's freezing,' Clem said.

'Yes . . . right.'

The forest was dark, the canopy having completely blocked the daylight. A trail of soft light flared between the trunks. I stopped again.

'Did you see that?'

'See what?'

I pushed my hand over my eyes. 'Probably nothing.'

ELEVEN

RAPHAEL TOOK US TO the church. It was at the end of a narrow glass road, in the shadow of the titan trees, where the air was much colder and frost glittered on the sunless side of the spire, which was lopsided and missing a patch of its terracotta tiles. Ivy had crept over the gap. Right up to the roof, so that the whole place looked like a cabin imitation of a church, the walls were covered by stacked firewood that parted in a grudging sort of way only to make space for the windows. They weren't big church windows, just ordinary ones. Near to it, the glass blocks of the road were being slowly prised apart by moss and sage. Everything was overgrown and dead poppies nodded in the long grass.

A little red windmill had been built into the roof, just like all the other houses. When I turned back, they made red dots all through the grey scattering of snow, catching the very last of the light as the sun disappeared beyond the mountains. I wondered what they were for but I had a feeling that if we asked Raphael about everything that caught our interest, we'd both be shoved into the river before dinner.

The forest stretched out for as long as the river did on either side. It had looked dense from further off, but close to it was primordial. It wasn't the sort of forest that could have been cleared with men and axes. Standing there, it was less strange that the people had decided to build out on the stacks. There were monkeys around the roots and they weren't big, but they didn't move when they saw us. There must have been bigger, more dangerous things there that didn't mind people either. Further downriver, there was nothing else. No road or other towns or a column of smoke. There were the trees, the snow, the cliffs, and that was it.

The church's back door was half the width of an ordinary one. Clem had to turn sideways. Instead of the vestry I was expecting, there was a kitchen, Quakerishly bare and very cold. Raphael pulled open the stove door as soon as we were inside. Next to it, sitting in a larger bucket of water as if it were gunpowder, was a copper bucket of sawdust. He threw in a handful, struck a match against the stove's grate and pushed the grille shut straightaway. Inside, light popped into life like fireworks, flashing and crackling for a good few seconds before the heat caught on the logs and settled to a more ordinary glow.

'What was that?' I said, a little flatly, because I already knew but it was frustrating to meet someone who knew all about it when we had muddled on in uninterrupted ignorance and blown up half the house.

'Whitewood. It explodes. If you light a fire, only use the wood that's stacked outside. It's kapok, from the other side of the river. Didn't you say you had some, at your house?'

I was surprised he had paid that much attention at Martel's. 'Yes. We . . . had a bit of an accident recently.'

He swept his eyes down me as if he would have liked to throw me out and lock me in a well-ventilated igloo before I could explode anything important. 'Try not to do it again.'

'I won't, but – what makes it explosive?'

'I don't know. But all the gantries in town are made of it, so no smoking, unless you want it to go up in your face. Or in here.' He pointed upwards.

The inside of the spire roof had been fixed neatly but often. The old planks, which must have patched over the first holes, had darkened and crumbled in turn and now they were interspersed with newer planks themselves. And all that was a repair of the original roof, which must have fallen in completely at some point, or else been pulled down when the place was made into a church.

Raphael brought cheese and salted meat down from the cupboards and put them on glass plates on the table. He disappeared outside briefly and came back with a pineapple, which he diced up so fast he must have done it every day, then tipped the pieces into a glass bowl. When I tried it, it was the sweetest I'd ever tasted. He opened the grate again once the fire was going, to let some of the heat out, then pulled away a peg that kept a pulley from moving. The ropes disappeared up through the ceiling and down through the floor. Up above somewhere, something creaked and turned squeakingly. After a few minutes came a rush of water just under the stove, then a hiss as it hit something hot. The cliff curved inward, so the ropes must have gone down through it to the open air and then the river to bring up water. It seemed bizarre until I tried to think of another way to get water on glass stacks. There would be no wells.

Another few minutes later the rush of water came again and this time there was a muttering as it poured into pipes I hadn't noticed. They were bronze and glass, and they went all round the walls, close to the floor and under it; I soon felt the heat coming up from the tiles. Raphael stood still, watching them.

'If you see anything leaking, say. All this should have been lit up last week.'

'How do you mean?'

'Before the frost. Cold pipes break if you heat them up too quickly.'

I nodded, but nothing burst or broke, only rattled. In the quiet, I noticed we hadn't heard from Clem in a little while. He was collapsed over his arms, still damp. When I nudged him, he mumbled about the altitude again. As gently as I could, I undid the buttons on his wet coat and got it mostly off him, so that it wouldn't block the heat from the fire. The lining started to steam.

Raphael had turned back to the stove, which had a separate boiler compartment. He dipped a pan in and tipped quinoa grain into the bottom with a soft sandy hiss. As soon as it was on the stove top, it started to bubble. While it did, he pulled open a glass-handled drawer in the base of the stove. Inside was a metal tray where salt had dried in bumpy white waves. He poured it carefully into a glass bowl, already half full. I watched him put it back.

'Is that a distillation oven?' I said. 'How did you get that up here?'

'I didn't, it was made here. Everyone's got one. This place has been here hundreds of years. They've always made salt.' He leaned forward to touch the wall, which had been built in two stages. The base was all irregular polygons. They had been fitted curiously around a natural outcrop of the bedrock, some of which was swirled through with glass, like a splash. Into its gaps, the masons had eased specially carved and curved bricks, even though it would have been much easier if they had chipped down the original rock. The upper half of the wall was much more standard, all straight bricks, but the irregular ones blended into them. It seemed like a painstaking, unnecessary effort to make the wall look as if it had grown up out of the ground.

The firelight threw into relief a frieze carved over the brickwork. There were pictures of trees and what might have been animals or tree gods, and mountains, and the shape of the river – our river – made simple and blocky. It was ancient. The only thing to say we weren't in a real Incan house was an alcove that must have been carved into the wall later, because it interrupted the line of the bricks. Inside was a shrine of the Virgin Mary, only the size of a doll. She was gold, but her robes were blue glass. They swam with shadows in the firelight, and then more strongly when Raphael lit a candle from the stove and set it beside her. I touched the edge of the map, which had been worked in geometric patterns.

'It's like a . . . what do you call it, those omnibus maps where they square off all the roads.'

Raphael rocked down into the chair next to mine and took some pineapple too. 'Listen. The snow's still coming. If it's thick in the morning, you're stuck. The path will be snowed shut and the river will freeze.' He touched the wall again as he spoke. He was showing me the section that was us. Bedlam was marked over the river. Below it, a long path snaked round the bend.

'Where are the cinchona woods?'

He traced the path all the way west around the riverbend, which was so steep that it would in the next few thousand years become an ox-bow lake, right to a point almost directly opposite Bedlam through the forest, due south.

'It looks good on there but that path is narrow.'

'So that's . . .' I was sitting with my back to the forest, facing the stacks. The town lights winked and glowed behind him through the window. 'Over there.' I pointed left, through the map wall.

'That's right.' He picked up a pencil and drew a neat compass on the stone. The map wasn't quite orientated north; it was north-east, but they had shifted it to make the dragon shape of the river upright. When he marked on the points, he wrote the letters in schooled, old-fashioned loops.

'Is it not possible to go straight through the forest?' I asked. 'Cut off the river, go due south? The snow wouldn't matter under the canopy.'

'No. The border I told you about is here.' He drew a line right below the town, so close that I looked round to see if I could see through the window. There was only blackness outside in that direction, but the way he had drawn it made it look as if it could hardly be a hundred yards behind the church. He pointed the end of the pencil behind me too. 'Chuncho territory. Do not cross the salt border. You'd be shot and hung up in a tree.' The wind howled, ruffling loose tiles in the roof. Fighting against the cold, the hot water in the pipes muttered and clattered more loudly. Over it all, the windmill had a rhythmic squeak and in the lulls I could hear the wind pulling at its sails. 'I don't know what the weather's playing at this year,' he said quietly. 'This is summer. It should be warm until April.' We were still only at the beginning of February.

'There's a solar storm.' I took out my compass and put it in front of him so that he could see how the needle was skipping. 'It's still going. We saw the southern lights in Peru. I think it's affecting the weather.'

Raphael looked at the compass and then me, not uninterested, but he must have reached his capacity for conversation that day because he lifted his bag on to his lap and took out the clocks from Azangaro. Gently, he prised the cases open and began to disassemble the clockwork, one piece at a time, with a pair of tweezers. I leaned across to Clem to see if he was awake, but he wasn't.

'Is there somewhere for him to lie down?' I asked.

Raphael pointed with the tweezers to a little door that would lead into the other arm of the church's small cross. When I went through to see, it was a tiny chapel, empty except for three or four beds neatly turned out on the stone floor and another alcove-shrine, a saint this time, although I couldn't have said which. He was gold and glass too.

Clem got up with some help, but he was dizzy and damp and it took a while to manoeuvre him into fresh clothes and then into one of the pallet beds. I'd thought it would be cold, but the pipes ran around the walls here too, and they must have been under the floor, because it was warm enough to have heated the sheets through. They felt like they had just come off presses.

'Is there a light?' I called. Because it was dark in the chapel and light in the kitchen, the steam drifting in through the doorway glowed.

'Above you. Twist the key. Like on a clock.'

I didn't understand until I straightened up and found what I thought was an oddly made oil lamp hanging on the wall from a piece of rope. It was made out of an old fishing float, but there was a clock's key in the side. I turned it and heard clockwork skitter. Inside the glass ball, a dusty gold glow trailed a clock's second-hand turning disembodied from a clock face. The light strengthened with each tick of the brass hand, and by the time a minute had swept by, it was much brighter than a candle. When I held it close to my eye, I could see the matter of the light; it was tiny particles, floating like luminous icing sugar.

'What is this stuff?'

'Pollen.'

I turned the lamp round in my hands. I didn't hear what he'd said for a long lag. It knocked around inside my skull for three or four bounces before the thinking part of me caught it. 'Pollen? From what?'

He didn't answer.

When I came back into the kitchen, he had lit more lamps and put one on the table to read by. The light cast long, criss-crossing shadows over the dismantled clocks where it shone through the mesh of rope that caged it. A cluster of lamps, little ones, ticked near the door. The quinoa was bubbling gently, but it wasn't even half-ready, given that the water was boiling so low. The stove was burning down too. Raphael was perfectly still and he didn't look up when I came in.

'Mind if I put some more wood on the stove?'

I waited, but he still ignored me, so I put in all the wood from the scuttle. The stove was by a window that turned the corner of the room. One side faced the town and its lights, the other towards the forest, along the treeline. It was black except for a faint glow somewhere inside that was the same colour as the lamps' pollen. The new wood sent out a fresh wave of heat and I almost thought about taking off my coat. Raphael was sitting in his shirtsleeves. In all the time I'd been pottering, he hadn't turned the page. I sank down in the other chair to look at the light on the table. The pollen floated and furled, brightest at the edges of a set of tiny sails stitched on to the clock hand. It was hypnotic. My fingertips itched to open up the bulb and see what the pollen did if it was allowed to float free, but I didn't want Raphael to punch me in the face so I sat without touching it, my hands trapped between my knees.

It was a little while before I realised he hadn't moved at all, although he was still holding the tweezers and the clockwork. I'd assumed he was only thinking, but it was perfect motionlessness.

'Everything all right?' I said.

He seemed not to hear. Slowly, I stretched forward and waved my hand under his eyes. Nothing happened. I was starting to feel uneasy when I remembered it had happened before. He had ignored us on the jetty earlier, sitting as still as this, when I'd thought he was going to kill something. I caught his wrist and lifted it gently. It wasn't difficult to move him, but when I let him go, his arm didn't thunk back down again. It fell at nothing more than the speed of relaxing tendons until his knuckles brushed the table edge and rested there.

He looked up suddenly. I'd never known anyone to be frightened to see me before, but he was then. I sat back slowly to put some more space between us. He had clenched his fists. 'Is everything you needed there?' I asked.

His eyes slipped down to the clockwork again as though it might have moved since he last saw it, then nodded. He got up and drained the quinoa into the sink. When he came back to the table to serve it, he rested the edge of the hot pan against his hand. I waited for him to realise and snatch it away, the muscles in the back of my neck tightening more and more the longer he didn't, until I had to put my hand out to touch the pan rim. It burned even in a split second.

'Christ, put that down. Can't you feel that?'

He put the pan down to examine his hand. There was a red mark but the burn hadn't broken the skin. 'No.' He looked nearly worried when I reached out to stop him lifting it again. 'What?'

'Don't.' I took it off him and touched the handle experimentally, then had to pull my sleeve over my hand. He sat down to get out of the way. 'Were you born like this?'

'It's nothing.'

'Analgesia isn't nothing. Nor is catalepsy. Have you been to a doctor?'

He gave me another brief glassen stare, more like himself again. 'The doctor here is an empiric with some army ants and a hacksaw. What do you think?'

I sighed. 'That the Quechua medical profession is not all it could be.'

He tipped his fork at me by way of agreeing.

'Did you say empiric?' I said after a second.

'Is that wrong?'

'No, I just haven't heard anyone say that since I was small.'

'What do you say now?'

'Quack,' I said, interested. He must have learned English from passing expeditionaries when he was young, although it was such an ancient slang word that it must have been an old man who'd taught him even then.

He let his eyes drop and I felt awkward. I hadn't meant to tip him into language fatigue but he didn't say anything after that. It was clicking silence, because he was putting the clockwork back together again inside another glass fishing float he must have had ready and waiting. It was split in half neatly and when he had finished, it fitted together around a tiny hole, for the piece of string on which he had suspended the clock mechanism. There was no pollen inside yet and he wound the string round the ball and left it in a bowl between us filled otherwise with lemons and differently coloured maracuya, which must have had an English name, but I didn't know it. He saw me looking at the latter and cut one in half to show me. You had to eat it with a spoon, which made it seem more like a purple egg cup of rice pudding than fruit, though it was much better than rice pudding. We saved some food for Clem, but he was so deeply asleep that he didn't even stir when I shook his shoulder.

Just as I came back, a singing bell rang from beyond the closed door to the nave. I thought at first that it was something I'd made up, but after a little lag, I heard it again, a sparkling noise that carried clear over the wind. Raphael was looking at the door too. After the second pause, it sounded once more, much longer.

'Has someone been in there all this time?' I said.

'No. They wait in the woods until they see lights in here.' He sat still, looking exhausted, but he never lost the rigidity down his spine. I had never seen him slouch, not even sitting on the floor at the miserable little inn in Crucero.

'Who?' I asked.

'The . . . I'm not saying Chuncho any more, that just means wildman. The people who live in there. The ones who keep the border.' When the bell stopped, he stood up. 'Come with me,' he said. 'Bring the lamp.'

TWELVE

THE DOOR THAT LED into the nave was frozen closed and Raphael had to push his shoulder into it. Ice cracked on the other side. When I went through after him, up a steep step and down again into a blast of cold air, I saw why. The main church was open like a cloister on all sides except ours, held up by pillars mostly invisible under the vines, which were red and dying. The normal order of things was inverted; we didn't come out behind the altar but by a font. The altar was at the other end, at the base of the cross shape the church made. There were three candles on it, inside glass jars, and a bundle of blankets. Beyond was the open air and the looming blackness of the forest. Snow had blown crosswise across the nave, enough for us to make footprints.

The bundle was a baby, wrapped up against the cold and tucked close to a rag doll. She was asleep. From behind the altar a beautiful marble statue stood watching and shielding it from the wind. The statue was holding a bell. Raphael lifted the baby up. It yawned and woke but didn't seem to mind.

'What?' I said, bewildered. 'Where did she come from?'

'Look over there. Put your hand over the light.'

I wrapped my hands around the pollen lamp so that it looked like I had a star between them, the light seeping out from between my fingers. He blew out the candles. For a few seconds all I could see were dim yellow bursts where the light had been, but then there was a glow somewhere under the trees. It flared and then faded, slowly, easily the size of a person. It startled some birds and suddenly a whole flock of them took off through the branches. Each one left a swooping trail of light. Nearer the ground, there was a soft haze of more muted light. They were vines, like Chinese lanterns, fragile and translucent and twined around the roots of the trees, which were as tall as me. They were dying now and hardly more than botanical skeletons, but inside they glowed, just. It was too soft a light to have seen from the well-lit church. The bright wake shone again, further away. There was a brilliant puff as whoever it was walked through a patch of the vines.

'It's the – pollen,' I said, staring. 'There was someone there. Just now.'

'They leave crippled children here. I can't see what's wrong with her but there'll be something. Where are you going?'

'That's the most fantastic thing I've ever seen, is it – what are these vines? I've never seen anything like . . .'

'Candle ivy, but stop, don't go any further in. The border's just there, it's in front of you. They'll kill you if you cross it, *stop walking*.'

'I've stopped.' I swung my hand to and fro in front of my face, because there was a weird, after-firework glow whenever I moved. 'It's thinner here, they were further in . . . bloody hell,' I laughed, because a hummingbird had just dived down to snatch something from a tangle of candle ivy just in front of me and shot back again so quickly that it left a hummingbird ghost in the pollen. 'Come and show her this.'

'She'll see it every day.'

'How often do you look at it? I live a mile from a beach but I've never swum there.'

He looked like he might have accused me of childishness if he had had the voice to spare, but he came after me and let me take the baby. She was like a hot-water bottle and she squeaked and laughed when I waved a zigzag pattern into the pollen for her. Well up ahead, through the trees, whoever had brought her came into view again, or his pollen trail did. There was another one too, more off to the left, and another on the right. They came together while we watched, person-height half-ghosts. The light gleamed on something shiny on the ground: water or ice. I climbed up into the roots of the tree beside me to see. It was a straight line, the glass road, continuing well on into the trees. The light hung above it a long time after the pollen stopped flaring. When I eased back down again, the wind was stirring Raphael's hair and motes of pollen floated by us like cinders.

The baby cheeped and tried to catch one, which only set more off. Raphael touched my shoulder to turn me back towards the church.

'Go inside. I'll be with you in a minute.'

'Where are you going?'

'To find some milk, go on.' He gave me a push, very light.

Although I hadn't taken off my coat and he had come out without his, he didn't seem worried about the cold and went to the bridge in only his shirtsleeves, without even putting his hands in his pockets. I cupped my hand over the back of the baby's head. The cold was already taking the feeling from my fingers, and the skin across my knuckles felt like it was cracking even while we walked. I wound the rope of the pollen lamp round my wrist so that the baby could hold it and tugged the church door back open with my free hand. She pressed the lamp against her eyebrow to see the pollen move. I dragged a chair in front of the stove.

When I sat down, I balanced her on my knees and put the lamp back on the table. She was just about old enough to sit up. She clapped twice and grinned when I copied her, then leaned forward to pat her hands against mine.

'Clapping game?' I said. I couldn't tell if it was deliberate or not. She was the first person I'd met who was so young.

She clapped again and waited for me to copy her, then looked irked when she tried and missed her own hands. I snorted and helped her.

'Nothing wrong with you, is there?'

She smiled. She was just starting to grow some teeth. When Raphael came back, he tipped half the jug of milk he had brought with him into a new pan and stretched to fetch down a glass beaker from the middle shelf of the cupboard. He was much smaller than whoever had put the cupboards up; he could only just reach.

'Crippled children left here,' I prompted him.

'They leave three or four a year.'

The milk started to boil before I would have expected and he moved it off the heat. Somewhere in the oven's complicated interior, hot water and steam were singing and plinking. There was a sigh as a new bucketful rushed into the pipes. Once the beaker was full, he held his hands out for her. I gave her back again and touched the beaker to be sure it wasn't too hot for her. The baby settled with it in Raphael's lap. He had his hands around her ribs, which were so tiny he could lattice his fingertips together. Next to her, he looked pale and mistreated. The ring finger on his right hand was too stiff to move much, broken once and never quite set properly.

'Why?' I asked.

'This place is a hospital.'

'With . . . one doctor with a hacksaw and some ants.'

'Somewhere for them to live,' he said impatiently. 'Together. Being looked after. Not slowing down anyone who isn't already slow.'

The baby held out the empty beaker, just like anybody else would have, though she wasn't old enough to seem like a proper human being yet. He gave it back to her again once I'd filled it. She took it carefully because it was too heavy for her. While she drank, she put her ear to his ribs and I had a feeling she was listening to his voice through them. When he wasn't speaking, she looked up.

'Bizarre thing to do, leaving them here,' I said.

'Is it?'

'Yes. Slinging unwanted babies off a cliff isn't bizarre. That saves time, food, labour over someone who's never going to be useful. But leaving them somewhere . . . they're not saving themselves anything, are they? They must have spared people to look after the first ones, and people here farm land and take up space and territory, same as they would if they hadn't been left here – they might as well keep everyone together. Same effort.'

He had been looking at me, but he turned his head slowly away while I talked. 'I wouldn't try and talk about Indians and common sense at the same time.'

'I hate to break it to you but . . .'

'There is a tribe,' he said, over me, 'about sixty miles up the road who decided it was a good idea to make women give birth alone in little huts two miles from everyone else, on the edge of a cliff. They're well on their way to killing themselves off. Leave humans in a place like this for ten thousand years and you breed a special sort of moron. We're not very impressive, as a race.'

'The Inca were pretty bloody impressive,' I protested.

'The Inca lived in Cuzco, not in the Antisuyu.' It wasn't the first Quechua word he had used since coming back inside, I realised suddenly, but my hindbrain had parsed them without noting them. The Antisuyu was the land beyond the mountains. Anti, Andes. He had more of an accent now that he was tired too, with sharper consonants and those tiny sharp pauses mid-word which sounded profoundly more dextrous than English. However ambivalent I felt about his company, I could have listened all night. It was like hearing the moment when a ballerina stops walking and begins to spin. 'We are not them. Are we?' he said to the baby, who seemed not to hear. 'Maybe she's deaf,' he murmured.

'What happens to her now?' I said. 'And can you call her Ivy, please, because it would be a shame not to.'

He almost smiled. 'She isn't mine to name. We'll find her a family in the morning.'

As if she didn't like that idea, she began to cry. I gazed at them both and felt bleak about trying to sleep in a house with a crying baby in it. I saw Raphael's nerves fraying with it too, but he didn't shake her. Instead he only touched the back of her head to settle her again, then gave her a little toy horse. I didn't see where he had taken it from, but she seemed pleased with it and bit the stitching on the saddle interestedly.

'I'm going to bed,' he said once she was quiet. 'I'll leave a light on the ladder.' I looked, because I hadn't noticed a ladder before. It led up into the belfry, which must have been where he slept. There were no more rooms down here. 'There's an obsidian razor for you in the drawer behind you. They stay sharper than metal ones. Soap on the third shelf of the cupboard.' He was losing his voice again. 'There's a basin below that.'

'Thanks.'

It seemed odd that he knew exactly where everything was until I remembered how orderly you can be, living alone.

He got up slowly, the baby on his hip. She sat straight, looking around, then seemed to run out of steam and bumped her nose against his chest again. He put the toy horse softly down on the table on his way out. I tried not to feel envious when he climbed the ladder smoothly and one-handed. The baby had her nose resting against his shoulder, so I could only see her eyes, but they narrowed when she smiled at me. I waved and she put her head down, embarrassed.

When I went outside, snowflakes settled on my hands for half a second each before they melted. It had never quite gone from the air and in the light it was blowing like the last disparate bits of fluff from old dandelions. A tiny kelly lamp burned in the outhouse to keep the intricate pipes from freezing. I didn't remember his having gone to light it. On the church roof, the windmill kept on its uneven staccato creaking in the wind, and every couple of minutes new water rattled into the pipes.

I fed the fire again once I was back and then sat down with a book, easily tired enough for bed but wanting to give the baby time to go to sleep before I tried. I jumped when I saw something fall off the table from the corner of my eye, then thought I'd imagined it when nothing clunked. I leaned down to see.

It was the toy horse. It was a rocking horse and it was rocking gently on its runners. It hadn't made a sound. When I tried to pick it up, I misjudged the distance and only knocked it. It spun gently, still silent. Wondering if I was going deaf, I poked it, and felt it sink and knock into the floor. As I took my hand away, it lifted again. Distrustful of myself, I got down on my hands and knees to put my temple right against the floor. The toy was floating a quarter of an inch off the flagstones. I could slide about twenty pages of the book under it, and the cover. Once I had, the horse sat on that. Eventually I picked it up and rinsed it off with boiling water. I put it in the middle of the table where it couldn't scoot off again. It sat there like anything else would, rocking gently. It made me think of the statue at home again, whose closing hand I'd shunted off out of real memory like it had happened in a dream. I should have knocked it off the table again to make sure it fell properly this time, but I didn't dare.

THIRTEEN

I WOKE UP OF MY own accord, not too early, and nothing hurt. Because the room didn't look in daylight how I'd thought it would, I didn't understand where I was at first and had to lie still while I pieced it together. Instead of proper windows, there were glass bricks in the polygonal masonry, about one to every twenty stones. They let in irregular patches of light, tinged green and blue and, sometimes, where some sort of metal had melted into the vitrifying flow, a coppery gold. All together they made colourful light pebbles over the floor. A pipe must have run right beneath where I was lying, because although small shadows fell through the light where the snow was still coming down, there was deep, gorgeous heat under my spine. I sat up and linked my arms round my knees, feeling like someone had sewn up all my worn-out patches. Raphael must have leaned in at some point, because there was a candle burning beside the little shrine in the wall.

Clem was breathing hard, even in his sleep. The air was better than it had been in Azangaro or Crucero but it still felt diluted. I folded his blanket back to move that small weight off his chest. I'd left my jumper out, but it was so warm now I didn't need it. I leaned on my cane for a minute once I was standing, waiting. My leg was sore, but not half as bad as I'd expected. When I checked, the scar was much less angry than it had been in Crucero. It wasn't until I saw how much better it was that I realised how much I'd been worried about it, or how I'd been seeing everything through the penumbral soot of a fear whose coals I hadn't let myself look at, though I'd been carrying them – that if it got worse, there would be nothing to do out here except cut the leg off. Of their own accord, my shoulders relaxed. I hadn't known I'd been holding them stiff. I felt like I'd surfaced from a mine.

The kitchen smelled of laundry powder and fresh vapour, because there were shirts draped over the glass pipes to dry. The baby, who was sitting on the table, burbled at me and held up a wooden building block, either to stretch or to show me. I went over to tickle her and she laughed a deep viola laugh that sounded like it ought not to have come from something so small. She had new clothes, white, and Raphael was dressed like a priest. It was odd to see him neat all in black. He looked like someone else. He didn't say anything and I didn't blame him – it was only just past seven and that was early for a third language – but he touched the little brass tap on the stove to say there was hot water. By the stove was a bowl of ground coffee and a little triangle stand with some calico stretched across it to make a filter.

The corner window next to the stove had a hazy view of the town. Because we were so hemmed in by mountains, the light was still dim and our lamps cast my reflection in stronger colours over the view. Everything was covered in snow. All the thatched roofs were white triangles now, the windmills brilliantly red. The trees on that side weren't the strange pines, just conifers and sickly kapoks whose ambition had exceeded their tolerance for the altitude, and the snow in their branches made a thick new canopy. I polished the glass, which was clouding from the drying laundry. Up close, the panes were all odd thicknesses and irregular sizes – they were chipped-out shards, not blown and moulded.

'The snow's heavy,' I said at last.

'The river's frozen.' Raphael let his hands drop and the bones in his wrists thumped against the tabletop. The baby looked down to see what had made the vibration. It didn't make her jump, though it did me. It was loud, one of those broad things that already broad men do to take up more space. However much he had mellowed yesterday night, he didn't want me in his kitchen now. 'You're stuck here, unless you walk back to Azangaro.'

I clenched my hands when I found I'd backed myself almost into the window. I had to force myself to turn away and trust he wasn't going to make any sudden movements. Out of all the difficulties my leg brought, the limping and the tiredness and everything else, that anxiety was the stupidest and most wearing and I was starting to think that what I really needed was to just get into a proper fight, win or lose.

I forgot about him when I saw the woman standing outside. She was in the long grass between us and the bridge, stock still. Her back was curved forward and she was propped up with a cane. It made her look old, but she was my age. She was staring at the house.

I had to reach for the thread of what we'd been saying. 'Well, we'll pay you for however long we're here.'

'Mr Martel wouldn't hear of it.'

'No need to tell him then.'

He frowned as though it was hard to think of Martel not knowing something.

When I turned back to the window again, the woman had come right up close to it and her face almost against the glass made me jump. I bit my tongue rather than make a noise. She had only come to look at me. After a second she limped away. The ghost of someone else was coming over the bridge, a man. He was huge, and he was dragging one leg behind him. I could hear it through the window, the grinding noise it made on the stone. He must have had metal encasing his shoe to keep it from wearing through. I stepped away from the window, not sure what was happening. Raphael must have heard the noise too but he ignored it. He was playing with the baby. She had his rosary and she was trying to find the end of it. Whenever she came to the cross she giggled. On the fourth or fifth time it sent her off into a burst of that deep laughter again. He smiled too.

'We'll see how it goes,' he said at last. The baby was cheering him up. 'It might all melt again this afternoon.'

I'd made two cups of coffee. When I passed him one, he frowned as if I'd offered him something dead. I didn't move, ready to tell him not to be rude. But then he seemed to remember himself and took it.

'Thank you.'

'Who are those people?' I nodded at the window.

'There's a ceremony soon, to choose her new parents.'

The huge man with the bad leg had stopped next to the woman. They waited close together now. Two more people had appeared in the meantime too, a young couple. The man was in a wheelchair. It had been made from an ordinary chair and wheels from a perambulator, but somebody had fixed wooden skis to the wheels so that it moved more like a small sleigh. His wife's shoulders were uneven, so much that it must have been painful. It made pushing the sleigh-chair difficult.

'Right; shall we go?' Raphael said to the baby. He touched the top of her head so that she would know she was being spoken to and took her tiny hands, very gently, giving her time to get used to the idea that the rosary game was finished now. When she smiled, he took the beads back and lifted her up. He had put a fur blanket around her. 'Up you come. Let's go and find your new mama.'

'Where are you going?' Clem asked. He had just come in, bleary but better. When he wasn't feeling well, his hair was less red. 'Whose baby is that?'

'About to find out,' said Raphael. As soon as he opened the door and the cold poured in, I realised I'd only seen the latest arrivals. What I'd thought yesterday was open grass beyond the kitchen door was really an overgrown courtyard, and it was nearly full. There was no noise except for the sigh of the trees and the birds. I got up again too, at first to shut the door, but I stopped on the threshold, because there had been a tiny stirring when they all saw the baby. Clem pulled irritably at my sleeve and I explained about the bell and the church.

While I was talking, Raphael was too. He was keeping to Spanish which, even in such a short time, was starting to sound official. If he had been chatting it would have been Quechua. He was saying that the baby seemed not to have an impairment except maybe deafness. It caused another stir. Some of the people nearer the front clasped their hands. There was barely a straight figure among them. They were all twisted, or missing limbs or eyes, or whole but strangely made.

'He wasn't joking about its being a hospital colony, was he?' Clem said by my ear.

'No,' I murmured, quiet because I'd had a sudden unexpected lash of envy. It was hard to be always the slow one and the one who everyone else made allowances for. If I'd lived in a place like this, I wouldn't have felt so pointless. It was probably only a fantasy. I'd felt worse living with Charles. But it seemed different to that, the arrangement here.

A boy of about twelve hurried up to the front with a glass bowl, a nice one with strands of blue all through it. One by one, ten or eleven people, mainly women, came and dropped in a little piece of knotted string. I glanced back at Clem, who looked at me too with light in his eyes.

'That's Incan knot-writing,' he said softly.

When he had mentioned it before, I hadn't envisioned it properly. I almost said that I'd seen Raphael doing it on the way here, but I realised in time that doing so would mean a joyful explosion halfway through an otherwise serious public gathering.

As each person put in their string, they left something else too; a little basket of pineapples, or jars of pepper or cocoa pods, cloth.

'Priests aren't paid by the Church here,' Clem explained. 'They're freelance. You pay them per ceremony, usually in money. He'd be rich in Azangaro, but I can't imagine they see much in the way of real currency up here. In fact it's probably a way to prove they have the means to look after a child, a valuable offering.'

'Maria, you said you wanted a baby,' Raphael said to someone. 'Don't be so shy.'

'But she's mad,' someone protested.

'If she wins she gets help then, doesn't she.'

A short, round woman crept out from the crowd, holding her string too tightly. Raphael had to persuade her to let it go, then nudged her back to the others. She put down the pelt of something white and soft on her way. An older woman put her arm round her. Raphael glanced down at the pelt as if it was too much.

Once all the names were in, the boy held the bowl out to Raphael, who spun the strings around three times one way, three times the other, then drew one out. He didn't have to look at it; he must have been able to feel the knots. Clem's fingers closed hard over my arm.

'God, it's like seeing into the past. This is incredible.'

'Juan and Francesca Huaman,' Raphael said.

The young woman at the front, the one whose husband was in the wheelchair, clapped her hand over her mouth then half-ran forward for the baby. Everyone else cheered and clapped, and things turned to a Spanish-Quechua mix that I couldn't understand. Clem grinned.

'They're saying good luck. Christ, look at that, what is that?'

People were holding little glass vials and lobbing what was inside towards the Huamans and the baby. It was the same pollen that was in the lamps, and as soon as it was out of the vials it floated up, haloing them, and a brighter glow began to trace all their movements. Raphael gave the baby to Francesca very carefully, not in the sack-of-corn way of people who are used to children. Once Francesca had her safely, he stepped back and clenched his hands. He looked worried, and sad, but nobody noticed. They were all too taken with the baby. It felt like unusual attention; there was a kind of awe, that she was so perfect.

'It's pollen,' I said to Clem. 'It's in the lamps in here too. Boatloads in the forest.' I told him about the pollen ghosts from the night before.

'They went into the forest? Chuncho then?' He looked sparkly at the idea.

'I only saw pollen trails.'

'But that's interesting,' Clem murmured. 'If someone's keeping up a colony, then the colony must do something for them. Otherwise it would be Spartan-style over the cliff.'

'I said that. Raphael says not, though.'

'I think Raphael would withhold interesting facts just to be irritating.' He went out to congratulate the Huamans.

Raphael came back to the door as everyone else closed round the new family. He went straight to the stove to make himself some more coffee. Outside, people were leaving over the bridge. Someone was playing a guitar. While he waited for the slow tap to fill his cup, he pulled the lacing of the cassock open down his back, his arms bent behind him and his fingertips precise on the strings. He had laced it crosswise so that he could get out of it himself, although it didn't look as if it had been made for that. It had a red velvet ribbon in the back of the collar.

I'd always thought it was gaudy, but standing there watching him beside the gold and glass shrine, I realised that his was a candlelight faith. It didn't work in the clear unforgiving light in London or Scandinavia, where even the dust in the cathedrals showed. But in the warm dimness and the shadows, what would have been tasteless at home made sense. The shrine looked like an oil painting made into real substance. So did he. England's was a reading religion, one it was difficult to understand at the bleak unimpressive first glance, one that needed books to explain itself. But his was images and images, the same as the old stages, in a place where not everyone could read and good light was expensive.

He had an ordinary shirt on underneath. He pulled the sleeve over his knuckles and pushed his hand over his eyes.

'That was astonishing,' Clem laughed, tumbling in from outside. He brought snow and cold air in with him. 'People can write their names on *khipu* – is that a revival or unbroken tradition since the Inca?'

'Do I look like I've got a time machine in the cutlery drawer?' Raphael said, halfway into the waistcoat he had left draped like a tea towel over the oven door. It was old, but the lining was new. It was blue Indian chintz, the best sort, handpainted with birds. I'd seen it before; it was the same as the lining of Dad's coat sleeves. But that coat had been old by the time he had it. It had been his father's. Harry Tremayne must have brought a bolt of it here as a present for someone who had used it sparingly enough for there still to be fresh offcuts. Seeing it new made me feel as if I must only just have missed him.

'Shocking,' Clem said, disappearing into the chapel with a very purposeful stride.

Raphael took his cup from under the tap and didn't look when there was a clunk from the chapel, Clem tipping his bag out on the start of a pencil hunt. His eyelashes looked blacker because they were still starred.

'If you can't feel heat,' I said.

He lifted his eyes. They were raw. Three or four children a year, he had said; hard if he wanted children. I didn't ask, but pulling his own name from the strings seemed like the kind of thing a priest wouldn't be allowed to do.

'Does coffee not taste the same, hot or cold?'

'I can taste if it's boiled or not. And steam has a smell, so . . .'

'Oh, right.'

'Off out,' Clem chirped, on his way back and halfway into his coat. He had his journal too and a pencil sticking out of his waistcoat pocket.

'No you're not.' Raphael put the coffee aside. He hadn't drunk any of it. 'I'm taking you to see the forest and where you can't go. I'm not having anyone say I didn't make it clear to you.'

'Honestly I tend not to get much out of topiary, it's altogether more Merrick's thing—'

'There are six markayuq out there,' Raphael interrupted.

'Lead on.'

I lagged behind them with my cane hooked over my arm while I buttoned my coat up. There was new snow even since everyone had left. It creaked as we walked. Like last night, Raphael went without his coat and I realised that he couldn't feel the cold any more than burns. After another few steps came a following thought I should have had earlier too. He was keeping the house warm for us; he would have needed the stove to cook, but whether the heating pipes were going or not wouldn't have made a blind bit of difference to him. I looked hard at the firewood stacked round the church so that I'd remember, when we came back, to find out how much it cost, or at least, how much time it took him to bring it all in.

FOURTEEN

THE TREES CAST EVERYTHING into shade. The canopy had blocked the snow, but frost crunched in the grass and our footsteps stayed frozen in it behind us. The spider webs strung through the grass snapped and fell whole, winking where tines of light cut down through the branches. When no sun filtered through at all and we were past the first of the trees, each of their roots as thick as an ordinary birch, a shimmer started to follow my cane hand, like yesterday but much fainter and only as bright as the imprint of the sun on closed eyes. Ahead of me Clem was waving his hand to and fro in front of his face.

'It's the pollen,' I said. 'It's thicker further in, you'll see.'

Raphael looked back. He had left the ghost of a wake that looked more like a less shadowy patch of shadow than its own light. 'If you can ever see by it, you've strayed too far.'

When we were both paying attention to him and not doing light experiments, he pointed to a broad line of dead earth, which was greyish although the soil wasn't clay, then above it, to the animal bones hanging in the trees. It stretched in both directions for as far as I could see, disappearing into the hazy morning on one side and round the cliff on the other.

'This is the border. You can't miss it. Salt, bone,' he said, pointing down and then up. 'It's well maintained for fifty miles in either direction. They're always here; they always watch it, and they'll see it like a lighthouse if you cross. They'll kill you.' He stood on the salt line and lifted both arms. It gave him light wings and showed the red in his hair. While it lasted, just for a few seconds, he looked like his namesake must have when archangelic work still hinged on wrestling prophets. 'Please don't wander,' he said quietly.

'Oh, God.' I jerked back from what looked like a man clawing his way out of the ground right beside me, but it was only a clever carving in the roots of the nearest tree. Something about seeing it shifted the way I was looking at the trees and then I saw them all. They were everywhere: howling carvings straining away from the salt. I stepped back again, then shuddered when something cold dropped down the back of my collar.

Clem touched the grain of one, which made me flinch. They weren't for touching. The one he had chosen was a man contorted like a monster, tendons standing out hard from his throat. 'I've never seen dendrographs like this.'

When the wind furled down through the trees, it moaned in the carvings. Raphael came back from the salt line and dropped the backpack he had brought among the roots of the closest tree. The thump made the pine needles on the ground jump.

'That's all I wanted you to see.'

'What about these markayuq then?' Clem said. 'I was promised anthropoid markayuq, damn it.'

Raphael hesitated but after a second he pointed to our north-west, then north-east, then east. They were there, perhaps forty yards apart, statues seven feet high and standing just before the border. I could see the ghosts of two more further away through the morning haze. People who had been at the ceremony were walking towards them too, some very slowly, having trouble in the cold. Soon the first of them stopped in front of the closest statues and began to pray. I couldn't see the sixth markayuq at first. It was closer than I'd thought, just by the church but beyond the border, its back to us. It was looking over a little clearing of glass crosses and cairns.

'Don't swear in front of them,' Raphael said. 'If you go up to one, give it some salt.' He held out a handful of little vials to us, full of white crystals. It was exactly what the Indian man in Crucero had given to him. Along the border, glass flashed where other people were holding vials too.

'No, no, no,' Clem said. 'Come on, show me properly. I want to see a proper prayer.'

'I'm a Catholic priest,' Raphael said.

Clem laughed. 'I know how people round here are with religion. You're like Italians with cheese. I know you must pray to these things too, don't be shy.'

'I'll tell you how to do it.'

'Shy,' Clem said happily. 'Do you consider it more private then, the native side of things?'

'I consider it not sanctioned by Rome or the Cuzco bishropic,' Raphael said. He inclined his head at the nearest markayuq. 'He might have been built by Indians but officially that's St Thomas. Do you want me to tell you or not?'

'Tell, tell,' Clem said. He was bouncing on the balls of his feet, which was sometimes a restive habit or an enthusiastic one or both. Raphael took him to the statue and I half-meant to wander, but Clem caught my sleeve and said firmly that it was Culture and that a man couldn't subsist altogether on chlorophyll. Raphael gave him a salt vial. Close to, the statue was looming, a head taller than me.

'Why salt?' Clem asked.

Raphael lifted his jaw towards the forest beyond the border. Because we were so close, the pollen trails we left were brighter and it was possible to move only slightly but leave a clear line in it. There was no need for anything as strong as pointing. It would have looked like a firework. 'It's an offering for the people in there, in exchange for the children. It's worth as much as silver this far from the sea. Are you doing this or not?'

I looked again at the border. Martel had implied a tribe of angry savages, but something about that didn't ring true. They had carvers, salt traders, and if they didn't use all the salt, money. Guards for a hundred-mile border and enough children to reject three or four every year. That didn't sound like a tribe. It sounded like a town, an organised one. If the other expeditions had assumed they were facing a few hunters with spears and then run up against half an army, it would explain a lot.

As Clem held out the salt, the statue lifted its hand, palm up. It made us both jump.

'My God,' Clem smiled. 'They're clockwork. Hence the real clothes, is that right? Covers up the joints?'

The statue was still moving. I thought it would stop to be given the salt, but it extended its arm sideways to invite Clem to put the salt vial into the glass amphora just next to it. There was no sound but the creak of leather. I stared at it for a long time.

'Can I – so they do move, do they?' I said.

I'd thought Raphael would ask why I was being so dense, but he seemed to recognise what I might be talking about. 'You've seen one before.'

'We've got one in the garden at home. My father brought it back. I saw it move its hand and I thought I was going mad.'

'Your father stole a markayuq?' Clem laughed.

'He didn't steal it, he was asked to take it,' Raphael sounded like he was measuring out words with great care now and he paused while he waited to see if the scales would tip. 'The villagers . . . considered that it was unhappy here and ought to be taken somewhere else.'

'They believe these things are alive?' Clem said shining.

Only half-listening to them, I looked along the line. Other statues were moving too. The next one along only shifted fractionally, but the one after that had put both hands right down, because the little boy talking to it was too small to reach the amphora. There was one that didn't move at all, and the people praying to it were easing the salt vials into the amphora very quietly, as though they were edging around somebody who was asleep. Close to us, Maria, the unhappy woman who was shy about joining the lottery for the baby, had stopped to wait for her turn with St Thomas. She passed her salt vial to and fro between her hands, her eyes a long way off.

'There you are, Em, not mad at all,' Clem said to me. He dropped the salt vial into the amphora. It clinked somewhere near the bottom. As he straightened up, he looked at the tooling on the statue's clothes. 'So these designs are native, but the statues themselves . . . well, they're obviously Spanish church marvels, aren't they. So they were shipped over here as saints, and then reclaimed as markayuq?'

'No. They're from here, they were here hundreds of years ago.' Raphael moved his hand forward as he spoke, like he was pushing something well away from himself. It was such an emphatic thing to do, and completely contradicted what he had just said, that I was confused for a second before I understood. Hundreds of years ago was about forty yards in front of him, near the graveyard statue. He had done the same thing at Martel's, forward for the past, back for the future. 'The Jesuits claimed them as saints.'

Clem tipped his head. 'You're telling me that an Amerindian culture had, in the sixteenth century, invented clockwork set off by pressure pads?' He bounced on the springy ground to see if the statue would move again but it didn't. Pine needles skipped.

'The first missionaries here wrote about them in their – *don't* touch them,' he said suddenly when Clem reached out to move the statue's sleeve aside.

'Catholic priest,' Clem said, laughing. 'They're as important to you as anyone. I'm an anthropologist, not an inquisitor; you can just say, you know.'

Raphael looked tired. 'I don't want you interfering with St Thomas any less than anyone else wants you interfering with a markayuq.'

'Of course, of course. But I'm not making a report to Rome, honestly. Right! Merrick, stay there: daguerreotype time.'

We both watched him rush back to the church.

'What's a daguerreotype?' Raphael asked.

'A sort of photograph,' I said, then saw he was still waiting. 'Which . . . is a way of recording an image on glass. The glass is treated with a light-sensitive chemical and when it's exposed to the sun, it reacts to light in front of the lens, which makes a black and white image. Light and dark. It's much more accurate than drawing. I don't know exactly how it works. But it doesn't affect the thing in the image any more than painting it would.'

He had been listening carefully. 'How long does it take?'

'A few minutes.'

'Minutes,' he said.

'You don't have to be in it if you don't want to stand still for that long,' I said, and then realised he hadn't meant that minutes was a long time.

He was looking at St Thomas with a strange unhappiness, but he said nothing else.

'Is it all right to have a picture of them?' I asked.

'Why wouldn't it be?'

'Some people don't like it.'

I had thought he had a habit of staring hard at whoever he was talking to, but I saw his focus change then. He was only thinking; he just didn't look away to do it. Instead he retreated behind some closed doors inside his own skull and left the rest of himself exactly as it had been before. I saw him come back too. 'Are those people usually stupid?'

'Y . . . es.'

'Maria?' he added to the woman, who was still waiting. He moved a little aside to show the statue was hers if she wanted.

She didn't. She shook her head quickly and showed him a string she was knotting. 'Not finished,' she said in a child's Spanish.

'Can I?' I asked.

He gave me a vial. The statue did the same thing again. However it was made, it had been done better than any of the clicking little automata I'd seen in London. My heart was going fast and a startled animal part of me was sure it must be alive, but I hadn't travelled enough to have seen proper church marvels before. There were saints who cried blood and moved in Spanish cathedrals still and lots of people believed they were real. They must have been convincing too. I stayed where I was to watch the statue let its arm drop again. Its sleeve moved gently, the creases levelling out into darker diamonds and lighter borders round them.

Clem came back, the daguerreotype box under one arm and three sticks the same length to make an improvised tripod.

'Got it!' he called. 'I think the light looks all right, don't you? Good and even? This pollen is a gift. Raphael, come and tie some string around this for me, there's a good fellow.'

Clem fussed and adjusted as the sticks tipped and didn't quite do what he wanted, and eventually Raphael smacked his hand away and banged the tripod into the ground. It sunk an inch and a half and stuck.

'Christ, what were you before the priesthood, circus strongman?' Clem laughed.

'Get on with it, he's standing there on one good leg.' Raphael said.

Clem frowned, puzzled. 'Did St Thomas only have one leg?'

It came out sounding like a joke, but it wasn't his sort of joke and because I was watching I saw his ears flush when he understood. I tried to catch his eye to say I didn't mind, but he was tying the camera into place.

Raphael looked like he was listing all the Christian reasons not to kick Clem in the head. When he glanced at me and the statue again, his expression opened.

'Stay still,' he said.

The statue was moving again. I'd half-seen it from the corner of my eye, but it was so slow I hadn't recognised it. It touched my chest, fingertips first, then flattened its hand to my breastbone. I shut my eyes to listen, but even so close I couldn't hear cogs. Off to my left, Clem made a delighted squeaking noise. I heard him take the cap from the daguerreotype camera.

'Stay absolutely still,' he murmured, concentrating too much to have heard that Raphael had already said that.

'What is it doing?' I asked Raphael. I could only try to throw my voice a little towards him, not confident I could turn my head without blurring the picture.

'Just a benediction. He won't hurt you. It's good. They don't do it to everyone.'

'There must be a counter in the pressure pad,' Clem said. 'You know: reach out to every fifteenth person who stands there long enough, or whatever. How often is it, have you noticed? Of course you haven't,' he said when Raphael shook his head. 'However often it is, it's bloody clever. I suppose you wouldn't be amenable to my digging to find the—'

'Touch that ground and I'll sacrifice you to something made of teeth,' Raphael said flatly.

'Not so wholly Catholic after all then, are you?'

'Clem,' I said.

'Merrick, old man.'

'Less needling of our only guide?'

'Oh, do shut up,' he said, not as warmly as he could have. I did shut up, and felt bleak about the chances of their not having a furious row before the week was out. It was hard to see how Clem could have spent so much time in countries like this but never noticed that success or failure depended on being a water boatman, skimming, instead of a diver and getting everyone wet with an enormous splash whenever anything interesting passed through the deep water. Standing near him and Raphael together felt a lot like standing on the banks of a half-holy lake somewhere lost in the mountains, with a St Bernard dead set on winning a swimming medal.

The statue still had his hand over my heart. If he had been a person, he would have been able to feel it beating, because it was going fast, or it had been at first. The longer I stood there, the more it eased. I felt as though there was calm coming up through the ground, and although I knew the statue was clockwork, the magic of it worked all the same. The tendons in his hands were standing and there were fine lines around his blank eyes. It would have been a lovely thing to believe in, if I could have believed in anything at all.

Very gently, the statue gave me a little push. It must have been a way of moving people along if there was a line, but it felt like the pat doctors give you on the way out to promise that you aren't made of glass after all and you'll be all right in the end.

'Clem, can I move?' I said. It wasn't until I spoke that I noticed they had been bickering all along. I hadn't heard any of it properly, for all they were ten feet away. 'He's— I mean, it's pushing me.'

'Y . . . es. I think that's long enough.' He dropped the shutter.

I stepped back and the statue let its hand drop.

'Incredible,' Clem said. 'Absolutely incredible.'

Maria, ready now, edged up to Raphael and gave him her salt. He reeled her back in by her sleeve and took her by the hand to St Thomas instead, who didn't move this time.

She hesitated, then wound her length of knotted string around the statue's wrist. She stopped and turned away before she had quite finished when someone else came up beside her to put in some salt.

'Maria,' Raphael said. He gave it a Quechua intonation this time, which sounded regions warmer than that formal religious Spanish. A nickname would have sounded wrong in that. I wondered how the hell I knew. It was far too soon to have anything like a proper sense of register, but it had a weird, deep pull already. I twisted my hand to and fro on the hook of my cane, feeling, again, like I was brushing up against something I had used to know but had lost.

She said something about her mother and hurried off. Clem was dismantling the daguerreotype box, but she didn't pause to look.

Raphael touched the trailing cord on the statue's wrist and pulled his fingertips down it. 'It says if she wins a baby next time, he's invited to the baptism. I'm rigging the next lottery,' he said.

'It says that exactly? With a conditional and . . .?' Clem asked. He looked like he had found heaven without having to go to the trouble of dying first.

'No,' said Raphael. 'Conditional invitations are expressed indirectly with numerical adjectives and sheep.'

I snorted and then tried to pretend I hadn't.

'No need to be snippy. There was never any evidence for anything else. There's not a – I don't suppose they all learned from a particular person – you know, a proper khipukamayuq. Sorry, Em, that means master-of-the-knots—'

'There are no proper *scribes* here any more,' said Raphael. 'You're three hundred years too late.' He swept his hand forward again. The far past, far ahead, into the forest again.

Clem hadn't seen him do it at Martel's. I understood much too late that I should have said something, but I was so busy thinking about how it worked, the past ahead, that it didn't occur to me what it looked like to Clem, who gazed over the border, in the direction Raphael had motioned at. Without knowing what he meant, it seemed as though when he thought about an older, more complicated culture, he thought of the people in the woods.

'No, you're right,' Clem said. 'But this is a hospital colony, you told us, and it's being replenished all the time by someone. There must be a lot more of them out there than there are of you here; maybe they still have scribes.' He was over the border before either of us understood. Almost as soon as he was across, the pollen flared much more and he left a real wake.

There was a yell from almost everyone who saw, and a surge towards the salt that jerked short like someone had wrenched their strings.

Clem waved his arms to make the light flare. 'Hello! I say? Anyone here?'

People were turning back to Raphael and half-sentences came at us, all interrupted by the others: *what is he*, *you have to*, *he'll be*, *for God's sake*. It was real shock and it only lasted a moment before Raphael went after him. He didn't go quickly. He came up behind him and tapped him on the shoulder.

'Markham.'

When Clem turned round, Raphael punched him in the face. It floored him. Raphael caught the collar of his coat and dragged him back over the salt. He threw him the last yard and Clem landed in a spray of pine needles, still conscious, just. No one seemed startled. Instead there was a collective easing. Some of the women sighed and turned away back to town. A few young men hovered near the border, watching the forest like they expected something to come howling out.

'Jesus Christ,' Clem coughed. 'You – raving *lunatic*—'

'Shut up.' Raphael pulled him up and dragged him back towards the church. Clem twisted, but Raphael was exactly as immovable as he looked and none of the struggling swayed him so much as half an inch.

'Put him down,' I said. I sounded like a Navy officer still. 'It was a mistake.'

'I'm not going to hurt him, I'm going to rebaptise him.'

'You'll hurt him by accident. Stop.' However badly balanced I was now, I was still taller and I thumped my forearm into his chest to make him stop. He thought about making me move and I saw it, and then I saw it fade, but not altogether. He leaned back slowly.

'It was a misunderstanding,' I said. 'He thought you were pointing to the people in the woods when you talked about scribes. He hasn't seen you talk about time. He was unconscious at Martel's.'

'People won't talk to him unless he's baptised again,' he said, much more quietly. I felt like I was trying to stand directly in front of a furnace. It was worse for knowing he was justified; Martel had said that everyone here would be killed if Clem were. 'Get out of my way.'

I stood aside, and helped Clem up. He was too heavy for me to support and still foggy, so Raphael took him by the arm, not gently but not roughly either. The new baptism wasn't much more than having his head dunked into the font, but when I looked back people were watching.

'*In nomine* of whatever you think is looking after you. There. Congratulations.' He dumped him on the ground, protected from any accusations of unceremoniousness because nobody else spoke English. 'I'll find you a towel.'

Clem propped his wrists on his knees. 'He's bloody strong.'

'I saw.' I knelt down too, slowly, then had to sit and cross my legs. 'Are you all right?'

'I'm fine. I suppose being attacked by the natives is part and parcel of the job. Minna will love it.' He cracked his jaw and winced. 'I thought he was going to kill me.'

'You're all right.'

'No more getting in the way of psychopaths, hey?' he said, nearly smiling, but not quite. 'He could have hurt you.'

I nodded. He could have. But it felt good to have stood in front of him without flinching and, however stupid it was, I wanted to do it again. 'He didn't though.'

'God, I really thought . . .' Clem had the shaken look new recruits have when they see guns go off for the first time at a real ship instead of a hulk in the Bristol Channel. 'He's mad, isn't he. He would have done it if I'd been too far in to drag out.'

'I think he could have dragged you quite far,' I said. I found his handkerchief and scooped up some snow with it so that he could hold it to his chin. 'But I don't think he's mad. Martel will raze the place if anything happens to us and everyone certainly thought something was about to happen.'

'Yes.' He sniffed, then winced. 'That was interesting. That was fear-of-God shock, not fear of some fellow with a bow and arrow. Or Martel. You know, I've got a theory about this place.'

'What?'

He pushed his wet hair back. I'd never noticed before, but he was beginning to lose it, just up from his temples. 'You know the Incas practised human sacrifice? You find the bodies sometimes, miles up in the mountains. All the victims are children. Completely perfect children, which isn't a coincidence in a society that didn't know siblings marrying was a bad idea. Perfect teeth, virgins, everything. The idea is, you see, nothing impure for the gods.' He lifted his eyebrows. 'Notice it was him who fetched me. No one else crossed, even though it was an emergency and they wanted to. He's the only healthy person we've seen here. That's why he can go over. It's holy ground.'

I looked back at the town and the ragged line of people limping over the bridge. 'So cripples and invalids are . . . impure.'

'Right, exactly. So not allowed. They're left here, past a clearly marked line, in salt, which in itself is all about cleanliness, isn't it. And the graveyard, and the altar, look – both beyond the salt.'

I hadn't noticed before about the altar but he was right. It was exactly on the salt, or where the salt would have been under the church floor. Standing in front of it yesterday, Raphael and I had still been on the Bedlam side, but the statue behind it wasn't. Which was why, I realised, the church's layout was inverted, with the altar at the wrong end of the cross. The building was a lot older than the Conquest; it must have been a native shrine long before it was a church. When the Jesuits arrived they must have tacked on the spire and kept the old altar in place.

'That's interesting,' I said dutifully. 'Was testing your theory worth being punched in the head?'

'Are you joking? There are about fourteen academic papers in that, which you'd know if you ever stirred yourself to join any societies.' He looked back at the border. 'I wonder why he went in after me.'

'Martel.'

'I bet he could get away with losing one of us,' Clem muttered. 'One could be an accident.'

'You're right, I probably could,' Raphael said. He pushed the door open and dropped a towel on Clem. 'So don't do that again.'

'Is that what happened to the last expeditions?' I said. 'They crossed the border?'

He nodded.

'Why would they do that?' Clem asked.

'Because the cinchona woods are that way.' I pointed. 'Through the forest. The river path traces a big loop. They thought they could save time.'

Clem looked towards the salt line again, then the path that stretched on around the river – or what should have been the path. It was nothing now except a space where snow heaped five feet high against the tree trunks. 'How long did you say the snow would be here for?'

'I don't know,' Raphael said, 'but I doubt it will be long. It's summer now, it should be warm. Why? Just be patient; it won't kill you. Crossing the border will.'

'No,' I said. 'It's not impatience. We're going to have timing problems if we wait too long. If we hit the Indian monsoons, we won't be able to plant anything. They start in June and last until September. We need to be well clear of them, which means we have to arrive in Ceylon at the end of May, at the latest. It will take a month to get back to port from here, and another three weeks at sea, if everything goes smoothly. If we're to have any kind of safe leeway, we need to leave in three weeks. If we don't stick to that, we'll reach India with nothing but a handful of very expensive firewood, even if we manage to retrieve cuttings.'

He watched me for a second and I thought he would hit me. I leaned both hands on my cane and decided he would just have to do it, because I wouldn't be moving.

'That it's problematic for you doesn't change anything. You can't cross the border.'

'Can we employ someone to help clear the snow on the path around?'

'No. People here aren't fit enough and you can't take the fitter ones from the cocoa farm. They have to hit their quotas or Mr Martel won't pay. Just wait,' he said quietly. 'Wait another week. No one knows what the weather's doing. This might all be gone tomorrow. This is summer. There shouldn't be snow at all.'

'Then I can write to Martel and ask him to send men to help clear the path,' I said, aware I was rubbing him up the wrong way but I didn't want to think of what I was meant to do if we couldn't get through. 'We can say the coffee we want is down in the valleys.

After this snow, the stuff you grow around here is definitely dead now.'

'Someone would have to walk on the river back to Azangaro for you to send a letter to him,' Raphael said, a little dangerously.

'We can pay. Money isn't in short supply,' Clem broke in. 'I think that's an excellent idea.'

Raphael didn't reply at once and I could see him making a survey of the possible futures. If he forbade us from sending the letter and the snow stayed, there would be no choice this time next week but to try through the forest, and he couldn't watch us for every minute of every day. If he said yes, we would wait for Martel. He didn't seem angry about it any more; we were making him anxious. Not even anxious. He was starting to look frightened.

'You won't make yourself any friends if he comes in two days' time only to find the snow has already gone,' he said.

'I'll say I made you. He can't be angry with you.'

'Fine,' he said, almost too quietly. 'Ask around town, find someone who has the time.'

He had brought his bag out as well as the towel for Clem and he went back to the St Thomas statue to wind Maria's prayer around its wrist properly. Once he'd done that, he took out the same glass-handled brush and wax he'd used on the way here. When he began to clean the statue's breastplate this time, though, his hand left soft trails in the pollen and before long there was a perfect geometric pattern hanging in the light.

Everyone had gone by then and the morning mist had cleared just enough to show the farmland. It was a patchwork of allotments, crammed into the space between the cliff and the border. I helped Clem up.

'Let's write that letter and see if we can't find someone to take it,' he said. 'I'd feel a damn sight better with twenty strong men keeping an eye on Raphael, even if they can't do much about the snow.'

'Yes. Good idea. And we should send off your maps too. And make a sketch of the one on his wall.'

'Why?'

'Because then if we're killed, the India Office will still have their charts. Which is what will be important, for whoever comes next.'

He looked queasy at that. 'They do train you up a particular way, don't they,' he said.

'I know, I'm sorry. But we still should.'

'No, no, you're right. The map's done.' He paused. 'Em, what the hell are we going to do? It will take days for Martel to come, if he even feels like coming.'

'Settle in, do some drawing.'

'And wait for his temper to fray?' He nodded back at Raphael, then winced and mouthed a much worse word than he would have said aloud. 'It's pretty damn frayed already and we shot ourselves in the foot telling him about the cinchona plan. All he has to say is that we were here for quinine after all and judging from what you told me, Martel would be only too glad for us to be killed by Chuncho instead of caught by quinine barons who might hold him responsible for letting us through in the first place.'

'If he were sure Martel would believe him, he wouldn't be so worried—'

Clem was already shaking his head. 'No. We can't bet our lives on that. Look, he has to like one of us at least and it's not going to be me.'

'I'm not his favourite soul either—'

He caught my arms too hard. 'Just – you need to find a way and you need to start now.'

I looked across to where Raphael was still cleaning the statue. 'Right. All right, I'll try.'

'Good,' he mumbled. He made himself another snow poultice. 'I'll go and draft that letter to Martel.'

'You should go.'

'What?'

'To Martel's. Raphael can't hurt you if you're not here.'

Clem swallowed. He wanted to go.

'I don't want to leave you here with him, Em. I don't like this at all. He doesn't want foreigners here – he certainly doesn't want us round the border or the markayuq and I think it might be verging on sacrilege for us even to be asking about them, never mind disturbing them – and there are so many accidents that could happen in snowy weather if he gets it into his head that you're pushing too much or . . .'

'No, look – it's better if you go. Then you can courier the maps to Minna too. I'll be fine.'

'Are you sure?'

'Fifty-fifty. It's good enough.'

'All right.' He deflated, relieved. 'I shouldn't be more than four days.'

I crushed the little boy in me that was frightened of being left behind. Clem wasn't a coward. Someone had almost killed him and if he stayed, he would be resentful, which would annoy Raphael even more. He had to get away for a while.

'Well, you go inside, I'll . . . be with you in about ten seconds, I imagine, after he's thrown something at me. There's something I want to ask him.'

Clem patted my arm and turned away and into the church. He went slowly, holding his head at a careful angle. I crunched over the frosted pine needles towards Raphael and the markayuq and stopped two yards shy of them.

'If you're trying to be quiet, you're not,' he said without looking around.

'No. But . . . listen. The statue – the markayuq, I mean – that my father brought home. My mother thought it killed her dog when I was small. Went to an asylum for it. Could a markayuq do that?'

He didn't seem to think it was an unusual question. He went back to the waxing, and I thought he wouldn't speak again, but he did. It sounded unwilling. I wondered why he bothered to make an effort. Martel hadn't said he had to be polite to us. 'What was the dog doing at the time?'

'Biting me, I think.'

I'd been sitting with Dad, outside. It had been a hot evening. Heat is a difficult thing to remember in cold but I'd only had one jumper at the time and I hadn't been wearing it, and there had been flowers everywhere. The dog had been a gigantic thing that, like Caroline, was well meaning but had a snappish disposition. It had come up to us calmly enough and tried to nudge me away from Dad, who it didn't like. When we tried to chivvy it on, it caught my sleeve firmly enough to drag me up. I pulled back and it had clamped its teeth round my arm instead – that I remembered clearly, because now, under the anchor tattoo on that arm, there were still tiny scars. Caroline came out from the house to see what the noise was about and they argued over my head.

And then they'd both yelled, and the dog was dead on the ground. The crack of its neck had been like a thick twig snapping hard.

I still wasn't sure if Dad had killed it, or me, or someone else.

'You set them off standing near, never mind having a fight with a dog,' Raphael said. 'They move slowly but if they catch you wrongly they'll break your arm. Certainly kill an animal.'

'Are you sure?'

'Yes. Write to the asylum. She's not mad.'

I nodded, although I couldn't imagine that Charles would believe me even if I told him.

By then, Raphael had been standing there for long enough to set the clockwork off again. The statue put its hand against his chest to give him the same little push it had given me, but instead of stepping back, he leaned into it, letting his weight hang forward against the stone. More than anything the statue looked as if it had just picked up a rag doll, a good one, but worn out. I went to another to watch it move. Clem had sneered at the idea that Indians had made them, but the Ancient Greeks had had clockwork temple marvels, hydraulic doors, steam-engine toys, everything. There was nothing to say that somebody else, undisturbed by Christians burning the libraries, hadn't thought of it too.

PART THREE

FIFTEEN

ONCE CLEM HAD WRITTEN the letter – I said he needn't bother since he was going himself, but he pointed out that if he was laid up by mountain sickness again he would need something to pass along – we waited for the hazy sun to reach noon for a sextant reading and spent an hour or so going over the map, adding latitude lines as best we could estimate them. I drew Raphael's frieze map and annotated it as much as I could, with a guessed scale and an explanation of the border and the size of the stacks, and how the lensed light through them affected the river route.

I saw Clem off from the base of the stacks. He knew where he was going and he had a revolver, but four days in the Andean highlands alone was not a stroll from Hyde Park through Kensington, and when we parted we were both nervous-brash and brief. I sat down on a glass boulder to watch him go, my heart thudding still too quickly in the thin air. Between the massive cliffs and the sweep of the river, he was miniature. He had to go carefully at first because the glass of the stacks had intensified the sun and melted the ice in long strips, but after a few hundred yards he was past that and out on to the river. He was walking near the bank, the side where the salt wasn't. The ice looked likely to hold; or, if it didn't, the water there was only knee deep anyway. He turned at the sharp bend and waved. I waved back but stayed where I was, not sure what to do now. The sun had come out for an afternoon foray and the glass near me was heating up, the river steaming.

I had to move before the water started to boil, and by the time I was at the top of the stacks again I was frozen. I retreated back to the church. Raphael came in before long and asked what

I'd done with Clem. For a second after I told him Raphael stood very still, then nodded and cooked some lunch. He didn't mention it again, but the terseness he'd had at Martel's was back, although I couldn't tell why. I'd thought he would be glad to have only the slower of us to watch.

'Do you have a barrel of pineapples somewhere?' I asked, for something to say, when another appeared.

'Mm. Help yourself. On the left without.'

'Without what?'

He pointed outside.

'Right,' I said, feeling stupid. 'Thank you.'

He coiled into himself like a fern, and I gave up and tried to concentrate on eating. I would have gone out to explore the town but I couldn't face the idea of risking the ice on the bridges again. The heel of my hand already ached where I'd leaned too hard on my cane on the way back from seeing Clem off. It was starting to bruise. I was relieved when Raphael went out instead. Part of me knew it would be hard for anything to happen to me if I stayed inside by the stove, so I did, and drew one of the pollen lamps to show Sing. Raphael was out until dark, when I saw his pollen trail coming back from the border. I hid in the chapel and wondered what he had been doing out there for so long.

The snow didn't melt. In the morning there was another new, brilliant layer, and the cold was deeper and sharper. Clem was right to have gone; there would be no thaw soon. But with the pipes in the chapel running hot, I slept well again. Impatient with myself for feeling worried about walking into town, for all the nearest stack and the houses perched on it were thirty yards away, I went out with my sketchbook to draw some of the howling carvings on the border. There was mist again and they were eerie where they faded off into the white, which glowed sometimes where things had disturbed the pollen.

I jumped when a pine cone landed in my lap. It was stone solid and completely closed. I sat back suddenly, annoyed with myself for not having understood sooner.

'Of course they're bloody explosive,' I said to St Thomas. 'They're sequoias. And we're sitting on glass cliffs in damp weather.'

It should have been obvious as soon as I saw the obsidian stratum in the stacks. The glass lensed the sun hot enough to burn ordinary wood and grass, so any other kinds of tree that grew here would be periodically wiped out. But sequoias love fire. Here, because the climate was wet and fires otherwise might not have caught often enough, the whitewoods helped the process along. Something in the heartwood was inflammable. The big trees had bark like armour, so they survived, but the pine needles and the twigs went up like dynamite. The whole forest floor would blaze, damp or not. The fires opened the fallen pine cones and the heat rising into the canopy opened the unfallen ones. All the other vegetation would be burned off, which left the new whitewood seedlings room to grow. They were perfect for the place. I couldn't think of another tree that would manage forest fires and rain or snow at the same time.

'Well. Do you suppose my brain will grow back or that I'm permanently slow now?' I slung the pine cone over the border and into the denser pollen, where it cometed away into a patch of candle ivy. St Thomas managed to look sympathetic. I smiled a little. The markayuq were all unsettling, but there was something kind about the way his eyes had been carved.

He turned his head. I only had time to think I hadn't moved enough to set off his clockwork, and that there must be someone behind me, before whoever it was hit me hard over the back of the neck and knocked me forward into the pine needles.

His clothes smelled of charred honey, the same as Raphael's, and for a second I was sure it was him; but in a spinning-penny moment of clarity I remembered that Raphael was smaller than me and whoever this was most certainly wasn't. The man let me collapse and did it again, and then everything exploded into a bright black. By the time I could turn over, whoever it was had gone. St Thomas was still looking beyond the border. Knowing it was a terrible idea in the snow, I let my head touch back against the ground and waited to be able to move.

*

When I opened my eyes, it was raining under the trees: big, painfully heavy drops that felt like someone had spilled a case of bullets on me. I was half-frozen to the ground and I had to tear free to turn onto my side. The pine needles were all gullied by tiny silver streams. They didn't look like water at all, shivering and shining as they sank into the earth. Little rivulets ran off my coat too and plinked as they hit the ground. I rubbed my eyes and winced when I felt the bruises shift over my ribs. Someone had been shouting my name for a while but it was only then that it sounded distinctly separate from a dream.

'Merrick.' It was Raphael, right next to me now. He was kneeling in the pine needles. He gave me a cigar case. It must have had embers in it, because it was hot. Pins and needles soared down my hands when I took it, and then the feeling came back. 'Can you sit up?' he asked. The Quechua edge that had been in his consonants yesterday night and earlier this morning was completely gone. His English was cleaner now than mine, which had brine and jetsam in it. He was concentrating, to be as clear as he could; I must have looked concussed.

'Someone came up behind me. I didn't see.' When I was upright, my ribs panged and I had to stand with my hand pressed to them. He brushed pine needles off me. I wanted to say I was shaking because I was angry, not frightened. A few years ago no one would have been able to do that to me, nothing close, and never without my seeing. 'Stop, I'm fine.'

'They don't want people on the border. Markham will have set them off yesterday.' He said it softly, as if someone might overhear. The back of my neck crawled with the certainty that there was still a man behind me. I twisted around, knowing there wasn't really. There was only the empty air, then the carvings on the border. Things moved beyond it, but only little ones with little pollen trails.

'I've lost my sketchbook,' I said, trying to look about, but it was difficult to turn on the spot. My leg hurt. I'd fallen awkwardly.

'It's here.' He had found the pencil as well. He swept the moss off them both before he gave them back.

'Thank you,' I said. It came out annoyed-sounding and I tipped my hand, trying to say I wasn't angry with him. He nodded before

I had to scrape together a sentence and walked slowly so that I could lean on his shoulder. At the church, he hesitated.

'You'll be better coming down to the river. It's hot down there and the water is salt. You can go under once and you don't have to spend half an hour cleaning every cut.'

I wanted not to move any more. 'Will I?'

'You have to. Or you'll have a . . .' He sighed. 'This is wrong; tell me what the word is.'

'Say what you think?' I said, glad to have something to think about that wasn't a complete failure to keep myself safe.

'Calenture.'

'Fever. No, I know. You're right.'

'Hold on,' he said, and went inside. He came out again straightaway with his coat. I thought he would put it on, but he took mine from me and gave me his instead. It was lined with a fine pelt which might have been sealskin or something more foresty, but it was twice as warm as mine. He had broad shoulders and I didn't particularly, so it fitted well even though I was taller. It smelled of beeswax. I had to look behind me again. The trees were talking now that the sun had been out for a while – the green cluck of settling wood – but there was nobody there.

'Mine was all right—'

He had hung it over the woodpile, where it dripped, although I hadn't been aware of its being wet. It was too cold. 'There's mercury in the pockets.'

'There's what in the pockets?' I said, still slow anyway and not improved by the bang on the head.

'M— doesn't matter.' He steered me towards the cliff, but away from the bridge. 'It isn't far. Straight down there.' He pointed to a place just along from us where the surface caved in, into a narrow blowhole, although it couldn't have been, there being no tide. He took me to the edge, where there was a little winch, much smaller than the main one on the last stack and perched on the cliff like a gallows. Far down below was a little loop of the river sheltered by a cave, the water turquoise and steaming. It was just shy of one of the glass shadows of the stacks; the current must have moved it just enough to cool it down.

The winch lowered us to the rocks just by the pool. Raphael had brought a bag of laundry as well as his rifle and as soon as we were down he left me to it and went to the main river to scrub the crumpled clothes out. None of them were his. It was as much privacy as I would get. Further on from us, around the base of the second stack, there were fishermen. They threw the nets out like Scandinavians do, standing thigh deep in the water. Behind them, on the beach, the river boiled where it touched the hottest parts of the glass.

The water was as hot as a bath. I eased down on some rocks that had been polished smooth and made into steps. It was a pool, with walls. I couldn't tell if they were natural or not. On one side was a fine mesh to keep fish out, or perhaps something worse. The water, though, seemed mostly dead, and I wasn't surprised. It was so salty I could feel the buoyance, and it stung, sharp and clean, in all the grazes I hadn't known were there along my ribs.

Quartz crystals sparkled on the rocks just next to me. They had formed in perfect cubes, slightly stuck to the rocks, but one of them came off when I pulled. It wasn't quartz; a corner ground off easily. Salt. I'd heard of it forming that way on the banks of the Dead Sea, but not anywhere else. I took a cube back to my things to show Clem later.

'What happened there?' Raphael said suddenly. It made me jump.

'Where?' I looked around, expecting to see him pointing somewhere, but he was watching me. He spun his hand in the air to tell me to turn around again. He meant my back. I couldn't feel the lash-scars. 'Oh. Clem happened. We were in the Navy together.' Looking how I did now, I heard how like a lie it sounded. I turned my arm around so that he could see the anchor tattoo over the veins between my elbow and my wrist. It had been done much better than I'd paid for and it hadn't faded or blurred yet.

'What did you do?'

'Insubordination.'

I couldn't remember why. It was one of those lighthouse memories around which everything else was dark. All I could remember was that it had been drizzling on the day. Clem had been new on board and I'd shouted at him about something even though he had outranked me, something that must have mattered immensely at the time – there had been a child, one of the cabin boys – but I couldn't reach it.

'And now you're . . . best friends,' Raphael said.

'Is that strange? People who clash at first often get on later. He was always interested in Peru. Then he found out my father had come here a lot . . .'

He watched me for what felt like a long time. 'Places like this amplify all the things that have ever gone wrong for you. There's no insulation, no trains or doctors or space to get away from someone. It's bad enough with people who once fell out over late rent, but it would be dangerous to go into the woods with someone who once had you publicly flogged.'

'We didn't know each other then; it wasn't falling out. We don't fall out. He gets cross and then he forgets about it. He's got a quick temper, but it's quick in both directions. He forgives people within fifteen minutes of shouting at them. If you were to take an average he'd work out as straight as a spirit level.'

'So would these mountains,' Raphael said, with a little razor blade in the lining of his voice. I had to concentrate not to shy away from him. Having to argue had sharpened things and the memory came back. The cabin boy had stolen bread. He was meant to be whipped for it. That was the row.

'If he so much as shakes his finger at you, you're both going back to Azangaro.'

'That's not . . . he will shake his finger. He will lose his temper. That doesn't make him bad. He's just a bit of a Cleopatra.' I didn't feel too indignant. I was enjoying how much he disapproved.

'It's hard to trust a man in his thirties who still loses his temper.'

'As opposed to one in his forties who lives in a permanent state of having already lost it,' I said, waving at him. 'Come on, he deserves the benefit of the doubt. You've only known him ten seconds and nine of those have been while he was mountain sick.'

I thought he would be angry, but he smiled. 'If you say so.'

'I do. What are you worried about, anyway? That we'll start bickering at the wrong moment and be eaten by jaguars?'

'No. That there will be a moment, another one, when one of you has to help the other, and you hesitate, and I'm eaten by jaguars.'

I laughed, because I couldn't remember the last time I'd disagreed with someone and not offended them. 'He's all right. You'll see.'

He made a doubting sound and turned back to the washing. I dropped my head against my arms. The salt took my weight and the current tugged me gently to one side, but not enough to move me. The heat had reached my bones. I could feel all the vertebrae down my spine and they were bending more than they had for months. Like a warm pressure on the back of my neck, I could feel too that he was watching me. It snuffed out the lingering suspicion that there might be someone behind me, or at least, any sense that it would be important if there were. He would have shot anyone who was. I must have fallen asleep there, because it made me jump when he tapped my shoulder with the back of his hand. He was just in front of me on the rocks, smelling of laundry soap. He would have to take it all back up to the top to rinse it out in fresh water if he wanted to get rid of the brine, which confused me, because it would have been easier to do it in the church to begin with, until I realised he had only brought it so that he could look busy while he kept an eye on me.

'I'm going back up. I'll send the winch back down for you,' he said.

'Thanks.'

I watched him go, then I climbed out and dried off on my shirt. The heat stayed with me even once the winch came back down and lifted me up into the cold air beyond the glass shadows. I rode sitting on the bar rather than standing, my cane over my knees and elbow locked over the rope beside me. By the time I got back to the church, Raphael had the stove built up and open. I took a bowl outside to rinse the salt off my skin and then caught sight of my reflection in the window when I turned. There was only one bruise on my face. I went back in, pleased. I could say to Clem that I'd bumped into a tree or something, if he noticed. I didn't even want to touch the idea of telling him someone had attacked me from behind and I hadn't seen one solitary atom of them.

Raphael had climbed up the ladder that led up to his attic to start hanging the damp things over the rungs. There was a clothes-line too, between the side of the ladder and the nail that usually held a crucifix on the wall. The crucifix had been relegated to the top of the coffee jar now. I climbed on to a chair to help.

'Get down,' he said.

'I'm fine.'

'No, it's rude here. You let the strongest work. You shouldn't even be making me coffee.'

'I . . . don't care if it's rude.' I shifted when he frowned. 'Look, the most frightening thing I can think of isn't losing the leg, or getting shot or beaten up by angry Indians. It's the moment I think yes, I should be sitting down, and he should be doing everything for me.'

He gave me some pegs. 'By the hems.'

'I know. I do it at home.'

'Aren't you rich?'

'No. It's me and my brother and a part-time kitchen maid who thinks I don't know she calls us Walking Cain and Nearly Abel. He has polio,' I explained.

He nodded, then smiled. 'You're Abel, aren't you?'

'Oh, shut up.'

He pegged my sleeve to the line, which made me laugh, partly because he didn't seem at all like someone who played and it was a relief to find that he did.

'Is it worth all this, for cinchona cuttings?' he asked after a while. The bruise must have been darker by then. 'You can just leave.'

'I can't. If I don't do this I'll have to rot in a parsonage in Truro. Am I in danger in here too?'

'I don't know. You should have been all right even sitting on top of the border, never mind where you were. Markham must have made them nervous.'

'Well, we'll hear if anyone breaks in.'

He was quiet, but it was the strange hollow quiet he had when he wanted to say something. Whatever it was, he swallowed it. I thought suddenly it was lucky to the point of unlikely that he had come to find me in the twenty minutes it would have taken before I died of cold. He'd had no reason to look for me, unless he'd known something would happen. It explained why he had been so gentle when he found me. Guilt is a good propellant for kindness. But I wasn't sure enough to accuse him. Or perhaps I wanted too much for it to be real kindness.

SIXTEEN

IT WAS THE TAIL end of the afternoon and I was starting to wonder what to do about food when I saw that Raphael was watching me again. I'd been drifting through the kitchen, trying to keep moving but near the stove at the same time, turning over the idea of pineapple versus going into town to see about fish.

'Come with me,' he said, from nowhere. 'We're going to see the carver.'

'Carver – what?'

'You're driving me mad, get your coat. And bring that carrot.'

Not sure what was going on, I gave him the carrot from beside the stove and then followed him out to fetch my coat off the woodpile. I had to shake the frost from it. 'Why are we going to see the carver?' I tried again.

'To see if we can do something about that,' he said. He swept his eyelashes down at my leg.

'How?'

He looked as if he would have explained, but his voice was fracturing, and he moved his hand to say I'd just have to trust him. He led the way out to the bridge, slowly again, so that I could keep up.

The second stack seemed to be where most people lived. It was biggest, and all along the twisting path and the gantries that led through it was a jumble of miniature shops. None of them were anything more than canopies set up over people's front windows, with a few upturned crates outside instead of chairs. Raphael tapped on someone's shutter. A woman opened it and beamed when she saw us.

'You must be one of his new foreigners,' she said happily to me. A goat bleated somewhere beyond her. 'I saw you go by yesterday, didn't leap out at you; I hope you're grateful. Where are you from then?' She spoke fine clear Spanish and I relaxed into being able to understand.

'England. I'm Merrick, it's nice to meet you.'

'Other hand. You won't get much from this one.' She only had one, her left, so I swapped over to shake that instead. It was still only partially formed. She had fingers, but not full length. 'Merrick. Now we all used to know a marvellous man called Jack who had a little boy called Merrick. You're not him, by any chance?'

'Jack was my father.'

'Good. You look just like him, but then I worried that white people might all look the same anyway, so I didn't like to say. Welcome home, took you long enough. Come here and apologise for being away.'

I laughed as she hugged me over the counter. 'I'm sorry, ma'am.'

'Inti, I'm Inti. I was named after your grandfather, actually,' she said, and didn't explain. There was no time to ask her and I was getting used to being confused and tired most of the time. It didn't seem to be improving, even if the dull pain in my ears had gone now. All the stories we'd heard on the way about acclimatising to altitude after a few days were rubbish. 'I shall call you . . . Merry-cha, that's excellent I think. Oop, milk, thank you,' she added to an invisible Raphael somewhere on her left. He had gone in through a side door while we'd been talking. 'Coffee?'

'Yes, please,' I said, still laughing. 'Pleased to meet you.'

'Yes, I expect you are.' She gave me too much sugar, but I had a feeling that not everyone got any sugar at all.

Raphael came back rubbing his hands dry. It was getting dark now and all around us, inside the haphazard houses and out, hanging from the eaves, were pollen lamps. The ones Raphael made were small and neat, but some of them here were much bigger. Hands from what must once have been sturdy outdoor clocks turned inside them, churning the pollen. Some had a deep ambery glow, but some had had their mechanisms altered so that they ran fast and spun much brighter light. Hanging as they were on different levels and in different sizes and shades of gold, it was like sitting in the middle of a star field. Inti put two glass cups on the counter in front of us, and a bowl of diced pineapple. I wondered who had cut it up.

'Have you met the markayuq?' Inti said, as if she were talking about local landowners whose unofficial permission I'd need in order to stay.

'Yes, yesterday. They're fantastic. I've never seen statues like them.'

She laughed. 'They're not statues. Nobody could make anything like that. They're people who turned to stone. Didn't your father tell you anything?'

'Why would they do that?' I said.

'Do what?'

'Turn to stone.'

'Stone lasts longer than a person. They do it so they can watch over a special place. We're extra-special. We have six.'

'Did it use to be seven? I . . . know my father took one when he was here.'

'Yes, yes, seven before, but St Matthew was unhappy. He wanted to go with Jack, see somewhere new, and everyone thought it was for the best.'

'How could you tell, that he was unhappy?'

She had been winding up more lamps while she talked, little ones whose clockwork hummed rather than clunked, setting them alongside our coffee, and one in the empty pineapple bowl. 'Nearly walked off the cliff.'

'Oh.' I found myself doing what I'd always hated seeing other people do in China: glancing at Raphael for a secondary translation. The words made grammatical sense, but the undersense was hard to catch. Chinese tea farmers had always looked at my interpreter that way, it being broadly and well known that even quite fluent white men were nonetheless mad and not to be trusted with things like numbers and adding. They had used him like a cultural limbeck through which to filter everything I said, even though we had all been speaking Chinese.

Raphael didn't see, though, because he didn't look up.

'Do you not have markayuq in England?' she said.

'No. Or I don't think so.'

'That's unlucky,' she said. 'Perhaps they had to leave.'

Raphael was still watching the rainbow bubbles in his coffee and I felt sorry. To live wading through little myths and trying to hold markayuq and saints together in overlay for a congregation who thought statues lived because nobody could possibly put together stone like that, when he must have known that somewhere out across the sea was Rome, must have seen etchings of the Vatican – it was bleak.

'But what happened to your leg?' Inti said, motioning at my cane with her own cup.

'Shrapnel.'

'Are you in the army then?'

'No, no, I'm a gardener. It was just an accident.'

'Gives you trouble?'

'Yes. But the doctors at home say there's nothing much they can . . .' I tried to check with Raphael again, but he didn't help.

'Oh, no, don't be silly. Measure round above where it hurts, mark the place with your finger.' She held out a length of red string.

'Pardon?'

'Do as I say. *This* is the biscuit of co-operation,' she added, setting a biscuit down on the counter by my cup. I laughed and she winked. 'Oh, Ra-cha,' she said when I took the string. 'Upstairs is getting a bit, you know, and I was wondering . . .'

'I was going to ask . . .' Raphael disappeared inside again and left me none the wiser.

She lifted her eyebrows at me. 'Measure?'

I did and gave the string back to her with my nails pinched over the right place. She took it folded there and flicked a knot into it one-handed. She smiled.

'Soon have you sorted out.'

'In . . . what way, exactly?'

'Oh, for a manacle. It helps with bones, you know?' She held her arms out to show me the wooden bands around her wrists. They were whitewood, carved in forest patterns. 'Grow you tall, if you wear them when you're little, help with strain when you're older.'

'How does wood help?'

'It's a sort of magic. Anyway, come in, come and see the shop properly. Bring your coffee. I only make coffee so people will sit here and I can persuade them to buy things,' she added, grinning. 'It's a lot of bother, with the goat, but it works out overall.'

'Inti,' Raphael's voice said from somewhere above us. As I ducked in through the trapezium-shaped door, I passed a steep ladder that led up to a loft like the one in the church. The rungs to about head height were hung with dry laundry. Raphael had nudged things aside to make a narrow way up through the middle. 'There are two black guinea pigs up here.'

'I'm selling them to the doctor,' she called 'Give them some corn.'

'I am not feeding them so the doctor can dismember them over an idiot with a chest cold.'

'Oh, but—'

There was a clunk and a rush of cold air, then a firmer clunk. Inti winced. She was much taller than I'd expected her to be, nearly as tall as Raphael – everyone here was tall. 'Did that sound to you like a man liberating two quite valuable guinea pigs onto my roof?'

I nodded.

'The doctor pays quite a lot for them,' she said, looking wistful. 'Black ones have special properties, you see. But Ra-cha doesn't approve. I suppose he's right. It is a bit cruel,' she concluded. 'Come in.'

The smell of sawdust met us on the next threshold. For some reason I'd expected a toyshop, but it was more like a cabinetmaker's; there was a section of banister along one wall, stacks of wood air-drying, planks with glass insets that looked like they were meant for another gantry. Low tables, stools – some very simple, some finely worked – door handles and bowls. There were toys too, tiny ships and spinning tops, and everything smelled of new sawdust. It was hard to see how she could have managed, but she had; the glass handles on her tools had all been shaped irregularly, to fit her good hand. As she led me through, something pattered against my ankle. It was sawdust. It floated an inch above the floor.

'Inti – how is it doing that?'

'It's whitewood.' She gave me a rough-cut chunk of timber. It felt much too light for its size. When I held it up, it was porous, full of miniature honeycomb chambers, the same as the wood at home. 'Never put that in a fire, it—'

'Explodes,' I said. 'I know.'

'Don't forget. All the gantries are whitewood. One match and whoomf. That's why we have heating pipes instead of open fires indoors.'

'Why are they whitewood, if it's dangerous?'

'To take all the weight of the buildings. It bears much more than kapok.'

'It's not even a hardwood,' I protested. If I pressed hard I could put a clear nail mark in the grain, if it could even be called grain.

'The forest is blessed by the markayuq. It's one of their miracles.'

I gave up.

Raphael dropped an armful of laundry down the ladder and followed it. He disappeared briefly into the kitchen and I heard him grating soap, and then he collected up the clothes and came through with it soaking in a bowl of steaming water. He turned sideways to get past Inti and opened the next door outside with his elbow. Beyond it was a tiny garden with a goat and a vertiginous washing line, hung at either end with lamps. When Raphael set the bowl down in the snow and knelt to start washing everything, the goat clopped across to investigate, looking dangerously close to eating the laundry. Raphael threw the carrot we'd brought into the far corner to make it go away. It clopped off again, more enthusiastically. The whole thing had the look of a long-established protection racket.

'You might as well stay for dinner now,' Inti said happily. 'It'll take him a while to get through all that and my son will be back soon.'

'Oh. I don't want to intrude,' I said, distracted because Raphael had sunk his hands straight into the hot water. If it was from the stove, it was boiling.

'Rubbish! We hardly ever have proper guests.' The front door closed. 'Oh, that's Aquila now. Now you have to stay. He's Ra-cha's clerk; he'll be a priest one day. He needs to practise his proper Spanish.'

'In that case – yes, sorry, hold on.' I tapped on the window. It was thin enough to hear through.

Raphael looked up.

'Put some snow in that. It's too hot.'

He frowned but did as he was told.

'He can't feel it,' Inti said.

'But it must still be burning him.'

She looked sceptical but didn't have time to argue.

'I'm here, Mum,' a boy's voice called through from the kitchen. 'I've brought Maria, I think she'd be better for a hot meal, so – oh?' he said when he saw me. He was about twelve and I couldn't see anything wrong with him; he was glass-bright and tall. The same boy who helped Raphael at the ceremony in fact. Behind him, Maria was hunched in her coat, hugging a doll.

'He's come with Raphael,' Inti explained. 'Merrick, this is Aquila; Aquila, Merrick. They're staying for dinner,' she added.

'Hello,' Maria said tentatively to me.

'Come and sit down, come and sit down,' Inti told them, pleased to have more people. She opened the window next to us. 'Ra-cha, probably better leave that to soak actually; will you make us some more coffee instead?'

'Yes.' He came back and narrowed his eyes at the goat when it bleated at him. 'Christmas dinner,' he said to it. 'That's what you are. No bloody turkeys round here.'

'He speaks English when he's unhappy,' Inti explained. 'Apparently it's a good language for swearing. What's he saying?'

'He's abusing the goat,' I said.

She snorted. 'It's good for a person to be terrorised by a goat. Hard to get too high and mighty when there's something chasing you for vegetables.'

I went to help him find cups.

'Oh, sit down,' Inti said, alarmed. 'Aquila can help him.'

The boy was on the edge of getting up too. He looked as worried as his mother.

'No, I need to keep moving anyway. Let's see your hands,' I added in English once Raphael and I were alone together in the little kitchen.

'Why?' he said.

'Why? I wouldn't be confident of burns not being infected in Kensington, never mind the land of flesh-eating yuck and insects so big they have to file plans with the Admiralty before they set out – come on.'

'I'm not burned.' He held his hands out anyway.

They were covered in small scars; tiny burns and old grazes, even faint lines where he had pulled string too tightly and cut himself. His knuckles were red, but he was right. There was nothing new. He met my eyes but not for long. He was starting to seem like a skittish thing when there was nothing pressing that required him to be frightening.

'All right. Where's her coffee?'

We found it and he ground the beans while I ran hot water into a jug. Everything had to be washed up first; Inti's approach to dishes seemed to be the same as mine to slugs in that she'd slung salt at them and hoped for the best. Raphael cleaned as we went. I nudged him with my elbow towards the stove so I could scour the worktop. There was only salt to clean with and it made everything smell of the Navy. I caught myself smiling at the brush, pleased to be doing something that was easy and useful at the same time.

Inti's boy came in to shake hands. He was very cold, because he had gone out without a coat, although like Raphael he showed no sign of feeling it. I wondered, because they looked very alike, and wondered again because, although he was plainly pleased with the novelty of a new guest, it was Raphael who Aquila wanted to see; he was flustered and happy to have him there, and embarrassed.

'I was going to clean everything up this afternoon. If you can believe it's got like that since yesterday, she just—'

'It's your house,' Raphael said, and Aquila wilted. Raphael gave him a cup. 'Coffee.'

'Thanks,' he mumbled.

We carried the rest through with us. In the warm room among the pipes and under the creaking windmill it was cosy. Raphael went back outside to finish the laundry, but it turned into a dinner party once he returned and Aquila had finished cooking, which he did quickly. Inti brought out some wine and something brewed locally that tasted like turpentine and soon it was all a warm, laughing haze. Maria giggled when Aquila made her doll dance and gave it a voice, and Inti conjured a puppet to give it a dance partner. The dark came down outside and more lamps flared on around the stacks.

'We had better go,' Raphael said at last.

'No more coffee?' Inti said.

'No, Maria needs to get home. And I need to take Quenti's baby things over to Juan and Francesca. That reminds me, Aquila.'

The boy looked afraid that he'd forgotten to do something else.

'I've got my hands full for a while, so you'll have to go down to Azangaro at the end of the month to fetch the farmers' wages from Mr Martel. This is a letter for him, it explains who you are.' He passed a sealed envelope across the table. He had beautiful handwriting. 'Give it to him and don't take any rubbish from Quispe.'

Inti frowned. 'He's a bit young to be off by himself; can't—'

'It's time he got used to it,' Raphael said, not ungently, and there was a strange pause at the end of which Inti nodded, looking reflective.

Aquila couldn't have seemed more pleased. 'Should I bring more clocks if I can?'

'If you can.' Raphael didn't sound overly fond of him, was briefer with him even than with me or Clem, but warmth seeped through the lines round his eyes. I couldn't decide what had held him back. If he wanted children and Aquila wanted a father – there was no evidence of anyone else in the house – then it was hard to see the difficulty.

Maria squeezed her doll to make it lift its arms. 'Do you think they might take you away again soon?' she made it say to Raphael. 'Is that why Aquila has to go?'

He made a sound that might have been anything.

'Take you away?' I echoed, not sure I'd heard properly.

Inti nodded. 'Priests, you see,' she said. 'They always disappear in the end. The people in the woods take them back. They're only borrowed, to help us. We thought Ra-cha had gone years ago, and there was nobody to replace him then. Everyone panicked; we thought we'd been abandoned. But then, pop, back he came, as if he didn't know seventy years had gone by—'

'Seventy *years*?' I said.

Raphael stirred irkedly. 'It was my uncle who was here before, how often do I have to say it was my uncle—'

'My grandmother said it was you. She said you didn't like goats then either,' Inti laughed. 'He thinks foreigners don't know about magic,' she added to me. 'So he lies, so you'll believe him about staying back from the salt and not think he's mad.'

'Inti . . .'

'It's sad,' she said over him. While he was opposite her, it was difficult to see how he could be intimidating. It was plain that even if he had snapped at her, he'd only be told to settle down and finish his coffee. 'But you know about it, don't you? I expect your grandfather told you.'

'No,' I said slowly. 'I didn't know him.'

'We really are going now,' Raphael said. 'Come on.'

As we left, Inti stopped me to pass on her best wishes to my mother and I thought Raphael would have gone by the time I came out, but he was waiting for me outside with Maria. Like a little girl she reached out to hold my hand too, though she already had his.

'Aquila seems like a nice sort of boy,' I said, in Spanish still, because it would have been over Maria's head otherwise.

'He is.'

'Is he yours?'

'No.' He didn't seem offended. 'We're probably related, but they don't leave family histories with you on the altar.'

'Does that not cause . . .'

'I've stopped worrying about it,' he said.

'Are you sure you shouldn't start worrying about it again?'

We took Maria's weight between us as she swung up the steps. She giggled when we lifted her up the last. She was round, in shiny good health, but she was tiny and it wasn't much more difficult than lifting a real child.

'We don't know until it's ten months too late,' he pointed out. 'And then what do you say? I know you've been married for years and you're devoted and you're desperate for children, but that's an especially deformed, especially stupid baby, so maybe stop at one, just in case the next one turns out to be a crocodile?'

I laughed and he looked surprised before he smiled too.

'This is my house,' Maria reported.

'Keep the fire lit at the church or the pipes will crack,' he said to me, before I could offer to come in and help.

'I will. Night, Maria.'

Her mother met us at the door and asked in an unhappy voice if someone couldn't come and cook some soup.

'Night night,' Maria said, hugging her doll. When she didn't make any move to turn inside, Raphael towed her in backward by her apron strings. As I set out back to the church I heard them talking through the window. He was telling her how to cut vegetables, and her mother to sit down and be ill properly. I pushed my hand over my face, groggy with tiredness and Inti's lethal wine and not sure I could have been trusted with a vegetable knife. Maria started to sing a song. It was the nursery rhyme whose words I'd forgotten, the one about the dragon. I hadn't been able to fit the words to the tune because I'd been trying to do it in English. The Quechua fitted beautifully.

SEVENTEEN

I MADE SOME COFFEE AT the church and drank it watching new snow float down outside. The wind spun it and the pollen in great frozen firework undulations between the pines, which creaked and leaned. I hoped Clem was all right. If he managed to keep up a good pace, he could have reached Crucero by now, although the snow must have slowed him down. With any luck, it hadn't been so bad in the valleys.

Raphael came in with a blast of cold air and stray pollen motes. When I gave him some coffee, he looked at me in the way Navy wives do when their husbands get too much sea in them and start offering guests wine in mugs, but he drank it.

'What Inti was talking about,' he said, unprovoked. I turned back, surprised. I had been heating more milk for myself, hovering over the pan because everything boiled so low. 'My uncle was the priest here seventy years ago. He was the . . . it's complicated. There were thirty years between him and my mother so it's odd, but he was my uncle. We look alike, says everyone. He disappeared in the woods. Priests do. We're the only ones who can cross the border, and no one can cross to find us, so we tend to die out there. There are bears, wolves. That's all it is.' He sighed. 'And people like telling stories. It's not like there's a playhouse to go to.'

'Uh, shame. I was thinking how well you were doing for a hundred and ten.'

Raphael smiled, not wholly, as though it were a new and odd notion, to smile about it, with people who didn't believe he had been stolen by fairies.

Not wanting to go to bed yet, I sat by the stove sketching a whitewood twig. He put a jug of water down next to it by way of telling me to be careful about sparks, so I put it in the jug for good measure. Opposite me he took out a ball of thread and tied one end of it to a hole bored in the table. He had *Don Quixote* open in front of him and he turned the page every so often. On to the main string sometimes went smaller strings, as if the main thought were having a side thought, and then sometimes the side strings had ancillary strings too, but not often.

When I moved my sketchbook, the letter in the back fell out. I was about to tuck it back in again when I realised it didn't belong there any more. It came to me slowly, because it was the first time we had been sitting quietly without a baby or other things to do, and because it had slipped so far from the front of my mind that he was the priest at New Bethlehem. When Caroline had said the letter was for the priest, I'd imagined a tiny old Spaniard in a broad hat.

'Oh. I forgot,' I said into the quiet. 'My grandfather wrote a letter. It's for your uncle, I think.' I hesitated. 'But I said I would deliver it, so if I could just give it to you I can say to my mother that I did.'

'Let's see, then.'

I held it out.

He let the knots fall over the edge of the table, where they looked like nothing more literary than a tassel, and scissored the letter between his first two fingers. Having held the seal to the fire to give the wax some flex, he eased it up with the edge of a knife without breaking it.

I watched him unfold the thick paper, much thicker than Charles would ever have bought now. When the stove light seeped through it, there was only a line or so of text, written in the middle and ordinarily sized despite its isolation, but I couldn't make out what it was. He turned the paper around for me to see.

Raphael

I find that I cannot come myself as I promised, and so I send you my son, who looks very like me, in the hope that he might stand in.

All my love,
Harry

'Family name?' I said.

'What? Oh. Yes.' He set the letter on his knees and seemed to struggle with something. I was nearly sure it was the idea of asking anything. It was too close to asking *for* something. 'What . . . happened to him, do you know? Your grandfather.'

'He was shot in India somewhere before I was born. I'm sorry, I don't really know. I think he was caught in one of the rebellions.'

His shoulders stiffened as though that was a horrible thing to hear. I had been going to guess at dates, but I stopped, uncomfortable and suddenly not sure if the friends of older relatives here had an importance they didn't to me. He didn't explain why he was interested and only sat looking down at the letter for long enough to have read it twice more. Instead of throwing it in the fire, he folded it up again along its old lines and then once more, to make it small enough, and put it into his breast pocket.

'Is it important?' I said. 'I could find out what happened to him exactly, when I get back.'

'No. None of my business, sorry.' He flicked open his book again and wound up a pollen lamp to sit on the opposite page, then the new one, the one made from the clocks I'd bought, to hold like a torch. The clockwork was loud in the quiet. His sight must have been bad, because on a white page the two lamps together were almost too strong.

'I'll go to bed,' I concluded, too tired to think in a straight line any morc, never mind around intergenerational connections across the Atlantic. There was no need for any more hot water, but he put another log on the fire.

I pulled the chapel door to behind me but not shut, because the latch was rusty. Through the glass pipe that came up just beside the frame, a little translucent salamander glided by on the current, smiling, then disappeared into the dark further along the wall where the pipes were only a gleam. In the kitchen, Raphael was leaning forward, watching the fire with his wrists hanging from his knees. Where I was standing to change into my night things, as close to the pipes as I could get without burning myself, I could still see him, just through the half-inch gap between the door and the wall. He took out the letter again and I thought he would burn it, but he only sat holding it open. Abruptly he held it wide of himself. I didn't understand until he set it down and pressed his hand over his mouth so that he could cry without making any sound. I tipped the door open, just enough to make it creak. It made him jump. I put my hand out to say I hadn't meant it to.

'What's the matter?'

'Aren't you going to bed?'

'Not now, no.' I went back to sit with him, then put my arm across him when he tried to get up. 'If you say you're going out for firewood or something I'll follow you, so don't, my leg hurts and I still can't breathe properly.'

He looked like he might argue, but didn't. I leaned both hands on the hook of my cane.

'Have you been to India?' he asked after a while. The grit and the broken stones in his voice were gone. He sounded much younger. The fire clicked.

'I have. I used to live there. I was an opium smuggler.'

'You were a what? I thought you were in the Navy?'

'I grew up in the Navy. But the family have always been gardeners and I was sharked quite young by the East India Company and their expeditionary arm. But India, yes. For about a year. I used to oversee a poppy plantation and then take the opium to China. It's nice there. Hot, but nice.'

'Is it common, then, to . . .'

'To live in India, very. Part of the Empire. Everyone speaks English, so it's an easy place to live.' I hadn't meant to say any more, but he scanned the cinders for something else to ask, so I tried to sift through some memories of it. 'Most people go in through Malabar. Which is . . . the army garrison, so every second white man is in a red coat. It's bloody odd, it feels like being on a battlefield, but there's no fighting there now. And there are lovely guesthouses and hotels everywhere, for all the East India Company clerks. It's rich, because everyone from abroad spends their money there. I think it's the best place I've ever lived. The first week, before I moved north, I had to wait for my manager at a hotel, and there was a swimming pool. In the room. And they had a tame tiger in the foyer. It was a sort of joke on new people. Everyone thinks it's a rug and then it sits up and answers to Gregory.'

He smiled. 'Is there such a thing as a tame tiger?'

'Tame or stupid, I don't know. It liked it when guests gave it wool to play with. And then if it got used to you, you'd open your door in the morning and outside would be a hug from an unexpected tiger.' I paused, feeling strange, because I'd never told anyone about it. There had been no one to tell. Charles hated that I'd left the Navy and wouldn't hear a word about the EIC, and Clem and Minna knew it all already, because they had travelled even as children and had no sense of the exotic, only the less worn-out. 'I've forgotten a lot. If you go somewhere . . . very different to home, even for a long time, the memory feels like a dream when you get back. But the general impression is hot and flowers everywhere.'

In the time I'd been talking, his breath had evened out again but there was, like the stacks, a brittleness in him and a glass core. I didn't ask him again what was wrong. It was none of my business. He twisted his wrist to move the cross on his rosary out of the way, then pushed his abused fingers together, slowly. I didn't think he was praying.

'All right?' I said, even though I knew he wasn't.

'Mm. See you in the morning.'

EIGHTEEN

HE DIDN'T SEE ME in the morning. For the next few days, he was already out before I was up, and still out well after I'd gone to bed. The snow stayed. Each morning, the top layer was crackly where it was frozen fresh and the only evidence I was sharing the church with anyone at all was the single line of footprints that went out to the forest and, sometimes, if the wind fell, his pollen wake weaving between the trees on his way to the markayuq. I wanted to ask if he was avoiding me, but it was a stupid question, because he was, and he was straight enough to say yes and keep on doing it.

I was avoiding dark windows but I had to look at myself shaving. There were marks on my neck, bruises like I'd expected, but there were grazes too. Whoever had caught me had been wearing something rough over their hands. The bruises down my ribs were nearly black in places, deep, though the ache was a clean sort and I didn't think anything was broken. Having spent my twenties perpetually battered and flung about it made me feel more like myself again, but the feeling of being watched kept coming back when I went outside in the mornings. I didn't go near the border again. Instead I went to see Inti. When I asked her to speak some easy Quechua for me, we were both surprised to find that I understood. I couldn't have produced it, but in the last few days of hearing it here and there, something in my mind had clicked back into place. Dad had told all his fairytales in Quechua. I'd forgotten that, even if I'd remembered the stories. Hearing it aloud after so many years felt like organ music coming up through the glass deep under my feet.

There was a lot of milking of goats too, not just Inti's. There weren't many other people about during the day who were healthy enough to do it. Apart from the fishermen, most of the fitter people worked on Martel's farm, the produce of which fed the village; all except for the cocoa, which was shipped downriver to Azangaro and sold for five English pounds per stone and a half. Three or four farmers took care to confirm the numbers, as though it was a fortune, which it wasn't. Sometimes I saw Raphael in gardens, with laundry or broken crockery, or stitching tipped towards the sun in a way that made me sure he was quite near-sighted. And always, in the end, back to the endless waxing of the statues. If I'd been braver I might have gone to find him, but whenever I thought about it, I got one of his thousand-yard stares. It made me very glad of Inti. Without her, those days would have been a bubble of isolated silence. Everyone else was too busy or shy to talk to me and I was too feeble to help with any proper work.

I'd almost convinced myself that Clem wouldn't come back. When he did, early on the fifth morning and completely without fanfare, having slept the previous night in one of the warm salt caves about a mile upriver, I was so surprised I dropped the cup I was holding. He laughed and hugged me. There was frost on the lining of his hood that crackled when I squeezed him.

'Em! I was sure he would have murdered you by now.'

'I was sure you'd have been eaten by a bear. How was it? Are you all right?'

'Oh, fine, but I do smell. Sorry.'

I put him in a chair and ran a bowl of hot water for him from the stove as he started to peel off his coat, then had to start the long process of easing down onto my knees to pick up the pieces of the cup. I found the biggest and collected the rest up into it. 'Did you manage to see Martel?'

'I did. He seemed very surprised to see me; I think he was convinced Raphael would do us in too. Anyway, I wanted to come straight back, but he shouldn't be far behind me. Two days or so. He's bringing men.'

'Oh, thank God.'

'Snow's still here, I see,' he said, nodding towards the woods.

'Never warmed up once.' I paused, stuck, because I had a handful of glass and I needed both hands to push myself up again. I had to stretch to put the glass on the worktop beside the stove. The floor, I noticed, was scoured clean.

'Where's himself?'

'Out. I don't know. I upset him. I haven't seen him properly for days.'

He snorted. 'Only you. Only you would manage to upset someone you're supposed to be charming into not shooting you. Nicely done.'

'Yes,' I said, feeling inept. I managed finally to get myself into the chair next to his. 'But he hasn't shot me, at least.'

'Right, but let's say the jury's still out on that one?'

'Probably.' The joy at seeing him had deflated. He was right. It had been abundantly stupid. I wanted to say it wasn't my fault that a letter for a relative Raphael could barely have known had upset him so much, but it was the kind of thing I should have guessed. Family in places like this was important. There was so little else.

'Oh, it's so warm,' he said happily. 'God, I love this place. I wish Minna were here.'

I looked away. Something else he thought was my fault. He was annoyed about having had to go by himself. I didn't point out that he had wanted to, at the time. It never helped, to quote his own motives back at him.

'Listen – give me an hour to sit down, but then take me on a tour, yes? Say you've explored the town, Merrick,' he said when I hesitated.

'Yes,' I lied. 'Of course I have.'

The first stop was Inti, and I was relieved when she seemed just as pleased with Clem as she had been with me. She was soon telling stories and, unlike me, he knew what to ask. Over fresh coffee, without milk because I couldn't chase down the goat this time, she explained how the village had come to be here. One of the markayuq, the eldest, was supposed to have conquered it from some wildmen who had lived here before, then petrified to watch over the spot. I would have taken it at face value, but Clem was keen to unearth a hitherto unknown pre-Inca culture. He found a likely looking place in the steep public garden on the second stack and set to digging a trench to see if he could uncover any older walls. It was bitter in the snow, but the children loved it, and the dig soon became a sort of show to watch while people ate their pineapple and drank their coffee. He dug deep, in steps, right down to the glass stratum about eight feet under the surface. Towards noon he found the corners of an old building, but it was from Inca times. He showed the children, and me, how the bricks had been worked into the bedrock, just like they had at the church.

'Typically Incan,' he explained. 'Look at that. Marvellous. The skill it would have needed.'

'What was the point of building like this?' I asked. 'It would have been easier to cut the rock away.'

'Because the bedrock is *alive*,' he said. 'You don't know who you're chiselling into, do you? You heard Raphael talk about the mountain. It's alive, the markayuq are alive, the creation story is that people were made of rock, not clay; it's all the same thing. Stone lives.'

A small rock we had already put aside fell back into the pit and he leaned down to move it, but there was a murmur above us and one of the children, a little girl with unevenly arranged limbs, hurried to take it from him. She showed it to Inti.

'What's the matter?' Clem called up.

'It could be a living stone. It fell on you twice,' Inti explained. She held it up to the light to see.

'How can you tell?'

'They're very white. Yes, check with Father Raphael,' she added to the girl. Some of the other children darted off after her, as if a little rock were the most fascinating thing they had found all year.

'See?' Clem said to me.

The tiny tremor, which I hadn't even realised was a tremor, that had disturbed the white rock before, became the rumble of a real earthquake right in the bones of the mountain. They made a sound, a kind of mechanical thrum. Stones tumbled on the mountainside and a sheet of snow swept towards the river, where it waterfalled off the edge of the cliff. A few people made a bow towards the peak and crossed themselves.

'No wonder they think it's alive,' I said.

Clem's spade chinked. 'I'm at the glass,' he said. 'I don't think anyone could have built much on that. There's nothing but plant matter caught in it, no sign of habitation. Shame. I wanted some pre-Incan wildmen. Hard to tell what's a story and what's not, isn't it? I wish they'd stick to the facts. Still,' he said suddenly, frowning, 'it's interesting, isn't it. That the markayuq . . . change the history of the place they watch over.'

'Is it?' I said, because I was freezing.

'Yes. Think about it. Everyone here agrees with Inti; this ground was conquered, even though it demonstrably, archaeologically wasn't. The man who did it is right over there; they think he turned to stone to memorialise the occasion. The statues are little loci of local history, but it's false history. So in the moment a markayuq is made, your history changes. There's more importance to a place. Important things happened there. Even if they . . . didn't. A markayuq is a desirable thing partly because having one means you're entitled to a more glorious past. History is malleable here.'

'Or when you live in the middle of bloody nowhere with nothing except pineapples, "I came, I saw, I conquered" is a much more interesting story to tell your children than "I came, I thought it would more or less do, settled down",' I said. 'Can we go inside?'

'No, no, you must draw the dendrographs for me, before it gets dark.'

'Clem, I might die of cold,' I said. I hadn't told him what had happened to me the last time I had tried to draw the carvings on the border. Having offended Raphael was bad enough. I wasn't sure I could cope with looking any more useless.

'Oh, don't be silly. It won't take you half an hour,' he said. 'Besides, you shoved me in the river and then you made me go back to Azangaro by myself. Consider this penance.'

I stayed quiet about the second part. I was too tired to fall out again. Once we had climbed out of the trench and I started for the border, I stopped when Clem didn't come. 'Are you . . .?'

'I'm staying here,' he said cheerfully. 'Inti's giving me a Quechua lesson.'

'So I go out to the border in the freezing cold to draw *your* dendrographs while you sit and learn Quechua in the warm?'

'Come on, old man, we might be off any day, and it would be such a waste not to have some record of them. I've already used my daguerreotype slides. And I've a singular resistance to drawing lessons.'

Raphael would be on the border. I wondered if I could finish my original drawing from memory, or through some binoculars.

'All right,' I said, but paused as the children came running back. They all climbed straight down into the pit to start sifting through the soil at the bottom in a clatter of sharp happy Quechua. They were looking for more of the white stones, and one of them said something about pieces of an old markayuq. One of the girls held up a piece to her ear in the way I'd listened to shells when I was that age. I watched them, full of the feeling that Raphael had told them it was something interesting so that it would be a good afternoon for them.

I couldn't find any binoculars, so I went to the trees but not right up to the border, and sat down on some roots by St Thomas, my back to him so that no one could come up behind me again. Inti had made me a carving of him from glass, tiny and perfect. It was a good-luck charm – he was the patron saint of gardeners, according to the local church – and I'd had it in my pocket for two days. She said that nobody knew his real name any more, but before the Spanish arrived, he had been a bodyguard for the King in Cuzco. When he first came to Bedlam to escape Pizarro's men, he had told stories about the Inca courts, but nobody could speak to stone now, apart maybe from Raphael, who evaded the subject. More magic for children, probably, but I couldn't fault it.

I had been there for a while before I noticed Raphael was just beside the next markayuq on from Thomas. He was smaller than the statue, so he fitted inside its silhouette. He was watching me.

'If you want to avoid me, don't stay stuck there, just walk fast,' I said. 'I can only chase you for about eight feet.'

He ignored me. 'Are you sure it's a good idea to sit there?'

'No. But Clem wants pictures of these and I don't want to annoy him again.'

'Even less than you want to be beaten up and left half-dead on the ground.'

'I wasn't half . . .' I sighed, because I'd breathed too deeply, which still hurt my ribs. 'He got back this morning. He walked for four days, I didn't. It's the least I can do, isn't it.'

'For a whingeing little prick who quietly hates you for not being able to walk? I could probably manage less, if it were me.'

'Which is why you've got queues of friends outside the church door,' I said easily, because it was nice to be sympathised with, even in his annoyed way. 'But listen, he got there. Azangaro. Martel should be sending men soon.'

He let his weight tip back a little as if the idea of Martel was exhausting. 'Good.'

'If they can't clear the way—' I began.

'I'm not taking you across the border.'

'I know. But you can cross. If I taught you to take cuttings, then perhaps you could go? We'd . . . make it worth your while.'

I thought he would ask what could be worth ending up like the thief on the cliff and I was ready to say we could take him to India with us if we had to, but he didn't touch it.

'Maybe,' he said. He stood so still I thought it might have been catalepsy again. He had been working with his waistcoat undone and a breeze pushed it back to show a flash of the Indian lining. It wasn't catalepsy. He let the same wind turn his head as if the bones in his neck were on as fine a balance as a weathervane. 'Maybe,' he said again, in a deadened echo.

I hesitated, not sure where we stood with each other any more. 'I'm going for some coffee soon, I can't feel my hands.'

'Right,' he said. He stepped backward over the border, one slow step, and then walked away into the graveyard. If he said anything else, I didn't hear him. I waited, but after half an hour he still didn't appear and the snow was blowing in from the river. It sparked coldly in the pollen. Thinking he must have come out further along and gone home without me, I turned back for the church, expecting to find him in the kitchen. He wasn't. The fire had burned down to embers. I built it up again and settled to finish drawing.

I didn't notice the dusk falling until I started having trouble seeing the pencil shading. I wound up a pollen lamp without thinking and then stopped as it began to tick around. I leaned back to see through the window to the forest. The wind was gusting in the pollen still, but there were no trails. Suspecting that Clem had stayed at Inti's for dinner, I cooked myself some quinoa and a cut of the venison someone had brought for some ceremony or other Raphael had performed earlier in the week. I did enough for Raphael too but even after I'd eaten there was still no sign of him. By then the dark was inky. A point of light came over the bridge from the stacks. I thought it would be Clem, but when I opened the door it was Francesca, the baby tied to her back with a green shawl. She looked unsettled to find me and not Raphael, and when she spoke she did it in careful, halting Spanish.

'I was wondering where Father Raphael was,' she explained. 'He was supposed to come and see Juan this afternoon, but he never – has something urgent happened?'

'No,' I said. 'He's in the woods still, I think.'

She leaned back from me, startled. Her uneven shoulders moved back different distances. 'He shouldn't be at this time of night.'

'Is there anywhere else he goes?'

'No, he's the priest,' she said, as if that meant he was chained to an anchor caught between the stacks. She stepped back to see more clearly into the trees, whose white trunks looked amber in the glowing pollen. There was no sign of anyone inside. 'God, they've taken him again. It could be years.'

'Or he can't feel the cold and he's collapsed somewhere,' I said. 'If he can't be anywhere else, we need to look for him. Can we find some people to help?'

'Yes,' she said. She brushed past me to the ropes that stretched up into the dark of the church tower, above the loft space where Raphael slept, and rang the bells. They sang out and it must have been possible to hear them for miles through the trees, but still nothing moved there.

NINETEEN

STARS OF LAMPLIGHT BEGAN to come over the bridge to the mainland. When Francesca explained what was going on, there was a weird stir, more interested than worried, as if none of them believed at all in the chance of hypothermia or falling over a tree root, or bears. Even though she said we would have to look for him, they all ignored her and went automatically to the markayuq. The statues looked alive in the lamplight and they moved their hands to take things, almost constantly – salt vials and shells and knotted prayer strings – because whatever pressure pads were in the ground were being bumped on and off by everyone around them. Maria had propped herself against St Thomas, her fingers closed over his sleeve, watching the crowd with unhappy eyes.

Inti took charge when she arrived and organised a long line down the border. Maria hung back. Her mother was nowhere I could see. I fetched her out from behind the markayuq and took her with me. She held my hand too tightly at first, and I gave her our lamp so that I could hold onto her and my cane at the same time.

The pollen was just thick enough in the air to leave strange, half-visible illusion trails behind us. Further into the forest, beyond the border, the trees stopped the wind and it was possible to see where the bats were swooping, invisible themselves but leaving tangles of gold light behind them.

The trees skittered. Sometimes a stream of pine needles fell down when something passed overhead in the canopy, and every now and then stingingly heavy drops of water fell and splashed on to us. Everyone was walking slowly down the border, calling and moving their lamps, or throwing pine cones to make light arcs in the dark. Maria slowed right down after a little while. We were at the back. She had a cord tied around one of her coat buttons and she was putting new knots into it, upside down if the way Raphael did it was normal.

'Do you want to leave a prayer with one of the markayuq?' I said.

She shook her head. 'My knots aren't very good. And my hands are cold.' I liked talking to her. Her Spanish was exactly at my level, about a middle-sized child's. 'I've spelled it wrongly.'

'I'm sure you could just tell it to him.'

She twisted her nose and then shook her head. 'Nobody can talk to markayuq any more. They don't understand.'

'Why don't they?'

'They're old. They spoke another language in those days.' She was watching a big pollen trail in the forest, the wrong shape for a person.

'Maria, Raphael is strong. And he can fight. I don't think anyone has taken him anywhere. He's here somewhere, we'll find him.'

'He wouldn't have had a choice,' she said, sounding suddenly far more adult.

We still hadn't found him after half an hour. If he had gone back to town, he couldn't have missed the lights; if he was anywhere nearby and conscious, he certainly couldn't have missed them. After barely half a mile, the front of the line reached a place where there was only a narrow path between the border and cliff, blocked with snow. Inti turned everyone back the other way and still there was nothing.

Clem came to walk with us.

'Where do you think he's gone?' he said quietly. 'I don't buy that he's been snatched. We would have seen something in the pollen, or you would have.'

'I think he went out without a coat and it's minus God knows. He can't feel heat or cold. There's something wrong with him.'

'Christ.' He looked out through the trees. 'We should be looking over the border.'

'We can't go over the border.'

He made a face at me. 'Gone native, have you?'

'A bit,' I sighed.

'Well, let's put it to Inti.'

But when we did, she shook her head. 'No. You'll be killed.'

'But if he is out there, he isn't very far in,' I said. 'I saw him go. He'll be only just out of sight. It's bitter out here, it's a miracle nothing's ever happened to him before. He was just in his waistcoat and shirt. I saw.'

She was shaking her head again. 'No. If that's what happened then – then it's what they wanted.'

'Who, the people in the woods? Why is what they want so important?'

Clem caught my arm. 'They don't see them like people, old man,' he said quietly. 'Listen to her. I told you, it's religious. The salt line isn't just about crippled and not crippled; it's about unclean and holy, humans and angels. Flesh and stone.' He nodded to the markayuq. 'You and I are thinking of a town in there with gutters and markets and weavers, but that's not what it means here. They're looking at it like heaven, or Eden, and Raphael is a kind of Nephilim with one foot in either world. You're running up against God's will, almost. Am I right?' he added to Inti. He had said it in Spanish.

She nodded, and looked faintly appalled that I hadn't understood before. 'Well – of course. Merry-cha, if they want him, you can't try and fetch him back.'

'Inti,' I said. 'For God's sake. They don't. They don't even know he's there. He could be dying.'

She caught my arm before I could cross the salt.

'You can't cross,' she said, as if I were talking about going to the moon.

'I can see him,' Maria said, not loudly. I almost didn't hear. She broke away from me and ran over the border before anyone could stop her. She had a bumbling, little-girl run and she laughed as she went.

Inti yelled and so did everyone else. Maria didn't come back. I started after her but Inti caught my arm and a man with one eye snatched the back of Clem's shirt. He was her brother, or I thought I'd heard her call him that.

'For God's sake, she can't—'

'Inti—'

'Wait!' she said over us. 'Just wait. They might bring her back. She's really just a little girl; they might bring her back.'

We could all see Maria's pollen trail. It wove as she tried to find whatever it was she had seen. People were calling to her but if she heard she paid no attention and I had a sinking feeling in my diaphragm. She was about seven, on the inside. No amount of calling would have made much of a dent on me when I was that age if I'd seen Dad over an arbitrary line in the ground.

Another trail flared as it came out from behind a tree.

Clem caught my sleeve. 'Christ, is that him?'

I shook my head. 'Can't tell.' But it was moving wrongly for Raphael, and although it was difficult to judge in nothing but light and black, I was nearly sure it was taller than me. Other people thought so too and the shouts took on a raw edge. Inti was quiet.

When the man reached her, Maria's pollen ghost straightened up as if someone had said something to her. They came back together. Whoever it was shepherded her, slightly in front of him. He didn't come all the way but stopped just behind the roots of a tree to watch her keep going and around him the pollen started to fade. Maria's light trail resolved into Maria herself as she came into the lamplight. Someone snatched her back over the salt.

'Maria, you silly girl,' Inti burst out. 'What will we tell your poor mother?'

Maria seemed not to mind. 'I saw Raphael,' she said. 'It's all right. He isn't stolen.'

'Who brought you back?' I said.

'St Thomas did,' she replied, and everyone seemed to think that was a perfectly good answer.

'Well, you're damn lucky he recognised you,' Inti said, still shaken. 'Come on, let's find you some holy water.'

I stared hard at the place where the man beyond the border had stopped and moved away from the crowd so that I'd see the last of the pollen glow undrowned by everyone's lamps. It was there, just, an afterglow still hanging in the air where he had walked. I lost it behind trees sometimes because they were so broad, and sometimes it looked as if he had walked under their high roots, but I followed the trail in stops and starts along the salt. It turned towards the border about halfway along, a straight right-angle of half-light whose end I didn't see before the wind gusted and sparked the pollen fresh, destroying the tiny glow that had been left. But the line had been there and I followed it. I had to bypass another tree before I could see where the trail would have come out, if it had come out. It was where St Thomas had been standing before, but, although the grass and the frost were dented from the weight, there was no statue there now.

Clem had hurried after me, and Inti's brother.

'How did they do that?' I said after a long silence.

'They could have . . . moved the original statue behind a tree and dressed a man up,' Clem said slowly. 'Make a bit of a show.'

I couldn't imagine anyone being able to move a markayuq with any subtlety. 'What for?'

'To prove there's someone there. To prove to *us* that there's someone there. To keep us out.'

I had closed my teeth too tightly and when I spoke again I heard a tiny crackle of cartilage inside my jaw, like I'd bitten a few grains of sugar.

'Sounds to me,' Clem added when I didn't say anything, 'like he's gone talk to them about us, doesn't it. Perhaps give them a bit of a warning to watch out, if we can't clear the snow on the path. I suspect he's less missing than we think.'

Rather than go back to her own house, Inti stayed with us at the church and sat by the stove for a long time. She must have known I was on the edge of crossing the salt, because she brought her brother, who could have stopped me just by standing in the doorway. He was a quietly mannered man, polite, but there was no escaping why he was there and in a graceless and resentful sort of way I made them both coffee and watched them wince over it. Neither of them had as much difficulty moving about as I did.

'We're going to have to get his things together,' she said to me. 'Aquila will live here now.'

'Inti, it's been less than a day,' I said. 'He might—'

'He disappeared for seventy years last time,' she interrupted. 'It doesn't get shorter. If he comes back at all, it won't be in our lifetimes.' Then, more gently, 'He's gone, Merry-cha. Everyone knew it would happen sooner or later. Honestly, I think he was just holding on until Aquila was old enough.'

'So you're going to move everything of his out and install Aquila? What if he does come back?'

'We'll put it all back again. But he won't come back. And I don't think he's got much, anyway. I'll get started in a minute.'

I knew I couldn't claim to have got an especially detailed understanding of him in a week, and he might not have minded in the least, but it struck me as something Raphael would mind a great deal, for Inti to see where he slept. He was in and out for twenty hours a day, with no privacy except in that tiny loft beside the bells. It would have been horrible enough anyway that he should have to offer that up as well, but given that he must have vowed chastity as well as poverty and service, it was infernal. I couldn't think of anything less sacerdotal than letting a brisk pretty woman go through his clothes. The idea of having to explain it to him when he came back made me push my fingernails into the wooden ladder.

'I'll do it,' I said.

'No—'

I hooked my cane over a rung of the ladder by way of staking a claim. When I climbed up to the loft, I expected it to be full of the furniture and clutter that wasn't downstairs, but there was hardly anything at all. There was a bed, a pallet exactly the same as the ones set up in the chapel, and by its side was a falling-apart copy of the Bible in Latin. Opposite, built into the wall, was a wardrobe, which was bare. There were shelves under the round window, empty and dusted. In the corner, once I'd wound up the lamp, I found a box. There were books inside, packed up, all in Latin. The bookplates on the flyleaves had the seals of the Vatican printed on them. Raphael's name was written in, although they were thoroughly second-hand; the publication dates were from the seventeen hundreds. Harry's letter was there too, and some sewing things; leather like the statues wore. He was making something for one of them, halfway through the riveting of a seam. Under those were his own clothes, clean and folded. That was it. I had to keep my head down because the bells were right above me. They moved slightly in the draught, not nearly enough to knock together, but the bronze hummed and gave a metal edge to quiet.

'There's nothing left to do,' I called down. 'Just a box. He's . . . packed everything away already.'

'Well, that's something,' Inti said unhappily from below. 'All ready for Aquila then. He must have known it would be soon.'

'Mind if I visit?' Clem said.

'Plenty of space. But mind your head.' I propped my cane against the wall and sat down on the bare floorboards. It was cold. There were no pipes. The ladder creaked as Clem climbed, and when he appeared his breath steamed. He looked around and then lifted his eyebrows at me.

'Heavens. He really has packed up.'

'He knew he was going,' I said. 'Did Inti tell you the story, about how the priests always disappear?'

'She did.' He came to sit next to me on the floor. Together we looked like something from an abandoned toyshop. He was all round and gold and I had to sit with my good leg folded and the bad one crooked, like a puppet someone had dropped from a height. Listen, 'I don't think there are wild Indians in the woods, Em. I think there are henchmen from the quinine barons. There'll be a semi-permanent camp out there. They feed the border myth, which is the perfect excuse for them to shoot anyone who strays in, no questions asked. We've been planning to go around, but we might not be able to, if Martel's men can't clear the snow. So Raphael's gone in to warn them we might try to go straight through.'

'But I don't see why he would be packed up like this.'

'He probably wants to get out of here as soon as his duty's done. It must be coercion. He's clearly not getting a cut.'

I pushed my hand over my face. 'But it would be dangerous to keep a camp out there. I mean maybe it is quinine men, but there *are* Indians round here.'

'How do you know?'

'Martel said it was . . .'

'What if they've been cleared out? It's such a good set-up. The people living here keep anyone from crossing the border because they believe it's blasphemy. It's self-policed; it's brilliant. They're not surprised if someone who crosses doesn't come back, so there's no murder accusation. Stop seeing the frills and look at the actual result of what's going on. Someone inside the forest is stopping people from crossing, and killing those who do. What do we know is on the other side? Quinine. Come on, Em. Wake up.'

I pulled my clasped hands apart and then again. It made the joints hurt but I couldn't keep myself from it.

'He could have just told us that. Don't go in the forest here, there are quinine thugs with guns. That's far simpler than Indians and abandoned children and walking statues. And . . . much more likely. I'd have believed that.'

'Yes, but Em, what an Indian man born and raised in the middle of nowhere imagines to be likely or necessary isn't what you or I would. I should think he didn't think quinine men sounded frightening enough.' He paused. 'Look, take it from me: there's almost no point in trying to work out why the natives do some things. Their way of thinking is so far from ours that no effort at translation will ever have more subtlety than smoke signals over a canyon. There will be factors here we don't know, cultural, religious, all sorts. He speaks English but he thinks like a Quechua Indian, you know he does. Think about that past-in-front business. That won't be the only difference, just the symptom of something much wider.'

I didn't say that I thought Clem was a bad translator, or that I didn't believe there was any such thing as an impassable gulf in the thinking of two human beings. Of course you couldn't translate everything, but you could damn well explicate, particularly if you both spoke such a sprawling monster of a language as English. 'What's gone before you, and what will come after,' I said instead.

'Beg pardon?'

'The past ahead. Time is like a river and you float with the current. Your ancestors set off before you did, so they're far ahead. Your descendants will sail it after.'

'No need to nitpick, old man, you know what I mean.'

I nodded, not wanting to have a fight under the bells. It would have resounded. 'Sorry.'

'Actually, this is rather good,' Clem said cheerfully. 'I think we ought to seize the day, don't you?'

'How do you mean?'

'I can set off through the forest now, say I'm looking for Raphael if anyone tries to stop me. And I assume I won't find him – what a shame – but we'll have our specimens.'

'Christ, Clem. If there are suppliers camped . . .'

'Then I shall see them a mile away in the pollen, shan't I?'

'And they'll see you.'

'Are your tools in your bag? You know, the knife to take the cuttings, string, all that?' He was already on his way down the ladder.

I tagged down after him just as he emptied out the last of my pack on to the windowsill in the chapel. Inti, who had been talking to her brother by the fire, plainly hadn't guessed what we were saying. 'They're in that roll. But Clem – they're going to see you.'

'From a distance a person looks like an animal in that pollen, I'm certain, and I'll see a big group of men long before they see me. I'll manage.'

'I don't think you will. People have disappeared; half an army battalion disappeared in these woods.'

He came past me into the kitchen to take some food, which he did calmly and vaguely and must have looked, to Inti, as if he were only foraging for some dinner. 'Yes, exactly. Whole expeditions, battalions, clunking about and setting off the pollen and the markayuq. Of course they were caught. One man is quite a different story. Stop fretting.'

'We don't even know how far it is. There's no scale on that map, if it's to scale at all—'

'I'll manage,' he said again, with too much emphasis, like he was talking to a child. He came back with enough fruit and bread for a couple of days if he was careful.

'No – Clem. Even if it's near, you never managed to take a decent cutting on the ship. It will be wasted effort.'

'Well, if I don't try, no one will, will they,' he snapped. 'You can't go and you frightened Minna off. There's no one else to do it.'

'I didn't frighten her—'

'For God's sake, of course you did.' He rounded on me much faster than he usually moved and pulled the chapel door closed behind him so that Inti and her brother wouldn't hear that we were arguing. 'You've been worse than useless since the start. First Minna, and then you had one thing to do, one: convince anyone we ran into we were here for coffee. And you told Raphael we were here for quinine the second he asked. Then I said to keep an eye on him and what did you do? You upset him so much he's barely spoken to you for days. Of course he's gone to tell the quinine men that we're here. You can't pretend you've been anything less than a catastrophic influence on this expedition. Much as I love you, get out of my way, calm down, and see if you can't think of something to say to anyone who asks where I am, if they notice. Can you manage that?'

'Clem, wait. What if you're wrong? What if there's something to these stories—'

He smacked me with the roll of tools he was holding. It snapped my head sideways and made me see stars.

'You're hysterical,' he said. 'Local priests are not spirited away by elves or fairies or whatever, and for God's sake, Occam's razor. What's the simplest explanation for this border? An Inca-related culture so advanced they built clockwork statues in the whatever-teenth century and still police a hundred-mile stretch of border watching over their rejected and less holy children, or some men guarding the quinine woods and feeding some old origin story from years ago, with the sense to order in a few Spanish church marvels and tell everyone they're local miracles?'

'I'm not saying elves,' I said, slowly, because it was shocking how much it hurt to be hit in the face without having expected it, and on top of the old bruise. 'I'm saying, what if there's *someone* there? Organised people, not necessarily advanced, but organised. We saw those terraces in Sandia; there's nothing like that even in Rome and I wouldn't want to take on Romans. If this is their place, if they do watch the border – they'll find you a hell of a lot faster than a few quinine men.'

'Look, I know you had an impoverished education, but I'm telling you, categorically, the border is a piece of staged rubbish by people who know the locals are superstitious.'

'I didn't have an impoverished education.'

'Yes, I expect the Bristol naval academy was very thorough—'

'Hold on a minute. You didn't go to university either. Wasn't it some grammar school in the middle of—'

'I was surrounded by people who did, always! I've published books, Merrick, papers. I don't even know how many scholarly societies I belong to – look, I don't want to go through listing everything. Just – perhaps, for once, defer to someone who might actually know what he's talking about. I have to be honest with you, you're bloody jumped up.'

'Above my station, you mean.'

'Well, yes,' he said. 'I'm sorry, but it's true. You have a good name, and don't get me wrong, Tremayne is a very respectable name indeed, but a name makes not a gentleman. You don't *know* enough. You need to stop pretending you're anything more than an able seaman converted into an India Office smuggler. Things will go a lot less wrong.'

'You brought me because I'm qualified.'

'I brought you because you can keep plants alive anywhere in the world. Of course you're qualified for that, more than. Just let me fetch them, all right? I'm in charge of this expedition, so let me worry about the decisions. You concentrate on getting the wretched cuttings to India.'

I stayed quiet and saw the two ways ahead as clearly as memory. Down one, I turned around to Inti and her brother and told them what he meant to do. Inti's brother was big and between us we would be able to lock Clem in the chapel, and he would be safe until Martel arrived, although by then, if there were quinine men in the woods, the path around by the river would almost certainly have been blocked or blown up and we would go home. I'd never work again. Sing would be sent to file things in a cellar somewhere. Bedlam would stay as it was for perhaps five years, and then someone somewhere would find a reason to shell Lima until the Peruvian government agreed to let British troops into Caravaya. If there were Indians, those troops would not wait about wringing their hands. They would burn the forest.

Down the other way, I let Clem go, and perhaps he came back with cuttings, but probably he would be caught and killed, like everyone else. There would be no cuttings, but his death would be all the reason the India Office needed to send a legion; any idiot would be able to see that. If the army's arrival was a clear inevitability rather than a vague threat years in the future, it could be used as a bargaining chip. Someone in the supply line might let through some cuttings if the only other option were British artillery regiments camped over the Andes.

My cheekbone still throbbed and I stood paralysed for what felt like minutes and minutes. I wished he hadn't hit me. It was hard to see past that and hard to know if the reasons for letting him go were good ones or just an excuse for revenge.

'Yes,' I said finally. Even as I said it, I had a terrible feeling that I'd decided for no better reason than that this was what Sing had told me to do, and the mountain air had stolen any capacity I might have had to imagine not doing it. I looked without meaning to at the jagged black shape outline beyond the town in stars and had a stupid vision of a cave somewhere in those razor crags where the logic of everyone who had tried to take things from this place lay stacked in little glass boxes. 'You're right. You'd better go to bed for now. I'll play cards with Inti. They can't stay here, there's nowhere for them to sleep. They'll have to go eventually.'

He let his breath out. 'Yes. Yes, good. We'll try and keep it a secret once I've got the cuttings.'

'What are you two nattering about?' Inti asked as we came through.

'Gardening,' I said. I dropped into the chair next to hers and played cards with them while Clem went to get some sleep. They lasted much longer than I'd hoped, long into the night, but

eventually they went home. Before they left, Inti made
not to go anywhere, so I swore and then went to wake C
As he disappeared into the dark, I stood in the doorw
both hands on my cane, waiting to see the pollen flare as h
into the woods. Although I was breathing and my heart wa
ing, my ribs felt hollowed, like there were no organs left
having all been scooped neatly out and left in canopic jars
where. The pollen flared beyond the markayuq. I went out a li
way to see the town. The last week had been like being allowed
visit somewhere imaginary. I'd thought it was imaginary: the gri
forest and the glass, the man who disappeared. People sang song
and told stories I knew from being a child, echoes from that gold
jumble of half-memories that were all I had from before Dad died.
Inti had said, welcome home.

I had no idea if I was helping Bedlam or if I'd just destroyed it.

TWENTY

India and China, 1857
(three years earlier)

The shelves in the Stacking Room at the Patna warehouse went up to twenty-five storeys. From the steps that zigzagged up the wall, there were gangplanks over the huge drop down to the floor. Checking crates fifty feet off the ground brought on a certain sharpness of mind that lasted for a long time afterwards. The crates were small and inside each one, the opium balls looked like rocks tucked in their sawdust, but if you cut one open, they were made of smooth, shiny gel that could be melted and smoked. I was cutting every fiftieth ball in half to check the consistency before we shipped everything down the Ganges to Calcutta, and from there, to China.

Beyond the high windows, fields and fields of poppies made white waves as the wind came in over the mountains. They were just starting to wilt now and the petals were everywhere. Someone was brushing them into piles against the wall where they had blown inside. Keita, my interpreter, who was twelve, was playing with one of the plantation boys and there was a burst of still-baby laughter as they fell over in one of the piles. It echoed up around the warehouse and I smiled. He didn't usually play at all, which worried me sometimes.

It was a strange job. I had been hired originally for tea. In the forbidden districts in China, there were rare types that the East India Company wanted for its own plantations in India but the Chinese growers wouldn't sell. When I'd first come, a year before, I'd been based in the Hong Kong office, at the mouth of the Pearl River, and had gone for weeks-long trips into the interior to steal

samples. Those samples, though, had to be smuggled out and taken round to the Himalayas. We had struck an agreement with another EIC operation, who were shipping silk out of Canton – which was, if you were coming from inland China, on the way back to Hong Kong anyway. The smuggled tea went in with the silk cargoes. It had all been straightforward enough at first.

I'd never dealt with opium before, but the poppy fields were in the same region as the tea, and Sing had pointed out in his efficient way that I might as well take the opium round to China on my way in for the tea samples. Gradually the tea side of things disappeared and orders from the Company headquarters at Hong Kong hinged around looking after the poppy crops. After six months on the job, I was nine-tenths an opium smuggler. We made a run every month, starting in India, across the South China Sea, past Hong Kong and into the Pearl River, where, after seventy miles on the strange, murky water, we arrived at the Canton wharves and the silk warehouses. By that December, we had made the journey seven times.

The colossal distance soon seemed ordinary and easy enough, but every now and then tiredness caught up with me, which it did on the morning our steamer sighed past Hong Kong and into the massive estuary of the Pearl for the eighth time. I'd found for years that if I moved around enough and if I was tired enough, I stopped remembering how I'd got to be in a place. It felt as if I'd just appeared there. Trying to think of the voyage then, I couldn't picture it. I felt as though one moment I'd been in the warehouse in India and the next here we were, again, on the ship, in China, three days and hundreds of miles away. It was nearly Christmas, just after the rainy season. The river was swollen and muddy and the water was viscous as it passed through our water wheel. Despite not being very interested in the soggy scenery, I was sitting outside on the rail. I would have had to even in the pouring rain. Any crew coming in with something illegal needed a blond person to be conspicuously British under the Jack, to keep Customs officials from searching the ship. They weren't allowed to touch British ships.

I watched Hong Kong go by. I could just see the office on the hill. The tripartite cross flag snapped out on the warm wind and

I felt then as though I spent my life going past things and never inside. The East India Company had made me into a sort of gypsy. I didn't dislike it, but just then, the miles I had to go before I would be able to stop seemed like too many.

My interpreter tapped me and gave me a rice cake with honey on it.

'You haven't eaten anything,' he said.

'Thanks. Share?'

He climbed up too. I'd found British clothes for him, so that he would obviously belong with me when we were with strangers. He wore them a lot more comfortably than port officials did and he had the knack of being always in a state of slight but not scruffy dishevelment. It implied that he had just come away from doing something useful.

A Customs ship glided by near us and we both watched it. I never felt completely safe, although we had never been stopped. The legal way to pay for silk was silver bullion, but if the EIC kept giving them that, Sing pointed out, it would end up paying more and more in real terms as silver devalued in China and became rarer in England. Opium, though, was an endless resource, and worth a thousand dollars a crate once it was on the Chinese mainland. When I'd mumbled that maybe opium wasn't the best thing for people to trade, Sing had told me to get it into my stupid flowery head that the effects of goods were not the Company's business. The point was favourable trade, and not crashing the British economy, and if one in twenty Chinamen had chosen to addict himself to something so idiotic, that, thank you, was his own fault. Availability of goods never forced anyone to buy them, however Gladstone might roar in Parliament. The devil could have roared at Sing and got nothing for his trouble but a newspaper in the face and a summary of the morning stock exchange.

One of the men on the Customs ship looked back at me, a flat look that said he knew exactly what we had in our hold – if it had been legal, there would have been no need to bother with a visible Englishman – but the ship kept going, away from us, towards one of the little jetties on the shore where a Chinese junk was waiting for inspection, one of its red sails stuck half-unfurled where a line had caught.

We came into a deep, cold shadow. I was still looking at the island and the Customs ship, but beside me, Keita leaned back.

'Christ,' he said in his adult way, which was all the odder because he was half the size an English boy his age would have been. He was a Japanese runaway who spoke fluent Chinese and English by means he had always managed not to disclose.

It was a British Navy ironclad, towering above our little clipper. It had five masts, the sails furled, and the gigantic waterwheels were stopped, but the engines were thrumming and there were still the last dying wisps of steam from the funnels. It must have just moved into place. I could see they weren't manned or ready, but I felt nervous as we sailed past the gun ports.

'They're not ready to fire yet,' I said, unnecessarily. 'We'd better get out quickly, though. I think it will be today or tomorrow. They won't hang about long.' While I was talking, a little supply boat steamed up to the hull and started to load person-sized shells up to the waiting winches.

He thought about it. The hems of his mind dragged a long way behind him. It took a while sometimes for him to look at all the briars caught in them and find which were relevant. 'I think today.'

'Why?'

'Just a feeling,' he said. He had a long history of accurate feelings. He always knew when it would rain. He always knew when Sing was coming, even though Sing was a great believer in arriving unannounced. I'd never asked him straight out if he had some real sense of things to come – it felt too close to an accusation of madness – but it had happened often enough now for me to pay attention. He shifted anxiously as if he didn't like being near the guns either.

'Before or after we get through?' I said.

He was quiet for a long second. He went tauter and tauter, then shook his head as if he didn't want to say. 'After.' I thought at the time that he sounded like he was lying, but I couldn't think, then, of a reason for him to do so and wrote it off the second it crossed my mind.

'I know it's itchy, cutting it so fine, but—'

'But Mr Sing will do worse than run a Navy ironclad at us if we come back with no silk, I know,' he said. If he had been any other child I would have put my arm around him, but he would have stiffened and hated it.

'Look at those idiots,' I said instead.

He looked, then smiled when he saw what I meant. There was another clipper over the other side of the river, flying a faded and aged Jack above a very Chinese crew. They had dressed a tiny European boy in an officer's uniform. It was hard to tell if they were taking the piss or if it was all they needed to avoid Customs these days. Nobody wanted to touch anything that could possibly have been a British crew now. Technically the Customs men had the Emperor's authority to search and seize any suspicious cargo, but they had tried that on a British ship last year and the Admiralty had gone ballistic – was still in the process of arranging its ballistics now – hence the gunships. Permission to fire on Canton until someone apologised had come through from Parliament this week. We finally passed the last of the guns and I felt easier, which was stupid, because it would have taken a clear fifteen minutes to load them from nothing.

Like always, Keita had a tangle of clockwork in his hands. He was adding to it fast, with a pair of fine tweezers and a little jar of cogs hanging from the rail on a loop of string, unaffected by the small motion of the ship. It was nothing like the painstaking way I'd seen watchmakers work before. He dropped things into place, never had to wiggle a pin, never fumbled anything. He had gone back to it while we talked, but he stopped now. 'I think we ought to go inside.'

'Are you cold?'

He pointed at the ironclad.

Just as he did, its engines roared and it started forward. The wave from the hull knocked us sideways and I nearly fell off the rail, though Keita rode it well. He didn't seem surprised. We climbed down on to the deck and he unhooked his jar of cogs, to carry by the loop like a lamp. Back beyond our wake, which had wobbled, there were smoke plumes on the horizon too big for the clippers and nothing to do with the little red-sailed junks pottering in wind-tack zigzags. It was another gunship. One I knew. One of the plumes was bumpy, from a stuttery funnel. 'Jesus. That's the *Thunder*. Sixteen guns. I thought the Navy would just fire a few warning shots but they mean to raze the city with all this, don't they?'

Keita made a small reproachful sound as he bumped into me, thrown forward by another wake wave, this time from a clipper racing in the opposite direction. I put him on to his balance again, wanting to pick him up. All around us now, more clippers were running for Hong Kong, back the way we had come. A few of them steamed close as the river bottlenecked. Keita looked too little to be in the middle of it all and I nudged him inside. He was shaking in the tiny, buzzing way mice do. He didn't like sailing at the best of times. Ships, he always said, were an unforgiving form of travel. If a horse went lame you could usually dismount and walk away. If a ship went wrong you usually drowned. I settled us in the little mess room and we played backgammon until we pulled in to the long wharves at Canton that evening, thankfully well out of sight of the ironclads. There were soldiers on the bridge over the river. Keita watched them unhappily.

I climbed down on to the wharf before the gangplank was lowered and lifted Keita with me, wishing I'd had the sense to leave him in India this time. He was normally such a collected person that it hadn't occurred to me he might be frightened now. He didn't mind storms, tea farmers shooting at us, mandarins threatening us. The Navy, which usually aimed well, hadn't seemed any different.

'If you'd tried to leave me in India I'd have settled down in the hold, thanks,' he said flatly.

'Stop talking to what I haven't said. How do you do that, anyway?'

'You've got one of those faces.'

'That makes no sense.'

'On purpose,' he said.

'Fine,' I laughed. 'Let's get this over with. Stay in front of me,' I added, because the wharf was crowded, not with stevedores but ordinary people holding children and bags, trying to reach Hong Kong before anything happened. We wove through them as best we could, up to the warehouses, where somebody who wasn't our usual silk trader came out to meet us. Above the roofs, on one of the garden gantries that seemed to float with all its struts lost in wisteria, a beautiful, impassive woman smoked a tobacco pipe while she watched the river. She was in her fifties; she must have seen it all before.

'Mr Tremayne! Mr Wang sent me out to see you. He's, er . . . fled,' the new man explained. 'Nobody knows when it's all going to start.'

'Soon,' I said. I had a decent grasp of Chinese. Keita was there for when things became too specific or for the people who didn't quite trust that I knew what I was saying, which was a wholly reasonable doubt to have. 'There are gunships coming up from Hong Kong now. Shall we get everything swapped over?'

'There's an extra condition,' he said quickly.

'You're coming with us, of course you are.'

'Thank God,' he said, half-crumpling. 'Do you suppose we have time?'

'I think so. It'll take the gunships two hours at least to get here. They don't go fast. Come on, let's get going.'

Most of the warehouse men had fled, so we had to unload the opium crates and then load the silk bales ourselves with the crew, but some of the trader's men hurried round with a cart while we did. The opium disappeared onto the back of the cart, which sped straightaway towards the bridge, while there was still a bridge. Keita stood just inside the hold and directed. He was good at even distribution and making the best use of space, whatever the mad shape of whatever we were loading. Halfway through, he froze and his head snapped to the side, towards the river, as if he had heard something huge, but there was nothing but the rattle and chatter of the crowds. He stayed like that for a long second.

'Is it starting?' I asked quietly.

He nodded. 'Soon. We'll have to sail through it. But they won't be aiming at ships; it should be all right. That can go over there,' he added in his courtly Mandarin to two of our men who were bringing more silk bales. Behind us on the wharf, people were waving money at the captain for a place onboard.

'That's going to have to do,' I said. If I had been a better man, I would have jettisoned the silk cargo to make room for more people, but I was too frightened to lose the work. I had nothing else, and would have no references if I made Sing angry enough. Leaving behind cargo was exactly the kind of thing that made him angry. 'Mr Shang! There's space.'

Shang, the captain, had been waiting to see if he could let people aboard. He had already moved women and children to the front. He put the gangplank down again and waved them across.

I shepherded Keita up the ladder to the deck to see if anything had changed on the river. There were no more incoming ships now. 'We have to go. They've blocked the river further up.'

The engineer had seen too. The smoke from our funnel thickened as he stoked up the coal.

Shang climbed back into the cabin and pulled a throttle, and we leaned out into the current. The people he had let in through the hold began to come up on deck. He must have packed them in below, because it was quite a crowd. I felt the ship rock and sent the bigger men back down, to be ballast.

'Is silk really important enough to start a war over?' Keita said to me when I came back. He already knew the answer, but when he was worried he asked things like that in the way other children asked to be told fairytales they already knew off by heart.

'Sit up here,' I said, tapping the rail so that we could hear each other over everyone else talking and fretting. He climbed up and I put my arm across him in case one of the other ships bumped us. They were close. 'It's not about the silk. It's about not pissing about with the East India Company. If you try and dictate terms of trade to them – if you say you can only buy silk with silver bullion – they make sure you do something stupid. They'll run obvious smugglers, like us, until someone snaps. Some poor bastard from Customs boards a British ship to try and put a stop to it, like they did with the *Arrow*.' He nodded. I explained it in the same way every time and sometimes he filled in parts if I left space, but he didn't now. He sat back against me, fitted to my chest like he never usually would have. I squeezed his arm, worried. It was starting to bother me that he was frightened of shots that wouldn't even be aimed at us. In the near future hung the shape of something else, something he wasn't saying, but there was still nothing unusual on the river.

'That's a violation of treaty. They can't touch our flag. So the Navy comes, shells the hell out of everything for a week, and when the Emperor folds, Britain dictates the terms of the peace treaty. This time it will hinge around the legalisation of opium.' I could smell iron; the ship was running hot. 'It's a new kind of war. There's no need to lay a siege and take someone's capital city any more. You just have to make them sell underprice. That's . . . I don't really have the right sort of mind for all this, but it's how the British Empire works, I think. There's a queen, a prime minister, and the East India Company board of directors.'

Keita nodded. He had absolutely the right mind for it. 'Quinine next. They're selling it too dear, aren't they, in Peru?'

'Damn right they are. The sooner someone shells Lima and makes them trade the sodding stuff for tea, the better. I'm sick of getting a cough and worrying for a fortnight if Sing will spend the money on us if it's malaria.'

He was holding my sleeve hard and looking, not at the other ships, but down at the water. I could feel his heart through his ribs.

We were passing the crocus fields just outside the city and I was starting to feel like we might just have got away. Between the crumbling buildings and above the flooded streets – it had rained all last month – great swathes of dyed cloth swam yellow from lines strung thirty feet above the ground. A melon seller was still going about his ordinary business close to the shore and so, around him, was everyone else. The dyers and saffron pickers had nowhere else to go. The chances of their having helpful relatives in Hong Kong were the same as my having them on Mars.

'It's none of my business,' I said, 'but can I ask why you signed up for all this rather than staying safe at home like, you know, an ordinary child?'

Keita laughed, but not much. 'Really it was the cook. I don't like him.' He narrowed his eyes. 'He keeps post under his wig. I mean, when he collects it he brings it back like that, even if he isn't carrying anything. And it's just . . . if you wear a wig, that's an effort towards ordinary hair, isn't it? But there isn't much in the way of a verisimilitudinous illusion if there are envelope corners sticking out of it. I don't know. I feel like he might be a stupid person and the postal wiggery typifies the stupid. Does it?'

'Yes,' I said.

He looked uncertain. 'Usually I'm being unreasonable.'

'No, I think that sets a worrying standard of behaviour. Don't go back, stay with me. Japan sounds bloody dull anyway.'

He tensed well before the shell screamed over us, although it was completely incongruous. There had been no warning; we were too far from the ironclad to hear them beating to quarters. The shell smashed into some buildings on the riverbanks and blew them to pieces, some of which crashed into the water right up close to our hull. I twisted back to wave at Shang and point towards the middle of the river, but every other ship was doing exactly the same. He shook his head and we sped up to bypass it all, but we were dangerously close to the banks. Another shot blasted a dyer's. I saw a vat of saffron fly whole across our path and land in the water, where the dye spiralled out and made a floating, bright yellow patch.

We swerved, and I felt Keita slip from under my hands. Later, I was sure that he had pushed himself from the rail on purpose. His balance was so good and I'd been holding him so tightly that he couldn't have fallen. I stared at the empty patch where he had been for a second, then dived after him. Because the water was exactly the same temperature as the air, it felt for a bizarre second like hitting a denser sort of mist.

The shell must have been a stray. They wouldn't have aimed at us, and there was nothing close to aim at anyway. But the reeds about twenty yards from me exploded, and I felt myself lifted up and hurled backwards in the water. At first I hung still, not sure which way was up, or what had happened. When I understood at last, it was because Keita was next to me and dragging my sleeve.

We broke the surface together. Bits of blasted reed floated around us, and chunks of mud torn from the riverbank.

'Swim. I can't help you, you have to swim,' he said, as unlike a child as I'd ever known him in all his history of unchildishness.

I did, because at the time I couldn't feel anything wrong. It was only when Shang swung back to find us that I saw what had happened to my leg.

When I woke up properly, I couldn't tell where I was. It was a good room with a big piano taking up half the far side, which usually meant Hong Kong. A while ago, a firm in Manchester or somewhere had been certain that every one of the thirty million or so moneyed ladies in China would want a piano now that trade was more open and so they'd shipped a silly number out, only to find that the climate was all wrong for piano strings and nobody was interested anyway. In an effort at charity, all the British diplomats and EIC writers had bought two apiece and fitted them into whatever corners they could. On the wall was an oil painting of some tea clippers.

Sing was in the chair beside me.

'You'll be lucky to walk again,' he said, and I had a strange wave of gratitude that he had got straight to the point rather than edging around it. He was pale. 'The bombardment started half an hour early. It was a mess. They ended up catching French troops in the crossfire too. I'm surprised they didn't hit Hong Kong by accident.'

'I'm sorry,' was all I could think of to say.

'So am I.' He let his breath out. 'Just get better the best you can. I do not want to send Horace bloody Spruce out to the Amazon. He'll spend half his time coming up with Greek names for all the new kinds of cinchona he misidentifies.'

I laughed, which sent a pulse of bone-deep pain twanging up through my spine. 'Yes. Right.' I could already feel it was never going to be better, but never is a broad thing to understand in the few seconds after waking from an opium sleep. I could see the idea, but I couldn't hold it or feel it.

He watched me for another moment and then stood up, which brought Keita into view where he was sitting in the window. 'I'm going to arrange passage for you back to England.'

'Can't I stay here?'

'Only until you're well enough to be moved,' he said quietly. 'I'm sorry. We're not the Navy. There's no invalid provision. If you're not working we can't keep you.'

He left in his clipped way and I sat very still, knowing I was in that strange, long space between being shot and feeling it.

'Come over here,' I said to Keita, to give myself something to do. 'Are you all right?'

'Yes.' He was. Somebody had found dry clothes for him, Chinese. But he didn't look like a coolie's son. He was too healthy and too clean, and he had a slow, unskipping way of moving that might only have been his own character, or old-money tuition. I'd never asked. 'Does it hurt?' he said.

'No, I'm up to my eyes in opium.'

'I've got to catch a ship in an hour.'

'What?'

'They don't need me here,' he explained.

'You mean you were here with me and they don't need me any more. You can come with me to England. I'm not having you go where you don't want to.'

I saw something go from him; it was hard to say what, but when he spoke, it was more slowly than he usually did, and although his voice was still small, the measure of it was grown up. There wasn't any little boy left in him.

'There are things you wouldn't do, if you had a motherless child waiting at home. Or with you. Places where you would turn back.'

'What are you talking about? I won't be going anywhere. Probably never again.'

'You will.'

'You know you can't make sweeping statements just on the strength of being exotic and foreign.'

He nearly laughed. 'Of course you'll go. You must. People are like bees. They're all workers who could be queens, with the right stuff, but once a queen-making has begun, it can't be reversed. A bee that's halfway a queen can't turn back into a worker. She'd starve. She must keep growing and then she must leave.'

'Someone's cryptic this morning. And I'm not a bee.'

'I know. Sorry. I'm not much good at all this. Look, the point is, I'm going home. I've already been away too long. I know you've never asked, but I do have a family. Lots of brothers. They'll be worried. This is my address.'

He gave me a sheet of Japanese, the flyleaf of a Bible. The picture signs were almost the same as Chinese and I could understand, though I couldn't have said them aloud. Clover Castle, in a place called Longshire.

'You needn't write, but there it is, if there's an emergency. Or . . . well. The post isn't very reliable anyway.'

'I see,' I said.

He looked hard at a point on the floor as if he were suddenly dizzy.

'What's the matter?'

'I will have forgotten in the morning,' he said.

I shook my head slightly. Will have forgotten; there were English children who couldn't have said that.

He lifted his eyes again. They were full of tears. 'I had better go or I'll miss the ship. I'm glad to have met you, Mr Tremayne.' He gazed around the room once more as though he were leaving it after years, not hours. I saw him catch himself and put on a smile. What he would look like in his thirties was clear, just briefly. He would be a late-bloomer, odd until middle age, but then he would come into himself properly and he would be lovely. I could feel them, all the lost years I'd never see.

'Keita, wait—'

'No,' he said, but he stopped. He was struggling with something. In the end it made him thump the doorframe. 'I don't like doing this, but I don't want you to have to live thinking there was no reason.' He was looking at my leg where it was set straight with a cage under the blanket. 'You don't know what this means yet, but listen anyway. When Mr Markham crosses the salt at Bedlam, you must not. But it's no good saying must not to anyone, so I've made it cannot. I'm so sorry, but if you were well, you would go with him and I want you alive at the end of it all. This was the only way I could think of to make sure of it.'

Everything had warped into the feeling of an opium dream and even knowing I was awake, I couldn't tell if I was hearing something real. 'What? How do you know Clem?'

'I don't. Get some sleep. Good luck.'

I could have made him stay. He was a little boy; if I'd told him not to talk such nonsense and to sit down, he would have. But I was opium-fogged and I felt like I was drowning, and I couldn't gather together the presence of mind to do it.

TWENTY-ONE

Peru, 1860

THE CHURCH WAS ECHOING without anyone else in it. The dark pushed up against the windows and so did the cold. I kept the fire going and the pipes running, but although I'd plenty of things to do – half-finished sketches and Spanish to learn – I couldn't settle to any of it and ended up by the window instead, with its diagonal view of the border and the streams of light where animals paced beyond the salt line. I saw a bear, but never anything tall enough to be a person. All I could think was that the border was a clever idea. It might as well have been Hadrian's Wall, but they had taken the idea and distilled it down to all that was actually required of a wall in a perfectly policed world: a line on the ground. I wondered if it was perfectly policed.

Eventually the lamps' clockwork ran down and I had to wind them up again. Moving about brought me back to myself and I was thinking about cooking something when the bell in the nave jingled.

I leaned to the window. There was nothing in the pollen, although I wouldn't have seen anything from here unless they came at an angle. After a second, the bell rang again, then again, for longer, then silence. I put my coat on, and my shoulder to the door. It was frosted shut and I had to push hard. The idea of carrying a baby across the icy bridges made my ribs tighten.

There was only one candle lit on the altar, but it was enough to show that there was no baby. It was the body of a man, half-laid-out, half-dropped, and the candlelight made his hair brilliantly red.

I leaned against the edge of the altar and felt the rough places in the stone digging into my palms. It took me a long time to push past the feeling that I shouldn't touch him. When I did, he was as cold as the altar. I had to cross my arms. He didn't seem like himself, because he was never so expressionless, even asleep. Although I waited to feel sad or angry or something decent, all that arrived was fear, not of the woods or God but of Minna. I'd have to explain what had happened and I didn't think I'd be able to lie, but I couldn't decide what the truth was. When I tried to run through the memory I couldn't tell if I'd let him go because it was right or because he had hurt me.

It was Raphael's voice that I heard at the back of my mind, asking what the hell I'd been doing. Since we had left the Navy, Clem had meandered about on archaeology expeditions while I'd been forged into a machine on the anvil of the East India Company. I was the stronger of us by far but I'd forgotten, because I was too used to feeling broken. Then I'd lashed out, and it was so much worse than anything he could ever have done to me. And I'd done it in the church of a man who was orders of magnitude stronger than the people around him but spent his life doing their laundry. I'd never felt shame like it. It burned, silent but concentrated like a welding torch until something in me vitrified. I had to burn myself on the altar candle to shock myself out of the certainty that I'd go mad with it. It helped, and I started to think more clearly.

There were marks around his neck, deep and dark. Shaped like fingers. I measured my hand against them without touching him. They belonged to someone with a bigger reach than mine. I lifted up his hand. His fingertips were grazed. He had scratched at something hard. I tipped my lamp to his nails, some of which were broken, but if there was anything under them I couldn't see it. Certainly no blood. Whoever had caught him, they had been wearing something substantial. I glanced out into the trees, where there was no light, though there should have been if someone had run back after ringing the bell. There were only the markayuq. No one and nothing had moved.

Because the cold seemed a better idea than underfloor heating, I left him on the altar with the candle and crossed his arms over his chest as well as I could with his muscles stiffening. I went back inside and leaned back against the door, my fingers tapping at the hook of my cane. I wanted to fetch Inti, but there was nothing she could have done but insist Catholicly on sitting a vigil in the snow. It was only wanting to talk to another person.

'You let him go,' I said aloud to myself. 'Live with it.'

I went to sit by the stove and play patience.

In the morning, I let myself out once it was light, which was late, because the mountains hid the sun so well, and walked up to the border. There was something maddening about deducing things from light trails in the dark and I wanted to see the trees in ordinary light, looking ordinary. It wasn't until I reached it that I saw the heaps of fur on the ground. There were dead wolves everywhere. They were all around the markayuq, some just on our side of the salt, some just before. Their necks were broken. I'd strayed in among them before I saw them and I stood still, listening hard, because it seemed too unlikely that they were all completely dead. But I didn't hear any breath except mine.

They must have come for the body; they would have known it was there from half a mile away. The top half of my spine seized at the thought of having slept through it. Wolf packs weren't quiet. They would have been calling to each other through the woods and I hadn't heard, even though I was sure I'd only dozed. And then someone had killed them all, and still I hadn't heard. It made listening seem very futile now. In front of me, the salt line had taken on a weird anti-magnetism. Even if I had decided to, logically and carefully, I couldn't have crossed. For a long time I stood looking into the trees, straining to see anything – a spark or a dying pollen trail, something moving – but it was all dead and silent.

I heard leather creaking. When I turned my head, slowly because I didn't know if I wanted to see what was there, the two nearest markayuq had twisted towards me. One was St Thomas and like always he managed to look less accusatory than curious.

'I'm not crossing,' I said aloud.

'Who are you talking to?'

I swung around. Raphael had paused on the border to re-arrange his bag of markayuq-cleaning things on his shoulder beside the old strap of the rifle. Once he had moved it, it left a red stripe where it had pulled his shirt to one side. He was so pale from the cold he might have been Spanish, but he was very alive.

'Where have you been?' I said. It came out flat.

'In the graveyard cleaning the – you watched me go in, why are you asking me?'

'Seventeen hours ago.'

'Seventeen . . . hours.' His eyes went past me to the town, where the morning light was only just coming past the mountains. Some of the houses had glass roof tiles and they sparkled.

'Where have you been?'

'I haven't been anywhere, I was just . . .'

'For God's sake,' I said, nearly laughing. 'Clem is dead on the church altar. You're telling me you just wandered off for a night-time walk? Or did you disappear so that we'd cross the border looking for you and everyone would swear to Mr Martel it wasn't you who killed us, and you could get rid of the idiot foreigners bothering your markayuq?'

Of all the imbecile things to do, confronting someone who might have murdered half the expedition should have been high on the list. But I was ashamed enough and angry enough not to care if he was dangerous. I was dangerous too. Clem had made me remember that. I knew I could take the rifle off Raphael and shoot him with it if I had to. I was almost a head taller. People talk about seeing red, but I didn't. I only saw in greater focus.

'He's what?' His voice cracked and he put his hand to the mossy tree trunk beside us.

'Was it you?'

'No! Stop – stop.' He was having trouble talking; he was breathing too fast and too shallow. Where he was holding the moss, his fingernails had lost all their colour. There were pine needles caught in the folds of his shirt, and pollen; whenever he moved, it glowed away from him in wisps, more where the wind was catching him down his left side. He might have been evanescing into the frozen morning. I frowned. It was hard to think that he'd look like this if he had been set up in a tent somewhere. A spider peeped around his collar. I scooped it off him and showed him, although not for long before it bounced out of my hand and on to the tree. He jerked away and then opened his hand properly. Strands of web stretched between his shirt cuff and the first joint of his fingers. He scrubbed it off, fast, then stayed very still. His breath was almost gone.

'Come inside,' I said at last.

'I can't move.' He was nearly too quiet to hear. 'I'll be along in a minute.'

Further towards the border, where the pollen was thicker, it made those cold cinder patterns. It was difficult to believe there could be so much of it in the snow, but then, the vines in the trees were barely dead – the frost had killed them only this week. It was supposed to be high summer. My leg panged from having been still and cold for too long, but I couldn't bring myself to sit down in the roots, which were all grey with rime. He was holding his fingertips two inches off my chest, to stop me coming any nearer. They shook.

'Tell me what happened,' I said. 'And please be convincing.'

'Just – same as always but longer.' He was struggling in English again and I saw him reach for the word, but he couldn't catch it. 'It is sometimes.'

At first I didn't understand, but then I fell very still and realised I was either being told the honest truth, or a lie he had been preparing since he had first frozen by the statue on the river in Sandia.

'Catalepsy,' I said for him. 'For that long?'

'There are long spells. Longer than this, but I didn't expect . . . I wasn't due one. Or I would have told you,' he said, much more hotly than before. 'I would have told you to watch for it.'

I tried to decide. He didn't meet my eye again. At Martel's house he had been like something from a goldsmith's, but he was as pale as me now and somehow even his hair was faded. It was brown, not black. All that seemed certain was that he had been outside for all that time. I couldn't tell if it was a feat of endurance someone strong enough and zealous enough might just manage on willpower.

'If I'd killed him, I wouldn't be *talking* to you now,' he said softly. He had to go into Spanish. If he was pretending panic, I'd never seen anyone pretend so well or so accurately. 'I'd have shot you. No?'

'There are a thousand things here I don't know. I feel like we've been edging around a set of laws nobody can explain since we arrived.' I motioned at the border. 'I'm not nearly in possession of all the facts, I do know that. I don't know anything beyond the border. I don't know who you talk to in there, I don't know how the hell they make statues look like they walk or why, I don't understand what your religion is, or what it might require of you. None of it makes any sense. I am in no position to make grand sweeping deductions about what you might or might not have done.'

'I swear to you, I didn't do it. I thought I was only gone for ten minutes until just now.'

There was nothing to say one way or another. Only whether or not I wanted to believe him. I did want to. The ferocious clarity that had let me stare him down before left me, draining into the pine needles, and without it I felt exhausted. Slowly, I took off my coat. He took it without arguing and shook out the last of the pollen and the needles from his own clothes before he shrugged into it. Without it, the wind cut straight through my waistcoat.

'Thank you.'

'Seventeen hours. You should be dead. You should have been dead sixteen hours ago, dressed like this. Were you sheltered?'

'No. Just in the graveyard.'

He pushed his hands through his hair. There was frost in it. He frowned when he noticed what was around us. 'Wolves. When did this happen?'

'I don't know. I didn't hear anything. I think they came for Clem's body.'

'They will have been – they won't let a pack of wolves into Bedlam.' He motioned back over the salt line to say that he meant the people inside. 'The border works both ways.'

I scanned the trees again. I couldn't see how they could possibly stay hidden always. The pollen showed everything that moved; everything, even moths. Even trained soldiers had to shift and go for a walk sometimes.

'Well – better go in,' I said. I leaned against the tree to turn round on the uneven ground, which was all bumpy with roots. 'Can you move now?'

He glanced up and nodded. At Martel's his eyes had been black, but now they were shot through with grey penny-scratch lines. He was losing his colours. It had been happening all week. I thought of how often I'd seen red in his hair when there shouldn't have been any, when it had been so black at first, like everyone else's here.

'Why did Markham go out? I've spent all week telling you not to.'

'He thought that there was a camp of quinine suppliers over the border, not Chuncho, and that you'd gone to warn them we were here.'

He didn't seem indignant or worried or even surprised. 'Everyone who comes here thinks that before long.' He sighed. 'We'll have a funeral tomorrow, if you're happy for him to stay here.'

'Is it not possible to take a body back over the mountains?'

'It wouldn't be dignified.'

'Tomorrow, then,' I said. I heard my own voice like it came from a long way off. I hadn't thought I would have to leave him behind.

'Wish it could have been you instead,' Raphael said absently, cat's-cradling his rosary.

'What?'

He spun the cross once. 'You're quite light.'

I smiled. He pulled the church door open and turned back to help me up the step. I took his hand and let him pull me inside, the backs of my shirtsleeves cold and damp with the snow blowing in from along the valley and my teeth aching from having been set hard for too long. I still couldn't decide whether I should believe him or not. But I was too tired and too cold to argue, and for that moment at least I loved him for having made the idea of the funeral that bit less heavy, like he had put his shoulder under mine to share the weight.

TWENTY-TWO

WHILE WE HAD BEEN talking, I'd heard chinking and voices in the background, closer than the village, but I hadn't paid any attention. They must have arrived just as I was leaving, because when we went through into the kitchen, it was full of people, and so was the flat land just outside. Martel sat back and smiled. Hernandez and Quispe were with him, still in their coats. Beyond them, through the windows, ten or twelve men were clearing the snow to stake up tents. They had already started cooking fires with the efficient domesticity of people used to moving miles between meals.

'There you are,' Martel said, standing up. 'My God. We arrived and Mr Markham was dead and you two were gone and the wretched carver was telling us mad stories.'

'I was only out for ten minutes just now,' I said. 'Raphael was coming back when I went.'

He smiled. 'Coming back from where, my dear?' he said to Raphael. 'Just at the moment one of the expeditionaries dies and ends up on your altar. Think about it carefully.'

'I was in the forest. I lost a day and a night.'

Martel must have known about the catalepsy, because he didn't question it. 'And what happened to Mr Markham?'

'He tried to go into the woods last night,' I said. 'They brought him back about an hour later.'

'So, Raphael. Did you kill him or did you only tell someone else to?'

'Neither. It was just – I was just stuck. It's happened before. You know it has.'

Martel's gun was on the table, a pretty revolver with filigree work on the handle. When he picked it up, around the barrel, I thought he only meant to put it away, but he hit Raphael in the face with it. 'Not good enough. I'm afraid I've got to arrest you. We're going back to Azangaro.'

'I don't think—' I began, less because I was sure of Raphael's innocence than because it wrenched at something in me to see how the blow had spun him. 'He'd have killed me too if—'

'In a world that ran on common sense, yes. But he didn't want to kill you. He did it because Mr Markham crossed the border, nothing else. It's held a particular kind of sacrilege and you haven't seen gibbering religious madmen until you've seen these people and their border. But we can't go now, we've just walked up the river. Quispe, keep an eye on him, make sure he doesn't kill anyone else. If that door has a lock on it, use it,' he added, nodding towards the chapel.

'I need him for the funeral,' I said.

'Then we shall go straight after.'

It was the moment to tell him about the quinine, but I couldn't stand there talking any more. Raphael looked like he was about to collapse and I had a strong feeling they would have been happy to leave him on the floor. He had turned his head away just in time and the butt of the gun hadn't taken out his eye, only grazed the bone below it. I couldn't tell if he had felt the pain, but he had definitely felt the impact. I levered him out by his elbow to get some snow against his eye and the rest of him away from Martel. I took him into the chapel and put him by the pipes to warm up, and a blanket around him. Quispe followed but he kept back. He looked worried, like he had just watched a boy flicking pebbles at something in a zoo with flimsy fences.

'I'm fine,' Raphael said quietly, but he sounded hazy.

'You can't feel what you are, don't be stupid. Stay there.'

'Wait. Harry, don't . . .'

'I'll be back. Torment Quispe for a few minutes.' I stayed where I was for a second, my heart thudding. I'd believed him about the catalepsy. There was no need to try and make me believe in fairytales too.

If the catalepsy was a lie, it was one he had thought through very well and maintained despite everything. As if he were just carrying on the day he had lost, from mid afternoon and not early morning, he was exhausted by six and in bed by seven, though usually he was up until midnight. He got up at three in the morning, his internal clock still apparently skewed by hours. There was no lock on the chapel door to keep him from walking straight past Quispe, who was asleep in a chair by the threshold. Like always, Raphael was quiet, but something about the pitch of the water bubbling in the stove woke me up. Half to see if he really was as awake as he would have been at a normal time, half to see if he was all right, I dragged myself up to have a cup of hot water while he made himself coffee. When he saw me, he took down a little jar of rich brown powder and handed it over, with its own small spoon. Because he had been over the border for so long, breathing pollen, it had seeped into his blood and showed now in the veins in the underside of his wrist.

'Cacao,' he explained. I'd started to avoid saying cocoa too. It sounded too close to coca, and coco, which meant coconut, and since we both dropped Spanish into English and English into Spanish, it was a bit dangerous.

I didn't take it. 'Everyone says that might as well be gold dust.'

'Someone gave it to me. It'll help you sleep, anyway.' There was half a jug of milk almost frozen on the outside window ledge. Raphael tipped it into one of the bronze pans. He paused with his fingertips still on the handle, then picked up a tea towel and folded it across his hand before he moved the pan, which was already hot from having sat on the stove all evening. I smiled, much more pleased with that than I should have been.

'Four spoons,' he said, nodding at the jar. 'It's already mixed with sugar.'

He had taken his coffee back to the table and, while he let it cool down, he started to rivet together a new seam on what was going to be a set of markayuq leathers, the same I'd seen upstairs. The pegs were all gold but never the same shade and all shaped differently: puma heads and leaves, acorns. Although he had two pollen lamps ticking just in front of him, he was slow with the rivet gun.

'Why aren't you escaping?' I asked. 'If he accuses you of murder . . .'

'He won't. He knows I didn't do it.'

Outside, in among the tents, a couple of fires were still burning, though I couldn't see anyone moving about. Martel's men had put their tents up in an interlocking row so that they all shielded each other from the wind. There was still lamplight inside one of them, and the silhouette of a man reading.

When I came back to the table, Raphael watched me as if he was about to talk, didn't, then started after I'd almost forgotten that I'd thought he might. 'I've been putting off the bees. We've a hive, for wax. I need to take out the honeycombs before we go. Could you help me?'

I put my cup down. Part of me thought I shouldn't be going into the dark with him while I still wasn't sure what had happened to Clem.

'I hate bees,' he said, and I believed him then, because he was too rigid and too proud to have chosen that for a lie.

'Let me find my coat.'

He was rewinding the pollen lamps and gave me one once I came back. I put it in my pocket while I got my scarf on and the buttons done up, and it glowed a little even through the thick wool.

'If I do anything you don't like, shoot me.' He gave me his rifle too. The strap was much older than the gun; it was so well-worn that the leather was soft, even at the stitched edges. I looped it on and felt strange to have the familiar weight against the back of my ribs again after so long. It made the bruises ache.

When I followed him out, he took me to the front of the church and the cliff, where the view of the town was full of lamplight that glittered in the glass places. A little stairway in the rock led to a small plateau. There wasn't room for much, but it was full of useful things – opium poppies, a dense crop of them, dead now in the snow; cooking herbs; a stout coffee tree, planted to one side so that it would have room to walk; and, screened by that, a beehive. He hung his lamp over a hook in the side. It had a glass front. Inside the bees were sleepy but moving, just, in a way that didn't look like it was supposed to be seen. It was more like the peristalsis inside one big thing than lots of small ones. The bees stirred more when they saw the light.

'Can't someone else keep a hive, if you don't like it?' I asked as he hinged up the lid. The bees mumbled.

'The wax is for the markayuq, and the knot cords. It's hieratic.' He took his hands back too quickly. 'You take out each rack and scrape the wax off. They won't hurt you. Just go slowly.'

'They're lovely,' I said, stroking a big one with my knuckle. It wiggled. They were black and a fine deep red. Peruvian bees were stingless, I knew from somewhere, although they did bite.

He gave me a pipette. 'Sugar water. Put it in the leftover cells.' He stood back with his arms folded. I ran his knife down the combs and watched them crumble. The honey was sticky enough to make them fall slowly, slowly enough for me to catch it all in a bowl. The quiet welled and I didn't break it, waiting for him to say why we were out here.

'Martel is a quinine supplier.'

I looked back.

'You have to come back with us to Azangaro. Tell him you've given up and it's not worth all this. Don't argue with him, don't try to arrange another guide. The men he's brought, they are not here to help clear the path. The path doesn't go anywhere. They blew it up years ago. He isn't angry with me because Markham's dead. He's angry because you're still alive and still here. He never believed you about the coffee; he knew what you came for. Those men are here to find you if you run. They'll kill you.'

'Did you kill Clem?' I said again.

'No.'

I foundered. 'But if you were just supposed to kill us both – why did Martel send us with you in the first place? He could have just let us wander off and get shot by someone like Manuel.'

'It isn't impossible to go through the forest,' he said, very quietly. 'People have come out alive before, with quinine. I was supposed to make certain that you didn't. Either persuade you to turn back or shoot you.'

'Then why did you keep us waiting, why did you say there was a way around? Why didn't you just let us go over the border when—'

'I hoped you'd give up and go home.' He let his breath out. 'I've been trying to keep you safe. I only let you send word to Martel because I hoped waiting for him would keep you out of the forest for another few days. That was a few more days to scare you into leaving. The – man who attacked you. I asked him to, I'm sorry.' He really did look sorry.

'I knew it. I was too bloody polite to say. Serves me right.'

'It seemed like the quickest way to make you leave. I didn't know you were going to stick with it like a donkey—'

'Or like a person who does his job properly—'

'God, you're mad, all of you from the bloody India Office! What, have they got your children in a shed somewhere?'

'I'm mad – what the hell were *you* thinking?' I said, feeling like I might drown in the senselessness of it. 'What if Clem had managed to get through? You were keeping us safe but – we were walking bombs for you, all that time! If he had got anything out of those woods, the quinine suppliers would have known it had to come from round here. High-yield quinine doesn't come from anywhere else! Bedlam would have been destroyed. Wouldn't it? Why in God's name didn't you shoot us the second we arrived? Or before, when Manuel attacked us? Letting us wander about, and when you have such powerful catalepsy you might not know if you'd lost an hour or five – we could have done anything! It was idiotic! What were you playing at?'

'What's the point of not taking innocent men into the woods and shooting them in the head?' he said sharply. 'How about not wanting to? I've had enough.'

I was already shaking my head, annoyed to be given a moral scruple instead of a reason from someone who was plainly used to doing whatever he had to, before I heard what he had actually said. 'Hold on. You've had enough – you mean you did it before,' I said. 'The Dutch.'

He nodded once. Everything about him exuded that old anti-magnetic pressure he'd had at Martel's, the one that said not to ask him anything else about it and to leave him the hell alone, but I had a decent resistance to it now, like the altitude.

'Why are we different?' I said, still softly, because a shadow had come into the window of the church above us. Quispe, fetching a glass of water.

'If you don't believe me, stay.'

'No, answer the question. If I turn back now with no quinine, I'm finished, so I need to know. Because it sounds to me like you don't want foreigners tramping through your holy woods, so you're telling me the one thing that will force me to leave. I can't march up to Martel and ask him if he's a quinine supplier; he'll shoot me if he is. I only have your word. Come on. What's different? Your village depends on it but you can't bring yourself to kill me despite having done it before – why? Do you need me for something? You want me to go back to the India Office and tell them nothing's here? I can't. Half of India is dying of a disease that can only be cured by the medicine in those woods, so—'

'Because I knew your grandfather,' he snapped, and then all the fight went from him as fast as it had come and he only looked hopeless. 'And you look like him.'

I couldn't face him and think at the same time. I turned back to the hive and edged the last of the honey wax on to the plate. The bees had come to explore my hands, but it was a nice feeling. From the corner of my eye I could just see Raphael watching fixedly in the way I would have watched someone performing surgery on his own eye. 'Take the honey,' I told him. 'I can't carry that and the cane at once.'

I held the door open for him on the way back in. He set the honey on the table, then took out a bottle of Jamaica rum from a cupboard and poured us both a glass. Once he had given me mine, he stood breathing the fumes of his and I realised he didn't like the smell of the honey. Of course he didn't; he spent every day of his life smelling of beeswax from cleaning the markayuq. Which accounted for his hating the bees as well.

'Where did you find Jamaica rum out here?' I asked, picking up the bottle. It was three-quarters full still, although the date on the label was from the middle of last century. 'This is what the smugglers at home bring in,' I said.

'I know.'

I felt the way I did when I was about to dive into deep water. The last pause was to look for shadows that might be rocks. There were plenty that might have been, but nothing broke the surface and the more I looked the fewer there were. 'Which is . . . why you speak last century's English. And you recognised me. At Martel's. And . . . that letter was for you, not your uncle.'

He nodded once, very slightly.

'Inti's story was true. You disappeared for seventy years.'

'Yes.'

'Where?'

'Just . . .' he waved towards the forest. 'About half a mile inside. It was the same as yesterday. But longer.'

'Jesus, Raphael.'

'What was I meant to say?' he snapped.

'I'm not Jesusing at you. I meant, what a bloody horrible thing to happen to anyone. What happens, how do you not starve to death? Or – age?'

He lifted his shoulder. 'It isn't sleep. You stop, it's like being frozen. Blink and it's gone. When you wake it looks like the light changes suddenly.' He was quiet for a while. 'You go out for a few days at first when you're small, then a month, then a year, then three; little intervening spells in-between – fifteen minutes, twenty – but those get longer too when you come up to a big one. Anyone here will tell you, everyone knows how priests are, everyone . . . counts, from the second you arrive.' He looked tired. 'Harry soon found out. I mean your grandfather. He was here when it happened.' He was looking into the rum. 'When I came back there was a letter from him with his address.'

'Did you write?'

'No. Inti said his son had stopped coming. It seemed a bit late.'

I poured us both some more rum, thinking. 'How long can it last? One of these . . . frozen spells.'

'A hundred years, if you're healthy otherwise. If not . . . two hundred. Longer. You never wake properly.' He sounded like he was staring into an endlessly deep gorge. I didn't ask if he knew anyone who had slept for two hundred years.

'So all priests have it . . . how?'

'Other way round. If you have it, you become a priest here.'

'How do they know which children to send? The – people who bring children, I mean,' I said, not wanting to say Chuncho when he didn't like the word. 'You wouldn't know if a baby had catalepsy.'

'They bring us when we're ten.' He breathed between sentences, for long enough to let me squeak if I wanted to, to make him say what was in the forest, who the people were, but I didn't want to. 'There are only a few families left that carry the disease, so they know more or less who to watch. It's rare now; sometimes you wait a hundred years for a child to manifest it. Which is why it was so late, before they brought Aquila. He'll be next, after me, when he's old enough. Well. He almost is. I was his age when I took over.'

'And when he can take over, what happens to you?'

'I can leave.'

'And go where?'

He nodded towards the forest where the pollen glow looked black-striped, because it silhouetted the trees. 'Home. You do your time in Bedlam and after that they take care of you. There's a monastery.'

'We're not talking about some little tribe of raiders getting ratty about their territory, are we?'

'No.' He hesitated as if he wouldn't go on, but he was only choosing words. 'The border isn't about territory, exactly. It's a quarantine line. Sick people on this side, healthy people on the other side. It's a religious . . . do you know?'

'Clem said you have to be whole, for the gods. He said human sacrifices were always healthy virgins, in Inca times.'

'Oh, they still are,' he said, shaking his head. He put his hands up a little when I widened my eyes at him. 'I knew a boy. But yes. And that's holy land, in there. Like the Vatican. So. If you've got a limp, you're out. But priests are immune to everything; it's something to do with what we already have. I don't know. So we've always been sent out to the hospital colonies.' He was rubbing his hand down his other wrist like he was pushing away something crawling. 'Then there was smallpox in Cuzco and it became much stricter. No one from this side could cross. Then the Spanish arrived too and they closed it permanently. There used to be half a dozen hospitals all along this river but Bedlam is all that's left and they only maintain this place because they need the salt. I'm not supposed to be talking about it,' he added abruptly.

'It's all right. I don't care who they are. I was only asking because I was trying to tell if by monastery you mean a hut on a cliff somewhere or a nice place with hot water and proper doctors.'

He smiled. 'It's not a hut.'

'Good.' I finished my rum. 'Do you mind if I have some honey?'

'Have the lot, get it off my table. I only want the wax.'

'Thanks.'

He watched me spread the honey over some bread. 'Are you drawing a bee?'

'Y . . . es.' I tipped the bread so that the head-splodge would run and make antennae, then showed him.

He laughed. It showed how he had been when he was younger. Mild-mannered and handsome. In a shilling-spin of an instant I realised that he wasn't crude work but the ruin of something fine. The same as everything else here. I felt ashamed for not having noticed before. There was a knack to seeing how things had used to be but I'd never had it; I was no archaeologist. The new understanding lit up the edges of my mind and like always they were closer and more worn than I would have liked or thought.

'Listen,' I said at last. 'Once I'm gone, get everyone out of here. The army will be coming. The British army.'

'What?'

'No one thought we would be able to do this. Come out with cinchona cuttings, I mean. The real point of this expedition was to make a good map and give the army a reason to come. Clem is Sir Clements; his death is a good enough reason, and they'll use it.'

He frowned. 'What would you have done if he hadn't got himself killed?'

'He didn't get himself killed, I did. I could have stopped him but I didn't because I had orders to do it if it looked like we wouldn't be able to bring out any cuttings.' It came out like a confession more than an explanation. I swallowed. He wasn't even looking at me now, but hard at the floor. 'I'm sorry. It was better than waiting for the Navy to shell Lima—'

'How the fuck is it better?'

'Because they won't come at all if I can bring out some cuttings now. Do you think Martel would help if I told him it was that or the army?'

'No, I think he'd shoot you for having made a fool of him.'

'What about you?' I asked, business-like and clear, and hating myself.

He straightened as if I'd let a little firework go off too close to him. I thought he was going to kill me; for being a snake, for bringing it all to his home – for not, in the end, being a thing like my grandfather, though I'd brought his ghost. When he did speak again, his voice was weakening. 'I can't take plant cuttings.' He looked up just enough to show me his eyes. There was a haze over the colour, those grey penny-scratches I'd noticed before but more pronounced even since this morning. 'I can't see small things close to. But I will take you through. We can go in daylight when the pollen trails won't show so much.'

'You can get us past . . . whoever watches the border?'

'Yes.'

I pushed my hand, still sore, round the hook of my cane. I was fitter than I had been at home, much, but miles through the woods and miles back was still impossible. 'Can we ride through?'

'No. But it will only take a couple of days, and I can help your leg.'

'How?'

'If I can get you walking, will you come with me?'

I frowned. 'Yes. But—'

'Good. Meet me by St Thomas after the funeral. Bring what you'd be taking with you to go back to Azangaro. I'll take the tent from Markham's things.' He was quiet for a second. I couldn't tell if he was angry. It was much worse than his normal bad temper. 'I can tell Martel you're dead. If you go back avoiding Bedlam and Azangaro once you have your cuttings, he'll never know different. I can show you how to go through Bolivia. There are Indians who will help you if you tell them you came from here. It'll take years to grow a quinine plantation, won't it?'

'Yes,' I said. Exactly what I'd hoped would happen was happening, but it was a Pyrrhic victory now it was here. I hadn't realised even when he had been gone that what he thought of me mattered. I'd been pleased, in that stupid little-boy way, that he had thought I was more or less acceptable even when Clem wasn't.

'By the time he hears of it, the cuttings could have come from anywhere.'

'Right.'

'Good then.'

I left him riveting the markayuq leathers, slowly, because he was doing it by touch. Before I went, I fitted a bowl over the honey and put it in the cupboard so he wouldn't catch the smell of it. In the little chapel I fell asleep wondering if he might just shoot me anyway now, whether I looked like his friend or not.

PART FOUR

TWENTY-THREE

THE ADMINISTRATIVE ORDINARINESS OF a death took over in the morning. The village was so small that there was no need for a delay before a funeral; Raphael rang the church bell and people came straightaway, wrapped in black shawls. I didn't hear any of it, because I slept right up until he came in and touched my shoulder and said it was time to go. It made me jump and I caught his wrist. He only kept still and waited for me to wake up properly. He was all neat and ironed in clerical black again. In the light through the glass bricks, his hair was red – much darker than Clem's, but still red. I didn't ask what was happening to him. I hated it when people asked too much about my leg.

I took my bag with me. Martel asked me why and I said it was because the church was always unlocked and some things had been stolen before. He seemed to think that was fair enough and left me with my heart going fast.

In a rush I wanted just to get back to Azangaro and go home. I felt burned through. I'd have to tell Minna what had happened and Sing would need to know about Martel but after that I could sleep without thinking someone might kill me.

But then I'd be packed off to the parsonage in Truro if it was still tenantless. Sing would lose his job. The army would come to Bedlam and trample it. I had to shut my eyes for a second. I'd told Raphael through the wall at Martel's house that I'd rather be shot by a quinine supplier than leave. I'd nearly been joking, but not really. Whatever Raphael meant to do, whether it was a bullet in the head or real help, it was going to be better than home.

Aquila had dug a grave on the far side of the border. It was a Latin mass, short, because everyone was standing and it was bitterly cold in the shade of the trees. It was a while before I noticed it was raining, and another lag before I realised how odd that was, when outside in the open, where the trees didn't reach, snow was still coming down. Just as I did, though, other people noticed too and looked up, hands open. A heavy drop landed on my sleeve. It wasn't water. It was liquid silver and the impact sprayed the big drop into lots of little ones that skittered away, off my arm altogether or under the cuff of my sleeve, shuddering. When I searched the ground, trying to follow one, the pine needles were covered in silvery beads. They were sinking into the earth, but for now it looked like someone had sprayed molten mirror over the whole graveyard.

'It's mercury,' Inti said. 'It comes from the trees. They drag it up from the graves and when it's cold they weep.'

I stared upward, because it shouldn't have been possible. Mercury, even if there had been pools of it underground, should have vapoured off through the tiny capillaries in leaves or pine needles, but the air was full of it. Inti caught a handful to show me how it juddered and ran.

'Lucky to see it,' she said. 'The forest must like Mr Markham. It's very lucky for the quicksilver trees to cry at a funeral.'

'I don't – how is there mercury?' I said helplessly.

'Oh, from the miners. You know Huancavelica? The mercury mine. Anyway, if you work with mercury enough, it gets into you. Drives you mad, kills you. Years and years ago a doctor set up a pilgrimage route so that miners who had served out their labour draft could come here and recover. Or die. Once they're buried, the bodies rot away but the mercury in them just runs downhill and hits the glass. It pools right around the roots of the trees. And – quicksilver rain.'

'But it shouldn't . . .' I gave up and sat down on a root of the nearest tree, next to a screaming face.

'It doesn't work with other kinds of tree,' she offered. 'Just whitewoods. That's her, by the way.' She pointed at the graveyard markayuq.

'What?'

'The doctor who brought the miners. That's her. She doesn't move much. There's something wrong with her. Mercury poisoning probably, Ra-cha thinks.'

'Oh . . . right.'

After the service, I made my way over to St Thomas, where Raphael was waiting among people praying or heading across to the other markayuq with salt and glass shells and knot cords. The clinking of the salt vials dropping sounded higher, because the amphorae were fuller than before. I put one in too, slowly, not sure what I was praying for. Past me, Raphael was watching Martel, Quispe and Hernandez going back to the church, where the men they had brought were taking down the tents. Quispe had stuck close to Raphael all morning, but he had eased back for the mass with a respect for the ceremony that made it clear he would have been unhappy, trying to keep a priest in a firm grip on holy ground. Once they were out of sight, Raphael caught my eye and nodded along the border, towards the river path, still blocked by snow.

'Have a walk that way. I'll come and find you.' He crossed the salt where we were, as if he were going to clean the graveyard markayuq. Where his steps left marks in the frosty grass, the mercury welled in the shape of his soles.

I did as he said and walked close to the salt where the snow was thinner. Nobody noticed, or if they did, they must have thought it was natural enough for me to want to walk by myself for a little while. He ghosted with me on the other side about thirty yards in. The pollen trail was faint and I wouldn't have seen it if I hadn't been looking for it. He was moving slowly to match me, and slower movement meant less of a pollen flare.

Once we were around the bend, he came back over the salt for me. Even such a short distance from town, everything was silent. The snow had muffled any noises from the woods and there was nothing except the sigh of the river, four hundred feet down the cliff. Most of it was frozen, but the three stripes of lensed sun in front of the stacks had melted it. Where it had run through to the other side and refrozen, the ice was mirrory.

'Right,' he said softly. 'I've got something to help you walk. It's from Inti. She measured you for it on that first morning.'

He lifted a wooden band out of his backpack. It was hinged and it had a bronze clasp, and carvings of dragons chased each other through vines and trees all around it. He held it straight between both hands, then let it go in the air. Instead of falling, it spun softly between his fingertips, as if he were holding a pair of magnets. He wasn't. He let his hands drop to show me. The gilt eyes of the dragons winked as the band moved.

'It's whitewood? But nothing in town . . .' I trailed off when I remembered the baby's toy horse, then Inti's sawdust.

He touched the tree beside us. 'These trees are young. That wood is from further into the forest. Fewer forest fires in there. The older the tree, the better the lift. It's how the gantries in town bear the weight of all the buildings. I don't know what's in it, but it works. Ready?'

I nodded.

He took it from the air again and held out the rifle. 'Take that.' He knelt down in the snow. 'When it's on, it will take your weight on this side. You have to lean into it or you'll fall over.'

I stayed still. He glanced up at me and then clicked the band round my bad leg, just above the scar. It did exactly what he'd said it would. There was suddenly no weight on my left leg. It was like I'd sat down; the pain in the scar vanished and I was nudged sideways, as though someone had started to lift me up, just from my hip. But I caught my balance in time, and like he'd said, I had to lean into it, or rather, spread my weight like I would have if there had been nothing wrong with my leg at all, but after so long limping it felt like leaning to the left.

When I touched the wooden band, it was smooth, with no honeycomb bumps, though the pattern was visible. Inti had sealed it and varnished it watertight. I took a slow pace forward. My whole balance felt askew, but nothing hurt. I thought too much about it and stumbled. He caught my elbows and balanced me like a coin, then walked backward a few steps and held his hands out to make me follow. I did, better this time.

'That's – it doesn't hurt.'

'Good. Try a bit further. Over the roots.'

I took his hand when he held it out and for the next few minutes he kept me balanced until I could manage properly by myself. He was cold, like always, though his coat was buttoned up. In bright light, with his hair turned that dark red and never having regained all the colour in his skin, he looked nationless.

'We have to go if we're going,' he said. He must have felt me shaking, but he didn't say anything about it. 'Are we?'

I nodded and couldn't keep a grasp of everything. I'd never been so happy, though an idiot could have seen that Raphael might only have given me the whitewood to make sure I trusted him for now, while a gunshot would still have been heard loud and clear in town.

I crossed the salt slowly. Even after only a week of being told not to, my heart tried to squash itself back against my spine. My breath steamed staccato because I was shivering. I expected to see arrows coming at us, but nothing did. Nothing moved in the trees at all.

'Come on,' he said. 'Whatever you see, don't stop to look at it. Keep going and stick close to me. They won't think you're a foreigner if we stay together.'

I nearly laughed. 'How could they think I wasn't? Look at me.'

He glanced back. 'Look at me. I'll fade a lot more than this; they've seen blond priests before.'

'What causes it?'

'Same as the catalepsy. Hurry up,' he said, as if we were on an ordinary road. I followed him, completely unable to tell if he was leading me to a burial pit somewhere or if we would have cinchona cuttings this time tomorrow. My leg still didn't hurt.

Within five hundred yards, the white trees stood closer together than they did at the border. The ground was always uneven with their roots, which tangled sometimes and made odd archways and lifts in the soil. The pollen traced our wakes more and more perfectly the further in we went and the thicker it became. It was still cold, but the only snow was the powdery stuff that had blown in from the cliff. When I looked back, the line of daylight already seemed distant. Under the canopy there was no light at all except the pollen. The branches were so thick I didn't think they would have let through much sunlight even without the snow roofing them.

There was life inside, much more than I'd thought. Above us the air was criss-crossed with light trails where birds flitted, and what might have been bats, and whatever insects had survived the cold. Somewhere, not so far off as I would have liked, a bear roared. Raphael slowed down, but not for that. There was a tree, half-choked by vines, just on the edge of what we were using as a path.

It had grown around something, the branches warped into curves not their own. In places, tiny rags were caught in the bark. The original something had been torn free. There was new growth and new, tiny twigs poking through where they couldn't have before, but as we came level to it, the shape of what had been there became clearer. One branch still held the outline of a person's ribs; another, half-broken outward, just about traced a shoulder and an arm. It was part tree and part candle ivy, in blossom still. The petals, as they fell, rained golden lines down through the pollen in the air. Raphael looked away. He didn't say anything and nor did I. He wouldn't want to hear that I'd seen a drawing of it or that I knew there were freckles across his shoulders. He wouldn't want to hear, either, that my father had gone over the border looking for him.

Some of the snapped branches were thick, but it was nothing an axe couldn't have helped. But then, that would have relied on having an axe, and on knowing that Raphael had been alive to help. I'd seen how pale he had gone after even one night out in this cold. It would have been forty years by the time Dad found him; forty years of being pulled slowly back into the tree, of moss and vines and pine needles, spiders, and all the small coiling ways the woods had of making things their own. It would have taken a long, careful study to see that he wasn't a carving and, even after that, it would have been mad to check for a pulse. This was sacrifice country. Dad would have thought he had found a dead man.

'How's the manacle?' Raphael said.

'It's good. Thank you.'

Where some petals had fallen across his sleeve he pushed them off. He was holding his rosary too hard. Some monkeys shrieked and shot away from us. Their tails left curls in the pollen wakes. It was hard to imagine that anyone watching could have failed to notice us by now, or notice that someone was there at least.

He overheard me thinking. 'We would have heard by now if anyone felt strongly about it.'

'But everyone else—'

'Came in here alone, without any permission, without a priest.'

I almost asked him who Dad could have come with in that case, but stopped myself in time.

We both looked over at a flash of person-sized movement a few trees away from us. I froze, because I thought there was a man standing there, but it was only a markayuq. It was turning its head as if it were watching us go. It looked like the one from the graveyard, but then, it made a sad sort of sense that the sculptors might have used the same model again and again, like Hadrian had – if they were all a lost empress, or someone's son.

'Aren't we a bit far away to have set it off?' I said quietly.

'No. Keep walking. Don't look at her. They're shibboleths. If you go up to them to see how they work, everyone knows you're not from round here.'

So I kept going, without looking to the side, although every so often, especially if we paused, which we still had to because while the whitewood band took the weight off my leg it didn't negate the pull of the scarring altogether, I saw slow movement from the corners of my eyes: markayuq being set off and shifting, never close.

'The whole forest floor must be rigged with clockwork,' I said after a while, feeling strange, because if it was rigged with clockwork it was too easy to imagine what else it might be rigged with.

'Just don't pay any attention to them. Let's stop properly. We'll eat something, and I want to teach you a prayer in Old Quechua. If you know it you're going to sound more genuine if push comes to shove. Like neck verse.'

We settled down among the roots of a tree full of dying blossom and candle ivy seedheads caging their tiny caches of pollen. While he taught me the words, he held a knot cord to show me how they were written too. It didn't sound like modern Quechua. Or, it did; it was recognisably the same language, but it had no Spanish in it, none of the Spanish rhythms that I hadn't even noticed before. It sounded heavy to me, although I couldn't have said why. The knotting was too complicated to understand in a twenty-minute sitting.

It was done in numbers, but numbers together formed codes that, like Chinese characters, ran together to make meanings. My brain stalled when he tried to explain it.

'It clicks one morning,' he said in the end. 'You'd see it if you looked at it for long enough. Anyway. All right to go on?'

I nodded. I felt peculiar, because I was starting to realise that if he meant to shoot me in a mile's time, he wouldn't have bothered to teach me prayers or knot writing. It wasn't even relief. In my mind I'd narrowed my expectations of the future down to about an hour. To have it open up suddenly, into what might have been days or years, felt like coming out from a wardrobe onto a great wide beach. Although I didn't understand it, I kept running my fingertips across the knot cord he had tied round my wrist, feeling the bumps and the grain of the twine. It was a reassuring thing to touch.

'So you're not angry, then?' It felt like a jinx to ask but I couldn't help it.

'Angry about what?'

'All this.'

'No.' He waited for me to catch up. 'Just – glad of the company.'

I didn't understand, and then I did. He didn't mean for the walk. The worst anyone else in Bedlam had done probably involved a bit of unkindness or some stolen pineapples. It would have been lonely to be the only one who had done worse.

Off to our left, a markayuq watched us go. It was closer than the last ones. Raphael veered away from me to give it a prayer cord too and came back without saying anything.

TWENTY-FOUR

CROSSING THE FOREST FLOOR was so slow we barely covered a mile an hour. I felt, in my foundations, which Clem said were magnetic ore, that we were curving. Twice we had to double back, and when we did I felt like we had cut too steeply into that curve. It was like tracing the outer edge of an hourglass. I wondered what we were avoiding, but I didn't ask. All the while, I didn't see anyone – not one solitary glimpse of an arrow fletching in the trees – but the sense of being watched never went away.

Despite the whitewood band, my leg started to feel sore after every mile or so and we paused often, never too close to a markayuq and always facing away from it, which felt itchy, but I was a lot better at this kind of thing than Orpheus and I never looked back. I started to enjoy the walk. The way tipped us gradually downhill and it was getting warmer – even the ground was starting to feel warm, which must have been something volcanic more than falling altitude, but either way it was lovely. The tree roots trapped the heat. There wasn't much space to sit comfortably and Raphael bumped down with his shoulder against mine, which propped me up just at the angle that kept my back from aching. I shut my eyes, not asleep but not sure I could go on much further either. As he knotted another string I felt the tendons in his arm moving. After a while he stopped and I straightened up.

'You're very pale,' he said. He was holding the cord wound over his hands like a garrotte, but slack.

'Just tired.'

'There are hot springs a bit further up, if you can make it. We can stop there overnight.'

'Is it safe to?'

'No one's objected so far.' He helped me up.

A gunshot went off somewhere behind us. Between the trees, a very straight, brilliant line of light arced out before the bullet thunked into a trunk. Other shots went off too.

'That's Martel,' I said. 'He's got a revolver. I saw it at the church. They sound like that.'

He caught my arm. 'Run. One wrong spark and everything in here will go up like a bomb, we need to be in the water if it does.'

'I can't—'

'You'll be surprised,' he said, and shoved me.

The shock of having to run was like being dunked in cold water and all at once I was awake and not tired. The air to our south-west was shot through with bullet trails, but we were too far off to see if they had hit anything. Even with the whitewood, running hurt. Without it, though, I would have crumpled on the first step.

Something smelled sulphury, and then suddenly we were on the banks of a little lake. There was an island in the middle and a single sapling whitewood tree, only about three times the height of a person and bound by candle ivy flowering happily in a moonbeam haze of pollen that swum and glowed on the thermals above the hot water. The banks under the moss, the pebbles on the lake bed and the boulders round the island were all glass. Raphael went out as far as he could on the land, slung his bag and coat across then dived in to swim the last. I copied him. Shouts came from behind us, muffled in the trees. I didn't notice until it seemed suddenly dimmer than before, but there was no pollen over the water; our trail stopped on the lake edge. The water was almost too hot. After the intense cold outside, my hands burned as the feeling came back into them. The pollen over the bank was a wall of diffuse light. Further up, some of the rocks had a yellow tinge where the sulphur in the water had crystallised.

Raphael motioned to say go round to the other side of the island. Once we were there, we held on to some smoothed-off glass. I half-curled up in the water, waiting for my leg to stop hurting.

'How was he following us?' I said.

'The pollen trails hang in the air a long time on a still day. There's a shimmer if you know how to look for it. Quispe knows; he's from this side of the mountains though he pretends he's not. He knows not to bloody shoot into it either.'

'I can't imagine Martel would listen to him.'

Raphael made a soft agreeing sound and then we both waited in silence, watching the warped view of the way we had come through a glass boulder and the fading light of the disturbed pollen. Small things were already zinging new trails through it, pulling the shapes to one side and the other. Something squirrelly traced a bouncing line of light halfway down a tree, then launched itself into the air and glided to the next. Its trail looked like a billowing flag. The ground sent up a high, sudden loop of brightness that must have been a jumping frog.

Slowly, my hands got used to the hot water and stopped hurting. Little aches washed up and down my spine. I felt like an old man and suddenly I missed how I'd used to be much more than I had for a long time. Three years ago I could have run for miles. Everybody says you don't notice health until it's gone, but I'd noticed, all the time, the same as I'd noticed warm sunbeams. It was probably just as well to have enjoyed it while it lasted, but I wished I could have been less fit then. It would have been less of a contrast.

There were no more shots. Gradually, I stopped expecting them.

The stream-bed was all glass pebbles, smoothed down until together they were like treasure. There were shells too, miniature, occupied by even tinier things stuck to the rocks. Nestled in the glass pebbles diagonally below me were a clutch of what looked like much more perfect pebbles, with yellow spheres suspended inside. Raphael saw too and dived for them. When he came back up with some, he set them gently on the rock in front of me for me to see. They were eggs.

'Water's not quite hot enough to cook them,' he explained. 'The ducks lay them underwater to incubate.'

I touched the curve of one, and it really was glass. Other things must have been mixed into it, because like ordinary duck eggs it was bluish close to. They were lovely things. He had left two in the nest; they had chicks in them.

We waited a while longer, watching the forest back the way we had come, but nothing else human disturbed the pollen. The silence began to sound less like silence. It had the ordinary clicks and creaks and hoots. The trees were so big that the wooden sound any tree will make in a place of varying temperature was more like muttering. Sometimes, when it turned to a staccato rumble of settling bark, it sounded like arboreal laughter.

'Can you see any?' he said at last. 'Ducks, I mean.'

I let the current of the lake spin me. I hadn't seen them at first because they were smart and black, and they blended neatly with the shadows in the pollen glow, but there was a little flock of them in the reeds on the other bank. He nodded when I pointed.

'I'll see if I can get one.'

I wanted to say it was all right, I wasn't hungry, but I was. I let my cheek rest against the rock to watch. My hands had started to shake.

One of the ducks had wandered closer to us, away from the others. Raphael eased up to it and it seemed not to mind. He clapped his hands hard by its head and it squawked and exploded. Or rather, it went up in white blue flames, and within about four seconds there were no feathers left, only a roasted carcass. He lifted it out of the water and tore off a leg.

'It's cooked, try it.'

'What . . . in God's name was that?'

'It's how they make glass eggs. They're full of flammable chemicals and then when the time's right . . .' He opened his hand to mime an explosion. 'But if you startle them they go off pretty well too.'

'They're phoenixes.'

'I suppose.'

'And you haven't made a fortune exporting them because?'

'I haven't got your fine criminal mind. Eat your phoenix. Christ,' he said suddenly, stock still.

I jumped when I saw the markayuq. She was standing on the edge of the lake, just where the hotter water tumbled down over the glass.

'Can't believe we didn't see that before,' I said. It was unsettling, not to have seen it, and I looked round again, expecting Martel and his men to be waiting for us to notice them beyond the island. They weren't. 'Well. I'll do the eggs.'

'No, hold on.' He went to the statue and unwound a length of string from its wrist, ran some wax down it – he always had some in his pocket – and started to flick knots into it, as fast as a fisherman tying netting, until most of the string was taken up. He wound it back round the statue's wrist. When he saw me watching, he shook his head slightly. 'Just a prayer. Give me the eggs, will you? Don't go too close to her.' He took the eggs carefully, but he looked unhappy as he carried them towards the hotter water.

'Don't burn yourself,' I said, anxious now.

'It doesn't matter if I do.'

'I talk to the air. Just because you can't feel it—'

I was cut off by more gunshots close by. I jerked behind the boulders again, but no bullets hit the island or the water. Raphael came back.

'They're going to spark the pollen in a minute—'

Exactly as he said it, the pollen ignited. It was like a flour bomb and I saw the edge of the flame race outward. It stopped when it reached the edge of the water, because there wasn't enough above the stream to maintain any flame, and in its wake it left darkness. Light did needle down through the canopy in tiny, fishing-wire beams, but not enough to see by. Raphael pulled himself up on to the island.

'Martel, you idiot, stop shooting before you set fire to the whole forest! Get over here.'

Nothing happened for a moment, except that the markayuq on the bank lifted her head. It was because he'd moved, but it looked for all the world like she recognised the sound of Spanish and didn't wholly approve.

Men came out of the dark, five or six, some patting at cinders on their sleeves. One was Martel.

'I'll get you out of here if you leave us alone,' Raphael said tightly.

'Excellent,' said Martel. 'Come along, gentlemen. What have you done with Mr Tremayne?' he added as he waded across.

The island was too little to hide on for long. 'He's here. Touch him and I'll walk you straight back the way you came.'

'Yes, no need to labour the point. Help me up.'

Raphael pulled him up on to the rocks and Martel squeezed his shoulder, pleased to see him despite everything and, I thought, reminding him who he belonged to. Around him, the other men were climbing up too. They looked rattled, and a couple of them were singed from the pollen blast. Here and there on the edge of the lake the grass smoked. None of it looked serious enough to set off the trees, but it was plain that was only luck. They set their guns gingerly against the whitewood tree.

'Hello,' Martel said when he saw me. 'You disappeared; we came out to find you.' He made an effort to sound offhand, but it came out brittle. 'I was worried something Indian might have gone through Raphael's head.'

'What happened to you?' I said.

'Attacked,' he said. 'There were twelve of us. Rather accomplished, really. I never once saw them, did any of you?'

There was a quiet chorus of no's and maybe's.

He sat down stiffly on the rocks. 'This wretched pollen. You think you can see, but you can't. You can only see what moves. They were waiting, not moving. Behind trees, among the roots. I saw trails, plenty of trails, but they know how to hide in it.'

'How many?' Raphael said.

I expected him to say dozens, but he looked pensive. 'I think only three. It took them some time. We lost the first man a few hours ago. It wasn't until the fifth that we saw anything at all.'

'Why didn't you turn back?'

'Well, we had to find you,' he said. 'You're heading to the quinine woods after all, I suppose?'

'Yes, and you aren't going to touch him.'

'Why would I do that?'

'You're a quinine supplier,' I said. 'Come on, Martel, you're up to your neck in it. You must be the richest man in Caravaya. You keep up the monopoly here, no one touches the *calisaya* woods, and the suppliers in the north pay you to do it. Right?'

He laughed, only a little, and I realised that he didn't altogether like earning his living that way. 'Well, no one touches the *calisaya* woods while the Bolivian border is closed. One would usually go round that way. But Bedlam is a good honey trap. It looks so much more straightforward than Bolivia. We find it's terribly good for catching unwanted expeditionaries.' He touched Raphael's shoulder. I thought Raphael would throw him off, but he only glanced at him and it was there in the lines and the small scars around his eyes, that he was glad Martel was all right. When I tried to sound out what would happen if Martel refused his terms and shot me, to see whether Raphael really would walk the wrong way and get them all killed, I found I had no idea. I almost didn't hear what Martel said next. 'Raphael keeps up the stories, and eventually everyone decides to try their luck in the forest, and generally they don't come out again, and since everyone thinks there are mad Indians here nobody questions it.'

'But there are Indians here. Why did you risk it?'

'You can get through if you go fast. I've seen that before. You lose some men, but if you keep going it's perfectly possible.' He nodded slowly, which sheened pollen light in his hair. 'Scientific expeditions do like to hang about looking at the distracting statues. When Mr Backhouse came a battalion went with him and half of them came back. Those are good enough odds for me when the alternative is so dire.' He watched me for a moment. 'I can't let you take those cuttings.'

'If I don't, the army will come.' I aimed it more at Raphael than Martel.

'Fighting on territory like this, a hundred miles from any decent supply line? Difficult prospect,' Martel said gently. 'I was an army man myself. A campaign like that won't last a month.'

'You weren't in the army that's coming,' I said. 'They don't care about difficult terrain. They'll force the interior provinces to open. You'll be bringing them the quinine yourself by the end of it. The Navy will come; they'll put everything along the coast under heavy artillery fire. Lima is on the coast. Cities can stand for a while under fire from ironclads but the Navy can keep it up for days. They shelled Canton for nearly a week not long ago. And then one day you'll get a very official order from your government to escort an army battalion up here and see them to the *calisaya* woods.'

'That won't be my fault,' he said seriously. 'Letting a crippled Englishman through my woods certainly is. It would be my head, if the monopoly were to break on my stretch.' He was still holding Raphael's shoulder. He looked shaken and I realised that knowing he had the reins of someone so strong was giving him a kind of strength too. 'My head last,' he corrected himself. 'After all the other parts of me. But let's not talk about it now. We're all tired and I should think there's some arrangement we can come to later. We've got plenty of food to go around. Is it possible to cook in this water?' he said to Raphael.

'Over there where it's hot.' He was quiet for a second. 'Don't touch the statue.'

'Oh, why would anyone touch your wretched heathen statue?' Martel said, but not rudely exactly. He sounded glad to have a familiar argument. I could imagine they had disagreed about the markayuq quite often. 'My God.'

So a bizarre sort of peace settled over the island. Some of Martel's men started to bring out food and Raphael took them into the water to show them how to cook it. The others began to hang some of their wet clothes up in the little tree. One kept watch, a rifle across his lap, his eyes on the pinstriped darkness back the way they had come. Out there, new pollen was just starting to smoke from the last of the candle ivy. They were visible only as after-image shimmers, but they were there. I watched them for a while, still hanging in the water. My leg felt better and I could have climbed up, but it seemed like tempting fate to sit too close to Martel.

The others were still eating when Raphael nudged me and gave me the waxed string from round his wrist. It was kinked from old knots but there were none in it now.

'See if we can't convince them you're one of us,' he explained as he wound it round my wrist over the other string, the prayer from before. He did it in a particular pattern, each strand criss-crossed over the last, then tucked the end under them all. I tried to make out the shadows in the trees, wondering if he had seen someone. There was no sign of anyone, but I was much less confident about seeing anything in the surviving pollen after hearing what Martel had said. 'That's for if you find a markayuq without his own cord. When you clean them, you wax the cord too. They're outside all the time. The cords rot if they get too damp.'

I nodded.

'Look.' He gave me the glass-handled brush I'd seen him use on the markayuq every day in Bedlam. 'You make a pattern in the pollen with it. Starts like this, see? Eights over eights.'

When I tried, I could do it, but it was difficult, like patting your head and rubbing your stomach at the same time, and satisfyingly hypnotic once I got the hang of it. He watched the pollen and nodded.

'Right. Go and try on her.'

'Going native, Mr Tremayne?' Martel laughed from where he and Quispe were sitting.

'Eat your food,' Raphael murmured. He took the wax jar from his bag too and gave it to me to carry across to the markayuq. He came with me.

The markayuq was on a steep part of the bank and it was hard to climb up to her. Raphael stood behind me; getting in the way of any shot from Martel. He watched me brush the wax onto the statue's breastplate past my shoulder. The pollen was so thick on her side of the water that our eyelashes combed lines into it.

I stopped, because the statue had lifted her hand. There was no hydraulic hiss, only the creak of moving leather. She touched my chest. I thought it would stop there, but her fingertips hooked over the top of my damp shirt and skimmed the uppermost button. She pushed at it until it slid open; then, just as slowly, caught the button and tried to put it back into its hole. I propped the brush into the wax jar and did it up again, hearing my own pulse inside my temples.

'How is it doing that?' I whispered. It didn't look like an accidental motion meant for taking salt. 'Is someone controlling it?'

'Tell her what they are,' he said.

'What?'

'Talk, I'll write it.' He unwound her string until he found a blank part. 'Go on.'

'It – they're buttons. You fasten up clothes with them,' I said slowly. He had to reach past me to tie the knots. He was far quicker at it than anyone else I'd seen, but it still took him almost a full minute. He wound the string back around her wrist.

'Good,' he murmured. 'Right, have you got anything you can give her?'

'I didn't bring salt.'

'Anything. Left hand,' he added, catching my right. 'Always the one that isn't natural; it's like not drawing a sword in front of the King.'

In my left pocket were matches. I took them out. 'What about these? I suppose nobody wants fire in here.'

'No, it's useful. But show her what they are.'

We both cupped our hands around the tiny flame. I blew it out quickly, although the pollen showed no sign of taking. When I put the rest of the book into her hand, her fingers closed over it.

'Good. Now come away.'

I heard her moving as we eased back down into the water. By the time I reached the island again, she had opened up her hands towards us, like the Bedlam shrines asked for salt. The matches were gone.

'Those things make my skin crawl,' Martel said.

Quispe was only watching. He looked worried. When someone laughed and threw a bone at the statue to see if it would move, he flinched. She didn't move. Raphael touched the small of my back as we came to the rocks.

'Can you get away quickly if there's a chance, in the night?' he said by my ear.

'Depends what you mean by quickly. I don't think I should try much more running. But I'll walk where you tell me.'

'Less conspiring,' Martel said almost comfortably. 'You won't get away in the night, I should say. There will always be someone watching, so put it out of your minds.' I wondered, unsettled, if he had recognised some English words, or if he only had a knack for guessing what we were likely to be saying. 'Raphael, come up here. I don't want to eat by myself. Mr Tremayne?'

'I'll be along in a second. My leg hurts,' I lied. Sounding worse off than I was seemed increasingly a sensible thing to do, although I hadn't thought beyond that.

Raphael waved to catch my eye again and then jerked his hand to one side. I moved more behind the rock, so that nobody would have a clear shot. From there, I watched Martel brush his knuckle over the graze through Raphael's eyebrow and ask how it was, like he hadn't been the one to do it. Raphael knocked his hand away, but not hard, and under his ordinary roughness he looked glad. I let my forehead bump down on my arm.

That night, Martel posted two men to keep watch, on us as much as for other people. The forest was still except for little animal trails on the pollen side. The dark where the pollen had burned clicked and chirped. I stayed awake a long time, but there was nothing to say that anyone was there, not even in the trees where the branches were broad enough to be walkways. Raphael sat reading just behind me, propped against the tree. I watched him through the open tent flap. He had given up on paper books and instead he had what looked, right up until you got close to it, like a neat ball of string, which he unwound through his fingertips and then round his hand, slower than I could have read by sight but not much. The knots were neat and almost invisible. If I'd only glanced at him and not known what he had, I would have thought he was spooling twine. Looped around his wrist like always, like another sort of knot cord, the cherrywood beads of his rosary clacked as he moved his hands and the cross plinked against the buttons on his shirt sometimes. It was such an ordinary sound that it made everything else seem less strange.

I did sleep in the end. Even so I kept expecting to hear the snick of Martel's filigree revolver.

TWENTY-FIVE

WHEN I WOKE, I didn't want to get up. The hot spring was heating the ground from below and the tent smelled of warm grass and canvas. The flap was still staked open. I lay watching the steam and the pollen twine in the air. After the snow, it was wonderful. I thought I was still deaf from sleep at first, but it was only quiet because no one else was up yet. I could hear the water well enough. The ducks were laughing further upstream. I closed my eyes again. I was so warm and so exactly comfortable that I felt like I was floating.

It wasn't until I shifted that I realised Raphael was asleep against my back, his arm across me so that it would have been almost impossible for someone, even standing right above us, to shoot me without catching him too. His rosary had imprinted a circle pattern in my arm, then a suggestion of a cross, just near the top of the anchor tattoo. I closed my fingers over the beads. It was the first time I'd been in bed beside anyone, having been tritely and pointlessly in love twice with other people's wives until I was too old to start. I'd thought perhaps I wasn't the sort of person who could have lived close to anyone else, but that was wrong, now I was here. It would have been good, always to wake up this way.

Because I was holding that old sadness too I didn't notice at first that there was a tremor in his hand. It wasn't shivering. I squeezed his fingers to see if I could stop it but I couldn't. It was a thrum, like he was lying close to a running engine from which I was insulated.

I'd never felt the absence of a medical dictionary before, but it was only a few seconds before I had to sit up, too frustrated to lie still. He was fading in front of me and the cause would be something well known. If I ever got home, there would be a doctor at a dinner party one day who would say, oh, yes, of course it would have been this; you know I didn't think anyone died of that any more.

All I could do was pull the blanket over him again.

Once I'd ducked out into the open, meaning to see about food, I found that the other tents – there were three and all open to let in the air – were empty except for Martel and Quispe. The others' blankets were still inside, but the men were gone. After everything that had happened to them it seemed especially stupid for them to have ventured off the island without Raphael, until I saw the shirts and waistcoats hanging over the lowest branches of the trees on the lake bank, on the pollen side. There hadn't been enough room for everyone's things on the island's small tree, and there were some clothes on the ground around the markayuq as well. She had dropped her arms now but they must have tried to hang things on her.

I frowned when I noticed that none of the blankets had been slept in. A few had been more or less shaken out but they held the last few square folds from having been fitted in packs. Watching the bank for any tall pollen trails, I lifted my shirt down from the tree. Although it smelled faintly of the sulphur in the water, it was dry and warm, like it had been in an airing cupboard. I stood holding it, surprised to be there and alive at the same time.

Raphael jerked awake. 'Merrick?'

'Behind you.'

He bumped back on to the ground again. His hair was auburn now. I blew the pollen near the tent flap to whirl it above his eyes. He waved his hand vaguely to say he was all right. I was still fastening my shirt when he sat up properly and came out into the light.

'Where are the others?' he said when he saw the empty tents.

'Not sure. Their things are here.' I rubbed at the rosary print on my arm, which still coiled across the anchor tattoo like rope. It didn't go away, but then I didn't want it to and stopped trying.

Raphael was looking at the clothes in the trees. I saw him fall still but I didn't pay any attention until he pointed down into the water, where Hernandez was floating face down, livid red marks around his neck. He had just drifted into view from beyond the rocks. Without deciding to, I went close to Raphael again and dropped his dry shirt into his lap, not wanting him sitting there alone and half-dressed. When he turned his head, the pollen light caught in vaults of his throat.

'I can't see very well,' he said softly. 'Where's the markayuq?'

I started to point to the statue's outcrop on the bank, but the space was empty. I turned around once, thinking I must have lost my bearings, but everything else was where I thought it was: the tree, Martel, even the ducks and the roiling steam above the hottest part of the spring. The markayuq was gone and there was a patch of flattened moss where she had been standing.

In fact, though, she wasn't gone. She was standing under our sapling whitewood tree. The hem of her robe dripped, the water beading on the well-waxed leather. I'd almost walked into her.

She caught my arm and slashed the pollen with her other hand to make it flare. It lit the anchor tattoo clear. She looked from it to my face and I saw her realise I was a foreigner, but she didn't have time for anything else before Raphael tore her hand away from me. She held on and it left grazes across my arm, and there was a strange unwilling creak of stone before Raphael shoved me to the island's edge.

'Go, go *now*,' he said.

I slung my bag and boots across and dived. The sulphur in the water stung in the new cuts and for a second all I could hear was my heart banging. When I twisted back in the water, she had moved again, was moving, across the island towards Martel and Quispe. The height of the rocks took her out of view. Raphael came after me. We were only just out of the water when a gunshot boomed and the ducks went up like firecrackers. The fires sent up sparks that ignited the sparse pollen above the island. I saw it burn, and when it was gone, there was a deep well of darkness around the little whitewood tree. I could make out a shadow near the trunk, but that was all, and it was impossible to tell if the shot had hit her or, if it had, whether a bullet could do any damage.

*

We slowed down eventually and the pollen flare faded a little.

'There aren't lots of markayuq all through the woods, are there?' I said. My voice came hoarse. I'd had a lungful of sulphury water. 'The ones from Bedlam followed us. Or she followed us.' Dead wolves on the border; no wonder. They had come straight between the markayuq. Arm's reach. 'What happened to the others? It wasn't just her.'

'They would have had to stop when the pollen on that side burned away. They need it to see by. She got to the island before, though. She was there just after us—'

'Why didn't you tell us about them straightaway?' I demanded, because I'd realised I didn't care what or how. I was almost shouting. I was less angry with him than with how wrong I had been. He had listened to Clem and me prattle about clockwork and odd religions when right beside him were stone men listening too. St Thomas had walked in front of me and still I hadn't thought it could be anything but a trick.

He stopped walking. 'Why did I not tell the foreign expeditionaries about our very rare, very holy saints, which are from a place I've sworn to keep secret? And say I had. Unless one had walked in front of you, would you ever have believed me? I can't make them walk. They almost never do. What was I meant to say, without sounding like another stupid Indian with stupid Indian neuroses? I sounded bad enough as it was, keeping you back from the border. If I'd sat you down and explained that the markayuq were real, you wouldn't have listened to me even for as long as you did. I couldn't have done anything that proved they were anything but good clockwork. Not without shoving one of you over the border, and they're not slow.' He glanced back. 'Especially not her. She's young.'

I wanted to argue, because in my mind I was much better than that, but he was right.

'What are they?' I asked at last.

'Just people.'

'But they stand outside all the time. They barely move, how—'

'They're like trees; they don't need to move. They do if they want to. It's just not often that they want to.' He was quiet for a space. 'Just . . . we'll be fine. All we need to do is keep out of their way. From a distance you look right.'

'Is it far now?'

'No. A few more miles.'

I knocked his arm. 'Well done, by the way.'

'For what?'

'You knew they'd do something to her eventually.'

For someone who had reduced the odds against us so efficiently, he didn't look pleased. 'I wish it had been Martel.'

I couldn't tell if he meant it or if he was only saying it to make me feel more confident. 'If he's still here, he won't be for long. Unless – do bullets hurt them?'

'Not usually.'

'Then . . .'

'Right,' he said.

The way was steeply downhill after that. There were steps in places, even the weed-choked ruins of little houses and towers sometimes, but never people.

When we came out at the river, it was sudden. I hadn't expected the sunlight or the heat, though I should have. We had come right down into tropical forest and the river was frisky, and over the far side, the trees weren't whitewoods but everything else. Kapok roots poured over the riverbanks, full of green parrots and big monkeys. Right under the kapoks, shaded in their canopy, were *calisaya* cinchona, tall ones, never cut down or barked. With their quiet colours, they looked prim and European among all the brilliant jungle plants. I brushed Raphael's sleeve and pointed, then put my arm round him and pulled him against me. He laughed.

The hand on my shoulder was nearly gentle when it arrived. Martel was strong and he thumped me back against his chest without having to pull much.

'Now then,' he said, and Raphael spun around. I'd never seen anyone look more helpless than he did then.

'Let him go,' he said to Martel.

'I'll let him go once we're in sight of Bedlam. Now come along.'

I closed my eyes when I felt the muzzle of his revolver press to my temple. It was cold.

'No you won't.'

'Of course I will. Now back through the woods, my dear.'

'You can't shoot into the pollen.'

'I won't be shooting into the pollen. I'll be shooting into his head.'

Raphael was still for a second, then came back towards us. Martel pulled me away from him to let him pass.

I let my breath out slowly and felt Martel's arm sink as my ribs did, then lift again with them. He was strong but he had been living easily. His gun was an old one, well kept but not meticulously, a clunky thing, beneath the silverwork, that I couldn't imagine had come from anything like the ferocious accuracy of the American workshops. He wouldn't be able to shoot Raphael with it from here, or not with any real certainty.

'You're taller close up,' Martel said to me in his friendly way.

'I know. I'd forgotten too. It's funny, isn't it.'

He laughed. I pushed my elbow hard into his stomach and twisted the gun out of his hand. As he lurched, I spun him onto his front on the ground and thumped down after him with my knee in his back. He was still stronger than me and so, although it might have been kinder to give him a moment or two to offer him some other chance, I wasn't sure enough that I could hold him there, or of what he had said about not firing into the pollen, so I pulled the knot string from round my wrist and strangled him with it instead. I waited until well after he had stopped struggling. When I sat back, my arms ached. Raphael came to us slowly and unevenly.

'Is he dead?'

'I think so.' I rubbed at the string marks across my palms. My fingers were stiff and pale from having had the blood stopped and I had to wait for it to come back, in pins and needles. When I swallowed, my throat hurt. I hadn't been breathing for almost as long as it had taken. The world cannoned into me, all the noise of the forest and the sound of my own breathing through the bones inside my ears, and it was all much too loud. Martel's body didn't look like a person any more. It might have been a clever sculpture. Something strange turned under my lungs and I felt as though someone must have done some kind of magic trick, swapping Martel for this.

I rubbed my hands again. My arms had stopped aching. It hadn't been difficult. Like it had before when I understood that Raphael wasn't going to shoot me, the future had an odd new breadth. That Bedlam was in danger from Martel, that Raphael was, had seemed immovable a few seconds ago.

Raphael knelt down beside me. He didn't touch Martel, but he nodded. 'Yes.' He inclined his head without lifting his eyes. 'I'm sorry,' he said. 'I've never done anything more useless than that.'

'You couldn't have done anything.'

'I would have taken that gun off anyone else.' He looked away and then seemed to have to push hard to look back again. 'I would have shot anyone else a long time ago.'

'Familiar devils are important after a while, though, aren't they? Better than nothing,' I said, and then shook my head. I could hear how incoherent I sounded but I couldn't see a way to sort it out.

Raphael watched me and I misread him. His neutral expression was a half-frown and it seemed cold. I had time to worry he was angry before he hugged me. I put both arms round him and had to rest forward against him, shaking now, though I couldn't tell from what. I didn't feel upset, but I could feel that everything I was thinking now was only skimming the surface of things, everything else shut off. He lifted me off the body and put me on my feet again. He was much stronger than Martel or me. He turned his head to his left and the rainforest beyond the river, his temple just resting against my chin.

'Who inherits his land?' I asked, for something else to say. I had my arms under his and my wrists resting on his shoulders, and they ached, but there was blood on my palms and I didn't want to put them down.

'No one. He didn't own it, it's someone else's. He said he paid rent to begin with but then he stopped and nothing happened, so he just kept it. I'd have to check with the land registry. I don't even know where that is. But whoever he was, he didn't come after the rent, so maybe he's dead.'

'Either way it will take a little while for him to hear. Especially if Martel stopped paying years ago.'

'Someone else will move in anyway. It doesn't have to be legal.'

'Take them for a nice walk in the woods.'

He laughed. 'Let's see your hands.'

I showed him, starting to feel raw. He had to hold them still. He found his flask and cleaned up the places where the string had cut me. I hadn't felt any of it. Across from us, an eagle swept down from the canopy and landed on Martel's body. It was a giant white thing with evil eyes but a downy hesitancy, just a baby still, and it blinked up at us to ask if this was ours, its wings flickering and ready to fly again. We didn't wave it away.

'All right?' he said quietly.

'I – if I were less all right, I think it would be better,' I said, not sure if I was speaking too loudly. The blood was still humming through my skull, electric. I'd never felt so awake.

He glanced up, without moving his head. 'Everyone feels like that. Everyone with any sense.'

'No, I mean . . .'

'I know what you mean. It was a bit good, is what you mean. That isn't evil. All it means is that you won't be one of those people who spiral off into guilty nightmares and never recover. Just . . . recognise the feeling and see the shape of it, and you won't aim it at the wrong person.'

'Are you sure?'

'Yes.' He watched the eagle and I couldn't tell what he was thinking.

'We haven't got anything to dig with,' I said.

'Have you heard of sky burials?'

'No. Sounds nice.'

'It's not. It's that.' He nodded to the eagle, which had settled now. 'But that's what we can say if anyone asks. Right. Let's go and fetch your plants. There's a crossing up there.'

So we walked along a little way until we found some rapids where there were rocks across the river in a kind of natural dam, although perhaps beavers had filled in the spaces. There, where the whitewood trees petered out, was another salt border. Once we were across, the relief at being on the right side of it again crashed through me like a cribbar and I floated for a while on the outrush. Raphael slowed down as we came to the rocks and the river.

'I could go back to Bedlam with you now, once we have the cuttings,' I said. 'Without Martel.'

'No. The markayuq knows you. We were lucky this time, but she'd catch you on the way back. We'd have to stop for the night again and she wouldn't. She's a foot taller than me. I can't fight her.' He looked ashamed and I wished I could say, without sounding like I was talking down to him, that I understood about Martel, that I didn't think he was a coward for not having fought, or for not risking it against a markayuq twice his size. But I couldn't think of a way and it just left a painful quiet before he shook his head at himself and pointed to the mountains ahead of us. They were close, very close. We must have come parallel to them. 'This is Bolivia. Those are the Andes. You can loop back to Lake Titicaca that way.'

'Is it possible?' I said, looking down at the rainforest, and it really was the rainforest beyond the river. Dense, unbroken, roadless jungle. 'When we planned the expedition we wrote off Bolivia quite quickly, it . . . we were told there was about to be a war. The borders are closed, they're not letting foreigners through. The roads are full of soldiers.'

'They're not letting foreigners through. But "they" is the Bolivian government. People who live round here have nothing to do with all that.' He managed to encompass the Bolivian government, modern borders, anything established by the Spanish, all in one bubble that ordinary people might look on with occasional interest but nothing more pressing. No government would be able to dictate anything much to people here. It was a simple matter of not being able to reach. They could stop foreigners using the roads, but there would be no way in heaven or earth they could put a man on every animal trail through the woods. 'There's a village of hunters about a mile south.' He pointed. 'I'll go with you that far and they'll take you over the mountains.'

'Will you be all right?' I asked.

'When?'

'Going back. You can't see.' In the shade of the trees where the daylight made the pollen invisible, he had been walking close to me to be sure of the footing, and hesitated if I'd stopped talking for too long.

'I'm fine.'

'How many fingers?'

He slapped my hand. 'Fuck off.'

'That doesn't work on bears.'

'Damn. Stalked as I often am by bears hellbent on ophthalmographical studies.'

'I'm not going through Bolivia and you're not walking through that forest by yourself. We already know there's a great chunk of it with no pollen.'

'No.'

'I didn't mean to imply it was your choice. And your English is hateful, I hope you know. It isn't decent to learn another language that bloody well.'

'I had to. Your grandfather was useless at languages.' He had laughed to begin with, but he lost it when he mentioned Harry. 'Come on.'

The way across the river came out almost straight into a cinchona glade. I had to sit in it for a while and look at the trees and the fallen leaves and fruit and roots to be sure they were the kind we wanted. They were, and there were thousands.

TWENTY-SIX

We had arrived at half past four in the afternoon, so I took careful cuttings and then spent a happy hour with the last of the good light splitting some kapok wood for cases and packing them with the reddish moss that grew everywhere. By the time it was dark, I had them ready so that we could go first thing in the morning. I propped the makeshift cases gently against some kapok roots on my way back to the little clearing where I'd left the bags and Raphael. I stopped when I saw that his pack was gone. He had left a lit pollen lamp propped on top of mine.

'Where are you?'

There was no answer, except for the hooting birds. When I picked up the lamp, worried he was frozen somewhere and meaning to go and find him, there was a note too. It directed me to the hunters' village, and said what to say in Quechua – they didn't speak Spanish – when I reached it. He had gone back over the river without me.

The lamp hadn't been to help me see. It was to stop me seeing littler lights. I did what watchmakers always say not to and forced the winder forward to make the spring uncoil too fast and run out, then pushed the lamp under my coat where it lay over my bag to block out the last of the light. For a moment everything was only black and I stood with my eyes shut. When I opened them again the sky was indigo, and over the river there was a soft pollen trail through the trees. It wasn't going back to Bedlam but east, further round the bend of the river. The very tail of it, faded and hazed, was still just enough to cast light on the graveyard markayuq where she stood on the riverbank, watching me. The grazes on my arm stung when I saw her.

'Raphael!' I shouted. I could still see, more or less, where the pollen trail stopped. He wasn't that far away. 'Where are you going?'

His voice wasn't strong enough to shout back and instead he traced letters in the pollen, slowly, to keep from sending it whirling off out of shape.

Home.

I looked further east, half-expecting to see the lights of a town, but there was nothing. He had been steering us away from the east all the time we had been in the forest. I thought of the empty room at the church, all his things packed up. He had never meant to go back to Bedlam.

'Right, good, and how far do you think you'll get, in the state you're in? Wait for me, I'll go with you.'

You can't. He drew an arrow under it, pointing back toward the markayuq.

'You can't see. What happens if you come to a place with no pollen?'

Not far.

'For God's sake, it clearly is!'

He didn't reply and the pollen faded until what he had written before only looked like the suggestion of writing. I stared at it for too long and stopped being able to see it properly. Aware of my heart in my eardrums I had to stand still to think and lean into the urge just to run after him. Things chittered and howled in the woods behind me, much louder than they ever had in the whitewood forest. At last, I wound up the pollen lamp again and tied it round my sleeve while I started to gather up the kapok planks I hadn't used for the cuttings. They were rough – I'd only split them with a little axe rather than sawn them properly – but the grain was straight and I had just enough knot cord to lash them together. It was fine and made of soft alpaca wool, but it was waxed and good enough. When it was finished, the raft wasn't halfway big enough to take the full weight of a person, but since the markayuq wouldn't know that, it didn't matter. I had to hunt about to find a branch about my height and, once I had, it took what felt like hours to make a rough joint and fit it on to the raft, then longer again to tie it into place.

Finally, expecting to see dawn at any second even though my watch said it had only been an hour, I tipped everything out of my bag that wasn't food or clothes and packed the bound cuttings in instead. Despite everything it was hard to leave the obsidian razor Raphael had given me and harder still to leave the little clutch of Clem's things I'd meant to give to Minna. But there was no space and something in my mind clicked into that gypsy way of thinking you get on long journeys, where unnecessary things stop mattering.

Very carefully, I carried everything down to the water. Once I'd tied the pollen lamp to the branch, at as close to the same height as my own breastbone as I could, I pushed the raft out into the current. I waited, afraid it was going to get stuck along the banks or in the dense reeds, but it found the central rip quickly and sailed away. Within a few yards it was nothing but the firefly point of the lamp.

On the opposite bank, the pollen stirred as the markayuq turned her head, then plumed softly when she started to walk after the light. I couldn't see her at all, only the glow, but it was where she had been, and it was the right height. When she walked, it was shockingly quick, as quick as an ordinary person might. I stayed exactly where I was, horribly conscious that the moonlight was bright enough now to give me a shadow on the rocks. I could nearly feel the pressure of it, a little silvery weight down my left side. It glinted on the gold leaf Inti had smoothed on to some of the patterns on the whitewood band. I put my hand over it, slowly.

She disappeared among the trees as the banks curved. The way over the river, which was all boulders and pieces of driftwood caught up between them, was difficult in the dark, even with the moon. I saw something big move in the water and almost fell in when I stopped to look at it. When I reached the top of the little cliff, which was held together by tree roots, it slid out on to the bank, but I couldn't tell what it was. Hoping that it couldn't climb, I set off in the paler pollen trail that still hung in the unmoving air, refreshing it with my wake but not as brightly as the markayuq had, because I wasn't going so fast. My leg hurt and it seemed best not to upset it again, though I wanted to run and let it hurt.

I lost sight of the markayuq's trail before long. Because I'd expected to follow Raphael for a while before I caught up, I nearly walked into him when the trail stopped just behind a tree, only half a mile or so from the river. He had stopped to sit down among some roots and frozen there. I put his coat around him. He must have been waiting to see frost before he put it on, but the air had turned cold again. It wasn't only altitude. The mountains had their own little climate that broke when it reached the river. Raphael wasn't the only one who hadn't quite noticed. A fabulous, iridescently turquoise beetle had come to visit him too, antlers tipped at a quizzical angle from where it sat on his knuckle. I moved it and clasped his hand. He was icy.

I found a me-sized dip in the roots and sat with my sketchbook to wait. My heart thunked and I tried to ignore it. A day and seventy years was a wide margin. I couldn't think what to do if he didn't wake soon. There was no one to tell, unless the markayuq came back, but even then I couldn't think she would be very interested in an ill priest when I was here desecrating her holy ground.

'Jesus *Christ*, Merrick, do you know what that looks like? I blink and you appear from nowhere, you'll kill me one day.' He jerked his hand close to his heart to show what he meant. 'What the hell are you doing?'

'It's cold,' I said, starting a list on my fingers. 'And you don't know when to put on a coat. This catalepsy happens with what seems to me like increasing frequency, and if it happens for long you need someone to tell someone else where you are. You can't stay out here for seventy years again; I don't care if you didn't die the first time, you'd be pushing your luck to try it twice. You can't see. If you come to a burned patch of pollen, which you will if there are any phoenix round here, you're stuck.'

'You've got other things to do,' he said flatly. 'You've got cuttings to take to India.'

'They're all right for a month.'

'There's a markayuq following you.'

'No, she's following a pollen lamp I floated off down the river.'

'Not forever she won't be.'

'Well, that's more my concern than yours, isn't it.'

'Merrick,' he snapped. 'You've known me for a fortnight. What are you doing? You're not my friend. You're not your grandfather, you couldn't be more different from him, and whatever you think, I am not very keen on having the grandchildren of someone I used to know kicking about in the forest. I am not a Tremayne family heirloom. Go home.'

'I am your friend, and my whole family has spun around you and this place for three generations, so I think you're pretty thoroughly my business, whether you want to be or not. And even if that wasn't the case, you can't do this by yourself. Do you want to get home or not?'

He stared at me for a second. 'If she catches you—'

'If. Now eat something,' I said, and threw some grapes at him, because it's much harder to be serious whilst trying to duck flying fruit. I'd found them growing wild with the cinchona.

'Why are you here?' he said.

'It's a few extra miles. Stop making such a bloody fuss. I didn't pay you for any of this except in clocks. I think you deserve some help now.'

'It's eight or nine miles.'

'Oh, well, in that case I won't bother.'

He smiled, unwillingly. 'What time is it?'

'Quarter past nine. I don't think I can go that far tonight.'

'No, me neither. We'll find somewhere to stop.' He helped me up.

'Will you die of this?' I said, not wanting to hear it.

He shook his head slightly. 'No. But it gets worse and worse. There's a place, that we all . . .' His eyes slipped away. They were wholly grey now. 'I should have been there years ago, but they sent no one to take over until Aquila,' he said.

'Can I take you there?'

'Yes. Please.' He was quiet for a second. 'Keep talking to me. I can feel it coming again. It's going to be long, soon.'

'But you had it for a whole day just—'

'There are short spells and long ones. The short ones are. . . five minutes, ten minutes usually. But then it's an hour, or a day, and that's how you know there's a long one coming. It's like foothills round a mountain.'

'I know you said it's like being frozen but – I don't understand how. How can you live through that?'

His expression lifted into something gentler and, for that second, he looked exactly like St Thomas. They were related. The resemblance was as close as mine to Harry's portrait at home. I'd never seen it before, but I couldn't understand now how I'd missed it. Or how I hadn't noticed that he wasn't fading but changing, or how I'd managed to make myself deaf to Inti's stories. She had told me that the markayuq had turned to stone, not been born that way, had been ordinary once. She had told me on the first day. 'How do trees?'

I must have slowed down, although I didn't mean to, because he came back to help me over the roots. The pollen was thick there and against my wrist his fingers were the same colour as the graveyard markayuq's had been. I climbed up after him and didn't know what to say, so I didn't say anything. My ribs ached with wanting to. Atom by atom he had managed to become more important than Clem or cinchona or anything else, but he was going to live for hundreds of years and I was nothing but another one in a long line of people he would never know well, who died like leaves.

TWENTY-SEVEN

IT WASN'T LONG BEFORE we found a road. It was glass and well maintained. Nothing had grown up through the brickwork and here and there were carved stones that looked like the kind Clem and I had seen on the ceques, the Incan highroads where they abandoned boulders in odd places.

'Seven miles,' Raphael said when he saw me looking at one. 'The salt traders use this road. It goes almost up to Bedlam. I was trying to keep you away from it before. It's watched more closely.'

'Salt traders?' I said. The cold felt deeper than before, although it was probably only having come out of heat on the far side of the river. The change was shocking. It had happened over about three miles, although all of those miles had been uphill. I hunched down in my coat, only just managing to follow the conversation.

'They bring children and take salt back to the monastery. Bedlam is a salt colony. That's why it is where it is. Salt is worth more than silver here.'

'That sounds . . . ordinary.'

'Should it not?'

It was no good. 'Do you mind if we stop soon?'

'There's a house up here, I think. Or there was. There used to be foresters, or . . .' He seemed to recognise something and stepped off the road.

I followed him more slowly. Trees had grown, or been planted, in an especially dense avenue on either side of the road, maybe to discourage people from straying, but even beyond that the way was difficult, full of little crevasses where boiling water ran and we had to find branches or stones across, and once a long wall that marked off nothing particular, crumbled and buried under vines. But eventually I saw it before he did – a round, haphazard house like a little tower. It was partly ruined, but only on one side, and there was still a clearer space in front of it that must have been the garden. There, beside a glass gravestone, a markayuq sat among the small mountain flowers, but even when we went close he didn't move. Raphael nodded and we went past, and found the door unlocked.

There was kapok wood stacked by the grate, old and spider-populous, but once I'd brushed it off, it burned beautifully and soon the fire was tall. The house stood in not quite a clearing, but a place where the trees were thinner and the pollen fainter, only just enough to see by without the firelight. The room was round except for a straight section where the hearth was. Cinders skittered over the slate as I fed in more twigs. Sitting on the windowsill, perfectly still and dormant, was another markayuq. Raphael had brushed the dust from him and waxed his clothes when we first came in, and the beeswax smell hung warm in the air.

'Raphael?' I said. He had disappeared while I was making the fire.

'Up here,' he said. His voice came from a doorway at the top of a tiny flight of steps in the far corner.

Wrapped in a blanket, because the cold had soaked me despite having been leaning over the hearth, I went to find him upstairs. He met me in the doorway and I jumped when I saw another markayuq behind him.

'Are you sure we should be here?'

'They're nearly dead; they're old. I think whoever's buried out there was looking after them and they've lost interest now he's gone.' He nodded past me towards the garden and the grave, which was framed by a window halfway up the little stairs. 'Ours is following us again, did you see?'

'No?'

He pointed past my shoulder and I saw her then, stopped still beside a tree, well shy of the house. I wouldn't have seen her at all if he hadn't pointed her out – the markayuq were the same white as the whitewood trees – and I was about to ask how he had known when she moved her hand suddenly to wave away a bird that had tried to land on her shoulder, which flared the pollen. 'She's waiting for us to come out.'

'Can you talk to her?'

'She won't talk back. There's something not right with her. I've never been able to get a word out of her. Thomas chats, but . . . I don't know.' He paused, because I'd mimed knotting, not sure how a markayuq could chat, but he nodded. 'She was at the mines. I don't know what mercury does to markayuq, but it makes normal people angry.'

'Why doesn't she come in?'

'She can't see us in here. Their eyes look black because they have – not cataracts. But they're meant for somewhere much brighter.'

He looked like he wished he hadn't mentioned the last thing, so I ignored it. 'Even with the fire?'

'If you walked right in front of it. Not if you stood to one side. It's easier to find us in the pollen. She knows we have to come out eventually and she's not in a rush, is she. I don't think she'll try to come in. Is it that cold?' he added, because I had pulled my blanket closed and huddled into it. Away from the fire it was bitter.

'Very,' I said. I had been feeling slowly more stupid since I'd found him, but it bubbled now. 'You know you could have told me you weren't burning and the cold wasn't hurting you, before. I would have nagged less. You only said you couldn't feel it.'

He could have interrupted me, but he let me finish before he even shook his head. He only did it once, an inch to one side. 'It was nice to be worried over. Look, come and see this.'

Behind him was some kind of weaver's workshop, full of looms, all threaded up in different shades and thicknesses of alpaca string. He wound a pollen lamp, which brought out the different reds and oranges of what I'd thought were loom strings. But they weren't the warp and weft of half-finished weaving. They were passages and passages of knotwork. It wasn't only cord but strips of rags and old cloth too – anything that would bear twisting, much dented where they had been knotted and unknotted and reknotted.

'My God. What does it all say?'

'It's how they talk to each other,' he said. 'I didn't know they did. I didn't know they wanted to.'

The nearest rack of string was vast, a whole tapestry; a whole novel. 'What's that one?'

He touched the first string. He couldn't read them by sight any more. 'Once there was a girl from the salt colony who . . . fairytale,' he said. He moved along. 'What does . . . July mean. It's one of the new months, it's in the middle of the year – what new months – the foreigners brought them.' He looked back at me. 'They talk about time a lot.' He was still reading while he spoke and he faded off and frowned. 'What year is it? I don't know. Quilka – that must be who's buried outside – Quilka says it's the year of the sun but I think they must have changed the measuring. In the salt colony they say numbers, counting upward, but I don't . . .' He had to stretch for the top of the new string, the markayuq all being more than a foot taller than he was. 'I don't know what it is they're measuring from. Perhaps the Sapa Inca's creation. No, too long ago. How long have you been awake? Only today. When are you from? From when . . . the mercury mines were open. This is her,' he added over his shoulder. 'The one who's following us, Anka.'

'What?'

'She's talking about Huancavelica. She was a doctor there. She didn't know when it was she was last here.'

'When was that?'

'They never decide,' he said. He ran both hands along the strings like a harpist would and shook his head. 'They don't know. It isn't that important to them, or not the older ones. They only know each other, so the way ordinary people measure time doesn't really matter to them. I think she leaves after this part. They go back to stories.'

'What sort of stories?'

'Long ones.' He sectioned off a whole sheaf of strings to show me and, looking closely, I could just see that the knots were all done in the same way, and different to the ones on either side; it was different handwriting. 'They're old, these ones. They sound old-fashioned; they're talking about the Inca courts.'

'The Inca knew about them?'

His shoulders went back. He didn't quite tip over into laughing but he balanced on the edge. 'Knew about them – half of life was arranged around them. The king's bodyguards were always stone people. Puruawqa, does that ring a bell?'

Carillons of bells. 'Knights. Praetorians.'

'Mm.' He didn't seem surprised that I knew, though I was. I was starting to see I hadn't brushed off even half of what I'd forgotten. I must have been fluent in Quechua as a child, given the amount I still understood. Inti had pointed out that it was Dad's first language. 'Anyway, someone here used to do that, he says he misses Atahualpa. He says he had wanted to go with him to his tomb to keep watch – they do that, a lot of the old ones are in catacombs now – but there was no tomb to go to.'

'Who was Atahualpa?'

'The last king. Pizarro killed him. Fifteen hundred and something.' He was still reading. 'This is Thomas. He told me he'd known the King, I thought he was joking. They go off sometimes. I didn't know they came here.' He swallowed. 'I've never seen anything like this before. I thought they didn't like talking. I would have set this up in the church if one of them had said.'

'Maybe the idea is to come away for a bit. And maybe others come here from the monastery. It must be a good halfway point.'

'No, you're right, probably,' he said, but he didn't look like he believed it. He looked tired, and left behind, and I was suddenly angry with the Bedlam markayuq. It must have occurred to them that he couldn't make friends with ordinary people; the best he could hope for there was to outlive them later rather than sooner. It seemed like a deliberate outcasting not to tell him about this place. But then, he wasn't like them; they were from before the Conquest. He would be one of the first in the new generation of hispanicised markayuq. However local he was by blood, he was a cultural foreigner and, even if they were polite, it was hard to imagine that they thought he belonged with them.

'This way of writing. Was it invented for them?' I came up beside him to touch the finer cords. The knots still felt clear. I did want to know, but I wanted to distract us both too, and to have a reason to stand with him instead of five useless feet away. 'They can't see marks on paper, they don't speak, they need something they can feel . . .'

He nodded. 'Invented by them. It's not too suited to ordinary people, it's bloody slow, but it's courtly so people wanted to copy it. Let's go back to the fire,' he finished suddenly. 'Before you freeze. Give me your hand. I can't see to get out of all this.'

I fetched him out. 'Another five minutes, before we go?' I said.

'No. We're staying until you're a normal colour.'

'I am a normal colour. Anyway, you don't know what a normal colour is for me—'

'I knew your grandfather. You look just like him and he was never that shade of blue.' He paused. 'You know when Inti said she'd been named after him?'

'Yes. I was confused. Isn't Inti a sun god?'

'Originally. It means sunny, now. People in town used to call him that. Because of his hair.' He inclined his head at mine.

'I've seen a portrait. What was he like?'

I saw too late that I shouldn't have asked. For me it was generations ago, and I had the same indifference to Harry Tremayne as I had to Queen Elizabeth, but it was still fresh for him and he looked away from me like he'd used to look away from Martel, as though by not seeing he could unhear.

'No, I mean there's no need . . .' I started, feeling stupid.

He interrupted. 'He talks fast. Talked. He quoted things a lot; I had to read all of Shakespeare.'

I smiled. 'How did he come to Bedlam in the first place? Dad said he was stealing quinine and then he had to lay low, but Bedlam is quite low. Even for out here.'

'He'd been shot. Bullets then were . . .' He held his fingertips apart almost to the width of a musket ball. I thought he wouldn't say anything else, but after a while, unexpectedly, he did.

TWENTY-EIGHT

New Bethlehem
1782

RAPHAEL WAS SKINNING A bear on the cliffside for the doctor's new hearthrug when the children came to find him and say there was a man dead on the beach.

He thought at first that they meant someone had fallen. It was rare, because everyone on the stacks had grown up on the gantries and the frosty patches were well known and banistered, but there were accidents sometimes in the winters, and that winter was howling. He only just remembered to scrub his hands down with snow on the way and ran trying to warm them up again. From the first bridge he looked down. The river was frozen and the snow was whirling in billows that were sometimes almost opaque and sometimes almost clear. The children were right, but he hadn't been. It wasn't anyone from the village. It was a foreigner in a Spanish coat, with bright blond hair that showed even from so far down. The man looked like he had come from nowhere. Later, some people said he did, although Raphael was more inclined to say he had run from Phara, which was equally impressive, because it was fourteen miles away.

He set the counterweight light so that he could get down fast and held the rope hard as it banged to a halt eight inches above the beach. For a second he couldn't find the man and felt a flutter under his ribs, because there were too many stories about ghosts in the snow that he didn't quite disbelieve. But then he saw he was almost standing on top of him. The man was under the ice. The water was shallow but the glass stratum below him was deep and littered with bits of ancient masonry so that he looked like he was falling, at an infinitesimally slow pace, very far.

The man opened his eyes and touched the underside of the ice, too weak for anything else. Raphael swore and slammed the butt of his rifle into it. It wasn't thick and when he hauled the man out, he choked, but not enough to have breathed the water yet. Although some of it had been washed away, he was still covered in blood. The sun came out again and Raphael understood at last. The man had fallen in the hot glass shadow, in the shallow water, and when the sun had gone in, it had frozen almost on the instant and trapped him there. He shook him to wake him up more and helped him along as much as he could back to the lift. It was difficult. The man was tall.

The children followed them to the church until he told them to go away. Inside, once it was warmer, the man explained in broken Spanish that his name was Henry Tremayne – Harry, for reasons he couldn't explain – and that he had been upriver somewhere near the mountains stealing quinine bark when he was caught. He had got away and run, but they had shot him in the shoulder. He was brave when Raphael took the bullet out, though he was no soldier and he shook for a long time afterwards.

Once Harry was warm and bandaged, there was time to notice that the children had moved a log under the window to see in. There was a row of eyes. When they saw Raphael they ducked, but not far enough. He let them be. They weren't making any noise. He opened the other window, the one that overlooked the mountain.

'Could you close that?' Harry said hesitantly.

'Can you see the mountain?'

'The mountain?'

'Just say hello.'

'Hello?'

'Good enough.' He closed the window again and wondered, for the thousandth time, if those half-sentient stones in the skeleton of the earth knew, still, when strangers came; if they were interested, or if they were only caught in deep rock dreams and unconscious even of the ages skimming by, never mind the people made of bones who flashed about too fast to follow.

Some Spanish men came later that week, looking for a foreigner. He hid Harry in the undercroft and said there was no one. They made a mess and searched the place anyway, but they didn't know there was an undercroft. They came again in the spring, to make sure, and the lie was more difficult because Harry had been about the village in the meantime, but a great advantage of the priesthood was mass and Raphael had taken the precaution of swearing everyone to secrecy weeks before. People liked Harry anyway; he was generous and strong. The summer was short and the next winter swept in fast, and although the bullet wound had healed more or less and Harry was worried about his family in England, Raphael kept him back, afraid he would only kill himself with the cold trying to trek over the Andes.

On the first day of real spring Harry jumped out from behind the woodshed and swung him around into the grass. Being nearly a head taller, he didn't have to try hard to do it.

'I think you'll find this is unobservance of the Sabbath. How about you stop rushing around for one afternoon?'

Raphael hit him, not very effectually. 'All right, Rabbi.'

'You should be grateful I haven't organised a stoning. Dear God.' Harry was laughing. 'It's such a lovely day. You can't waste it on the bloody markayuq.'

It was. The sky was blue and so was the river, and there was no snow anywhere but the peak of the mountain, which rumbled and sighed with a tiny earthquake like it was settling in the sun. Raphael snorted when Harry leaned across him to catch something in the grass. He had never known anyone so determined to look at crawly things. He'd tried to say once that there was such a thing as the proper use of a newspaper, but Harry had called him a savage and installed a green tarantula in what had used to be the coffee jar. It ate chicken scraps, or it had until Raphael had left it in the woods and told Harry it had escaped, with the jar, which he couldn't bring himself to go back out and fetch.

'I can't breathe.'

'No, I know, but it's worth it,' Harry said. He had caught a mouse and moved it to show him, his elbow sharp in Raphael's ribs. 'Look at this. I don't think anyone where I'm from knows he exists. I might write something.'

'Will anyone read it?'

'The flora and fauna of South America are a subject of fascination for everybody who's anybody,' Harry said, archly, because in fact it was an impression of his father. Raphael had understood that late, but he was pleased to have understood. Irony was a difficult thing to catch in a new language, and more so because not all languages had it, not even all local languages. He was nearly sure that if Harry had chanced on a village a hundred miles further east, he would have offended someone by now and been thrown in a gorge.

'Does that mean you and your four friends at your club?'

'I think four might be generous,' Harry laughed. He let the mouse go. It trundled off in no particular hurry. He had a knack with animals. He would poke and prod anything, but nothing seemed to want to bite him. Raphael was waiting to come in one night and find him playing cards with a bear.

Harry stayed still for a while, then sighed. 'You don't fancy coming to have a look at England, do you?'

'I can't go anywhere.'

'No, of course.' He sat up and leaned forward against his knees, looking out at the stacks and the mountain. The wind swayed the tips of his hair between his shoulder blades, although not strongly enough to tug any from the black ribbon. 'But you'll lose your English, you know. Real bugger to get so fluent and forget the lot.'

Raphael had started to learn after it became obvious that Harry had the linguistic abilities of a pigeon. He could stumble along in Spanish with the broadest English accent it was possible to have, but sometimes he forgot what he was supposed to be doing and lapsed towards the end of sentences into a weird mix of both. Quechua was too different even to try. Since English was only one more slightly westward hop after Latin and Spanish, it had been easier for Raphael to put it together than labour over trying to make Harry understand what grammar was. 'You'll have to come back.'

Harry smiled. 'I will, then.'

Raphael looked away at the flowers in the grass. It was only a story; no one would go to and fro between England and the

Peruvian mountains. But it was a good story. He could feel himself half-believing it, the same way he believed in heaven. It wasn't belief of the mathematical reasoned kind, only the sort that arises when the alternative would mean becoming one of those men who worked like machines and never spoke to anyone, old at forty.

The light changed. It was night and the galaxy was a stripe across the sky. Raphael jerked upright. The blanket that had been tucked over his shoulders fell into his lap. There was a light inside the church but no moving shadow. He got up and pushed the door open, his chest hurting because his heart wouldn't move. The last time had been ten years.

'Harry?'

'There you are. I'm cooking, not very well; I was hoping you'd come round in time to properly supervise. Or at least tell me how in God's name you're supposed to cook quinoa.'

Raphael pushed his hands together, because they were shaking. It had only been the afternoon. He folded the blanket over the back of a chair. 'Not like that. What's the point of you?'

'I'm ornamental.'

'Sit down and don't touch anything.'

Harry sat down obediently next to the stove. Even sitting he seemed tall. The lamplight had turned him all gold, sunspun. People called him that – Sunny, Inti – and he was. He didn't look like a human. He was too broad and too bright.

Raphael put a plate down in front of him and folded into the chair opposite, aware as he did of the stiffness in his joints. They didn't hurt. It felt as though whoever had made him had come back and tightened all the screws. He was starting to find that he couldn't slouch. Or not couldn't; but he could let his weight hang forward without moving his spine, and each vertebra felt as if it were strong enough to lift much more than it was.

Harry was editing some notes, probably about the mouse, going through in red ink and adding things in the margins. Raphael watched him write. He did it easily and quickly, for fun. It wasn't an unfamiliar idea, but there was still a novelty in seeing it.

'So the thing about mice here,' Harry said, without looking up, 'is that they rather resemble European voles, which is interesting, because they can't possibly be related. It implies that the shape of animals happens in the way bubbles do. A bubble will form in a sphere in Europe or Peru. They don't suddenly go square when you hit the tropics. It's starting to look like a mouse will always be mouse-shaped.'

'As opposed to tiny fluffy octopuses?'

'Well, exactly. Where are the cyclopes? Where are the one-legged men or the tripods, and why are there never mice that are blue or in possession of eight legs? You know? More things in heaven and earth than are dreamt of in your philosophy – except there aren't.' He paused. 'You don't care,' he laughed.

'I don't.'

'Happily that doesn't bother me at all. Are you turning into a markayuq?'

'What?'

'Well,' said Harry, as if they were still talking about mice. 'Odd thing number one: walking statues who are in fact men and women. Odd thing number two: you have lost almost as much time as you've lived – more if you count these smaller spells of yours. And they're getting longer.' He smiled a little. 'There are more things in heaven and earth than in my philosophy, but there are not *many* more. It would be extraordinary to find two at once and unrelated. It seems to me that it would make more sense for them to be in fact one, larger, odd thing. No?'

'Yes.'

Harry looked pleased. 'And all this stop-start exponential catalepsy is in fact a kind of stop-start metamorphosis, and each time you're a little different and a little stronger and one day different altogether. What a lovely creature you are.'

Raphael felt himself redden. 'Eat your bloody quinoa.'

'I am, I am.' He did for a while, then looked up suddenly as if a thought had bumped into him sideways. 'You swear damn well for someone who's only learned English for a year. You do all sorts of things well.'

'Languages get easier the more of them you speak—'

'No, no, no. You've got an incredible memory. Graven in stone, isn't it? You're made of different stuff and it works differently. You utter stinking cheating bastard.' He kicked him under the table. '*Oh, Harry's so stupid, Harry can't learn Quechua, look at my fancy English.*'

'Ow.'

'I'm going to read this essay to you,' he said vengefully. 'Tell me if it sounds clunky.'

'Oh, I don't want to hear—'

'Part *One*,' Harry said over him. 'On the idiosyncratic features of the lesser Peruvian mouse.'

Raphael sat still to listen. He had never known it till recently, but he liked being read to. The pollen lamps were running down by the time Harry had finished. He let them. Harry faded almost to sleep before he jerked awake and apologised and started getting ready for bed. It was only the ordinary routine but Raphael watched him while he still could, awake because of the lost hours. Once Harry was gone, it would be back to knowing the exact time to wind up the lamps in the evening, and noticing how that moment retreated or advanced by its weekly minutes as it tided up to and away from midsummer.

Harry dropped *Don Quixote* into his lap. They had been working through it in an effort to improve Harry's horrible Spanish. 'Your turn.' He sat down again and shifted his chair closer so that he could follow the text too, smelling of soap and a fresh shirt for bed. He wound up the lamps again.

Raphael found their place and didn't say there would be no need for it soon. Harry wouldn't stay much longer and he wouldn't come back. He had a wife at home, and a little girl. He wasn't a natural expeditionary; he worried about them and wrote letters he couldn't send. The quinine men watched the post.

'Still with me?' Harry asked after a little while.

'Yes. Just finding the place.'

'It's there.'

'I know that.'

'Read it then.'

'Shut up.'

*

Raphael didn't sleep and then went out early, resigned to being tired all day. Spring had thoroughly sprung; there were bees and big butterflies everywhere, even though last week there had been a frost. Over the border, the graveyard markayuq was missing. He hunted around for a while and then found snapped twigs and trudged after her.

They did wander every so often, for a change of scene, but it made him uneasy when they did. If there had been fires in the forest, or if it had been a harsh winter, they got lost in the deep patches of dark where the pollen had faded and it took days, sometimes, to find them by lamplight. The trees were soon denser and the new pollen flared around him. The warmth from outside was starting to seep into the woods. He had come out without his coat and didn't need it even in the shadows. Stirring through the trees, the wind was warm too.

When he still couldn't find her after an hour, he gave up. She would come back eventually and, if she didn't, he would go out again when he was awake instead of nearly sleepwalking. He paused, leaning against a tree, to brush a blue butterfly from the back of his sleeve. With his head resting against the bark he closed his eyes for a second, feeling heavy. He didn't usually mind being so bound to one place, but sometimes he could feel the weight of the anchor. The chain would barely stretch to Azangaro, never mind to England. When he opened his eyes, his breath steamed.

He couldn't move. He was clamped into place by something. It was a vine, candle ivy, thick and twined around his chest and his arm, pulling it behind his back. He wasn't standing; his whole weight was being held up, a foot clear of the ground, by roots that had grown up under him and formed round him. They were grey with frost. It was only panic strength that let him tear through. Once he had half-fallen out of it, the tree was a monstrous broken cage. He raked his hands through his hair. There were strands of frozen web caught in it. It was plainly winter and there was nothing alive anywhere, but it made him shudder so hard it hurt his shoulder when he thought of what summer must have been like. When he looked down at himself, his clothes were rags where the branches hadn't saved them from the weather, but he didn't feel cold. Ground frost crunched under him. The forest floor was springy with pine needles.

The trees on the way back to the border had changed. The roots had interlaced. He had to climb to get through, and when he found the graveyard, Anka was there, sleeping now; they had a different quality of stillness when they were asleep. He found the border, still well kept, and almost bumped into a little boy cleaning St Thomas. The boy stared at him. Thomas recognised him and touched his arm with one knuckle. He could be expressive; it had the quality of, you're late.

'Um . . . good morning, sir,' the boy managed.

'Morning,' he said. He couldn't tell if the boy was one he'd known as a baby, but he didn't think so. There was nothing wrong with him. They had sent one, finally. In another few years, he could leave. 'What – can you tell me what year it is?'

The boy was still little enough to be asked about arbitrary facts and he didn't stumble over it like an adult would have. 'Eighteen fifty-six, sir.'

He had to rock back a step. 'Are you sure?'

'Yes, sir.'

'Is there a priest at the church?'

'No, sir. The church is empty. No one goes in unless there are visitors.'

'I see. Thank you.'

Raphael left him there and went to the church. The door was locked but like it always would, a decent shove just at shoulder height juddered the latch open. Inside, everything was cold and still. Despite what the little boy had said, he had half, abortively hoped it wasn't real and that Harry would be there just the same, but he was gone. Nobody had been there for a long time. The air tasted undisturbed.

Everything had been cleared away, neatened up, but it was all there. *Don Quixote* was still on the table, closed on what looked like the right page over a letter. When he slipped it out, the ink on the envelope had faded to a strange brown. It was addressed to him. He opened it.

Raphael,

You've been gone for a month and I must go home. But I'll come back. Write to me when you see this.

Harry

There was an address in England underneath. He read it twice more and eventually he put it down and dragged himself up the ladder to see if his clothes were still there. They were, and the bolt of Indian cotton Harry had brought. He didn't look at it. Instead he found some warm things to take downstairs and draped them over the chairs to air while he set the windmill going and waited for water. He expected the rope to break after so long, but someone must have come in and kept it turning every now and then. He built the stove up very slowly, trying to ease the heat into the pipes instead of rushing it all in at once. They creaked but didn't burst.

He was cleaner than he would have thought but not clean. He scrubbed it all off, too hard, and had to stop when he scratched himself. He didn't feel it. He stood watching points of blood well in the mark on his arm and waited, but there was nothing. He could feel the pressure but not the sting.

More slowly, because his hands had started to shake, he got dressed again and then didn't know what to do next once he was. After a long, limbo silence, he sat down in front of the book and touched it gradually, afraid to set the weight of his hand on it, but it didn't turn to dust. He found the place easily, because the print was faded where it had sat for a long time in the sun. The paper should have been cold, but he couldn't feel that either.

Someone tapped on the door. He didn't say anything, because he felt four miles to the side of it all, but a woman came in. She was holding a flask and a bowl that steamed.

'This is for you,' she said. She waited until he took it. She was neat and quick as a robin, tall, with only one hand. He saw her scan him and the little lift of her head when she noticed he was healthy. 'My son told me that he found you on the border. He said that St Thomas knew you and that you enquired after the date?'

'Was it right, what he said?'

'It was. Twenty-third of July, eighteen fifty-six. Were you expecting something else?'

He nodded.

'You're him, aren't you?' she said. It wasn't a real question. She didn't sound surprised. 'Everyone wondered what had happened to you.'

'Delayed. Why is there no one else here?' he asked.

'No other priest? Nobody knows,' she said. 'There was no sufficiently healthy person until Aquila.' She looked around, worried. 'It should all have been maintained as you left it.'

'It's fine.'

'Are the pipes functioning properly?'

'So far,' he said, wondering why she was talking to him as if they were in an official report for Lima. 'I've got spares if they're not. Or I had.'

'No one's disturbed anything,' she said quickly. 'But I'm not sure it was ever inventoried, so perhaps a few items might have, you know, over the years . . .'

'I think it's all here.' He stopped, because it had occurred to him, piecemeal, that she wasn't being lofty at all. Her tone was wrong for that. The language had changed. There was more Spanish in it. 'Is that coffee?'

'It is.'

He took down a pair of cups and rinsed away the dust, and shared out the coffee between them. It steamed, but he couldn't feel the heat of it. He couldn't tell if he'd burned himself.

'You'd better eat, before it goes cold,' she said, nodding at the stew in front of him. It was rich. They must have been doing well.

'I'm sorry, I'm not hungry.' Breakfast had been seventy years before, but only an hour ago.

'You should eat it anyway. You'll be hungry in a minute.'

'Why?'

She nodded at the window, to the overgrown courtyard outside. People were starting to gather there in twos and threes. More were coming from over the bridge.

'You've seventy years of baptisms and confessions to do.'

He had to eat slowly, because his taste had changed, or rather, faded. It was barely there.

'I'm Inti,' she said, and his eyes must have caught on her for too long, because she twisted her nose. 'I know. I didn't select it. My mother wanted a boy.'

'Raphael.'

She nodded as if she already knew that.

He pushed his hand over his wrist without meaning to. He kept feeling spider webs. But his knuckles had gone red; the water must have been hotter than he'd thought, which meant at least that if there were any leftover spiders, they were cooked. He tried the coffee. It tasted bizarre now that he couldn't tell at once if it was hot or not, but not bad. It was strong enough to taste, at least.

'What's your boy's name again?' he asked at last.

'Aquila. I think he might be concealed in your woodshed. He wants to come in but he's terrified of being accidentally rude. Have I been accidentally rude?' she added.

'No.' He set the coffee aside. 'Right. Let's go out and see what we can do with everyone. But I'll need Aquila to help me. I don't know their names.'

He'd always felt impatient when old people waxed lyrical about it, but it was easy to spot people's grandchildren and great-grandchildren, and it was unsettling. There were eyes that never changed, deformities, and that was unremarkable, but there were other things that had swept down the lines too. There was a girl who spoke with her hands just like her great-grandmother, despite never having met her and her mother having nothing like the same style. He had gone out expecting strangers and some were, because a good third of them were altar children or the sons and daughters of altar children, but in the main it was a colony of ghosts.

By the time he had met everyone who wanted to be met, it was late. He locked himself in, although he never usually held with locking a church. With his back against the door he looked around at the room. It was all the same: the ladder up to the loft, the kitchen, the stiff side door into the chapel. But it wasn't the same, either. The roof had been repaired twice and needed it again. There were books on the shelf behind the ladder that weren't his. They were in English. His heart bumped into his diaphragm to think of Harry coming back to an empty church, but when he opened them, the Ex Libris notes said that they belonged to someone called Charles Backhouse. There must have been expeditions here; Harry had said there would be. It needled that they had been put up in the church, but then, they had left it all as they had found it and it wasn't as though there was a nice inn and coach house in town.

In the deep silence, the clockwork in the pollen lamps clicked. So did the wood in the stove. The windmill rope creaked around its pulley and under it was the roar of the wind in the forest. The winter must have been long already, because there was almost no pollen in the air.

For a long time he looked down at the letter without touching it. Harry had told him about Heligan. Somewhere in a churchyard on that side of the Atlantic were familiar bones.

Or here they were, in this place. Somewhere was another church – his – where Harry was cutting up pineapples, but it was too far gone. Harry had kept sailing while he had stayed still and there was no tacking ahead to find him again, no catching up, and there would have been no waiting, the current being too strong. He had fallen too far behind.

Not able to sit any more, Raphael went upstairs to fetch the Indian cotton and laid it out on the table. With all the pollen lamps lit, there was enough light to unpick the stitching on his waistcoat. After a few hours it was all undone and he lifted out the worn-out old lining to lay it over the cotton as a pattern. It was complicated, but he had always mended things and it was only a matter, really, of cutting straight, and an obsidian knife was as good as a scalpel. It was light outside before he had finished, but he did finish. Once he had he went straight out, because there were people he had promised to see and, even if there hadn't been, it seemed best to muck in. It would pass the time.

TWENTY-NINE

The Caravaya whitewood forest
1860

WHEN HE STOPPED TALKING, I gave him the little flask I'd brought from Bedlam. He frowned until he caught the fumes from it – I'd stolen some of his rum – and then laughed and shared.

'Thanks.'

I swallowed some too and sat still to let it burn its way down, just as hot and good as the fire. I didn't know what to say; I felt like more of a stranger than ever and I couldn't say that. It had been Harry's ghost keeping me safe. It was nothing to do with me.

'Better go soon.'

'Yes,' he agreed, but then his focus turned inward and he frowned. 'I'm tired,' he said, puzzled.

I was too, so much that I was only just upright. It was past eleven now, and hard to think that this morning, we had been on the island with Martel. But I could see what he meant. He was always walking and always working. He wouldn't have been unusually tired, if it were just the distance and the worry alone.

'I bet you are.'

'What? We've been sitting here for ages.'

'Well – not only are you changing, you're changing into something a lot heavier than you used to be. You're lifting more weight every time you move,' I said, and finished quietly, because I heard halfway through that it was what Harry would have said. It could have been a portrait of me, on the stairs at home.

'I hadn't thought of that.'

I looked out the window again. The light was just as dim as before. Anka was where we'd left her – I could see her pollen shadow. 'There's no reason to rush on if she's not coming in.'

He didn't say anything. It was like seeing clockwork wind down. He stopped gradually, and then it was that strange, absolute stillness. I watched him for a long time, hoping to God that it wasn't going to be years. I had a feeling it wasn't. Both the long spells I knew of had been when he was by himself, well away from people, and I would have bet money that the rest had been too, because otherwise someone would have accidentally buried him. The shorter spells, the ones I'd seen, came when other people would have daydreamt or dozed; he had been tired every time, and sitting still.

I went through our bags for some food. We had grapes and apples, and some phoenix eggs wrapped in a handkerchief. I cooked two over the fire, needlingly aware of the markayuq in the window, but he hadn't moved at all. It didn't come to me exactly, or not in the ordinary way of a cork popping to the surface of a pond. I must have known it since Raphael told me what they were, perhaps before, so it was sluggish, more like a cork in treacle. For years I had sat in a greenhouse opposite a breathing stone person who watched my father's grave. And who came inside when it rained.

I fell asleep thinking about it, propped in a nest of blankets by the hearth. I didn't know how long it lasted, though, before I came awake all at once. I listened, not sure what I could have heard. Raphael was still frozen. The fire was still going, just.

I jumped when I saw Anka outside. She was right by the window; right by the door. Not wanting to look away from her, I shook Raphael's shoulder but it didn't move him. The door opened gently. What had woken me was the catch. She was holding a tangle of candle ivy, full of glowing seed cases, each one as bright as a lamp. It was enough time to promise myself that she wasn't interested in Raphael, snatch up his rifle and run for the loom room. Behind me, she lobbed the vines so close that the light slung my silhouette against the wall as pollen burst into the air. The other markayuq was exactly where we had left him, unmoving. I pushed the door to, not all the way so that it wouldn't clank. I couldn't see her through the gap, but I heard the hiss of her robes as she crossed the floor.

The window opened when I pushed it. I climbed out and dropped down. It was a floor and a half, because the loom room was up a little set of stairs, and the jolt jarred my leg. I pressed both hands over my mouth to keep quiet and crawled behind the woodpile.

The sparse pollen flared whenever I moved too suddenly. I tipped my hand to and fro, more and more slowly, until I found a speed that was nearly invisible. Getting up was difficult but walking wasn't. What was hard was to stay so slow, much slower than she walked. My throat hurt with knowing I would be, to an ordinary person, in perfect, full view of the house, but no steps sounded behind me. Once I'd gone as far as I could bear, I knelt down to the level of the woods where the animals had eaten the shrubs back and shot through the clearest path I could find. The pollen trail of the bullet flashed brilliant and perfect and, because there was no wind so deep inside the forest, it hung there, almost without blurring. I walked fast to the next tree so there would be a person trail too, then stopped and forced myself to stand still. Then I eased back towards the house as she came out. Even going slowly was leaving a sparkle. I stopped again as she came nearer. She passed so close she almost touched me. A quarter of an inch more to the left and she would have knocked into my shoulder.

I stayed frozen there for a long time after she had gone. She was following the bullet trail. After I'd counted to fifty I started to move again. I kept leaving cinder snatches in the light, though never a whole ghost. She had left the door open and I felt absurdly resentful that she'd let out the heat. The cold had settled in by the time I got back inside, where the embers of her light bomb still breathed pollen on the floor. Raphael caught my wrist and pulled me up the steep step.

'Christ, I thought she might have—'

'She didn't touch me.' He pulled a blanket round my shoulders. 'She was looking for you. I saw the last half of that. You didn't try and snatch a coat before you went?'

'How much can they see?'

'They see you if you move.' He looked out into the woods. My rifle shot was still there, and so, more faintly, was her trail. There was nothing coming back towards us, although I divided the trees into imaginary quadrants and studied each one carefully in case she was doing what I had.

'If she's not coming now, I should change,' he said at last. 'If I stop anywhere in these clothes they won't last long.'

By the light of our pollen lamps, after I'd closed the shutters so that the glow wouldn't show, we changed his ordinary clothes for the heavy leathers he had been making. Once I'd fastened him into them, which was difficult because they were as thick as armour, he was only a few shades away from the colour the others were. I stepped back as soon as it was done. A fortnight was a short time for him to have conditioned me to wariness around the markayuq but he had managed it. It felt wrong to stand too close to him without a salt vial or a brush in my hands. It only lasted while he stood still. When he crouched down to find some wax in the pocket of his old waistcoat and run it down his knot cord he was only Raphael again.

'Is there a reason the others are tall and you're ordinary-sized?' I asked, because I couldn't stand the quiet any more.

'Whitewood,' he said. He traced a line down his ribs as if he were showing me the boning inside a corset. 'Put it on a healthy person and they grow as tall as the markayuq. We stopped doing that when the Jesuits arrived. Bad idea for native priests to be clearly identifiable. Right, let's go. Are you warm enough? You're not useful if you keel over.'

'Yes . . . yes, shut up, you pointless fossil.'

He pushed me gently into the wall. I tried to push him back and couldn't.

The trees grew closer and closer together as we walked. We kept to the glass road now, because there was no use, in the thick pollen, weaving through the trees; if Anka wanted to follow us, she would see, whichever way we tried. But if she was, I didn't see her, only the furls and switches of light where birds and bats floated between the branches. The path coiled upward, taking us slowly higher into new mountains I couldn't see, but the cold sharpened and the glass road clouded with frost. All the temperate plants that had grown between the trees faded away. The trees were titans and their roots had tangled through each other, interlocking sometimes in impassable brambles of foot-wide bark that encroached onto the edge of the road, and sometimes in patterns that arched right over it, which must have been guided and pruned once by an ancient forester. They made living tunnels where the air was warmer and the candle ivy still flowered, so thickly that the glow in the air looked like sourceless sunlight and we lost every last shadow. Sometimes, a corner of stonework or a hopelessly eroded carving peeped through everything, but it was impossible to say how old it was.

Every now and then was a clear patch in the pollen. Nothing seemed to have caused it exactly; it was like the abysses in deep space, the patches of darkness where the stars happened not to have scattered, and whenever we reached those, Raphael hesitated. He didn't ask for help, but I kept talking and steered us to the middle of the road.

I had to stop too when we came to a place where something had smashed down through the trees. It had left a hole in the canopy, a big one, and through it came a glimmer of the stars. Partly on the road was a gigantic chunk of masonry, old, part of an archway.

'What . . . in God's name is that? How did it get there? Catapult or . . .? Do people build in the trees?'

'Don't know. I haven't been here since I was little. Which was . . . more than a hundred years ago.' He looked brittle as he said it, like he might have slowed and never moved again if he stared for too long at the idea.

'Give me a hand,' I said, to bring him back to now. I climbed up on to the stone to see down under it. 'Well – it fell a good way, it's smashed the glass.' There was a great shatterweb in the road's glass bricks. Some of them had crumbled away, long enough ago for the rain to have worn down the sharper edges.

'Careful,' he said.

'Of what?' I asked, and then bumped my head on something as I straightened up. It didn't hit me hard and I felt it veer away. 'Ow. What was that?'

He climbed up with me and stretched across, past me, to catch it. It was a log, floating in the air, and when he let it go for me to see, it spun gently. Some moss tipped off the edge of it. I looked up. There were more of them, many more, half-branches, some of them still, some of them turning very slowly. The hole ripped through the canopy didn't have ragged edges. Some of the displaced twigs and pine needles had already risen that high and bumped into the broken branches, and started to clog the gaps. There was no breeze to chase the pollen back into the space, which was much darker than everything else, a column of dark that came down in straight lines nearly like sunlight would have. I stretched up to tap the log. I had to pull it to make it dip, about half the strength in my arm. It would have been strong enough for a child to sit on.

'Come on. Better not stay.'

I looked back. 'I haven't seen her.'

'It isn't her I'm worried about. I feel a bit . . .' He shook his head. 'The gates are just up here. You can leave me there. Someone should be about that way.'

'All right. We'll find someone and then I'll go.' I watched him slide down ahead of me and hesitated, because it was steep on the other side. He lifted me down. There was no strain at all in his hands now. I might have been a doll.

'Thank you.'

He let me go.

'Will you go back to Bedlam, once you're . . . finished?' I said.

'No. They've got their markayuq, and Aquila. I'm allowed to return, but I think I might go mad and end up in bits on the riverbank. I'll probably stay at the monastery.'

'Will I be able to come back to see you?'

'There are dispensations,' he said slowly. 'But I don't think you'll want to in twenty or thirty years, or whatever it is.'

'How do you know it will be that long? You've just come out of seventy years and you've only been awake for a few. Why do you think it will be . . .'

'It takes a hundred years to change. More or less.' He paused. 'If I'd been in a safe place and not out in the middle of the woods, last time – with Harry – I would never have woken so quickly. I shouldn't be awake now. These last few years . . . it's like waking up in the middle of the night.'

'So the next one . . .'

'I don't know. It could be half an hour like just now or it could be much longer. It's like falling asleep. It happens in snatches but you keep waking and then you don't.'

'And then after?' I said, not able to say what I meant. If I woke up in the middle of the night, even if I walked around the house and talked to the dog and opened windows, I never remembered it the next day, and always felt strange about the open windows when I saw them.

'And then afterwards if I'm lucky I'll be like Thomas. You know. Up and about if I want. Thinking, talking. Slowly.' He rubbed his hand over the knot cord on his other wrist.

I didn't try to say it wasn't what I'd meant. Asking if he would forget me, because I'd arrived in this tiny wakeful space, could only sound like bleating. He wouldn't give a damn if he forgot me; I suspected he might even be glad to. All I'd done was remind him of a dead man. 'Then what?' I said.

'Then they're awake usually but then they sleep for a few months at a time. Then awake again. Repeat for six hundred years and then you sleep more and more, and then you never wake but you don't exactly die either. They sink into the bedrock in the end. Dead markayuq don't look like people. You wouldn't know, usually.'

'Which is why people used to build around the bedrock.'

He nodded. 'You should have seen the fuss when they built the cathedral in Cuzco. Smack through the ground, huge trenches through the rock. I went once, when it was nearly finished. Gave me the creeps.'

I laughed. 'No one explained to the Spanish?'

'Of course they explained, but the engineers told them not to be idolatrous and to sod off. Only reasonable response, really. I can't think anyone approached them in a very measured or un-Indian way.'

'Why do you hate Indians? You know white people are much worse, don't you? It isn't as though there's some kind of international bar you're not reaching out here. We're terrible at everything. Lasting much past forty-five. Learning more than one language. It's a miracle, actually; sickly prematurely ageing worryingly inbred horsey idiots have managed to convince everyone else their way is best by no other means than firmness of manner and the tactical distribution of flags. I can't believe no one's called our bluff yet.'

He laughed. It always took me by surprise when he did and I had to fight not to look too pleased. 'I don't like bad translation. I don't like idiots who go around telling white men that the mountain's alive and it thinks things, and that villages are watched over by special people who turned to stone.'

'But that's what it is.'

'No it isn't,' he said, and smacked me in the chest with his knuckles. It was the very lightest tap but I could feel the weight behind it now. Any harder and I would have gone over backwards. 'That's terrible. That's not how you'd say it in Spain or England, is it? You'd say, there is a particular hereditary illness in the Andean highlands that causes petrification and eventually renders the sufferers inert in a kind of permanent catalepsy and apparently part of the surrounding rock, which has led to a cultural tendency to be very careful of stone, and a religion that reveres it. That's exactly the same thing, in the language that you actually speak rather than in Quechua but using Spanish words. Bloody Quespañol. Speak one or the other, or don't complain when someone smacks you over the head with a Bible and calls you a moron.'

I was still laughing as we rounded the bend and beyond it was an aqueduct, almost as tall as the trees. Four markayuq stood on plinths on either side of the columns that rose over the road and they turned their heads to watch us. They were much more like guards than the Bedlam shrines. Their clothes were different; it was the same leather, but it had been made in plates and greaves, and they all carried spears. Gold, because gold would never rust. They seemed wholly awake, as awake as we were. My heart bobbed up into the back of my throat. If they were keeping track of who went in and out, and when, then they knew only one markayuq boy had been delivered in the last hundred years and they knew he was only twelve. I might have looked nearly like a turning priest but the timing didn't add up.

But none of them made any sign to stop us. The one nearest to us only nodded a little. I thought he looked sad.

'They would have had whole retinues to bring them here from Cuzco when they changed,' Raphael explained quietly as we passed them. 'I don't think they like seeing people having to make the run from Bedlam alone. I remember . . . there was some trouble with them on the way out, when I was little. They stopped us, because there was no provision for getting back.'

'Shame Anka doesn't feel that way.'

'Anka turned in Bedlam. Or as far as I can tell she did. No one helped her; I can see why she wouldn't have much sympathy for someone else whose foreign friend's grandson arrived at exactly the right moment. It isn't fair.'

'Why didn't anyone from here go and fetch her? Why didn't they come for you?'

'There's no way of telling when we'll turn, or not without a doctor following you around. You can gauge it more or less, but I wasn't due, when I lost the time with Harry. And once we are asleep, it's illegal to move us. Even if someone had found her they wouldn't have been able to do anything about it.'

'That's a stupid law.'

'Where a markayuq stands is important. Everyone assumes you stood there on purpose. It would be like moving the altar of a church, or . . . I don't know. It is stupid, you're right.'

From vents up near where the water must have been, valves sprayed a constant, fine mist down into the trees. It had made a slick patch of black ice in the road. To keep a decent footing we went round, climbing over roots until the road was clear again. It led straight underneath one of the aqueduct's arches, where everything took on a tiny echo. On the other side the trees looked older. The water must have been to stop any forest fires from jumping into the oldest stock. Mist coiled around everything. The air was thin and I could sense that we were very high up now, but the forest was still the forest, too dense to see through even without the mist.

'Merrick . . .'

The life went from him, even though it left him standing still and upright. I sat down on some roots and waited, but half an hour ticked by on my watch, and then an hour. After that I stared at the second-hand, not knowing whether to wait or not. I'd started to write a note for him before I wondered whether he could still read it. I didn't know how to leave even a simple message on a knot cord. In the end I tied our cords together, one end round his wrist and the other to the loop of a root, and carved *Gone to find someone 8.15am* next to it. I left my watch wound up and open, balanced on the root. I waited for a few seconds after that, trying to think of a way for him to be sure of the date too, but my watch didn't show that. He would know at least if it had been more than a day. The springs would have wound down by then.

'I'll be back soon,' I said, in case he could hear me. 'But this isn't a busy road. I don't want to leave you here if nobody ever comes. See you in a minute.'

It felt stupid to speak to him. He wasn't there. It wasn't like speaking to a sleeping person but to a coat he had taken off.

Carefully, because in places it was icy, I set off down the road, expecting to see houses or walls at any minute, but there was nothing except a tiny tumbledown something on the left. It was overgrown completely, the stonework pulled apart by some local version of saxifrage. And then, on the edge of an outcrop, not sheared away but finished neatly in a straight line, the path ended. The outcrop overhung a valley and suddenly I had a sprawling view down. The forest went on and on in a great mist-ringed basin. There was no city, no people. I could see what had used to be a town. There were stone towers, but they were crumbled. Something gleamed between the ruins: glass, an obsidian flow that ran down from the mountainside. The forest had almost claimed it all back. Vapour clung in rags around the masonry. It had been years since anyone was here. Decades. There was a lake too. Nothing moved there except some birds.

The back of my throat gone dry and burned-feeling, I started down the valleyside. It wasn't steep. The tree roots made steps here and there that were good enough to get down by. I went down awkwardly, hearing nothing except my own breath and the squeak of the straps on my backpack, where the doubled-over sections under the buckles rubbed together. Outcrops of stone dotted the way. I didn't see anything in them at first but then I started to catch the turn of shoulders and suggestion of arms. If I hadn't known what I was looking at I wouldn't have guessed at it. The markayuq had blended into the rock, mostly. If it was possible for them to wake again at all they would have had to tear themselves free.

I'd hoped there were still people living there and the ruins were incidental, but there were no new houses or huts, or anything. There were dead people in the glass, sealed in like flies in amber. It must have rushed down when it came. A markayuq was caught in it too at the edge, waist high. I couldn't tell if she was dead or sleeping, or only thinking. The glass had splashed on the side it had hit her, which made her look like she had been frozen for ever just in the moment she walked into the sea.

Further on, some trees had grown over the flow of obsidian and cracked its surface where their roots pushed up, but since I didn't know how fast they grew, it was impossible to tell how long they had been there, or if the glass was a thousand years old or fifty. It would be useless to saw through a root. Whitewood trees didn't grow rings; the wood inside the bark was formed agelessly in those tiny honeycomb patterns. There must have been a way of telling – Inti would have known – but I'd never thought to ask her.

Raphael had last been here more than a hundred years ago. I sat down on the edge of what had once been a fountain, dry now, and tried to see any sign of the age of the place. I had no idea what people had worn here a hundred years ago or two hundred, or even whether it had changed much in that time. Not far away from me, a tower had collapsed into the lake. Chunks of masonry, big enough to walk around, with little stairways and archways that led nowhere, made an archipelago of stone islands. There were phoenix ducks there and petroleum-coloured feathers on the ground nearer to me. Whatever had happened, and whenever, there was nobody left now. I stayed away from the people in the glass.

Someone moved. It was Anka and she was watching me. I couldn't tell where she had come from.

'Do you speak Spanish?' I said.

She didn't move.

'I'm not trying to trespass. I'm here with Raphael. He's changing. I'm trying to find someone, to help him. Is there anyone left?'

She picked up a rock and I thought she would throw it at me, but she only used it to carve into the fall of glass beside her.

Holy ground.

'I know it is. But I can't leave him here in the middle of nowhere if there's nobody to help him.'

Leave.

'Is there anyone left?'

Don't know. Not awake for long enough.

'How long?'

I didn't think she would reply, but she seemed to think about it, and of course she had plenty of time. *A week here and there.*

'When . . . are you from?'

Born 1579.

'And you're only just properly awake now.'

Mercury. Turned after a miner's funeral in the graveyard. Her hand had shaken over the last part and my teeth hurt in their roots.

'It's been nearly three hundred years,' I said, because I had a terrible feeling that no one else had been able to tell her yet.

She didn't write this time. No wonder she hadn't wanted to talk to anyone, in her waking weeks. She must have known she was in the middle of a fractured sleep, like Raphael, but far worse. She didn't want to talk because they would all be dead when she next noticed.

'I need to wait. To see if anyone comes,' I tried again. 'They have to move him; he can't stand out here.'

You must leave. Bones cannot disturb stone.

It sounded like a translation of something that would have been well known if I'd been from here, but I caught the gist. I was an ordinary person, or less than ordinary with one good leg. It was a special sort of offence to try and move a sleeping markayuq. I could see her bristling and my heart sounded loud inside my ears when it occurred to me that maybe even thinking of moving one was illegal in itself. Like talking about the death of a king.

'No,' I said anyway, before she had finished writing. I would never have imagined that an argument as slow as this, where I had to wait for a stone woman to write on glass with a shard of broken rock, would feel urgent. But it did. Anxious heat had been building up in my chest since she began to talk and now my veins sang with the need to fight or run. She had to drag the rock around curving letters and the grinding noise of it hurt to hear.

Sacrilege.

'I don't care.'

She only set the rock down again. I watched her for a long second through my own breath, which was clear white. My leg already ached from having come downhill.

She started to move again and I got up and walked away as quickly as I could. She followed me, not in any rush. I struggled much more on the way up than on the way down and when I looked back she was still there, still following. Halfway up the valley the trees closed in again and the pollen was bright. I stopped at the top, waiting for the pollen to fade with my pulse drumming and knowing it wasn't going to fade enough.

I had been aiming back to the place I'd left Raphael, for no real reason except the fairytale chance he might wake if I was just desperate enough, but when I found it, he was gone.

I looked up and down for a pollen trail I could hide in, but animals seemed not to like the road. I started back along the glass towards the aqueduct. It stretched on further than I'd thought. Anka was closer now. She didn't make any effort to rush and she caught up with me slowly. When she did, she only reached out for my arm.

Raphael pushed me out of the way and hit her full in the chest. The noise was inhuman, stone smashing into stone. He was smaller than she was and he must have known he was going to lose before he even began.

She dragged him backward and hit him across his temple. If it had been me, the bones in my skull would have clattered into the nearest tree, but he had changed enough for his not to. I was still a good way from the aqueduct. The four markayuq sentinels watched quietly. They turned their heads as I came towards them, but they were so divorced from everything else that the fight must have been only a vaguely interesting flash in among the changing whirr of the seasons. Anka, though, wasn't coming after me. Raphael had kicked her ankle out from under her and pinned her down, but she was holding something and it took what felt like a long time to realise that it was my matches.

The pollen went up much faster than it had before. The trees were ancient and so did they. Explosions thundered like a whole fleet firing its guns at once. I ran back for the aqueduct and fell on the ice and skidded the last few yards underneath, but the fires were so strong that the misty fall of water there didn't make much difference. More trees went up, so hard the explosions shook the ground and knocked me over again. Shrapnelled bark tore down my arm.

Raphael shouted something, not in English.

Someone grasped my shoulder and pushed me down on to the ground, until I was crouching. As soon as I did, I stopped feeling any heat. It was still hot, but nothing from the explosions hit me. Wood clattered against something close. When I looked up, the four sentinels were standing around me, leaning down, their arms interlocked and blocking almost everything. They weren't burning. Their robes were singeing but not much, or not on my side. What did reach me though was the smoke, which smelled of chemicals, and I choked. The dark closed in on the edges of my eyes.

THIRTY

When I came to, I was in a proper bed with a velvet pillow under my head. It was soft when I moved. I lay still for a long time, very sleepy. Some of it was altitude, that same thick feeling I'd had in Crucero but worse. Once I was sitting up, my head spun, not unpleasantly. I waited for it to stop. There was a bandage on my arm and the room was too bright. It was hard to see at all at first, but when I could it was all windows. Some were doors. A brazier burned low next to me.

I got up slowly. It was painful, but not impossible. Standing, I found all the cold air, which had a real bite now. I leaned against the wall on my way to the glass doors. Raphael was sitting outside, facing the balcony. He was very still and I thought for a horrible second that I was too late, but he twisted back when he heard the door and got up to help me across. It was even brighter outside than in and, in the brilliant light, the haze over his eyes was translucent. I folded slowly onto the bench, the L of my hand propped to my forehead to keep the sun out of my eyes despite how everything around us was mostly lost in fog.

He looked better, healthier. I said so.

'It's the altitude,' he said. 'We were made for up here. It's twenty-five thousand feet. You won't feel well.'

'There are yak in Nepal that wouldn't survive at twenty-five thousand feet,' I grumbled. The fog made the cold cut-throat and someone had taken away my coat. He gave me a folded-up blanket I'd thought was a cushion. I hunched into it and then frowned. 'Twenty-five thousand . . . there are no mountains that high in Peru. Are there?'

'We're not on a mountain.' He pointed through the banisters of the balcony.

It wasn't fog. We were in the middle of a cloud bank. Where the vapour was thin I could just make out the corners and roofs of buildings. It didn't look like an ordinary city. Everything was on a different level, on whitewood gantries, and they didn't stand on any ground. A garden floated at five or six different heights, just ahead of us. There were trees and flowers I'd never seen before, and colourful things in greenhouses. In a pavilion made of intertwining whitewood saplings was a bronze telescope, pointing down. A skiff with red sails wove along through the air, between the buildings. Now that I was looking more closely, they all had wharves and posts to tie up ropes. A fleet of boats hung like hot air balloons above one of them, all tied to the same ring.

'Am I . . . allowed to be here?'

'There are only one or two of us in a generation now. They left me in Bedlam for a hundred years and they're feeling guilty,' he said. 'You can do whatever I want.'

'They?'

'The clerics in charge here, and the . . .' He had to search for the word. 'The Prior,' he said eventually.

I caught the smell of smoke and held on to the banister. 'Did they save the forest?'

He gave me a pair of binoculars. 'Still saving it. There are aqueducts that cut through; it's divided into fire zones. You'd never lose more than a fraction of it.'

I looked through the binoculars. There were ships below the clouds, waterships, moving slowly and spraying jets down on the still-smoking forest. I couldn't see any more fires. I could taste the smoke, just, but we were a long way above it and the wind was taking it before it could filter too far into the city. I felt dizzy and had to give the binoculars back.

'Jesus. Someone's going to stumble over this place soon. There are rubber expeditions starting out round here, and that's forgetting coffee and pepper farmers, and . . .' I trailed off and tried to shake some of the fog out of my head. 'Small countries with valuable resources always have to give them away in the end or they're crushed. You can't live in the middle of a nascent whitewood monopoly. Is there some kind of plan here to deal with—'

'I've been here two hours, I don't know. Calm down. It's been hidden for four hundred years; no one's coming in the next ten minutes.'

'No, I know.' I lapsed back on to the bench. 'This is . . . I'm too altitude-stupid for good adjectives. It's incredible.' I leaned forward with the heels of my hands against the edges of the rail. I wanted to go to sleep.

Someone tapped me on the shoulder, on my other side. It was a man with a tangle of knot strings.

'Oh, he doesn't want that,' Raphael said.

'You don't know. What is it?' I asked.

'Permission to come back when I wake. It's not . . .'

I looked at the knots and then back at him. 'You'd rather I didn't.'

'You won't want to. It will be years and years.'

'Well – I will, but that isn't—' I had to stop and try again. 'Look, I know I'm not Harry, I know I've been standing in. If you don't want me to come back I won't. But I want to come back.'

He watched me for a long time and then reached past me to take the tapestry from the now worried-looking man.

'What are you writing?'

'Your name and my signature. Not Harry – you're damn right you're not Harry. He would never have done any of this. He worried too much about getting home to do anything much at all.' He gave the strings back over my shoulder. The man retreated inside. 'That isn't binding to you, only to them,' he said quietly.

'I'll be here.'

'Yes, well,' he said. He didn't believe me and I didn't try to persuade him. I knew I was sure, but there was no way to measure that for him, or to prove it was permanent. He was still watching the scribe. Once the door swung shut, he touched my arm and held something out. It was a pine cone, one of the iron-strong ones from the whitewoods, but it was charred. The fire had cracked it open, and inside the seeds were loose. Some pattered into my palm. 'Souvenir.'

I took it carefully. 'Am I allowed to have . . .'

'No. But if there are other whitewood forests, no one will care too much about this one, will they?'

I sat studying the seeds and finally understood why Harry had planted an explosive tree at home. He had been seeing if whitewood would grow elsewhere. But it hadn't grown properly; the wood had been light but it had never floated. It had failed because Heligan was at sea level. The whitewoods would need mountains, high. The Himalayas.

Someone else came into the room behind us, a stewardly man who gave the impression he had been just outside all along waiting for the scribe to leave.

I got up. 'I'll make some coffee,' I said, a bit loudly, in case the steward had enough Spanish to guess at some English. 'Do you want some?'

'Please.'

While I looked in my bag to find the coffee, I slipped the seeds through a worn patch and into the lining. The steward had stoked the brazier and brought some water.

It only took me a minute to make some coffee, but it was too much. Raphael was gone by the time I went back out. I sat with him for a little while longer, in case vestigially he was still there, but I didn't think he was. Before anyone could see – I don't know why – I took his rosary.

I called to the steward, who called for doctors. I waited for half an hour before one of them explained in unsettlingly good Spanish that this wasn't one of the short spells.

Without him they didn't like my being there. I stayed close to my bag in case I had to run, though I had no idea how I was supposed to escape from a floating city, but when the soldiers arrived it wasn't to arrest me. The doctor translated, gently, that they wanted to know where I should be taken, because there was a heavy chance I would die of the altitude in the next twenty-four hours. Any visitor was usually required to stay on the mountain for at least a month before risking the extra height of the city.

'One of the markayuq told me I wasn't meant to be here,' I said, still slow and proving their point. The more I tried to speak the more I realised they were right. It was worse now than when I'd first woken.

The doctor winced. 'Correctly. The border is closed. But frankly to refuse a retinue for turning markayuq is idiotic, and an unintended side-effect of the quarantine laws. Unfortunately many of our laws are made by markayuq and so it can take . . . rather a long time to change anything.' He said it quickly, not liking to criticise them. 'You brought him home safely. At this point I rather think it would be political suicide for anyone to say you shouldn't have.'

I nodded and felt like I was going to cry. I must not have looked well, because the doctor gave me a cup of chocolate, spiced with something warm.

If Clem had been there he would have loved it. The soldiers had their hair shaved back from their temples and gold hoops around their arms that showed, I found out a lot later, their rank. They were the closest to Incan I'd ever seen in real life or in a book, but sitting there with them, I couldn't summon up any curiosity. They seemed just to belong to the place. I wasn't surprised to see orders passed along on knot cords; that the short swords they carried were made of obsidian, not steel; that their armour was gold-plated squares that rippled when they turned, or that they spoke that older Quechua which Raphael had taught me for the prayer in the forest. I had a faint, faint sense of being lucky to have seen them. It felt like having been dropped into a place where Rome never fell and there were still Caesars, but broad principles are hard to catch when the thing at hand is to work out how to read latitude on someone else's map.

They had brought me a Spanish map, but it was old and I struggled to find Arequipa on it. Once I had, I sat back and felt hollowed out. The doctor sent the soldiers away and they went, oddly too respectful. I had a feeling it meant something here, that I'd arrived with a markayuq, but nobody said what it was.

I left a note for Raphael with my address on it, the same one Harry had left, feeling hopeless, because I couldn't promise that anyone would still live at Heligan by the time he came around. They said it would be, by their best calculation, twenty-one years and six months.

They took me at night. The ship was small, but the sails caught the wind well and once we were above the forest, there was a blackout on board. I sat in the dark in a loop of rigging rope. I'd tied it myself and no one had stopped me. I swung gently, pushing off a little sometimes from the rail. There were lights under the clouds, a big spray of them that might have been Azangaro. I had been sitting straight, but something about seeing a familiar place took the last strength out of the bones in my spine and I let my head bump against the ropes.

Twenty-one years and six months. It was a long way. Looking at the distance made me feel so tired I didn't even want to begin. Even if it had been less, there was no one to walk with. It ought not have been surprising. I'd never thought there would be anybody and it was spoiled to imagine that I had any right to company. In a few weeks, or months, I wouldn't be sad any more and back to all my old indifference, which was ordinary enough, but just then it seemed monstrous. I squeezed the cross on Raphael's rosary until my hand bled.

They left me just outside Arequipa. The ship couldn't dip below a certain height – the whitewood lift was too much – but they let me down on a rope wound to a silent pulley. To anyone watching from the ground it would have looked like I was being lowered by a considerate cloud, though I don't think anyone saw. The fields outside the town were deserted. I walked the last of the road up to the house where Minna was staying. The upstairs window was alight. Although I stared at it for a while, I couldn't go up. I asked a beggar for the next nearest inn, where, because it was the off season for the herders, most of the rooms were empty and as good as free.

PART FIVE

THIRTY-ONE

Ceylon, 1861

When we met Sing in Ceylon, we had fifty-four cinchona cuttings in the Wardian cases, and three whitewood shoots. I planted the latter in the coldest set of shadows I could find, north-facing, and sat staring at them nearly as much as we all stared at the cinchona.

I'd never seen plants dealt with more seriously. The gardeners and I made paper cases to carry the sprouting cinchona cuttings out with their tiny new root systems and the soil around them intact, and planted them with tape measures against their stems to make sure we didn't bury them too far up. The ground Sing had acquired for us was perfect and they grew quickly. I stayed for almost a year to see them through. In that time, the whitewoods shot up like silver birches. No one else touched them, I didn't tell anyone what they were, but they were the first thing I went out to every morning.

It was late in the boiling summer when I found Sing sitting at the base of one with a book and the unflustered air of someone who had been born to Asian weather. After the mountains round Bedlam, it was scorching. People hurried inside to get away from the sun like Englishmen avoided thunderstorms. It was easy to spot white people, even from behind; we moved too quickly for the heat and ended up in exhausted heaps before mid-morning.

Sing had managed to acquire a little table and a tea set, with lemons. I died a bit at the thought of drinking anything hot and had to shake my head when he lifted the teapot towards me. Down in the valley below us, the wind ruffled the new cinchona canopy. The cicadas started up a mechanical shriek.

'So what are these?' he asked. I'd kept them out of my report. I'd left out everything after I'd followed Raphael to the city. I knew Sing must have seen gaps. My timings added up wrongly; it had only taken me a week to get back across to Peru with the cuttings, and there was no way I should have been able to do that without help from a cavalry regiment. Even then, someone should have stopped me and asked about Martel and his men, though of course I'd completely bypassed Azangaro, three thousand feet up. But Sing hadn't asked me. I was glad, because I didn't want to tell anyone. Whenever I thought about it, the idea felt like cutting off an arm.

I sat down beside him. It was awkward, even with the white-wood band, because the muscle was still damaged even if my weight didn't pull at it any more.

'I'll tell you when I know if they're doing what they should or not.'

He looked to the side. 'You've already taken cuttings from them.'

I had. There were six, much tinier saplings scattered about around them now. It looked all right so far – they had taken root – but the sawdust didn't float yet. 'If I'm right about them, they're going to be valuable. More than quinine. I was wondering if I could shanghai a plantation in the Himalayas.'

'For a mysterious project of unknown yield,' he said.

'Yes.'

'All right. Since you're the India Office's new golden boy. Speaking of which. I'm happy to hand off the cinchona to more junior gardeners soon if you are.'

I nodded.

'Good. Where would you like to go next?' he said, as if it was nothing. 'There are rubber expeditions going out in Africa now. Some Arctic exploratory stuff, if you wanted a change of scene. And the Foreign Office are mooing for anyone who speaks Chinese to get on the diplomatic service in Japan. It opened to trade while you were away,' he explained when I started to ask since when had there been a diplomatic service in Japan.

'Did it?' I said, surprised.

'Well, the Americans shelled them until they said yes.'

'Oh, right. Yes, Japan please.'

'Really? It won't be gardening.'

'Just – for a while. Can I?'

'Yes, of course.' He watched me for a second. 'But then we really will want you in the Congo.'

'Yes.'

We sat in silence. Down the hill from us, Minna was walking with the baby and the new ayah, a cheery girl who danced whenever she swept the veranda. Minna had had the baby a month early, which had nearly given me a heart attack but hadn't seemed to worry her. It was, she pointed out, far too hot to be penned up somewhere airless, even when that somewhere was your own mother.

'Is she going with you?' he asked.

'No. Why would she be?'

'Isn't that what people do, marry their dead husband's friends?'

'Awkward when I killed her husband.'

'No, you didn't. You allowed him to be stupid for the general good of mankind. And of that village, I might add, to which we now have no need to send the army. You're not going to have some sort of angst-driven breakdown now, are you?' he added warily. 'I'd encourage you not to.'

I laughed. 'No. But I can keep a secret from someone I see only occasionally. Harder to keep it from my wife.'

'No. True.'

He was looking at the rosary around my wrist, but he had never asked about that either. He had a pretty firm stance on religion, which was that the less people bothered about it, the fewer huffy trade impediments there were going to be. I pressed my other hand round it and squeezed until the beads printed my arm, and half the cross. I'd thought that I would stop thinking about it all after a few weeks, but I hadn't. I'd found that if I sat still for too long without doing something useful, the way ahead – twenty years – looked as far as the stars. To Raphael's way of thinking, you only had to sit still and the future would catch up with you from behind, but I was starting to feel like I was facing the wrong way. It got further away the longer I looked.

'Right, morning rounds,' I said, unable to sit quiet any more. We had slipped into talking about the cinchona plantation as if it were a hospital ward. 'Coming?'

'I think I'll stay here,' he said, for the first morning since we had arrived.

THIRTY-TWO

Cornwall, 1881

When I came in from the garden, Minna and Cecily were putting holly up around the house, which was now full of people because they had invited everyone they knew. There were trees and candles everywhere too. More than anything it looked like the garden had moved into the house for the holiday. There was a brandy, Christmas-cake smell drifting up from the kitchens and someone was playing the piano in the parlour, a beautiful version of a carol whose words I'd forgotten. I couldn't believe how warm it was with the roof and the windows all in good repair and the fires going. It felt like another house altogether. I hadn't been there often enough in the intervening years to have remembered it any other way than how it was when I'd left it before Peru. When I was in England, which was rare, I stayed with Sing. I could have bought a house of my own, but I didn't want to. Silence in empty rooms whistled.

Minna turned around where she sat on the stairs twining holly round the banister.

'Oh, Em, there's someone here for you,' she said.

'Who?' I said, confused, because I'd been sure that everyone I knew well was already here. Minna and Cecily had invited themselves and promptly redecorated because they said it was bleak, and I'd invited Sing, because it was a sort of unspoken pact to have Christmas and New Year together if both of us were in the same place, which was not every year. We were the only people either of us knew who didn't disappear off into extended families for the holiday. Even Sing's servant went back to the Netherlands towards the middle of December. Usually we would have been at Sing's house in London, but Charles had died in November and I'd been back at Heligan since then, going through everything. I had a feeling Minna was there more to keep an eye on me than to put up new wallpaper.

'He says it's a surprise,' she laughed.

'Where?'

'In the parlour. He's the one with the piano.'

'I don't know anyone who plays the piano. Do I?'

'You do, dear,' Cecily said. She sounded exactly like Clem. The red hair was glorious on a girl and in all the Christmas candles she might have been something shined up from Byzantium. 'But he's been keeping it secret.'

I went through slowly, looking at the candles and the decorations. The man at the piano was dark and slight, with a grey tweed waistcoat and shoes with a Japanese manufacturer's mark on the heels. He smiled at me. He was sitting to one side of the piano stool so there would be room.

'Keita,' I laughed. 'What are you doing here?'

'Surprise.' He finished the carol and let his hands drop into his lap, although he had hooked down the pedal and the sound resounded. 'I heard about your brother; I'm sorry.'

'You didn't come all the way from Tokyo for that?'

'Well, and it's Christmas,' he said awkwardly.

I smiled. I didn't touch him, though I would have if I'd thought for a second he wouldn't, Tokyo-ishly, take it as assault.

He was a changeable thing. He was a late bloomer just like I'd thought, and he was coming into himself more and more every time I saw him. He had been fragile as a young man, but he was in his thirties now and glowing. Nothing else about him had changed. He was still exactly the same pensive person he had been in China, and when I'd found him watching a cricket match at his school fifteen years ago.

There were women I didn't know taking up all the chairs at the other end of the room, so I took a tray of tea things and made it on top of the piano. He closed the lid over the keys so we could use it as a counter. Once the tea was poured and cooling, I saw how he was looking at my wrist, which still had Raphael's rosary wound around it. I rested the heel of my hand on the edge of the piano lid, the beads imprinting the underside of my arm. He didn't tell me not to, although it was a nervous habit he must have noticed before.

'Who are all these people?' he said instead.

'Apart from Minna and Cecily, no idea. Their friends.'

'Why are they inviting people to your house?'

'They invited themselves and then said it seemed empty. I think I might be Minna's winter project. She's worried that I'll be upset about Charles. And apparently when you say in a moment of good-willed absentmindedness that you'll be someone's godfather, it turns out that you're actually signing away all your worldly goods to her, including your house and any available Christmases. Actually I quite like all the noise,' I admitted.

He smiled. 'Me too. Listen, did I imagine that you're going to Peru in June?'

I hadn't told anyone, but that was no more a barrier for him now than it had been twenty-five years ago. 'No, I am. Why?'

Somewhere upstairs, where they had renovated Dad's study into a new, bigger parlour, Cecily had taken over the music. She played the violin and she had begun the same carol Keita had been playing, but she was pretending not to know all of it and, in the joking way musical people can, bridged the gaps with 'Ode to Joy'. The fireplaces here and there lined up and I could hear people laughing through the chimney.

'Could you send me some of the pollen from the forest? Only a vial.' He paused. 'I'm making some fireflies.'

I laughed. 'To Tokyo?'

'No, Knightsbridge, please.' He gave me a piece of paper with an address on it. Filigree Street.

'Holiday?' I said.

'No, to live. Not for very long, only a few years.'

'Lovely,' I said, and waited to see if he would say anything else, but he didn't. For his country he was a tall man, and he held himself like one, but every so often there was a fragility around him when he was coming up to something that seemed especially insurmountable. I poured him some more tea and watched the moving steam catch his eye and tug him slowly into the present.

'Is she playing "Ode to Joy"?' he asked at last.

'She is. She's joking. She means you should go upstairs and say hello.' They had met before. Minna had come on holiday to Japan once when Cecily was about four. Keita had taught her to read, in about two afternoons, with the efficiency of someone who didn't like children and wanted a proper human being to talk to.

'What?'

'Keita? Joy?' I said gently. He knew the translation of his own name but he still looked far away.

'Oh, yes.' He came back to himself properly. I saw him studying the possible recent future, the one with Cecily in it in full Christmas swing. He looked worried. 'I'd rather not.'

I laughed. 'Christmas spirit. It's why you're here, on you go. I'll come up in a bit. I just want the last of the light.' I motioned at Charles's old study.

His black eyes caught on the door. I thought he smiled, as if there were an enormous surprise party waiting inside, but he turned away too quickly for me to be sure and when I leaned in round the edge of the door, nobody burst out from behind the ferns.

I'd been excavating for a month. Charles had kept everything, from old, irrelevant account books to octogenarian financial newspapers, but it all had to be gone through. An accountant from Truro had been helping me, because I'd never kept a proper ledger in my life and I had no idea how it worked, and I didn't understand what bonds or trusts were, or how investment differed from gambling. What money I had, had come here, and what was left had gone to the bank in London, where the account was too little for them to bother asking me much. The India Office paid well, but well in modern terms; to fully restore a vast twelfth-century estate, created and then expanded in times when noblemen had been the equivalent to the millionaires of this century, was long work, and would have been even on the Prime Minister's salary. I was happy doing it, though.

We had found a lot of things: failed investments from Dad's time, where he had tried to get some of the mortgage money back by betting on the tin mines, which had promptly run dry, and a few from Charles too. He had never told me about those, too ashamed I suspected, though it wouldn't have made a blind bit of difference to me. The mortgage on the house had been astronomical and I'd only paid off the last of it a few years ago. I was trying to keep chipping at the records for an hour or so a day, even during the holidays, so that the idea of it couldn't grow too monstrous on the fertile soil of absence.

Carefully, because I still couldn't quite bring myself to trust the strength of the whitewood round my thigh even after twenty years wearing it, I climbed up on a chair to take a random pile of dusty things from the top shelf. I dropped them on to the desk and crumpled down after them. It was much nicer than usual, though, with the music coming through the ceiling, and happy voices, and the candles sparkling all along the stairs. The puppy yipped at me under the table. I lifted her out.

'I wondered where you'd gone.' She was barely a dog yet; at first glance she was an enormous ball of fluff with ears. Like a baby would have, she emerged with her paws curled up. I laughed and hugged her. She was called Quixote, because I was working my way through books as well as dogs. She was Gulliver's great-granddaughter. 'Come and help me read all this rubbish. What have we got, do you think? Oh. Could it be as exciting as – old receipts for lamp oil? I think it might.'

She fell asleep hanging over my arm. I laid her across my lap so she wouldn't hurt her back like that and held her to keep my hands warm while I read. I frowned when I realised that the pile was nothing to do with Charles. They were much older accounts in Harry's writing: ordinary household stuff. I put the first ledger aside. The next thing down was a slim envelope. When I opened it, the documents inside were flowery and official, in Spanish. The seal of the Peruvian government was at the bottom. My Spanish was good enough to scan them and my lungs caught when I first guessed the meaning, but I wasn't sure. After I'd spent another quarter of an hour with a dictionary, I knew I wasn't wrong. Not quite able to breathe properly, I went upstairs and looked through rooms full of festively dressed people until I found Sing. He was talking to one of Minna's friends.

'Could I borrow him?' I asked.

'If I can borrow that dog.'

'Yes. Trade.' I gave her the dog. Sing followed me out.

'Was I just bought for a St Bernard?'

'Comparable weight of goods. I, um . . .' We were in the corridor, still surrounded by music, but I couldn't wait. 'These are land deeds.'

Sing didn't speak Spanish, but he understood what he was looking at straightaway. There must have been a standard format for the documents, or else, he recognised how the numbers were laid out. Acres, price, tax. From what I could tell, the land had been bought just after Peru had won independence from Spain. The new government must have been selling off land in the interior to help recharge the treasury.

'So this is what your grandfather did with the money,' he said, after looking through a few pages. 'This must cover thousands of acres. All beyond the Andes.'

'This one is for all the land around Bedlam.' I fished out a deed from the middle of the sheaf to show him. Nueva Bet., it was abbreviated to, but it was there. 'Raphael told me that Martel had a landlord who had stopped asking for money years ago. I mean – that must have been Dad, he must have known about this, but I never thought . . . this is what I think it is, isn't it?'

'If you think that your grandfather bought the land to keep it safe in the event that anyone discovered what was there, and died before he could form any kind of legal protection round it – yes, it looks that way to me.'

Sing knew what was there. Late one night, out on the new whitewood plantations in the Himalayas, we had been celebrating. The trees, already the size of oaks, had been growing for perhaps five years, and for the first time that evening, one of the gardeners had pruned some twigs and found that they floated. Sing had known there was something odd about them before that, because they were volatile things to grow and we'd had to have heavy fire regulations right round the mountain, but I'd told him then what they could do if we could only grow them strong enough. It had felt dangerous to say it aloud, even though I had the evidence floating in front of me that we had just rendered any whitewood expedition to the Andes unnecessary. He had laughed, properly, for the first time since I'd known him, and said only that I ought to get some sort of award for shrewdness. None of it had felt shrewd. It had felt like tightrope walking, for years. I'd been ill for a while after that, with relief. There would be a whitewood trade, but not out of Peru. It would be India Office plantations, ours, and nobody would ever have to know about Bedlam, or what was in the sky above it.

I couldn't frame what it was I wanted to ask. For what had happened to Raphael never to happen again; for it to be impossible for the next Martel to hold anything over Aquila. For no one to march in and build a cathedral or a salt mine over the town.

'Is there a way to . . .? Can we ringfence it somehow? In . . . a trust, or – I don't know. Build a bloody great wall around it?'

'I'll talk to some lawyers,' he said. 'We'll be able to make it so that no one touches that place even if they find El Dorado out there.'

'I don't have much money to throw at something like—'

He laughed, not at me but softly. 'Merrick. You have what – a thirty per cent share in the Himalayan whitewood plantation? Hang on to it. The heartwood is almost mature. The Navy wants it. You're going to be very wealthy indeed soon.'

They weren't surprised to hear from me at Raphael's monastery in the new year. There was a post office box in Lima that they had told me about and correspondence took a couple of months, but we arranged dates and, like people tend to do in situations of limited communication, they stuck exactly to their word. At the Bedlam border, a salt trader met me and took me along the glass road, considerately with a horse. Anka wasn't at the graveyard and no one followed. Having been to Bedlam so often, I didn't have altitude sickness any more in the mountains and there was no delay. A little ship met us beyond the aqueduct and took us into the city. I stood by the rail and watched the clouds go past, and the first buildings, and then the huge docks where ships the size of cathedrals floated at anchor. Those hadn't been there before.

The monastery was a ghost in the clouds. Where the sun edged through, the walls shone. They were inlaid with gold. It wasn't that gold was fabulously valuable. They were, said the steward who met me, on the top of a gold mine. It was because in its earliest days, the place had been a sun temple, and gold reflected the light yellow. I'd been too distracted to have paid attention last time, but the halls he took me through were beautiful, and impossibly high, the masonry hauled upward by rafters and vaults of whitewood. In the heights were pollen chandeliers. They spun slowly, making tiny golden galaxies.

I'd come back to Peru often to see Inti. My Quechua was good enough now, although it sounded very modern here, even though I'd made her use only the oldest words, nothing Spanish. There had been a pronunciation shift. Up here it sounded sharp, but when the steward met me on the monastery steps, we understood each other. He seemed pleased, if terse. I wanted to say I hadn't come with an army, and there was no need to be nervous, but it wasn't me bothering him, or I didn't think so.

On the stairway up to the monastery proper, where everyone lived, there was a markayuq on a plinth, holding a human skeleton kept in shape by wires and slim metal rods. The bones were slight, a girl probably. The stone man's grasp stopped short of the bones, outlining where her body had been.

'That's what you have to be careful of,' the steward said, with a sternness I didn't deserve. He had stopped to say it and until then I hadn't noticed that two guardsmen had followed us, towering, grim men with condor designs stamped into their armour.

It was difficult to look at the markayuq and the bones. It was plainly meant to be awful, but its being macabre wasn't what bothered me; I'd never had any trouble with bones in themselves and these ones were kept very well. It was the same way I couldn't look at French postcards; a kind of pointless prudishness that came from never having married. Their heads so close that they must have been kissing when the markayuq froze. Whoever the girl had been, she was crippled. One femur was twisted. A Bedlam girl. I wondered if she had died by accident, trapped like that, or if she had done it on purpose.

'Is he awake yet?' I asked instead. 'Your letter said sometime this week.'

'He's been stirring for the last few days. The doctor has estimated that it should be some time this afternoon or in the night. Their pulses come back up to normal speed a few days beforehand. It becomes more like sleep than stasis, you see.' He paused, with a thorny quiet. He was worried about something, or something had gone wrong, but I didn't push. Before and now, the monastery stewards put me powerfully in mind of the Swiss Guards. It must have been a calling, and no one wanted to say anything difficult about the markayuq. Some boys sitting on the stairs stared at us.

'Sir, is there any . . .' They looked from him to me. They were asking about Raphael.

'Not yet,' he said. Then to me, abruptly, to get it out at once, 'Sometimes they never wake properly. Something goes wrong, and . . .' He lifted his hand towards the markayuq on the stairs but glanced up, to the next floor, and to the room beyond which was that balcony with its view over the city. He was nervous. They all were. One in a generation now; it mattered that Raphael woke and kept his mind at the same time.

'Is he showing any sign of that?'

'As far as we can tell, no, but it's never certain.' He swallowed. 'You are of course here at his invitation, but you must be aware of the protocols. Has someone explained?'

I shook my head.

I was allowed to touch a markayuq, but only with my undominant hand. Under no circumstances was I to let one touch me in a way that wasn't flat-handed; if there was an unexpected lapse, I would be stuck there, and nobody was going to cut through a saint's fingers just to save mine. Should it seem to be happening, I was to step back and say why. If I used Quechua, I was to use a register appropriate to their station. If I had trouble knotting messages, there were scribes who could help. And I would never be left in a room alone with any of them. The guards, he explained, were there for my safety. Markayuq were strong and didn't always remember that they were. The guards would help me should an accident happen. If an accident did happen, I was not to retaliate, unless I wanted to be quartered on an altar by tomorrow morning. I wondered how often it happened, if he needed to mention it.

At last, they let me go up to the room. It was just the same. I didn't go out on to the balcony. He was exactly where I'd left him, perfectly kept, his clothes like new. I felt as if the past twenty years had been nothing but a loop which had brought me back to the same place and the same hour. While the monastery had seemed dreamy when I'd tried to think of it before, it was everything else that seemed that way now. It was hard to believe that I'd lived more than half my adult life in the meantime.

The steward brought me some food and a brazier so that I could make my own coffee. The water boiled so low here that there was no other way to get at it fast enough while it was still hot. I watched the coal inside burn through a glass window in the front until I saw Raphael shift, as if he had just come out of a daydream, then made two cups, one black and one white, and took them out. I sat down on the bench with them rested against my knees. Behind me, near the door, the two guardsmen had stood up too. I hadn't seen before, but coming close to the stone banister brought me into view of the floating gardens. They had been much expanded, and they were full of people, waiting. Little boats had been tied to the gantries and moorings and there were more people in those. They were too far away to hear, except for a tidal murmur I had thought before was the sound of the streets below.

Raphael looked at me sidelong, starting to smile, then stopped. He watched me for almost half a minute. It was a brilliant afternoon and the light was hurting my eyes – it felt like the edge of snowblindness – so he must have been able to see how I'd changed. His eyes caught briefly on the rosary. The haze over them, complete now, didn't look like a cataract. It was more like a second lens, a necessary one, not to frown into the streaming sun. Otherwise he was just the same; his colours all gone but just the same. I gave him his cup.

'You like it black, don't you,' I said.

He laughed.

HISTORICAL NOTE

Clements R. Markham was a real person, and he really did lead an expedition into the Peruvian interior to steal cinchona trees in 1860. In real life, though, there was no Merrick Tremayne; Markham made it out alive but was unsuccessful. He went on to publish a Quechua dictionary, translations of various Spanish histories of Peru and an account of his own travels, which I relied on heavily when I wrote this book. A man called Charles Ledger got some live plants out eventually.

Peru is as real as I could make it until the expedition turns off onto the river that leads to Bedlam. After that it's imaginary. But most of the imaginary things are based on existing myths and fairytales about stone, and sixteenth-century Spanish accounts of the last surviving dregs of the Inca administrative system. Especially brilliant books are Carolyn Dean's *A Culture of Stone*, and *Narrative Threads*, edited by Jeffrey Quilter and Gary Urton.

The Inca really did write on cords. There are plenty of pictures of court scribes and accountants reading from them in Felipe Guaman Poma de Ayala's *Nueva crónica y buen gobierno*. The system was killed off with the arrival of the conquistadores, and while a few original examples do still survive, no one can read them any more. Current English scholarship suggests these cords were mainly for numbers or used as memory aids, but the second you speak to anyone Peruvian in Spanish they say yes, it was definitely writing. Although we have no Rosetta Stone for it – or Rosetta String – I'm with the writing camp. The people who built Machu Picchu knew the difference between magnetic and polar north, and they built earthquake-proof temples in the fourteenth century. I'm pretty sure that sending a letter wasn't beyond them.

Heligan is a real place and very much open to visitors. As I give it here, the history of the Tremayne family is completely fictional. Henry Tremayne did not (to my knowledge) meet a markayuq in Peru, so things turned out differently for him in real life.

ACKNOWLEDGEMENTS

First of all, I'd like to thank the Society of Authors. They funded three months of language school in Lima, accommodation, and all my travel in Peru. I wouldn't have been able to go without their help, which means about a third of this book would be quite different and much worse.

Just as important is Peruwayna Language School in Lima. In three months, they took me from 'hola' to conversations about possible theories on Inca sun religions, as well as a host of things between. Outside school, Spanish opened up some amazing conversations with Quechua speakers – they really do point forward for the past – as well as a lot of historical sources.

Thanks also to Gladstone's Library. As part of their writers in residence programme, they gave me a room for all of February 2016, fed me, kept me brilliantly supplied with copies of *The Illustrated London News*, and made sure I sometimes saw the inside of a pub rather than just my laptop keyboard. A significant chunk of this book was written in their cafe.

Finally, there's my mum and dad, who put me up uncomplainingly for all the time I wasn't in Wales or Peru, even though I single-handedly quadruple the heating bills. And thanks to my brother, Jake, who is able somehow to sort out all my narrative problems on the phone whilst doing a degree in something completely unrelated.

READING GROUP GUIDE

Questions for discussion

1. How does Merrick develop as a character depending on where he is across the globe? What new insights about himself does he encounter in each place? How does this alter his opinions on home?
2. Pulley employs flashbacks in portions of the novel. How do they help flesh out the characters and their backstories? How are they important to the events happening in Peru?
3. Does Merrick's relationship with Clem change over the course of the novel? Why does Merrick, despite his disability, respond better to life in Peru than Clem?
4. What is the role of women in *The Bedlam Stacks*? Is Minna's understanding of her gender a product of the society she lives in, and does it differ to that of the women in Bedlam?
5. Think about Charles and Merrick's relationship with each other, their father and their grandfather. What is the importance of family ties in the novel? How does nostalgia figure into these relationships?
6. What is the relationship between history and fantasy in *The Bedlam Stacks*? How does Merrick react to the magic around him?
7. How does imperialism function in the story? Is Merrick's experience in Peru changed at all by his race?
8. What is Raphael's role and how does his relationship with Merrick develop? What do they learn from each other? How does their relationship affect how they understand love?
9. Merrick's disability alters his perception of himself, as well as his career opportunities. How are the themes of illness and medicine further explored in Bedlam?

10. What borders – physical, spiritual, emotional, cultural, linguistic – do the characters encounter? Are they able to cross them?

Recommended reading

The Watchmaker of Filigree Street by Natasha Pulley; *The Bone Clocks* by David Mitchell; *The Miniaturist* by Jessie Burton; *The Essex Serpent* by Sarah Perry; *The Night Circus* by Erin Morgenstern

A NOTE ON THE TYPE

The text of this book is set in Bell. Originally cut for John Bell in 1788, this typeface was used in Bell's newspaper, *The Oracle.* It was regarded as the first English Modern typeface. This version was designed by Monotype in 1932.

ALSO AVAILABLE BY NATASHA PULLEY

THE WATCHMAKER OF FILIGREE STREET

THE INTERNATIONAL BESTSELLER
WINNER OF A BETTY TRASK AWARD 2016
SHORTLISTED FOR THE AUTHORS' CLUB BEST FIRST NOVEL AWARD 2016

In 1883, Thaniel Steepleton returns to his tiny flat to find a gold pocketwatch on his pillow. When the watch saves Thaniel's life in a blast that destroys Scotland Yard, he goes in search of its maker, Keita Mori – a kind, lonely Japanese immigrant. Meanwhile, Grace Carrow is sneaking into an Oxford library, desperate to prove the existence of the luminiferous ether before her mother can force her to marry.

As the lives of these three characters become entwined, events spiral out of control until Thaniel is torn between loyalties, futures and opposing geniuses.

'An assured and absorbing debut ... Immensely pleasurable reading ... Intricate, charming and altogether surprising'
NEW YORK TIMES

'Ten out of ten'
SPECTATOR

'A charming, quirky, clever tale, filled with intricate detail, and a plot that feels as deftly crafted as a precision timepiece'
JOANNE HARRIS

BLOOMSBURY PUBLISHING
LONDON • OXFORD • NEW YORK • NEW DELHI • SYDNEY

COMING IN 2019...

PEPPERHARROW

The sequel to the international bestseller *The Watchmaker of Filigree Street.*

Thaniel Steepleton and Keita Mori journey to Japan, where time, destiny, genius and love (not to mention a certain clockwork octopus) collide to electrifying effect.

BLOOMSBURY PUBLISHING

LONDON • OXFORD • NEW YORK • NEW DELHI • SYDNEY